SHANE'S HARMONY
CALEB'S CHANCE

by
Amy Durham

Shane's Harmony
Caleb's Chance
Copyright © 2017 Amy Durham
Published By Amy Durham

First Paperback Edition
(Previously published as two separate ebooks)

ISBN: 9780097495836
Editors: Dawn Laurent Bourgeois, Glenda Edwards, Justy Engle
Cover Artist: Tracy Stewart
Formatting: BB eBooks (www.bbebooksthailand.com)
Proofreaders: Teresa Reasor, Barry Blakeman, Cheryl Blakeman,
Kimberly Burton, Madeleine Estherby
Contact Information: amybdurham@gmail.com

OTHER BOOKS BY AMY DURHAM

"Hope" is the thing with feathers –
That perches in the soul –
And sings the tune without the words –
And never stops – at all –

~ Emily Dickinson

To survivors of sexual assault everywhere…
May you find the thing with feathers perched in your soul.

CONTENTS

Chapter 1

SYDNEY

WEDDINGS ALWAYS MAKE me cry. It's been that way for as long as I can remember. Witnessing the expression of love so strong that two people join their lives always turns me into a teary, snotty mess.

So, it's with reddened eyes and a handful of tissues that I excuse myself from the interior of Ugly Mug, the romantically-decorated coffee shop currently hosting Grace and Asher's wedding reception, and walk through the back parking lot toward my car.

I'm not so much afraid of social situations. They just make me nervous. It's like I don't really know how to act in a crowd anymore, even though I was once the life of the party. It's no surprise I needed a breather from all that sweet, sappy interaction.

Popping open the driver's side, I plop down into the seat and close the door. It's early evening, not yet six o'clock, and the May night is pleasantly cool, so I crack the window slightly. I also lock the doors out of habit.

I pull my phone from the small clutch purse that matches my bridesmaid dress and notice I have a voicemail. I press to play it and hit the speakerphone button.

It's my dad.

"Hey, honey. It's Dad. Give us a call when you're leav-

1

ing to head home, so we know when to expect you. Hope you've had a nice time. Love you."

I love my parents. I really, really do. And I especially love my little brother, Devin. But the constant smothering is beginning to get old.

Glancing at the clock, I know the happy couple will be leaving shortly to begin the honeymoon phase of wedded bliss. My plan had been to drive back home to Greyson. The drive is just under two hours, and since I'm home for the summer anyway, it had seemed like the easiest solution.

Except I just can't go home. I've been coming to that conclusion since the day I moved home from Phoenix, but Dad's voicemail just now confirmed it. I cannot go through another summer like last year. All the hovering and care-taking and treating me like I might break apart at any moment. Being home for the past couple of weeks since the semester ended has proven to me that no way can I survive another three months with them.

I *want* to be okay socially again. I *want* to feel like an adult, not a child with a curfew or a girl so fragile she needs watching over. I know nothing will change if I go home again.

I can't go back to Phoenix either. Amanda, my room-mate, moved out of the dorm and into an apartment for the summer, and offered to let me stay there and share rent. But that means going back to Phoenix.

I *cannot* do that.

Flagstaff is a nice enough town, and Grace is here. Or, at least she will be once she and Asher come back from their honeymoon. I know she'll be busy with her new job and new husband, but at least I'll have one friend in the city. A friend who is totally separate from my life in Phoenix and all the things I need to leave buried there.

I have enough money for about a week in a low dollar hotel, and I can eat cheap. Peanut butter crackers and canned ravioli are standard fare in college dorm rooms, and I know they can sustain me until I find a job. And I won't be too picky about a job. Fast food, waiting tables, even cleaning toilets will do just fine as long as I can stay here. I'll work on finding a place to live once I have a job.

Why not? Why shouldn't I stay in Flagstaff? I can't spend the summer in Greyson and expect things to change. I've got to push myself out of my comfort zone.

Mind made up, I shoot a quick text to my parents and tell them I've decided to hang here for a few days, and that I'll call tomorrow. They'll be a little baffled, but at least they won't worry when I don't come in tonight. Immediately my phone buzzes with an incoming call. I send it straight to voicemail. I don't feel like explaining myself right now, so instead I dial Claire's number. I know she'll understand.

"Sydney," her voice comes over the line and immediately soothes my nerves. Claire is ten years older than me and has become like a big sister I can turn to.

"Hey Claire." I take a deep breath and lean back against the seat.

"How are the wedding festivities?" she asks.

"Winding down."

"And how have you managed it all?" I knew she would ask. It's why I called in the first place.

"Pretty well, actually," I answer. "But I'm kind of exhausted."

"Social situations will probably be difficult for some time. What about the new people you met?"

"Everyone was really nice," I say. "Of course being around Grace was great. We've known each other all our lives. She's got so many friends here who love her and Asher, and they've all been really welcoming to me. I felt comfortable with them, which was kind of weird."

"You've kept mainly to yourself for over a year. It only makes sense that being a part of a group of friends would feel foreign to you at first."

"You're right. I don't want it to always feel weird, though." I close my eyes and just spit it out. "I think I'm going to stay in Flagstaff. Indefinitely. Until I figure out what I want to do next."

"Really?" she asks. "Have you talked it over with your parents?"

"No, not yet. I will. I just figure this is the first time I've felt okay in a group of people in a long time, and even though it's strange, I don't want to give that up yet."

"You're stepping back into the world," Claire says. "Beginning to find *you* again."

"You don't think I'm crazy for wanting to stay?"

"I think you're a grown woman and you know what's best for you."

"I'm going to get a hotel for a few nights, then get a job and look for a place to live." Saying it out loud gives me a quite bit of confidence.

"Call me anytime."

We say our goodbyes, and I pull up a browser on my phone to look for reasonably priced hotels.

I'm just about to place a call to the Super Lodge, a discount motel a few miles from here, when Shane Dawson steps out into the parking lot. His eyes, a startling icy blue, settle on me, and he starts walking toward my car.

Shane had served as Asher's best man today, and since I'd been Grace's maid-of-honor, the two of us had walked arm in arm up the aisle after the ceremony, and as such had carried on a few conversations. I'm not very good with conversations these days, so I felt completely inadequate compared to Shane's easy charm and quick wit. But he'd been kind to me, and I'm not in the habit of being ungrateful for kindness.

So, instead of being irritated that my motel reservations have been put on hold, I smile at him and give him a slight wave as he approaches.

"You need a break, too?" he asks, casually leaning a hip against my car. He taps a finger on the window, so I punch the button to lower the glass.

He's such a contradiction in the tux. I know from the short-sleeve shirt he wore to the rehearsal last night that his arms are full of tattoos. I also know that his blond hair is normally spiked or gelled in some kind of messy look. Today, however, his ink is covered by the long black sleeves of his tux jacket, and his hair is combed smooth. The only clue to his regular persona are the small piercings in his left eyebrow and the barbell piercing across the bridge of his nose.

I like both versions of him.

As tall as he is – probably six foot, three inches – he might look intimidating with the metal on his face and ink all over his arms, but as soon as he opens his mouth he completely disarms the people around him with his bubbly personality.

I'm sure girls just *love* him.

And I don't care how many girls love him.

Really, I don't.

"Looking for a motel room for the night," I say, keeping my tone neutral. "I was going to drive back to Greyson, but I've decided to stay in town tonight."

"You can stay at our place," he suggests, like sharing his

place with a virtual stranger is the most natural thing in the world. "Asher's already cleared his stuff out of his bedroom, but the furniture is Caleb's so the bed's still there."

Shane, Asher, and Caleb apparently share a three bedroom townhouse. Or at least, they did until this afternoon when Asher married Grace. Once the two of them get back from Hawaii they're moving into Grace's tiny little studio apartment until they find something bigger.

"Thanks, but I'm thinking I might stay a little longer," I answer, trying desperately to sound casual and not like I'm freaking out at the thought of staying at his apartment. "I might even look for a job and stick around for the summer."

He narrows his eyes and his brow furrows, as if trying to figure out how I could just throw something like that out there so flippantly.

"You might stay in Flagstaff?" he asks. "When did you decide this?"

"Today," I answer, because it's the truth. Opting for more honesty, I go on. "I've been trying to come up with a plan that doesn't involve staying home in Greyson this summer. I like it here, and I know a few people, so why not."

What I *don't* tell him is that I'm trying to come up with a plan that involves never going back to Phoenix again either.

I'm not a child. I'm twenty years old. I can make my own decisions. I can change the course of my life if I want to. I just have no idea what that new course should look like yet... or if I'll be able to navigate it successfully.

Flagstaff's as good a place as any to try and figure it out.

"Okay," he says, pushing away from my car and kneeling so his face is directly in front of me. "That settles it.

You definitely have to stay with us. We have the room, and we won't hound you for money."

"Shane, that's really sweet, but..."

He interrupts. "Seriously, Sydney, there's no sense paying for a shitty motel room when you can crash in Asher's old room."

"You guys have lives," I argue, though secretly I'm touched by his thoughtfulness. My reluctance has nothing to do with him and much, much more to do with *me*. "You don't need a strange girl hanging around."

"We'll come and go like normal," he says. "And you'll come and go however you need to while you look for a job. Maybe we can convince you to cook something every so often. Pizza gets old, believe it or not. Meanwhile, you'll have a safe place to stay."

Safe.

It surprises me how much I believe him.

Before I can talk myself out of it, I speak.

"Okay."

Well, I wanted out of my comfort zone. Looks like I got my wish.

Chapter 2

SHANE

GRACE'S MAID-OF-HONOR IS seriously gorgeous.

And seriously messed up about something.

I guess I'm a sucker for a pretty blonde with issues, because that's the only reason I can think of that I insisted she park herself at my place for the immediate future. Part of me regrets it already. This arrangement is going to put a damper on my social life for sure. I can't think of one girl in my list of contacts who won't automatically think something's fishy and give me some lame excuse why we can't hook up.

I pull in to my parking space in front of the townhouse, and Sydney parks next to me in Asher's old spot. I cut my eyes in her direction, and she looks at me with wary uncertainty.

I'm going to have to get to the bottom of what's up with her. It'll drive me crazy if I don't. Plus, digging around to figure her out should be all kinds of fun.

I force myself to behave like the twenty-three year old I am, rather than the randy teenager I sometimes act like. If Sydney's skittish about something, I don't want to add to it, so I'll be a gentleman. Despite what some people think, I'm familiar with the concept.

"Pop the trunk," I say, hopping out of the car. "I'll grab

your luggage."

"You don't have to do that." She steps out of the driver's seat and pushes the door shut, coming around to the back of the car.

The lavender bridesmaid dress looks fantastic on her. It only covers one shoulder, so the other one is bare, and her skin is smooth and creamy all the way from her neck to her wrist.

And yeah… I *so* should not be thinking about her that way.

"I can be a gentleman when I decide to be," I respond, grabbing a huge pink duffle bag out of the trunk. When she looks a little skeptical, I switch to humor. "Besides, pink is my color don't you think?"

She giggles, and dammit, I like the sound.

I know I can be… *a lot* sometimes. I joke around more than I act serious. I can be crude pretty often. I like to have fun, and I like girls who like to have fun. But does any of that preclude me being a gentleman also? I'd go to the mat any day of the week for my friends, so I don't think my penchant for off-color jokes and fun-loving girls is a black mark on my character.

From the back seat, Sydney retrieves an oversized backpack that looks like it's seen its better days. She practically has to hoist it to pull it from the car, so I reach out and take the strap from her, easily swinging it onto the shoulder opposite the pink bag.

"Is there a dead body in here?" I ask.

She looks at me with narrowed eyes. "Shoes, make-up, and hair accessories."

"The motherlode of girly stuff." I click the button on my key to lock my car and head toward the townhouse. "I'll treat it with care."

Unlocking the door, I motion for her to go in ahead of me, still being the gentleman I claimed to be.

I watch as she surveys the inside. To the right of the entryway is the staircase leading upstairs. "Master bedroom and private bath is up there," I say, nodding toward the steps. "That's Caleb's space. He was here first, so he got dibs."

Continuing down the short hallway, I motion to two doors, one on either side. "The door on the left is my room, and this one is the bathroom."

We step into the living room, which isn't huge, but isn't tiny either. The living area opens into the small kitchen on the left side. A door off the kitchen opens into the bedroom Asher just vacated.

Her eyes sweep across the living room and kitchen. It's fairly tidy for a bachelor pad. The sofa, love seat, and two overstuffed chairs – which all face the flat screen TV and gaming system cabinet – don't match, but they don't clash either. Seating is important when you host video game tournaments for the guys. In addition to the bar, that seats four people, we have a small table which can also seat four. Again, a necessity when ordering pizza for a house full of dudes.

"The door off the kitchen was Asher's room." I nod my head in that direction. "Guess it's yours now."

"For tonight," Sydney says, turning to face me for the first time since she stepped into the townhouse.

"No rush." For whatever reason, I like the way she looks all up in my space. I don't examine it too closely.

"Your place is nice." She smiles. "Not at all like I ex-pected."

"We're not slobs." I shrug my shoulders. "When you have to be tidy and precise in your professional life, it kind of spills over into your personal life, too."

"I guess that's true. Tattooists have to be pretty fastidious I imagine."

"We do."

An awkward moment passes, just a second really, when I realize that I'm standing in the middle of my apartment, a pink duffle bag on one shoulder, a backpack full of shoes and make-up on the other, talking to a smoking hot girl about how fastidious I am.

"Hey, I'm going to get out of this tux and have a beer," I say, breaking the silence and telling myself I'm just being nice. "You're welcome to join me if you want. Caleb won't be in for a while. He's taking Felicity home."

She shakes her head. "Thanks, but I'm just going to change and go to sleep. It's been a long couple of days."

"Okay." I choose to deny the disappointment that sparks inside me. "Let's get you settled in."

Pushing open the door to the now vacant bedroom, I notice that Asher re-made the bed with clean sheets. He's nice like that. I drop Sydney's bags on the mattress, looking around the room. The closet door is open, and inside it's empty. I'm certain the dresser is equally empty. Asher's been moving his stuff over to Grace's for the past couple of weeks.

"Plenty of space, so use as much of it as you need." I turn toward her as she puts her purse on the dresser and kicks off her silver high-heel sandals.

"Thanks," she answers. "I won't be a bother. I'll be out on the job hunt first thing Monday morning. I'll stay out of your way."

"You're not in the way, Sydney." I'm more than a little bit pissed at myself for the truth in those words, so before I utter any more stupid stuff, I back toward the door.

"Goodnight."

"Night, Shane."

I pull the door shut behind me and stand there like a dumbass, staring at the knob. After a few seconds I hear the lock click into place, the sound almost deafening in the silence of the moment.

Well, that's that.

I grab a beer from the fridge and place it on the table next to the couch. Once I shed this tux, I have a Heineken and round of *Call of Duty* waiting for me.

And a blonde in the other room who's either impervious to me or scared of me. I'm not sure which it is, but I should just leave it alone and let her be. But she's just so…

There's that thought again, about how Sydney's gorgeous and shy and alluring as hell. And since when am I into shy girls?

It's all the engagement and wedding stuff going on around here lately, I tell myself as I peel out of the tuxedo. I hang each piece of the tux carefully, getting it ready to head back to the rental place on Monday. The wedding madness has messed with my head. First Asher and Grace got engaged, then Gabe and Rachelle. Gabe and Rachelle practically eloped New Year's Eve. Well, technically it wasn't eloping since they took their moms, but they did go to Vegas to tie the knot, then came back to Flagstaff for a big party.

Grabbing a pair of jeans from my closet, I pull them on and think about all the wedding craziness of this week. Bachelor party. Rehearsal and dinner. Lavish ceremony and reception. Hell, even Caleb seems to be settling down with Felicity. Not to mention Bing and Kristy. It's only a matter of time before they get hitched and start the whole family life thing with Kristy's son, Ezra. Of course, the guys razzed me mercilessly at the bachelor party, which naturally was a video game marathon with pizza and beer... thus the Heineken still in my fridge. All of them – Asher, Gabe, Bing, and Caleb – told me over and over again that I was *next*. That my *one* is coming for me so I better get ready. Ash even nudged me and said he thought I was already ready, like the guys were giving me grief for still enjoying my unattached status, but he somehow suspected I was on the lookout for Ms. Right.

Could he be right?

I shake my head, exiting my room and making a bee-line for the beer next to the sofa. I take two huge gulps and decide they're all full of crap. It's just their happy ever after bullshit gone to their heads.

I'm the same Shane I've always been – over the top and life of the party.

I kill the beer and head to the kitchen for another one, then put all thoughts of women and relationships and all those unpleasant entanglements out of my mind.

It's time for *Call of Duty*.

Chapter 3

SYDNEY

I'T'S NOT YET seven o'clock. I set my alarm early, so I could make coffee before Shane and Caleb wake up. Also, I'd like to get in the bathroom first as well, to avoid any sort of weird bathroom overlap with Shane. I figure tattooists aren't early birds, so seven in the morning should be safe.

Riffling through my duffle bag, I find my comfiest pair of blue jeans and a long sleeve tee shirt bearing the name of my alma mater, Greyson High School. I take a moment to appreciate that I still fit into my high school clothes and that I did not gain the "freshman fifteen" everyone talks about, but rather had lost fifteen pounds before the end of my freshman year at Malpais College.

A year later, and I still haven't put those pounds back on.

Derailing that train of thought, I rewind back to last night and wonder how late the guys stayed up. I know Shane was up late. I heard him go back and forth between the living room and kitchen a few times, and even though the video game volume was low enough not to disturb me, I couldn't help but be aware of him, just on the other side of the door. Caleb came in sometime after midnight, presumably after dropping his girlfriend Felicity off at home. Felicity is a nice girl. During the wedding festivities I'd learned that she's a nurse and had ascertained that she's in her early to mid twenties. After hearing Caleb arrive home last night, he and Shane had engaged in a short conversation that I assume had to do with me staying in Asher's old room. It had been a quiet conversation and no voices were raised, so hopefully Caleb has no objection to my presence. It had been quiet in the townhouse after their conversation, but who knows how much longer the two of them were awake.

I grab my clothes and my bag of make-up and hygiene products, intending to stop in the kitchen long enough to start a pot of coffee before heading to the shower. I open the bedroom door and back out, tip-toeing and pulling the door closed silently. Then I turn toward the kitchen and realize I'm not alone.

A very shirtless Shane, wearing only a pair of low-slung jeans, stands at the counter measuring coffee grounds into the filter. His left arm is covered from elbow to shoulder with an enormous tattoo of a tree. It's bare except for a few leaves still hanging on, while wind whips through, spinning leaves in the air around the branches. The wings of a giant eagle spread across his upper back, the body of the bird covering him from shoulder blades to the bottom of his ribcage. In its talons, the eagle holds a scroll of paper, partially unrolled to reveal the word *strength*.

"Morning," he says, his voice still gravelly from sleep.

I snap myself out of *checking him out* mode.

"Shane." I'm surprised, but not startled, which is kind of astonishing in itself. "Hi."

I can't help but notice him. I've been noticing him all weekend during every wedding activity. There's no denying he's cute. Boyish in one way, but rugged and rough-edged in another. His icy blue eyes are piercing, and his blond hair is just messy enough to invite hands to run through it. Not that I'm ever going to do that. Shirtless, though. Yikes. Lean muscle and smooth skin, inked artwork on his chest and his sides. He's difficult not to look at.

And he's genuinely nice. Grace told me he was a good guy, even though he sometimes projects something else to the world. She also told me he plays the field… a lot. I think she was warning me. She has no idea that the warning is completely unnecessary.

"You a coffee drinker?" he asks as he flips the coffee pot switch on.

I nod. "I thought I was up early enough to make it. Didn't figure you or Caleb would be up this soon on a Sunday."

He shrugs. "I'm a morning person despite my best efforts. I try to sleep late, but it rarely works out that way."

"Me too, it seems." It's an honest answer, at least for the last year or so.

"You headed to the shower?" he asks, gesturing to the clothes and tote bag in my hands. He drops onto a barstool and props his elbows on the white and gray formica countertop.

"Unless you need to get in there first."

Shane shakes his head. "I'm in no rush. Go ahead. Coffee will be ready when you get done."

I've got showering in a hurry down to a science. When you live in a dorm with community bathrooms, you learn how to get in and out quick. When you're completely uncomfortable in that situation, you learn how to do it even quicker. I can wash and condition my hair, shave all the appropriate places, and soap the rest of my body in ten minutes or less. Today is no different, and I'm dried off and dressed in no time.

I dry my hair quickly, not bothering to smooth it out and definitely not going to the trouble of using my flat iron. Instead, I take my wavy blonde locks and pile them on top of my head in a messy bun. A small dust of powder on my face, and a speedy application of mascara, and I'm satisfied I look awake and alert, properly female, and yet not so made-up that it looks like I'm going to extra effort for some reason.

I don't know why I expected Shane to be gone when I emerged from the bathroom, but I'm a bit surprised to find him still in the kitchen. He has a cup of coffee in his hand and a forlorn look on his face as he assesses the contents of the refrigerator.

"There's not much in the way of breakfast, unless you want cold pizza," he says. "We do have a loaf of bread though, so I can make toast."

"You don't have to make me breakfast, Shane."

"I'm going to make myself some," he replies. "Seemed the polite thing to do to offer to make you some as well."

Ok Sydney. He's trying to be polite. Just accept it.

"Toast is great." I smile, and it's genuine, even if I had to force it.

I drop my tote bag back in my room, then pad back into the kitchen in search of a coffee mug. I don't have to look long, because Shane has already set one beside the coffee machine for me.

"Sugar's in the cabinet above the coffee, if you want it." He looks up from the toaster and nods towards the cabinet door. "And surprisingly enough the milk in the fridge is still good. There's just not much left."

"I only need a splash of it for my coffee," I say, bypassing the sugar and heading for the milk in the refrigerator.

The toaster pops up, and I see Shane remove two pieces and place them on a plate with two others. From a cabinet above the toaster, he retrieves a jar of strawberry jelly.

"Apparently someone wanted PB&J, but never opened the jelly." He slides the plate of toast and the jelly onto the bar, then pulls open a drawer and retrieves two butter knives. "Lucky for us, huh?"

I just smile in response.

For several moments we don't talk. We just drink coffee and eat toast with jelly. It dawns on me that even though it feels strange, I'm not freaking out. I decide that's an achievement.

"So where are you looking for work?" Shane asks, polishing off his last bit of toast and walking to the coffee pot for a refill.

"I'm not sure, actually," I answer. "I thought I'd go get a newspaper this morning, then scout around online today. I'll hit the pavement Monday and start putting in applications, but I'm not picky."

He returns to the barstool across from me. "I know a few business owners. People who've been to Resolution for ink. Mainly restaurants and retail. I'll call around today, see if anyone needs summer help. Lots of places hire for the summer since so many NAU students go home over the break."

"You don't have to do that, Shane." I can't help the protest that escapes my lips.

"You're going to have to stop saying that, Sydney," he says.

"I just don't want to be a bother."

He scoots his coffee mug out of the way and leans across the bar on both elbows. "You're Grace's best friend, Syd. That makes you part of our crew. You've got a place to belong here with us, so you're going to have to learn to accept help from us."

Part of their *crew.* A place to *belong.*

How long has it been since I felt either of those things? The start of my freshman year at Malpais College? No. It was before that. It was high school… with Grace.

I want those things so badly it kind of shocks me. But at the same time, I'm afraid to reach for them. I guess the first step is doing what Shane said… learning to accept help.

"Okay."

Chapter 4

SHANE

S YDNEY'S ALREADY GONE, in search of a Sunday paper, by the time Caleb rolls out of bed. I'm about ready to head out myself, so I nod toward the coffee pot as I grab my keys off the kitchen counter.

"Coffee's still hot," I say.

Caleb grumbles in response.

Unlike me, Caleb doesn't do mornings very well.

I slip my feet into my well-worn Converse and start toward the front of the townhouse.

"Wait up," Caleb says, just before taking the first hit of coffee. After a second gulp, he goes on. "Can we talk for a sec?"

I stop in the middle of the living room and turn back to him.

"Syndey here?" he asks.

I shake my head. "She went out to get a newspaper."

He takes a seat at the bar, his wrinkled University of Kentucky tee shirt reminding me that though he's now an Arizonian through and through, his roots are in Kentucky. He's got that serious look on his face, the one he reserves for when he goes all authority figure on me. He's only twenty-five, but since he's the oldest one of us, besides Bing, sometimes he plays the "I'm your elder" card.

"What are you doing, Shane?"

I narrow my eyes. "Excuse me?"

"With Sydney," he clarifies. "What are you doing?"

"I offered her our spare room for a few nights," I answer. "Figured it was the nice thing to do."

Caleb takes another long sip of his coffee, then sits the mug down. "You can't mess around with her. She's Grace's best friend. That makes her one of us now. You'll screw things up for the whole Resolution family if you get tangled up with her."

It worked for Gabe and Rachelle, I think, but I don't say it. First, because I don't want to antagonize Caleb and make this little confrontation any worse than it already is. Second, because I have no intention of going the Gabe and Rachelle route with Sydney.

"I'm not *messing* with her," I say, raising my voice a bit. I'm irritated and I want him to know it. "I'm helping her out. Like you pointed out, she's Grace's best friend. What kind of friend would I be to Grace if I let Sydney stay in some shit hole motel, when we have an empty bedroom?"

I know Sydney isn't the type of girl you mess around with, and it pisses me off that Caleb thinks I can't tell the difference between Sydney and the kind of girls I usually hang out with. Those girls know the score and are fine with it. They know I'm not in it for commitment or long-term. It's all about the fun. Sydney isn't that type of girl.

And what exactly does it say about me that I'm spending my time with the other type of girl?

I put that thought away as quickly as it floats through my mind.

Caleb nods. "That's understandable, and I'm happy the two of us can offer her a place to stay for a few days. But just be careful. Don't let her mistake your helpfulness for something else you can't follow through on."

Can't follow through on? Am I really that big of a jerk? I know I'm not exactly bring-home-to-mom material, but I've always been up front with girls about the no strings requirement.

I twirl my keys on my finger and look at Caleb for a moment, choosing my next words carefully.

"Will do," I sneer, saluting him like he's my commanding officer. "And thanks for the vote of confidence in my character."

I turn and walk down the hall toward the front door.

"Shane, I didn't mean…" Caleb calls after me.

The rest of his statement is cut off as I slam the door behind me and jump in my car.

SYDNEY'S CAR IS parked in Asher's old spot when I get back to the townhouse. Caleb steps out onto the front steps as soon as I put the transmission in park. He must've been watching for me to return.

Fantastic. He probably wants to continue that super pleasant conversation we had before I left.

I hit the button to lift the trunk on the used Audi I bought earlier this year, pull the keys from the ignition, and hop out of the car, bracing myself for whatever else Caleb plans to throw at me.

"I owe you an apology," Caleb says, meeting me at the back of the car.

I lift the trunk lid all the way up, blocking us from the window in Sydney's room.

"Yeah, you do." I turn to face him full on, not bothering to mask the frustration in my expression. "Before Felicity, you played around just as much as me, and I never gave you crap about it. I'm capable of being nice to a girl without trying to get in her pants. I'm also capable of being honest and not sending mixed messages. Give me a little credit."

"You're right." Caleb nods. "I was out of line. I know you well enough to know both those things."

Maybe he senses something is off with Sydney and wants to look out for her. I can't fault him for that. But I can tell something's iffy with her, too, and I'm not the kind of guy who would take advantage of that.

"What's in the grocery bags?" he asks, pointing to the trunk of my car.

"Our fridge is pathetic, man. Practically nothing but beer and pizza left from Ash's bachelor party. I got some juice and milk, and some bagels and a few boxes of cereal. Stuff like that. So at least we've got something to offer her while she's here."

Caleb pins me with a look, and I know he's wondering why I'm going to the trouble.

"Just trying to be a nice host," I say, handing him two of the grocery bags. "I doubt orange juice is the way to seduce her. Pretty sure she doesn't see me like that anyway."

Together we carry the groceries inside.

"She said hi when she came in but then went right into her room," Caleb whispers as we put the groceries away. "She's been in there ever since."

"Well, when she comes back out be sure you make her feel welcome," I say, keeping my voice low. "She probably thinks you're pissed because I sprung this on you without talking to you first."

Just then, the door to her bedroom opens and Sydney steps out into the kitchen. She looks back and forth between Caleb and me, clearly surprised – and maybe a bit uncomfortable – to be in the same room with the two of us.

"Hey, Syd." I keep my voice light. "I've restocked the fridge and the cabinets so maybe you won't starve while you're here."

"You didn't have to –"

"I told you to quit saying that." I cut off her protest. "We're glad to help. Right, Caleb?"

"Right," he says, picking up on my lead. "Grace would kill us if we let you stay in a crappy motel. You're welcome here as long as you need."

She takes a deep breath, and I watch her closely. All kinds of emotions are at war on her face. Happiness and uncertainty. Thankfulness and worry. It's like she's letting them all have a say before choosing which one to go with.

Finally, she says, "Thanks. I appreciate it."

Good. I'm glad she kicked uncertainty and worry on their asses.

"I'm meeting Felicity for lunch, so I've got to run. If you think of anything else we need for the kitchen, shoot me a text."

I nod. "Sure thing.

Before leaving, Caleb stops in front of Sydney and says, "Any friend of Grace's is a friend of ours, too. We're really glad to have you here."

"Thanks again," she whispers.

Reaching in my back pocket, I retrieve the paper with the names and numbers I jotted down for her. I made a few calls while I was out and found some potential jobs for her.

"These are some people I know who might be hiring for the summer. I talked to a couple of them and left a voicemail for the others, so they're all expecting to hear from you or see an application from you."

"Wow," she says, taking the paper from me. "Thanks."

I'm glad she didn't tell me once again that I didn't have to do that.

From the cabinet, I pull two plates and sit them on the counter. "I'm going to have some lunch and chill in front of the TV for a while. Join me?"

She hesitates, and I hate it. Good grief, does everyone here think I'm about to rip her clothes off every time I speak to her?

"Sydney, I'm not going to jump your bones," I say, reaching in the refrigerator for the meat and cheese I just put in there. "I'm being nice. You're Grace's friend, and that makes you my friend, too. I'm not offering a roll in the sheets. I'm offering a sandwich and a movie."

She looks at me, as if assessing the truth of my words.

Thankfully, it doesn't take long for her to decide I'm being honest, and she actually smiles at me when she says, "Okay."

Chapter 5

SYDNEY

IT'S JUST BEFORE eight o'clock on Monday morning, and I'm standing in my bedroom – my temporary bedroom – trying to decide what to wear. I don't have any actual interviews scheduled, but Shane says some of the people he contacted are expecting to see me, so I want to look my best.

Shane. What a wonder he's turned out to be. He's been kind and helpful, and I feel more comfortable with him than I've felt with anyone since…

Nope. Not going there.

But I will acknowledge and appreciate that Shane is a good guy, just like Grace said, and that he's been nicer to me than anyone in a very long time, for no other reason than because he's a decent man.

Decent men aren't easy to come by, so I'm thankful that I've met him and Caleb and the rest of the guys in their circle.

I've already had a cup of coffee, with Shane of course. I managed to beat him to the kitchen this morning, so I'm the one who made the coffee, but he came wandering in just as I hit the switch to turn the pot on. He pulled out a package of blueberry bagels and toasted one for each of us. It was easier this morning, sharing coffee and breakfast with him. I didn't find myself at a loss for words, or wanting to apologize all the time for inconveniencing him.

First major score since leaving my comfort zone.

I didn't call my parents yesterday, despite my promises to do so. I know they're both at work now, but my brother Devin is home, so I decide to give him a call. My parents will hopefully be satisfied that I called, and I'd rather talk to Devin anyway.

Picking my cell phone up from the mattress, I lay back on my pillow and dial Devin's number.

"Sydney, it's you," he says in way of answering the call. "I'm glad you called. Maria is here, and she's going to make cupcakes. I want ice cream with mine, but she says that's too much sugar and mom won't like it. Tell her to let me have ice cream."

Devin is thirteen years old. He's amazingly smart and jubilantly happy most of the time. He's also autistic… high-functioning. It's not uncommon for his stream of thought to come barreling out of his mouth, especially to someone he's familiar with. Maria is his occupational therapist, and I know the cupcake cooking lesson is a device to get him working on his attention span and fine motor skills.

"Hold up, Dev," I say with a laugh. "It's only eight in the morning. It's a bit early to be worrying about dessert don't you think."

"I know, but I like to plan out every part of my day," he says. "You know that."

"I do know that," I reply. "But give Maria a break. She's just following Mom's guidelines about sugar."

Devin doesn't answer. He just sighs.

"Hey, I need your advice," I say, which pulls him out of his pout. He loves to be asked to help.

"Okay." His voice perks up immediately. "What?"

"Well, I'm going out to talk with some important people today, and I don't know what to wear."

"You should wear your pink dress." His response is quick. He has my wardrobe memorized apparently. "You look good in pink. Did you know there are over twenty-nine thousand shades of pink? I like orchid pink and fuchsia the best, but the baby pink color of your dress is nice, too."

Devin fixates on things pretty often. Sometimes it's a historical event. Sometimes it's a movie or book. Lately, one of his fixations has been colors. Some people find his random bits of knowledge annoying, but I think it's cool. I've learned lots of things because Devin's gotten himself hooked on one thing or another and felt compelled to share it all with me.

"Twenty-nine thousand?" I ask. "That's a lot. Thanks for the dress suggestion. I'll wear the pink dress and my white sweater."

"Sweaters make you look like Grandma," he says, and I can't help but crack up. "Don't wear that. Wear the blue jean jacket. It's way cooler."

He's right. The denim jacket is cooler. "Okay, Mr. Fashion Designer. I'll wear the blue jean jacket."

"Who are the important people you're going to see?"

"Well, I'm hoping to get a job here in Flagstaff, and I'm really nervous."

"Why are you going to get a job in Flagstaff? It's a long way to Flagstaff. You should get a job in Greyson."

"You know how when I'm at college I live in Phoenix instead of Greyson?" I ask, knowing this is going to be hard for him to understand.

"Yeah."

"Well, I'm going to stay in Flagstaff this summer, kind of like I stay in Phoenix during school."

"Why?"

"Because I like it here. Grace is here."

"You don't want to come home and live with me?" His voice doesn't sound sad. He usually doesn't show emotions through the words he says. Right now he's gathering information in order to figure out what's going on.

"I love being with you, Devin," I begin. "But I'm a grown up now, and I'm not always going to live in Mom and Dad's house. Eventually I'm going to live in my own house. This summer is a way for me to practice. And once I have a place of my own to live, you can come visit me."

This grabs his interest, and he seems satisfied.

"You are awesome, Sydney. Those important people would be stupid not to give you a job."

"You're good for my confidence, Devin," I say. "I love you. I hope mom and dad are doing okay?" It's a statement, but my tone of voice makes it a question.

He doesn't tell me he loves me back, which isn't unusual. He shows love in other ways. "Mom and Dad are worried about you. I don't know why. I just heard them talking."

No, Devin doesn't know why they worry about me, and that's they way I want to keep it.

"I'll call them after they get home from work tonight," I promise. "I'll make sure they don't worry so much."

"Okay, Sydney. Bye."

And he hangs up, which also isn't unusual. When he's done talking, he's done talking.

Whatever uncertainties still hang over me, my conversation with Devin definitely boosts my mood. I'm still smiling when I step out of my room, dressed in the outfit

Devin chose for me, and find Shane in the kitchen.

He pauses, coffee pot halfway to his mug, and stares.

For a moment I worry that maybe something is wrong with the way I look, but then he smiles. "You look great, Syd."

I swallow back the comment that would've played off his compliment and simply say, "Thank you."

"Having one more cup before I head to work." He gestures to his coffee mug.

Shane is a tattoo artist at Resolution Ink, the same shop where Asher and Caleb work. Judging by the visible ink on all of them, including the owner, Bing, I imagine they're all ridiculously talented.

"I'm off on the job hunt," I say. "Wish me luck."

"Good luck, Sydney." He nods his head toward me. "You'll do great."

✧   ✧   ✧

Talking to Devin was good for me. Enough that after dropping off five job applications and meeting three potential employers, I feel like celebrating. Without much trouble, I find a place that does take out sushi and order two of my favorite rolls – spicy tuna and crab avocado – along with tempura vegetables. I'd pick up some for Shane, too, but I have no idea if he even likes sushi. Also, I don't know what time he'll be home. Tattooists don't exactly keep regular business hours. And last, I don't have his cell phone number to text and ask.

Step two in moving further out of my comfort zone… figure out a way to ask for his phone number without swallowing my tongue.

Once I'm alone at the townhouse, I change into gray yoga pants and an oversized sweatshirt that comes almost to my knees, then head to the kitchen to enjoy my celebratory dinner. I pull a can of soda from the refrigerator and hop up on a barstool.

Even though I'm alone, I don't feel lonely, and that in itself is a new feeling. I've been lonely for a long time, it seems, even in a room full of people. But sitting here in Shane and Caleb's townhouse, knowing that the two of them will eventually be here and that, for some reason I don't really understand, they care about me, I'm somehow filled with a sense of friendship and connection.

If I'd needed any confirmation that staying in Flagstaff was the right decision, this feeling is it.

After dinner, I accept that it's time to call my parents. I know Devin hasn't told them about my plans to stay in Flagstaff. He doesn't normally offer information about other people. If you ask him about someone, he'll talk, but otherwise, it doesn't necessarily occur to him to share something about me or anyone else with our parents.

Mom answers quickly, just like I knew she would.

"Sydney!" She sounds excited. "I thought we'd hear from you yesterday."

"I meant to call," I say. "I just got caught up and forgot."

"When are you coming home?" she asks. Way to cut right to the point, Mom.

I take a deep breath and decide to just dive right in. "I'm going to stay in Flagstaff, Mom."

She's quiet for a moment, like she's digesting what I just said. "Why?"

Just one word, but all the heartbreak of the past year is encompassed in it. I love her so much for being broken-hearted for me, for carrying me along when I couldn't carry myself... but I need to carry myself again. And staying in

Flagstaff is my first step.

"Mom, I have to start moving forward. It's time for me to stand on my own two feet. Staying in Flagstaff this summer is a good way to start."

"But where will you live?"

"I'll get an apartment once I find a job. In the meantime, I'm staying with some of Grace's friends that I met at the wedding. They're nice people, Mom," I reassure her.

"Are you sure about this, Sydney?" she asks. "Wouldn't you feel better working in Greyson and living here?"

I know she would feel better if I did that, but I would just be stuck.

"No," I tell her. "I want to feel independent again, Mom. It's time."

I hear her heavy sigh across the phone line. "As long as you're sure."

"I'm sure, Mom." I can feel her reluctance, but also her desire to let me choose my own path. "I know this is hard for you to understand. You and Dad have always taken such good care of me, and I'm so grateful, but it's time for me to start taking care of myself."

"All right, Sydney," she says. "Just know that you can always, always come home."

"I know," I answer. "And it gives me more peace of mind than I can tell you."

Chapter 6

SHANE

IT'S AFTER MIDNIGHT when my cell phone buzzes. I ignore it and let it go to voicemail. Despite knowing I'll wake up at seven, or earlier, I'm still awake and sitting on the couch, some random movie playing on the TV, nursing the same Heineken I opened an hour ago. Caleb turned in about thirty minutes ago, and Sydney's been asleep forever.

Sydney. In the space of the last week, she's threaded herself into my life without even trying. It's been completely unintentional on my part, too, but since the moment she arrived for Asher and Grace's wedding rehearsal, she's had my full attention. It's stupid to keep pretending it isn't true, so I might as well admit it, at least to myself.

We've established a bit of a routine in the four days she's been staying here. Since apparently we're both early birds, we have coffee and breakfast together each morning. Caleb never rolls out of bed until after ten, so it's a nice quiet start to the day, just the two of us. I'm kind of bewildered by how much I look forward to those moments each morning, but I just can't help myself.

I also can't help but wonder about her. Things like how many boyfriends has she had. How many of them were serious? Which one of them hurt her and made her skittish? What's it like to feel love from her, and why the hell would anyone hurt her?

I feel like a fool, but damn, she's nice. I know that's something guys say when a girl isn't super pretty, but with Sydney, it's the truth. She's nice, like in a way most human beings aren't. She's kind and soft spoken, and she looks at you when you talk to her, like listening to you is the most important thing in the world to her. And that notion that a girl who's called nice isn't all that pretty… total bullshit when it comes to Sydney. She's freaking beautiful. Blonde hair that just barely tinges strawberry in the right light. Gorgeous, deep green eyes that swim with all kinds of emotion. She's slim, almost too slim, but she's still got curves, and she's about a foot shorter than me, which means she'd fit nicely right up against my chest.

And… stop, Shane. Just stop. Regardless of the fact that I'm now being honest, at least in my own mind, about how much I'm drawn to her, Sydney Baldwin is off limits. Like Caleb pointed out, she's one of us now, and I only do casual when it comes to girls. And you just don't do casual when it comes to your friends. Friends with benefits is a myth anyway. Once benefits get involved, friendship eventually goes down the toilet.

My phone buzzes again, and this time I look at it.

Greg Dawson. My uncle. My mom's brother.

I haven't heard from him in months. We aren't estranged, but we've never been super close, despite the fact that I lived with him for several years. He calls every so often to keep me posted on my mom's *condition*, so the fact that he's calling must mean…

"Greg," I say, putting the phone to my ear and taking a long drink of my beer.

"Shane, it's your mom."

That could mean many things. It could mean she's in

the hospital again, with yet another side effect of her cocaine habit. It could mean she's been arrested again. It could mean she's decided to try rehab once more. Or it could mean something worse.

"What is it?"

"I hadn't seen her for several months, since not long after I called you last time," he begins.

The last time we'd spoken she'd wound up in the emergency room after passing out on the street in a pretty seedy section of Albuquerque. Someone called the cops, and she got arrested for public intoxication. She got hooked up with some kind of drug counselor after that, but if she dropped off the map and Greg hasn't heard from her since then, I'm certain the counseling had little to no effect.

"She's in the hospital in Santa Fe," he says. "It's bad."

It's always bad with Shaneen. My mother, Shaneen Dawson, has been using cocaine, and God knows what else, regularly since my father cut and ran when I was two years old. I really have no memory of him, and all I know is that his name is Trent, and he and Shaneen weren't married. When I was ten, she lost custody of me after the police showed up at my house to arrest her over a bunch of bad checks and found out I'd been home alone for a week. I'd been taking care of myself just fine without her, but of course, once child protective services got involved, I wound up in the system. Fortunately, Greg stepped in and saved me from foster care.

Shaneen would pop in and out of my life in random intervals after that. Since I was with Greg, she could see me if she wanted, and sometimes she even stayed with us for a few weeks at a time. But she always left again. We never knew when or for how long, and I learned early that she couldn't be counted on.

She's my mom, and I do love her, but trying to maintain a relationship with her has become a toxin in my life that I just cannot afford.

"How bad?" I ask, downing the rest of my Heineken.

"Lymphoma," Greg answers, the gravity in his voice evident even over the cell phone connection.

"What in the world is that? Some kind of cancer?" It sounds awful. Of course, most things that result from drug abuse are awful.

"Yes, it's cancer," he replies, and my stomach drops to my feet. "More specifically in her case, AIDS-related cancer."

All the breath seems to leave my lungs, and my chest feels like it could explode. No one should ever hear those two words – AIDS and cancer – in the same sentence. One is bad enough, but both?

"Shit." I sit up straighter, like being ready to spring into action will somehow make this conversation easier.

"No one's sure when or how she contracted HIV," Greg continues. "She has track marks on her arms where she's been shooting up, so it could've been a dirty needle. But God knows who she's slept with over the years, so it could be sexually transmitted. She may have been infected for up to ten years and just not known it."

I run a hand through my hair, pulling sharply as if to redirect some of my pain. "I don't guess it matters much how she got it. The result is the same."

"I had no idea until last week when the hospital in Santa Fe called me to tell me she was there. She probably had no idea either. With so many physical problems related her drug use, I'm sure a few new ones didn't even register with her."

I can't speak. I just wait for him to go on.

"There are a lot of treatments these days to help AIDS patients, but she's had the virus for no telling how long, and, of course, it's gone completely untreated. The cancer is a result of the virus, and it's already advanced and spread to the bone marrow, spleen, and liver. There's not much left to do for her."

Not much left to do for her. There's the answer to the question I hadn't asked. I drop my head, letting it droop from my shoulders, and exhale a breath I didn't realize I'd been holding.

"We're moving her to Albuquerque tomorrow, to my house, for hospice care." Each word hits me in the gut with the force of a canon. "You need to come, Shane," Greg says, his voice low and serious. "You need to see her. She doesn't have long."

"Greg, it's not that simple for me. You know that." And he does. Better than anyone, I imagine.

"I know, Shane, but she's your mom. And she's dying. As difficult as I know it is for you to be around her, if she dies and you haven't at least said goodbye, you'll regret it for the rest of your life." His words have a ring of truth to them that I don't want to hear. "I think you should come not for her, but for you. It's you I'm most concerned about."

"I'll think about it." It's the most I can do at the moment.

"All right," Greg says.

We hang up without goodbyes, because really, what would we say to each other under the circumstances?

I've always known the drug abuse would kill my mom, and I accepted it even though I didn't want to. But faced with the reality that what I've always known would happen, is, in fact, about to happen, something in me unhinges…

shifts irrevocably.

My mom is dying of AIDS because she either shared a needle or had unprotected sex with an infected person. Or both.

I know Greg is right. I should see her. But I don't want to go back and have to face all the crap that was a part of my life in Albuquerque. I don't try to hide what I came from, but every time I think about it I feel like I'm giving the past a little power over me, and I hate that. Where I am now is so much better than where I came from. I made a life for myself, created advantages I'd have never had in Albuquerque.

And hell... what will Sydney think if she finds out the truth about my past? I have no right to her, no hold on her, but damn it if I don't care what she thinks of me. I think I'd die if she thought less of me because of my past.

A weight settles on my chest, and my breath comes in quick gasps. I have no idea what I'm feeling, whether it's sadness or anger or something foreign that I've never felt before. All I know is that I don't want to feel it.

Silently, I walk into the kitchen and get another beer.

A few minutes later, still standing in front of the open fridge, I get another.

✧　　✧　　✧

I'M ON BEER number seven when I close the refrigerator too loudly. I hear Sydney stir in her room, the bed creaking as she gets up.

Shit. I woke her up. Her footsteps are soft, but I hear them as she gets closer to the door, and quickly I assess my state of mind.

I'm not drunk, but I'm buzzing enough to feel somewhat better than I did when I hung up with Greg.

Or worse, considering Sydney's about to see me in this condition.

"Shane?" Her voice is a whisper as she pushes the door open and peers into the kitchen.

And damn, does she look crazy hot. Pink boxer shorts and a white tee shirt that hangs off one shoulder, combined with sleepy eyes and pillow rumpled hair, and I'm in heaven. Or hell, depending on your point of view.

"Sorry I woke you," I say, my voice louder than I meant for it to be.

Her eyes dart from me, to the beer in my hand, and over to the living room where six empty beer bottles sit on the floor beside the sofa.

Shame is a living thing inside my chest. Stupid, careless behavior, and now she's seeing the worst of me.

Without a word, she slips out of her bedroom, quietly pulling the door shut behind her. She walks to the living room, her feet silent as they pad across the floor. She gathers the beer bottles in both arms, somehow managing to hold all six of them without clanging any of them together. I watch, stunned speechless, as she brings them back to the kitchen and hides them under the sink.

She looks at me then, without a trace of condemnation in her eyes. I'm so bowled over by the compassion she's showing toward me, even though she has absolutely no idea what's going on, that I take the partially drunk beer in my hand and pour it down the sink. After placing the bottle under the sink with the others, I face her once again, unsure what to say.

"What's wrong Shane?" Her voice is the same, sweet tone I've come to expect. I love that she automatically assumes that I've been drinking because something is wrong, rather than because I'm a guy who drinks excessively for the fun of it.

"My mom's dying," I blurt out. Until I heard the words I had no idea I was planning to say them.

"Oh, Shane," she says, reaching out to take my hand. "I'm so sorry."

It's the first time she's ever touched me, other than when we walked up the aisle together after Asher and Grace's wedding ceremony. I've just told her my mom is dying, and the only thing I can think about is that she's touching me. Of her own free will. And I freaking love it.

"It's been a long time coming," I reply, thinking maybe that'll be enough to stave off any further questions, because no way do I want to get into the nasty details of my mom's health decline.

She looks toward the living room then back at me. "Do you want to talk?"

Yes and no. Yes, I want to talk to her more than I want to breathe. No, I don't want her to know all the sordid details of my past. But I've had just enough beer to make me loose-lipped against my better judgment.

So, I nod, and not letting go of my hand, Sydney leads us to the couch.

She doesn't sit beside me, but rather on the other end of the sofa. At least she's on the same piece of furniture as me. Up until now, she's always made sure to sit in the furthest chair from the one I'm in.

"I'm really sorry," she says. "About your mom."

Then I talk. And by talk, I mean the words run out of my mouth faster than I can even think about them. I tell her about Mom's drug abuse, about living with Greg until I was sixteen, about mom's diagnosis and the fact that she's starting hospice care once she's back in Albuquerque. I don't know why I'm so comfortable with her, why I'm so driven to share things with her, but despite the fact that I know I'm crossing all kinds of lines, I feel a deep trust and affection for her. Confiding in her is easy.

Thankfully, I don't have so much beer in me that I forget to leave out what happened after I left Greg's at age sixteen. That's a story for another time. Like, never.

"Greg wants me to come see her," I tell her, once I'm finished with the details of her condition. "He thinks I'll regret it if I don't."

"He could be right." Her leg, which she curled underneath her while I was talking, stretches across the sofa, and she nudges me with her foot. "Or, he could be wrong, and you'll regret seeing her in that condition, regret drudging up all the unpleasantness of your relationship with her."

I grab her foot, closing my hand around it and noticing that she doesn't pull away, doesn't even flinch. "Would I be wrong to say no? To not go see her?"

Sydney shakes her head. "Not if that's what you really believe is best for you. No one can make this decision but you. Not me, and not your uncle. Just you."

I squeeze her foot but keep silent.

"Sometimes when something tragic happens, everybody thinks they know what you should do, how you should feel." The degree of understanding with which she says that is almost scary. "But only you know how you feel. No one should try to tell you, because they haven't walked in your shoes."

Her toes wiggle against my palm, and I swear on everything that's important to me that it's the most intimate thing I've ever experienced. I'm afraid to say anything or move, because I don't want her to take her foot away, so I sit still and quiet, my fingers still wrapped around her toes.

Closing my eyes, I decide to just enjoy the moment.

Chapter 7

SYDNEY

MY FIRST CLUE that I'm not in my bed is the fact that my feet are resting on something very warm and very solid. Cracking one eye open, I realize I'm lying on the couch. Shane is on the other end, which reclines. His legs are extended on the footrest, and my feet are resting in his lap.

It doesn't escape me that I'm asleep on the couch with a guy. A really hot guy. A really hot guy who had an awful night. I can't imagine how he feels, facing the imminent death of his mother, with whom he has a complicated, strained relationship. He looks so peaceful just now, his head resting against the back cushion, face turned slightly toward me. The light peeking through the blinds tells me it's close to seven o'clock, so I know he won't sleep much longer. Like me, he's an early riser even after a late night.

Slowly, I lift my feet from his lap, being as gentle as I can so that he can sleep as long as possible. When he doesn't stir, I swing my legs to the floor and push up off the sofa. I back away, tip-toeing to keep silent and watching to make sure he doesn't wake.

I slept the whole night, well, at least the part of it that didn't involve talking to Shane, without waking up. Without bad dreams. Without the feeling of fear that often accompanies me at night.

In the bathroom, I brush my teeth and throw my hair up in a ponytail. Creeping back up the hall, I find Shane still asleep, so I silently make my way to the kitchen. Taking the coffee carafe over to the sink, I run the water slowly, making as little noise as possible. I load the filter and the coffee grounds, and I'm just about to press start when I hear Shane stirring. Without a word or a glance, he heads down the hallway to his room.

I know he's torn up inside, waking up to realize it wasn't a dream and the terrible things he felt during the dark of the night are indeed real. I know all too well what a cruel prank a bright, new morning can be. There's an instant, when you first open your eyes, when things are fresh and rife with wonderful possibilities. But then reality comes crashing in, and all the awful things that hurt you are still there.

The coffee begins to drip, the pleasant aroma filling the air, and I hear Shane's bedroom door open, followed by the opening of the bathroom door. The shower kicks on a moment later. *Good,* I think to myself. Sometimes a shower can give you a boost... a different perspective... the energy to at least make it through the day.

With the coffee close to finished, I retrieve two mugs from the dishwasher full of clean dishes and sit them on the counter. Shane walks in a moment later wearing clean clothes, his hair still damp from the shower. I pour a cup of coffee and hand it to him, turning back to pour my own, stirring in a splash of milk. Wordlessly, we drink our coffee, stealing glances at one another over the rims of our mugs.

I'm not sure how we arrived at this no talking conclusion, but it isn't uncomfortable. In fact, after the events of last night and the heaviness of all we talked about, it's kind of peaceful.

When my cup is empty, I sit it on the counter and reach to open a cabinet, intending to get bowls for cereal. I'm stopped when Shane's hands land on the counter on either side of me, his arms brushing mine as his chin comes to rest lightly on my left shoulder. I'm complete boxed in, almost trapped, but it's not the least bit threatening. The fact that it isn't says a lot about how I feel about Shane as a person... and as a man.

For several seconds we just stand there, in this sort-of-but-not-quite embrace. I force myself to keep my breathing even. Nerves jump beneath my skin, not because I'm afraid, but because he's so close. I feel the heat from his body searing into the back of me, and his breath brushes softly along my neck.

"Thank you," he whispers.

I swallow hard, willing my voice not to tremble when I respond. "No problem."

He turns his head toward me slightly, so that his next words are spoken directly in my ear. "I was pretty buzzed last night, but I remember what we talked about. I unloaded way more than I should've on you."

"I didn't mind," I say, resisting the urge to turn my face toward his. "You obviously needed to vent."

"I did." I feel him nod. "And I didn't want to talk to anyone but you."

My stomach flips. "I'm glad I could help."

He lifts his hands from the counter and steps back enough that I can turn to face him.

"You're looking at me the same way you did before you knew the truth about my mom. You didn't even blink when I told you she was a junkie who now has AIDS."

I smile up at him, amazed that he would worry so

much about my opinion. "I'd never kick you while you were down. Believe me. I know what it's like for someone to hurt you when you're at your lowest. I'd never do that to anyone. Especially you."

He tilts his head and just looks at me. I can't begin to describe the look in his eyes. There's a brokenness that only comes from the kind of hurt that cuts you in half, but there's also hope... and longing so strong it reaches right into my chest and squeezes my heart.

I shouldn't want Shane Dawson. Shouldn't feel the things I do for him. I'm not ready. I don't know if I'll ever be ready. And even if I was at a place in my life where I could imagine a new relationship, I know he's not the one for that. He's young and free and unspoiled by the ugliness that can happen between two people. He isn't ready to settle down, certainly not with someone with as much baggage as I carry.

But knowing all that doesn't stop me from cherishing how beautiful I feel when he looks at me like he is right now.

He leans down, in that universal gesture that means *I'm getting ready to kiss you.* My heart hammers against my chest, and a little voice inside me screams *No!* I tell that voice to shut the hell up, because there's nothing in the entire world that I want more right now than for Shane to put his lips on mine. It may be all kinds of wrong and a bad idea all around, but I don't care. I want him to kiss me.

He doesn't.

Instead, he presses his forehead to mine, keeping his gaze locked on my eyes. Desire rolls off him like heat waves, stunning me with its intensity. That I inspired this reaction in him astonishes me.

His hands lift to my shoulders, then slide up my neck to my cheeks, leaving goosebumps in their wake. I press my hands flat against his chest, the thin fabric of his tee shirt doing nothing to diminish the firm muscles beneath it.

I've been with boys before, done my fair share of partying before my life fell apart a year ago. I know what it's like to be turned on, to feel that rush of passionate anticipation. But I have felt nothing like this. *Nothing.*

Not kissing Shane is more romantic and intimate than any amount of other physical intimacy I thought I'd experienced.

He leans closer still, his breath mingling with mine as his mouth descends. Though I don't know how it happened, I'm ready for the firestorm I know his kiss will bring.

Caleb's footsteps pounding down the stairs tear us from one another, Shane jumping back and stepping to the other side of the kitchen. He hops onto a barstool, and with shaky hands I quickly pour a fresh cup of coffee and set it in front of him. By the time Caleb steps in the kitchen, I'm working on pouring my second cup while still trying to get my breathing back under control.

"Morning," Shane says as Caleb walks toward the coffee pot, his voice steady and even.

Caleb grumbles something in response, then heads back upstairs with his mug.

I wait for Shane to turn around and say something, because lord knows I have no idea how to respond after what just happened.

But he doesn't turn around.

He gets up from the barstool and heads straight for his room.

Shocked, and more than a little hurt, I do the same.

An hour later I hear a car start. I look out my window just in time to see him backing out of his parking space, leaving without saying a word.

Chapter 8

SHANE

I'M TWO HOURS early for work. I don't have an appointment until after lunch, but here I am, sitting in the break room in the back of Resolution, pissed off at myself and feeling like garbage.

Bing's in his office doing important business owner stuff. Caleb's not in yet. My guess is that after his grumpy early morning coffee episode, he went upstairs and fell back asleep.

Not that I'd talk to him anyway. He'd just bust my chops over everything.

I nearly kissed Sydney. I knew it was wrong, knew I was being selfish, but I couldn't stop myself. She'd been so kind and sweet to me last night. She listened to the whole sordid tale about my mom, hadn't pressured me about going to see her.

It's almost like she understands what it's like to be in an impossible position where no matter what you do, you regret it. She's exactly what my heart needed… last night, this morning, and I suspect, in the days ahead, too.

Even now, all I want to do is get in my car, drive back home, and finish what we started this morning, before Caleb interrupted. I'd wanted to kiss her more than I'd ever wanted to do anything with anyone else. Ever.

No one knows I'm here yet. Rachelle's at the front desk, and I haven't dared to venture up there. No doubt she'll see something's wrong and pester the hell out of me until I either tell her what's going on or snap her head off in an attempt to get her to shut up.

I don't want to do either of those things, so I sneak into Asher's room. It's empty, of course, since Ash is in Hawaii on his honeymoon. The lights are off, and the blind in the window is drawn. I leave them both that way so no one will know I'm in here. Plopping down in his chair, I lean my elbows on the drawing desk and hang my head in my hands.

If Ash was here, I could talk to him. He's the only one besides Bing who knows the whole truth about my past. He's never judged me for it, and I know he won't start now. I could tell him about my mom – and about Sydney and my majorly conflicted feelings for her – and he would be kind. He wouldn't immediately give me the same stupid lecture Caleb did. I could tell Asher that it's not about being physically attracted to Sydney, although of course I am. It's about being attracted to all of her.

I know she deserves better than a quick make-out session in the kitchen, the kind we have to sneak in before Caleb wakes up. She deserves romance and chivalry and all that. Asher would tell me that I could give her all those things. I love him for believing in me that much, but I know I'm not the man to be all that she deserves.

Chapter 9

SYDNEY

I T'S ALMOST NOON when I leave my job interview at The End Zone, a sports bar not far from Northern Arizona University's campus. The manager was a really nice man, and I think he liked me, but the uniforms the waitresses wear are a total no-go for me. I'll never be able to wait tables for drunk college kids wearing booty shorts. Not happening.

If he calls me and offers me the job, I'll politely pass.

I'm still hoping to get an interview for a hostessing job at the nice Italian restaurant where I applied on Monday. I can handle black slacks and a white button-up. And customers who, for the most part, are looking for more than just beer and a good time.

With no other interviews scheduled and no other applications to turn in, I'm at a loss about what to do next. Going back to the townhouse is not appealing. I'd just be alone with the memories of that almost-kiss and all the worries about Shane's reaction afterward. I don't think I can deal with so much internal drama right now.

I remember the coffee shop Grace used to work at, and decide it's as good a place as any to grab some lunch and kill a little time. I have my laptop with me, so maybe I'll go online and take a look at some apartment options. If a job comes through in the next week or so, I'll need to at least have a plan. Thanks to Caleb and Shane's generosity, I have enough of my cash left for a deposit on a place of my own.

The gentle reminder about Shane's kindness toward me goes a long way toward shaking me out of my sour mood. So he was silent and awkward after our near miss in the kitchen. What right do I have to think he can't be weirded out by what almost happened? And why does all the responsibility for smoothing over all that awkwardness fall solely on him? I'm twenty years old, and while it's true that social interactions are still kind of hard for me, surely to goodness I can manage to let him off the hook so he doesn't think I'm mad or offended.

I find a parking spot along the street a block from Ugly Mug. Slinging the strap of my messenger bag across my body, I get out of the car, lock the door, and start down the sidewalk toward the coffee shop. I'm almost there when I notice the most gorgeous summer dress in the window of the boutique next door. It's sleeveless and flowing, with swirls of soft pinks and greens, like flowers in an Impressionist painting. I'm drawn to it immediately, even though I know there's no way I can afford it.

Glancing toward the door I discover that the name of the boutique is Beautiful Things. How appropriate. To the left of the door is a help wanted sign, and excitement bubbles inside me. It says to inquire inside, so I shore up my courage and push open the door.

A woman who looks to be in her early sixties looks up from the counter when the door opens. Her light brown hair is cut in a pixie style, and she's wearing pale yellow peasant-style shirt with long, billowy sleeves over a pair of faded skinny jeans.

"Welcome," she says. "What can I help you with?"

I take a deep breath. "I saw the help wanted sign."

"You're looking for a job?"

I nod, and she stands up and comes around to shake my hand. "I'm Kathryn Hill, the owner."

"It's nice to meet you," I say. "I'm Sydney Baldwin."

"Well, Sydney," she says, waving me to a small table in the back of the room. "Sit down and tell me about yourself."

I take a seat at the two-seat table that still allows her a view of the front door. Sitting my bag on the floor beside me, I take a brief moment to breathe and realize that although I'm nervous, it's a *good* nervous. I've noticed that a lot lately… that social and interpersonal interactions still make me nervous, but not in the way they used to. I think I'm nervous because everything seems important, like I want to make a good impression on people and to be comfortable carrying on a conversation. I don't mind *this* nervous feeling. It means I'm moving forward, and that's a good thing.

"I grew up in Greyson," I begin, making a point to make eye contact. "I just finished my second year at Malpais College in Phoenix, but I'm looking to relocate to Flagstaff."

I haven't said those words out loud to anyone until now. Not my parents, not Grace. Not even Shane. Even with Claire I only said I wanted to stay here indefinitely. I haven't told anyone that I'm not going to back to Phoenix when school starts in the fall. Perhaps starting with Kathryn Hill, who won't ask too many questions, is the way to ease into the idea.

"Well, I'm partial to Flagstaff, of course," she replies. "And you'll transfer to a school here?"

"That's my plan." Which is true, but I decide to give

her a bit more of the truth. "Eventually. I'm sort of at a crossroads, and I'm considering taking a semester off school to hopefully figure out which path is for me."

Kathryn smiles. "I think that's smart. If you're not sure what direction is best for you, taking some time to reflect and soul search may be just the thing you need. There's nothing wrong with honest work while you take that time."

Nodding, I exhale and feel a rush of gratitude for the understanding of this virtual stranger.

"Do you have family here?"

I shake my head. "My best friend, Grace lives here. She used to work next door at Ugly Mug. She just got married."

"Yes, I remember her!" Kathryn says with excitement. "I didn't realize she'd gotten married. How wonderful."

We converse for several minutes about Grace and Asher, talking about how beautiful their wedding was and how they're due back from Hawaii sometime this weekend. Talking to her is easy, and I'm relieved.

"Let me get you an application," she says, standing from the table and moving back behind the counter. "Fill it out, and get it back to me before closing time tomorrow. I'll be out of town until Tuesday, but I'll give you a call then and let you know what I've decided."

"Thank you, Ms. Hill," I say, taking the application from her. "I'll get it back to you today."

"Call me Kathryn," she responds. "And I'll look forward to it."

I'm sure the smile on my face is gigantic as I make my way toward Ugly Mug. I'm sure Kathryn has several applicants to choose from, but I can't help feeling that maybe she liked me enough to pick me.

✧   ✧   ✧

I ORDER A chicken salad sandwich and an iced coffee, then make my way to a corner table. The guy who took my order was nice, kind of cute even. His name tag said *Harrison* and indicated that he's the manager. Grace told me that Gabe used to manage the coffee shop, but that last year he bought it from the previous owners. I suppose now that he's in charge of the whole shebang, it's good to have someone else to manage the day-to-day stuff.

I'm halfway through the sandwich and reading through the application Kathryn gave me, when a familiar face plops down in the seat across from me.

"Sydney, right?" Gabe asks with a grin.

I nod. "Hi Gabe."

"Thought I recognized you," he says. "I didn't realize you were still in town."

"I decided to hang around, see if I could find a summer job. The prospect of staying with my parents in Greyson this summer just didn't appeal."

He smiles, knowingly. "Yeah, I remember when I moved to Flagstaff for college. I lived in the dorm even though my mom lives here. Sometimes you just know it's time to make the separation."

"So now, I just need to find a job so I can get an apartment."

"Where are you staying now?"

For half a second I wonder if I should tell him. I have no idea if Shane and Caleb have told anyone. But I figure there's no harm in telling Gabe. He's obviously part of their circle, and probably won't be surprised that they're being kind enough to help me out.

"Shane and Caleb have been letting me stay in Asher's old room."

"Hmmm," Gabe says with a raise of his eyebrows.

"Nice of them."

"Yes, they've been very nice. I just don't want to over-stay my welcome so I'm trying to be quick with the job hunt."

"Getting ready to fill out that application?" he asks, pointing at the paper on the table.

"Actually, yes," I reply. "On my way down the side-walk, I saw a help wanted sign in the window of the boutique a couple of doors down."

"Oh yeah." His eyes light up. "Kathryn's place. She's super nice."

I nod, agreeing.

"Put me down as a reference," he says. "All the mer-chants are friendly with each other and value each other's opinions. Maybe my two cents will give you an advantage."

It occurs to me at that moment that I've been sitting across from a man I don't really know, carrying on a completely normal conversation, and I've not been the least bit uncomfortable. I consider that progress.

"Really?" I respond. "Thanks."

"Sure thing." He stands up and starts to head back toward the kitchen. Turning before he's out of earshot, he says. "And if that doesn't work out, come see me. We always have extra hours that need filling during the summer."

I return his smile and say thank you once again, over-whelmed with the feeling of *welcome* that has enveloped me since I decided to stay in Flagstaff. Grace has landed among an exceptional bunch of people here, and they are no doubt the kindest – and coolest – people I've ever known.

And somehow, they've let me become a part of them.

Perhaps I've found my place… and the beginning of my new path.

✧   ✧   ✧

IT'S ALMOST DINNER time, and I'm still the only one at the townhouse. I'm sure Caleb's with Felicity. Things must be getting serious there. I have no idea what time Shane finishes his appointments. For a split second I consider texting to ask – because I did manage to ask him for his cell phone number – but decide against it.

I stopped at the grocery on my way home earlier and picked up supplies for a few days' worth of dinners. I decide to make spaghetti, because it's my favorite, and because it's good leftover too. If no one but me eats it tonight, it'll be in the refrigerator whenever one of us needs a re-heat.

Being in the kitchen is calming, both to my heart and my nerves. Obviously, at some point Shane and I are going to have to acknowledge what almost happened here. I've decided that I'll be the one to initiate the conversation because that puts me in control. It also makes me appear less awkward than I actually feel.

The pasta is in the boiling water, and the meat sauce is simmering in a pot on the stove when I hear the door. When the footsteps don't immediately head up the stairs, I'm pretty sure it's Shane. A moment later he's beside me at the stove, leaning back against the counter on my left.

He doesn't say anything, and this time the silence isn't comforting. I know he's weirded out about this morning, which is what I want to alleviate, so I just start talking.

"I know you probably feel strange about this morning, but you shouldn't." For lack of anything better to do, I grab a wooden spoon and start stirring the sauce. "It was just an overload of emotions after everything last night. Finding out about your mom and trying to decide what to do has you all twisted up inside, so don't think you need to apologize or explain. I don't expect it. Let's just try to forget about it, okay?"

Then I miss the counter with the sauce-covered spoon, and it lands with a splat on the floor between us.

"Damn it!" I exclaim, bending to pick it up. Shane stops me with his hand, getting the spoon himself and tossing it in the sink. He grabs a paper towel next and cleans the sauce from the floor.

When he stands to face me, he smiles and says, "Spaghetti?"

I nod. "Do you want some?"

"Of course," he replies with a grin.

And just like that, things feel right between us again.

We've just plated our pasta and taken seats at the bar, when he stuns me with his next words.

"I want to go see my mom."

I stop with my fork halfway to my mouth and look at him. "Are you sure?"

He nods. "I'm not expecting any kind of resolution or reconciliation, but she's my mom, and I think we both deserve a goodbye."

"When are you going?" I ask, turning my eyes back to my dinner, hoping to keep the conversation light.

"Leaving Saturday morning," he begins. "I had Rachelle reschedule all my appointments for the day. It's about four and a half hours to Albuquerque, so I'll drive up, spend a little time with her at Greg's, then crash at a motel for the night. I'll come home Sunday."

"If you're sure, and you have some peace about the decision, then I'm glad you're going."

We eat in silence for another moment, then Shane stuns me once again.

"Will you go with me?"

Chapter 10

SHANE

"ARE YOU SURE you want me to?" Sydney asks, turning her head so she's looking right at me.

"Yes." I shift on the barstool and face her. "I thought about it all day. You're the only one I've confided in. I don't want to talk to anyone else about it right now. I don't know if I can do it alone, so yes, I want you with me."

If Sydney only realized the affect she's had on me since she arrived on the scene. I've thought about her every day this week. At work, it doesn't matter what I'm doing... talking with a client, sketching a new piece... Sydney's always there in the back of my mind. I'm almost pissed at myself about it, because I know she's beyond what a guy like me should want, but I can't help it. I think about her all the time.

The thought of going to Albuquerque and seeing my mom scares the hell out of me. Not just because of the shape she's in, although that's certainly part of it. No kid wants to see their mother dying. But there's also the fact that we've never had the typical mother-son relationship. Even before she lost custody of me, I could never count on her. I don't know what it's like to feel that kind of bond with her. I never doubted that she loved me, but her love for me was never enough to make her change. Over the

61

years, I came to resent her as much as I loved her and that sent me down a dark path that could've ended me.

When I think about having Sydney by my side when I face my mom, it doesn't feel humiliating. It feels comforting. I think maybe I can do it if she's with me. It's like I want to show her the most vulnerable parts of myself, because somehow, some unexplainable way, I know I can trust her with them.

I'd been on the fence about whether or not to ask her, not because I'm afraid for her to see where I came from, but because I kind of hate the thought of dumping my family crisis on her, but then she dropped that spoon and cussed out loud. She was so flustered, and it was just so cute. In that moment, I knew.

"If you're sure," she says, her quiet voice floating in the air between us. "If you think I can help, then yes."

Relief spreads through me like wildfire, laced with something else. Something very much akin to anticipation and excitement. As much as the thought of seeing my mother in the shape she's in guts me, I'm also a tiny bit thrilled at the idea of spending so much time alone with Sydney.

"You mentioned a hotel." Her tone holds a hint of question. "Do you mean…?"

I hadn't thought that far ahead. Of course I'm not thinking we're going to hook up, but I'd be lying to myself if I said the thought of sex with Sydney hadn't crossed my mind. I'd just assumed we'd get one room, not because I expect anything, but because I'm not at all opposed to the idea of sharing space with her. In fact, I like the idea.

"I'll do whatever you want, Syd," I say. "We can get a room with two beds, or if you'd rather have different rooms, I'll be happy to reserve two. Just say the word."

She considers it for a moment, then answers. "One room, two beds. There's no sense spending the extra money for a second room."

The fact that she seems comfortable with the idea of sharing a room with me… yeah, it makes me ridiculously happy.

We eat in silence for a moment, then I switch subjects, moving away from the heavy subject matter. Plus, it occurs to me that I really don't know much about her, other than the fact that she grew up in Greyson with Grace. Definitely time to remedy that.

"So, what are you studying at Malpais College?" I figure school is a safe enough topic.

Her shoulder's tense, and she stops chewing. Maybe I was wrong about the safe topic. I don't say anything. I just twirl pasta onto my fork while watching from the corner of my eye as she swallows, takes a deep breath, then visibly shakes it off.

There's definitely a story there, something about college that doesn't sit right with her. As much as I want to know what it is, I'm not about to push.

"I'm still undecided," she says. "I had a couple of ideas about what I wanted to major in, but nothing seemed right. So, when I went back for my second year, I just finished most of my general education courses."

"I never tried college." I polish off the last of my spaghetti. "But I think you made a wise choice to not jump into something you weren't sure about."

"I'm hoping this summer gives me some perspective. I've been a little lost this past year." She lowers her lids as if it hurts her to admit that. "Kind of a wallflower with no direction."

"Wallflower?" I ask. "I didn't get that impression during the wedding. Sure, you're quiet, but that's just your personality."

"You didn't get that impression because you make it easy not to be such an introvert." She nudges me in the side with her elbow. "Your personality sort of fills in the gaps of my awkwardness. Plus, I feel really at home with all of Grace's friends here."

Something expands inside my chest at her gentle compliment, along with a sense of pride that in some way I've helped her feel comfortable around me. I want to tell her that I love the quiet side of her personality, that she intrigues me with the way she keeps parts of herself hidden away. She's a mystery I want to solve.

I know the grin that's on my face is of the big, stupid variety, but I can't help it. I'm sitting in my kitchen with Sydney, eating spaghetti that she cooked, and she just agreed to go to Albuquerque with me. Three weeks ago, I'd have said it would take a lot more to make me this happy, but at this moment, I can't remember *anything* that's ever been better.

Then Caleb arrives home. I've stopped expecting him home this early, because he always spends his evenings with Felicity, so it's a bit of a shocker when I hear his signature whistle as he comes in the front door. The surprise continues when he doesn't immediately head up the stairs to his room, but rather continues down the hall until he appears in the living room.

He's clearly perturbed to find Sydney and me together, and he eyes me with an expression that says *I know what you're doing, and I don't approve.*

I shoot him my own look that says *Screw you, Caleb. You don't have the first clue.*

It seems like we stare each other down for hours, but

I'm sure it's only seconds. Luckily, Sydney breaks the silence.

"There's plenty of spaghetti if you're hungry," she tells him.

"You cooked?" he asks, dropping his keys on the table and moves into the kitchen.

"I did," she answers.

I'm pretty sure she missed the tension between Caleb and me, or at the very least she doesn't know the reason for it.

He fills a plate with pasta, pulls a beer from the fridge. Making his way around the bar, he takes a seat at the table. "This is rather domestic for the two of you."

I want to punch him in the throat.

Sydney just laughs. "I made spaghetti because I wanted it. I figured I'd have tons of leftovers because the two of you are rarely home this early."

I level Caleb with another snarky look. *Take that, asshole.*

"But I'm glad you're both here to share it," she says, and her sweetness just slays me all over again.

"What's with you home so early, Caleb?" I ask. "Don't you normally eat with Felicity?"

"She's headed out of town with her sister, so we just grabbed a drink before they left." He takes a bite of his dinner, and I watch as he smiles in appreciation. "I was planning on a bowl of cereal and potato chips. This is way better. Thanks, Sydney."

"You're welcome." She looks back to her plate and a slight blush creeps up her neck. I love the way her skin flushes pink and promise myself that the next time she blushes, it'll be because of me, not my temperamental roommate.

"I had a job interview today," Sydney announces. "It went okay, but I'm not sure it's the right place for me. I put in an application at a boutique down the street from Ugly Mug, and I felt really good about it. The owner and I kind of hit it off. She's supposed to call me Tuesday, so hopefully that will work out."

"We'll keep our fingers crossed for you," Caleb says.

My feelings are mixed on the subject, because I know that once she finds a job it won't be long until she moves out. I know that's selfish of me, so I shove those thoughts away. I know finding a job is important to her.

"Absolutely," I tell her. "But don't be in a rush about an apartment. Don't settle for something crappy because you think you're in the way here."

To my surprise, Caleb agrees. "Shane's right. Be sure you find the right place. You can stay here as long as you need to." I suppose Sydney landing in a safe place is more important that Caleb's crusade to keep me away from her. "Occasionally Dex crashes with us, but he's not opposed to the couch."

"Dex?"

"He's a professional body piercer," I explain. "He lives in Sedona and works full time at a shop there, so he's only around every so often. Most of the time he just drives up for the day, one Saturday a month, but if he needs to spend the night, we let him stay here."

"Will I meet him?" she asks.

Caleb chuckles. "It's possible. Dex is a good guy, but he's a little unconventional."

"Says the tattoo artist with his skin full of tats and piercings." Sydney gestures at the gauges in Caleb's ears.

"Dex is even crazier than us, if you can believe it." I finish off the last of my spaghetti and take my plate to the dishwasher. "He has no filter and loves to tell stories about guys crying like babies when they get their dicks pierced."

"I think you like telling those stories as much as Dex." Caleb points his fork at me. "You're like a kid on Christmas morning when some dude comes in for a Prince Albert or Jacob's Ladder."

"I'm sorry, but it's damn funny. They come in all badass like it's not going to bother them, then whimper like toddlers when Dex comes near them." I rejoin them at the bar, then realize Sydney's eyes are wide in shock. "Crap, sorry, Syd."

Caleb clears his throat. "Um, yeah. I guess we're not used to having a lady in the house. Sorry."

Sydney blinks, then shakes her head. "I'm not offended or scandalized," she says, squaring her shoulders. "It was just quite a lot of visual all at once."

I can't help it. I crack up. I'd inadvertently planted the image of pierced male penises attached to crying adult men in Sydney's brain.

It takes a moment for the three of us to regain our composure, but I can't help but be thankful for the bit of humor that lightened the mood.

"How long is Felicity gone for?" I ask, hoping to move the conversation in a different direction, away from male genitals.

Caleb shrugs his shoulders, and answers in a grumpy voice. "A few days. Not sure how many. They're going to visit their brother and his wife and daughter in Tucson."

He sounds annoyed, which I find hilarious. "I suppose your foul attitude is because you're going to miss her?"

"My attitude's fine," he growls, finishing his spaghetti and taking his plate to the dishwasher. "And yeah, if you must know, I'm going to miss her."

Beside me, Sydney chuckles silently.

Caleb grabs his beer from the table and turns back toward us. "Thanks for dinner, Sydney."

Then he walks down the hallway, and I hear his footsteps ascending up the stairs. I half expected him to stay downstairs to chaperone the two of us, claiming some great desire to play Xbox. I suppose he'd rather sulk and miss Felicity alone upstairs.

"You play Mario?" I ask Sydney, clearing both our dishes.

"Are you kidding?" she responds. "My little brother and I play all the time."

I nod toward the TV and smile. "Let's go then. I'm gonna kick your ass."

She laughs, a full, deep down laugh. It's so beautiful that I vow to myself to find more ways to make her laugh.

Chapter 11

SYDNEY

"YOU SERIOUSLY MADE cookies?" Shane asks, eyes on the interstate in front of him.

"Yes," I answer. "Not from scratch. From a boxed mix."

"Like I care about that," he says, reaching for a chocolate chip cookie from the container in my lap. "If you cooked them in the oven, they're better than any pre-made crap I could've picked up."

We've been on the road for about an hour and a half, heading east toward Albuquerque. So far, Shane has been his usual, jovial self, but I'm sure he's over-compensating for the dread he feels about what's waiting for him when we arrive.

"There's also cheese, crackers, and grapes in the cooler," I say.

Having done my fair share of road trips with an autistic younger brother, I know how important snacks can be. Plus, I just like having them. It makes the driving part of the trip less monotonous.

"Between your snacks and the cooler of drinks in the trunk, we're set." He snatches another cookie, then looks back toward the road.

"Apparently, we were both struck by a wave of hunger

and thoughtfulness." I laugh as I snap the lid back on the cookies and put them in the back seat.

Shane chuckles as he finishes his cookie.

Riding shotgun in his Audi gives me an opportunity to study the ink on his right arm. His forearm is covered with an old-fashioned looking pocket watch, Roman numerals on the face, and the chain winding its way around his arm. Above the pocket watch, an angel with feathery wings sits, gracefully looking at the hands of the clock.

Someday maybe I'll have the guts to ask him what it means. Today, however, I stick to safe topics.

"What did you tell Caleb about this trip?" I ask.

Obviously, Caleb realizes we're both gone. I left it up to Shane how to explain it.

"The truth," he answers. "Or, at least, part of it. I told him I had a family crisis in Albuquerque, and that I'd confided in you about it."

"He didn't think it was weird that we're leaving town together?"

Shane just shrugs. "I'm sure he thinks I'm going to try to corrupt you, but he didn't say anything."

"He doesn't really think that, does he?" I ask. "I mean, surely he knows you're not a bad person."

"He knows I've played around a lot," he says after a long, silent moment. "And you're Grace's friend, so I guess he feels like he needs to protect you from me."

I think for a moment about how to respond. I'm not surprised to know that Shane has enjoyed his freedom. I'm also not offended by it. He's young, smart, and single. "Well, for what it's worth, I think I'm perfectly capable of protecting myself."

Across the console, I elbow him in the arm.

When he laughs, I breathe a sigh of relief. "Yeah, I

think you can take care of yourself just fine."

Surprisingly enough, I'm starting to believe it myself.

For the next couple of hours we chat non-stop. I ask him question after question about tattooing, and he asks me about growing up in Greyson. I tell him about my brother, his challenges, but also what an awesome kid he is.

Shane says he'd like to meet him someday.

And I believe him. I believe he means it… that he wasn't just saying it because it was the easy response.

It's the last hour of the drive when the subject of his mother comes up. I avoided all mention of his mom, intentionally, thinking it was best to let him bring it up if and when he wanted to. With each mile we move closer to Albuquerque, the tension in him coils tighter.

"I don't know what I'm going to say when I see her," he says quietly.

"Maybe you should let her talk first," I suggest. "Follow her lead. You don't have to say anything profound. Just be there."

He nods, eyes glued to the road. "Probably a good idea. If I start talking about my feelings, I'm going to wind up saying things about all the hurt and resentment I feel toward her, and neither one of us needs that."

I don't respond. He doesn't need me to. Instead, I shift slightly in my seat so that I'm almost facing him. Even though he can't look directly at me as he drives, he can still see that I'm listening, that I'm here.

"I've always felt really guilty about the resentment. It's so strange to love someone and resent them at the same time. Most of the time I just don't think about it, but now it's just all right there in front of my face."

"When did you see her last?" I ask, wondering if maybe there's a positive memory somewhere that he can grab a hold of.

"A couple of years ago," he answers. "She was at Greg's part of the summer. She was clean, or at least we're pretty sure she was. I spent a weekend with them."

"What was it like, being with her when she wasn't using?"

He shrugs. "It was okay. She tried really hard to do things, like cook dinner, buy me gifts, like that was going to make up for anything."

"No, it can't make up for all that you lost because of her," I agree. "But it was probably the only way she knew how to tell you she was sorry."

"I would've rather just had the words," he says. "To hear her say she was sorry about it all."

I reach across to where his hand rests on his thigh and place mine on top of it. He grasps my fingers in his like some kind of lifeline.

"It's okay, you know," I whisper. "The way you feel. The weird combination of anger and love. It's doesn't make you a bad person. It's normal to have those feelings. Don't beat yourself up about it."

My skin shivers as his fingers tighten around mine. There's something so affectionate and intimate in his touch. I know it's a reaction to our conversation, but my heart races just the same. It's been a long time since a guy touched me… a long time since a touch like this one made me feel good. So I can't give it up, even though I know it's all about his mom and not at all about me.

For a long moment we ride like that. Him with one hand on the wheel, the other holding mine. We don't talk anymore, but like always, it's a comfortable, companionable silence. My pulse thumps away beneath my skin, amped up because of the feel of his skin against my own.

After several minutes of silence, he releases my hand and whispers, "Thank you."

Then he takes the next exit off the interstate and heads south toward his uncle's home. Toward a kind of heartbreak I can't imagine.

Chapter 12

SHANE

THE SIGHT OF Greg's house is both familiar and foreign. The simple ranch-style house is ingrained in my memory from the years when I lived there, and yet it seems so long ago that the memories are like a hazy fog.

We step out of the car without a word, coming to stand next to one another on the sidewalk that leads to Greg's front door. My eyes are glued to the house, unable to look away even though I desperately want to look at Sydney instead, to feel the sweet comfort that's always present in her green eyes.

Sydney's hand finds mine, lacing our fingers together as if she's done it a thousand times before. The warmth of her touch sends a thread of peace winding through the unsettling tide inside me.

Together, we make our way toward the house, stepping up onto the front porch just as Greg slips out the door to meet us.

"Shane." He nods a simple greeting.

"Greg." He looks the same, just older. It's been over two years since I've seen him, and while his features are the same, his hair is sprinkled heavily with gray and a few more wrinkles reside around his eyes. His life hasn't been spectacular. He and Shaneen were raised by a single mom until she died when they were teens. After that, they lived with a grandmother who kept a roof over their heads, but couldn't exactly deal with the rebellious nature of two angry teenagers. Greg got married young, looking for a way to escape the monotony of his grandmother's house, but apparently he was a lousy husband and his wife took off with their son. I've always found it sadly ironic that he wound up raising me in much the same way his grandmother wound up raising him and my mom. The only difference was that my mom wasn't dead. She was just racing toward it at warp speed.

Now he's caring for his dying sister.

Whatever wrongs he committed in his younger days, his kindness to me and his compassion toward Shaneen have redeemed him.

"I'm glad you came," he says.

I don't respond, because I don't know how. I'm not glad I came. I also know I wouldn't have been glad to stay in Flagstaff. Instead, I introduce Sydney.

"This is Sydney." I turn toward her. "Sydney, this is my uncle Greg."

She smiles, the same genuine smile I've seen from her over and over the past week. Amazing how much comfort radiates from her smile.

"Pleasure to meet you," she says, reaching out to shake Greg's hand. "Though I wish the circumstances were different."

"Yes." Greg responds with a smile of his own. He looks at me then, asking without words if I'm ready.

I take a deep breath and clasp Sydney's hand tighter. "Let's go in."

Greg leads us past the living room and through the kitchen, my mind barely registering that the furniture is all the same. He stops in front of the door that leads into the guest bedroom. He doesn't turn around as he speaks.

"She sleeps a lot, so she may not be awake. She looks really frail. Just be prepared."

When the door opens, I'm struck by the sight of her. Her eyes are closed, but I can tell how sunken they are. Her skin is gaunt and pale. She looks sicker than any human being I've ever seen.

"Shaneen." Greg says her name softly, but in this silence of the room it's enough to rouse her. "You have some visitors."

I squeeze Sydney's hand hard in mine as I say, "Hi Mom."

Mom smiles weakly when I introduce her to Sydney. Greg moves out of the room to give us some privacy, and I wish he hadn't. I'm struggling badly, trying to find the words to say.

Sydney shifts around to face me, angling her head to force me to look into her eyes.

"I'm going to go get acquainted with your Uncle Greg," she whispers.

Oh God. She's leaving me alone in this room. The panic must show on my face, because she grabs my other hand and wraps both my hands in hers. Leaning down, she places a kiss on my knuckles, before looking back up into my eyes.

"You can do this," she says, her voice so quiet I doubt my mom heard her.

I swallow hard, then nod.

Sydney slips out the door.

Chapter 13

SHANE

"IS SHE YOUR girlfriend?" Mom asks, her voice scratchy and frail. "Cindy?"

"It's Sydney, Mom," I correct her. "And she's –" I start to tell her the truth, that Sydney's a friend. A good friend for that matter. Maybe even the closest I've ever felt to someone other than Asher. But I see the hope in her expression that maybe I've found someone who will stick by me, and I can't bring myself to dim it. "It's really new, this thing between us. But she's pretty special."

Mom smiles, and though her weakened state doesn't allow for a full-fledged kind of grin, the light in her eyes tells me she's pleased. I don't feel guilty for fudging the details of my relationship with Sydney, because I managed to keep Mom's hope alive without lying.

"Come, sit," Mom whispers, tilting her head toward the chair next to the bed.

I take a deep breath and oblige her, sinking down into the straight-backed chair Greg must've brought in from the kitchen.

"Where are you now, son?" she asks. "Still in Las Vegas?"

My heart sinks a little. She doesn't even remember where I live. I've never even been to Vegas, much less lived there. I guess when you live your life drowning in addiction, bouncing from one high to the next, you lose track of little details like where your offspring lives.

No point in bringing that up, though. It wouldn't do any good anyway. "I'm in Flagstaff now. I've been there for several years."

She nods, her eyelids heavy with each blink. For a moment I think she's drifted off to sleep, but then she speaks again.

"Do you have a good job?"

I could swear we had this same conversation the last two times I saw her. Rather than be a jerk about it, I just answer her questions. Telling her we've already talked about this isn't going to magically make her remember.

"I'm a tattoo artist," I answer. "I work in a really nice shop owned by a man named Bing Channing."

"You always loved to draw." Her eyes close again, and I'm glad. It gives me a moment to recover from the fact that she remembers anything about my childhood. She continues, without opening her eyes. "Tell me about the people you work with, and about your friends."

I wonder why she's asking now, when it's never mattered to her before. She's never appeared to care about how I spend my time or who I spend it with, but perhaps with death looking her square in the face, she wants to know I'm all right, that I have people in my life who will be good to me. Part of me says she's not entitled to that kind of reassurance after the shitstorm that was my childhood, but what good will it do me to be an asshole about it now?

It will cost me nothing to give her this bit of comfort.

"The tattoo shop is called Resolution. Like I said, the owner is Bing. I share a townhouse with one of the other guys who works there. His name is Caleb. My buddy Asher lived there with us until about a week ago when he got married to his girl, Grace. Rachelle is the receptionist at the shop, and she's married to Gabe. Gabe owns the coffee shop close by. Sydney just moved to Flagstaff. She grew up with Grace." Mom's breathing is evening out, and her eyes remain closed. "We're a family, Mom. It's the happiest I've ever been."

I think I see her nod her head, but it's hard to tell. I don't move, don't try to get up. Sitting there, watching my mom sleep, I think about the words I just said to her, and I know they are the absolute truth. I have a family. Not in the traditional sense, but a family nonetheless. I have people who I know would do anything for me, people I'd go to the mat for any day of the week. And I am the happiest I've ever been in my life.

A sense of peace floods through me, and I realize that in giving my mom the reassurance that I am, indeed, just fine, I've also reassured myself. The life I've built for myself is good, and I am thankful for every facet of it.

I'm not sure how long I sit there in silence, but eventually Mom rouses again. She grimaces as she wakes, and I can tell she's in pain.

"Should I get Greg?" I ask, certain he knows the protocol for her pain meds.

"In a minute." She turns her head toward me and opens her eyes. "I'm glad you came to see me, Shane. I know it's the last time."

I swallow hard at the bluntness in her words and nod my head, acknowledging the truth of her statement.

She slides her hand along the mattress, reaching toward me. Reluctantly, I place my hand around her small, sickly fingers. She smiles.

"You keep being happy, son," she says. "Keep making

me proud."

One side of my brain screams at me to tell her that nothing about what I've made of myself is to make her proud. I did this for myself, to pull myself out of the hell she created for me. But the other side reminds me that I made choices, too, and that I'm at least partially responsible for the desperate place I wound up before tattooing saved me.

And, damn it, part of me is happy that she's proud of me.

The swirl of conflicting emotions is suffocating, and all at once I cannot wait to leave this room. I'm relieved and enraged all at the same time, and as my mind whirls with excuses I could use to get up and leave, Mom drifts back to sleep, her hand going limp in my own.

I stand and step toward the door, but turn back at the last moment and just look at my mom. She's so pitiful lying there, her body finally failing her after all the damage she did to it over the years. *Choices.* She made a lot of bad ones and they defined her life... landed her in the shape she's in now. Somewhere along the way I made better choices. I'm not sure exactly how I managed to escape falling completely down the dark tunnel she did, but I'm grateful. So incredibly grateful.

I press a soft kiss to her forehead and leave the room, closing the door silently behind me.

I FIND GREG and Sydney sitting at the small kitchen table, which is missing a chair thanks to the one in the bedroom with Mom. Their soft conversation about summer weather in the southwest stops when they see me. I'm not sure how long I was in with my mom, but I hope it wasn't long enough that the awkwardness of being left alone with a stranger was too bad for Sydney.

Her eyes find mine, and she holds my gaze. She doesn't say anything, but compassion simmers from her, reaching into my chest and surrounding my heart.

"Was she able to talk much?" Greg asks.

I take a seat in the empty chair. "A bit. She slept a couple of times."

He nods. "That's normal, at least from what I've been able to tell since I found her in Santa Fe."

"Do you have everything you need?" I ask. "To take care of her here?"

"Hospice and the home health organization have both been really helpful." He leans his elbows on the table. "The goal is just to keep her as comfortable as possible."

"Greg, I…" I pause, not sure how to continue. I don't want to sound heartless or callous. "I want to help you, financially, if you need me to. Having her here in your house is a lot to take on."

"You don't have to do that," he says.

"Please," I respond. "I want to. She's my mom, and I want to be able to help you take care of her." I take a deep breath, shoring up my courage, and finish my statement. "Because I can't come back here, Greg. I just can't."

Beneath the table, Sydney's hand comes to rest on my knee, warm comfort radiating from her into me.

"I know that," Greg answers without a hint of anger in his voice. "You suffered the most from her choices, and I'd never expect you to pretend like that didn't happen."

"Part of me wishes I could," I admit. "But being here, it just hits too close, you know? So please let me help in the way I can. I know there are expenses that aren't covered by Medicaid. Even food and clothes and those things. I want to be a part of helping you through her last days."

He nods again, and I push to my feet. Sydney stands as well.

For a long moment Greg and I just look at one another, all the sadness and heartbreak of Shaneen's life passing between us in the silence. Words aren't necessary. We've felt it... lived it. Both of us loved her, and both of us have been hurt deeply by her. Neither of us escaped unscathed, but there's gratitude for the way our lives unfolded differently.

I reach out to shake Greg's hand, but he pulls me into a hug instead. It's strange and awkward, since hugging isn't something we've ever done, even when I lived with him, but given the gravity of the situation, it seems appropriate.

"I'm proud of you, Shane," Greg says, stepping back to look me square in the face. "I know if she could truly see the man you've become, she would be too."

I nod, hoping the look on my face conveys how much his words mean, because no way can I speak right now.

Sydney says a soft goodbye to him, her voice a layer of sweetness over the grief, then takes my hand as we walk out of Greg's house.

"I WANTED TO take you out to dinner," I say, as I maneuver the car through an intersection. "Somewhere nice. But I'm so drained right now I don't think I'd be very good company."

I promise myself I'll make it up to her. Nothing about the stuff back at Greg's house was pleasant, and she didn't have to come with me. She did it because I asked her to, and because she's nice. She deserves something special in the way of a thank you.

"That's sweet, Shane, but completely unnecessary." She shifts in her seat, and from the corner of my eye I see her sweet smile. "Why not just some pizza in the hotel room? I'd like that better anyway."

Relief washes over me. I don't have to pretend to be even marginally okay in a public restaurant, plus Sydney doesn't mind being alone in a hotel room with me. "Thank you," I say. "For understanding."

Her phone, which is lying in the console between the seats, buzzes with an incoming call. She looks down and sighs. "My Dad. I should answer."

She answers, and as I point the car in the direction of the hotel, I hear her end of the conversation.

"Hi Dad."

Pause.

"Things are fine. Really."

Longer pause.

"Of course I'm being safe, Dad."

Another pause. This time she shifts toward the passenger side window. Her voice lowers as well.

"No, it's not hard at all. I've made friends."

I guess it must be strange for her parents, her sudden decision to stay in Flagstaff, especially when they don't know any of the people she's associating with, except Grace and Asher.

"No, Dad, I don't want to come back to Greyson. Besides, I already found a job."

She got a job offer and hasn't told me? I know she's been looking diligently, but…

Of course, she's under no obligation to keep me posted on every detail of her life, but I'm sort of inclined to believe that what she just told her father isn't exactly true.

I try not to eavesdrop on the rest of her conversation,

although it's difficult when we're in the car together. At a stoplight, I notice a pizza joint that looks like a local flavor type place. Pulling out my phone, I take a quick picture of the sign so I'll have the phone number. Local pizza joints are always better than the big chain places. I'll ask Sydney what kind of pizza she likes once we're at the hotel, then I'll run back out and pick it up.

Sydney ends the call, but remains silent, her eyes focused on the floorboard of the car. I'm certainly not going to push her to tell me what's got her twisted up. If she got a job and didn't tell me, that's her prerogative. And if she didn't, but just needed to reassure her dad that she was doing okay, that's fine, too. Her reluctance to go back to Greyson is a personal matter. Her family issues are *hers*, and she can share them with me if and when she wants to.

Lord knows I've got no room to throw stones when it comes to handling family drama.

Chapter 14

SYDNEY

SHANE LEFT A half an hour ago to get dinner. While he's gone, I take the opportunity to shower so I don't have to worry with it in the morning. Not wanting to spend the time to blow dry my hair smooth, I opt for turning my head upside down and drying it just until it's not dripping. It'll be a kinky mess in the morning, but I can throw it up in a bun for the drive back to Flagstaff.

I pull on a pair of yoga pants and a tee shirt, then clear the phone book and complimentary paper and pen from the tiny table so that we can sit and eat once Shane returns. I'm just about to go in search of the ice machine when I hear Shane's key in the door.

Two plastic bags dangle from one arm, while the other balances a large pizza box.

"Here, let me." I take the pizza from him and sit it on the table.

"Your hair," he says with a grin. "It's kind of, I don't know, wild."

I feel myself blushing, but it's not unpleasant. I'm flattered that he noticed the difference and more than a little happy to see his sly grin.

"This is the *I was in a hurry* look." I crack a joke to hide the fact that his attention thrills me.

"Be in a hurry more often."

I can think of no witty response, so I just smile.

Shane sits the bags on the closest bed and grabs the ice bucket. "Sodas are in the bag. I'll get us some ice. Hopefully we've got some cups in here."

"I'll get them," I say, grabbing the plastic-wrapped cups from the bathroom counter as Shane goes for ice.

While he's gone, I unpack the bags and realize he not only bought pizza, but also salad and cookies. His words about wanting to treat me to a special dinner float through my mind, and I'm touched that even though he's been through the emotional ringer he took the time to make pizza in the hotel room extra special.

"Oh good, you found the salads." He steps back into the room, closing the door and clicking the deadbolt into place. "I hope you like Caesar."

"Very much." I take the two salad bowls and the plastic forks and set them on the table as Shane pours the soda over ice. "But you didn't have to go to that much trouble. I'd have been fine with just pizza."

"Wasn't any trouble." He smiles and winks, and my heart jumps a beat. "I figured why not make hotel pizza a little more high class?"

"Indeed," I reply, laughing as we take our seats and dig into our dinner.

I keep the conversation to a minimum while we eat. Instinctively, I know he needs the breather after what he went through at Greg's house. I think for a moment about the heartbreak of his family situation... how it's shaped him and changed him, but not destroyed him. My own crisis a little over a year ago changed me as well, but at least I had my family to depend on, smothering though they may be. Shane had had no one, until he landed in Flagstaff with Bing and Asher and the rest of the crew.

He's been strong and resilient, and I admire him so much for it.

He makes a joke here and there, and I'm glad that even though he isn't exactly jolly, he can still find that part of himself so soon after seeing his mother on her death bed.

Eventually, things turn quieter and I can tell he's ready to talk about his mom. He offers a few tidbits of the conversation he had with her, and from the sound of it, it sounds like not a lot was said.

I gently ask, "How do you feel after the visit?"

He takes a deep breath and closes his eyes. "I don't want to say I feel good, because that's not the right word. I'm glad I came, but at the same time I wish I hadn't."

"I figured it would be a mixed bag of emotions for you."

He nods. "I said my goodbyes, and so did she, but there wasn't any sort of acknowledgement of, well, anything. Not that I expected her to suddenly apologize to me for my shitty childhood or take responsibility for her actions –" he stops mid-sentence.

"But still you hoped for that," I whisper, knowing that was the closure he secretly wished for but knew he'd never receive.

"Yeah." His voice is nothing more than breath.

I reach across the table and take his hand. "For what it's worth, I think you did the right thing by coming. The right thing for *you*. When your mom dies, you won't wish you'd come to see her one last time. You won't regret that you didn't say goodbye. I know you didn't get the kind of resolution you wanted with her, but if you hadn't come, you'd have always wondered what she might've said if you'd seen her before she died. At least now you know."

"I know," he squeezes my hand. "Thank you for reminding me."

Together we gather the trash and move it all to the garbage can beside the door. Once that's finished, each of us takes a seat on our own bed.

I open my laptop, and prepare to search for potential apartments in Flagstaff. If I'm going to settle in Flagstaff, I'm going to have to make a plan. As the webpage loads, I take a moment to think back on the evening.

"You care if I watch some TV," Shane asks.

"Not at all," I answer, cutting my eyes toward him without turning my head. He's leaned against the headboard of the bed, long legs stretched out in front of him, looking all kinds of relaxed and sexy in his faded jeans with a rip in one knee and a plain white tee shirt that's *almost* too tight on his lean frame.

It doesn't escape me that I just thought of him as sexy. I'm a little bit proud of myself. It's been a long time since I applied that adjective toward a guy.

I scroll through apartments for rent as Shane scrolls through channels, and for a while neither one of us speaks. Like usual, the silence between us is soothing. I'm reading the description for a one bedroom place near NAU campus when the channel surfing suddenly stops, and Shane turns the TV off.

He stands up, and I think he's heading toward the restroom, but instead he walks in front of my bed and leans back against the dresser.

"Is everything okay?" I ask, wondering what it is that caused the sudden shift in his behavior.

"The other day you referred to yourself as a wallflower," he begins. "You said you'd been lost for the past year. And at first, I thought maybe you felt out of place because you didn't know us very well. But with me, and even with Caleb, I see how easy you've become with us."

My stomach pitches, afraid of where he's going with this. Has he figured out my awful truth? Is he going to ask me straight out?

"I know there's something keeping you from going to back to Phoenix and some reason you don't want to go home to Greyson. I heard you tell your dad on the phone that you'd found a job in Flagstaff, even though I'm pretty sure you haven't yet."

"I don't want to lie," I whisper. "I just don't want him to ask questions."

"Hey, I'm not judging. I figure you've got your reasons, and they're important to you. And you're well aware of my situation, so I'm the last person to judge anyone else about how they deal with their family." He pushes away from the dresser and walks to the bed, lowering himself to sit on the corner of the mattress. "We've kind of been dancing around this, you and me, and I'm not about to push you into talking about something you're not ready to talk about. But you've been really good to me. You've let me unload all my issues on you. You've listened and just been plain nice to me. So, I just wanted you to know, if you need to unload anything, I'm a pretty good listener, too."

I'm silent for a moment, long enough he thinks I'm not going to respond.

"That's all I wanted to say." He stands up and turns back toward his bed.

"Shane, wait." The words leave my mouth before the thought even forms in my head, but the moment he turns back toward me, I'm absolutely certain.

I *want* to tell him. The knowledge surprises me, scares me even, but it's true. I *want* him to know.

He returns to his spot on the corner of the mattress, and before I lose my nerve, I begin.

"I made a lot of stupid choices my first year at college," I say. "Drank too much. Studied too little. No pot or drugs, but lots of partying. It was the first time I'd felt free in my life, and I went a little nuts with enjoying it."

"I don't think you're the first to go that route," Shane replies.

I shake my head. "No. There are plenty of college freshman that do the same. I was popular. People wanted to hang out with me. Guys wanted to date me. It was addicting, the attention and the prestige."

"Most people grow out of that," he says. "It looks like you did."

"I didn't really get the chance to." My voice drops to just above a whisper. "It was a little more abrupt than that for me."

Shane's eyes meet mine, fear and concern and kindness swirling in the icy blue depths. In that moment I'm sure he knows, and I adore him even more for not asking me outright, but in his sweet, subtle way letting me know he'll support me.

"I was raped the week after spring break of my freshman year." I expect the words to slice through me like a blade, but they don't. Instead, it feels like dropping a heavy boulder I've been carrying for too long.

Shane doesn't flinch. The only visible reactions are the deliberate lowering of his eyelids and the deep breath he takes. When he opens his eyes again, I go on.

"It was a party at a house off campus. I'd been there several times before, so it was familiar. I thought it was safe."

The facts of the evening – the ones I remembered,

anyway – came rolling out of me then, the story washing through me like some sort of cleansing wave.

"I was drinking, naturally. That's what we always did at those parties. I'd gone with a group of four girls. Besides us and the three guys who lived in the house, there were a few other people, but it wasn't exactly crowded. Not like the way you imagine college parties to be. There was music. Some of the guys were playing video games."

Shane scoots closer, until he's close enough to me that this knees brush mine.

"One of the guys who lived in the house started flirting with me, which wasn't really anything new. He'd paid attention to me before. I thought maybe he'd eventually ask me out, but he never had. He sat down next to me on the couch. I was on my second beer. I wasn't drunk. I could carry on a conversation with him. Until I couldn't. He must've slipped something in my drink, although I've yet to hear any results from the blood tests they did at the hospital. I don't even know if any of the evidence they collected that night has been processed."

The words keep coming, matter-of-factly, and I find that with each syllable I feel a little more... *whole.* As if the brokenness I've felt for so long is somehow being mended by the fact that I'm unafraid to share the truth of it with Shane.

"I have no memory of how I got off that couch and into the bedroom. I don't know how I wound up naked from the waist down, whether I took my pants off or if he did it. I don't have many memories of the assault itself either. At some point, there was a loud noise from somewhere in the house, and I kind of came to. Enough to realize what was happening."

Shane says nothing. He just remains silent and grasps

both of my hands, enclosing his own around them.

"He was on top of me, and..." I don't finish the sentence. It isn't necessary. He already knows the truth. I take a moment to get myself under control before continuing. "I started struggling, though with whatever was in my system I couldn't do much. I remember saying the word *stop* over and over again. One of the other boys at the party stumbled through the door and into the room. He must've thought he was interrupting, because he just apologized and walked back out. That distracted the guy a little, and I was able to roll and push enough that he fell onto the floor. His pants were around his ankles, so when he tried to get up he tripped. Somehow I stood up. My underwear was around one ankle, and I managed to pull it up into place. I grabbed my jeans and stepped into the hallway and ran into one of the girls I'd come with. I guess she saw the panic on my face, because she yelled at the other girls to meet us at the car."

He finally speaks, squeezing my hands as he says, "Did you go to the police?"

"The hospital first," I say, recalling the misery of the car ride as I tried to put my jeans back on while at the same time trying furiously to block out the reality of what had happened to me. "My friends just sort of took over. Thankfully, we'd had the sense to decide on a designated driver, so she drove. When we got to the emergency room, they went straight to the nurses' station and quietly told them what had happened. After that it was just sort of a blurry stream of people, talking to me, examining me, talking to me again. A police officer showed up at some point, along with someone from the campus security department."

I watch the muscles in his throat work as he swallows

hard, his hands still gripping mine tightly. I can tell there are a thousand questions he wants to ask, but he doesn't. He just waits for me to continue.

"What happened after that is a really long, drawn out story that basically amounts to nothing." This is the hardest part of the story. The aftermath. The enormous insult added to my already horrific injury. "The campus security officer spoke to me briefly that night in the hospital, then referred me to someone on campus he said was a counselor who would walk me through the next steps. So, I went to her office the next afternoon, expecting that she would help me. She didn't. She asked me what I'd worn to the party, and when I told her jeans and a Malpais College tee shirt, she asked how tight the jeans were. She wanted to know how much I'd had to drink and did I make it habit to flirt with boys at parties."

"Shit," Shane mutters under his breath.

"She told me that she would talk with the others who'd been at the party and get back with me in a week or two. The only people she talked to were the guys who lived in the house. She didn't speak to the girls I'd gone there with, and even if she had, I'm sure she'd have dismissed anything they said because technically none of them saw what happened. After a couple of weeks, she called me into her office and told me that the police department didn't know how long it would take to process evidence and complete an investigation, so I shouldn't expect charges to be filed anytime soon."

Shane lets go of my hands to run his own through his hair, pulling slightly at the ends of his blond locks as if to ease some of the tension.

"The boy who raped me," I say tentatively, "is really wealthy. Or at least his parents are. They own the house where the guys were living. His dad is an alum of the college and apparently donates a lot of money every year. He's also a pretty powerful attorney in Phoenix. I'm sure Malpais and the police department didn't want to piss him off, so his son is still enrolled and is on campus every day. I did everything I was supposed to. Went to the hospital, called the police, and reported what happened. And nobody helped me."

"Sydney." The slight crack in his voice almost undoes me.

"I went back to Greyson that summer and tried to pretend like everything was fine. I tried to just put it away, ignore it, and go back to my regular life. But I couldn't pull it off. I knew my parents could tell something was wrong, and eventually I had to tell them. Reliving it through their eyes was brutal. They cried. My dad started calling the Phoenix police and the college almost every day, trying to find out if my rape kit had been processed, asking if the college was ever going to take any action against the rapist. I felt like I was experiencing it all over again every single day. I thought this summer might be better, but when I went home for a week before Grace's wedding, I knew I couldn't stay. They love me and they mean so well, but they're still in super overprotective mode, and I need to start standing on my own two feet."

"It's been over a year," Shane whispers. "Have they still done nothing?"

I shrug my shoulders. "I've stopped asking. I went back to school for my second year, against my parents' wishes. They had all kinds of ideas about how I could finish my degree while living in Greyson with them. But I was determined not to let *him* win. I thought that going back to school would show them all that I wasn't weak, and that it would spur the investigation along. I tried to tell myself that the university would do right by me in the end. That it was just a process that took some time if it was going to be done right. So, I'd check in every week or so and ask if anything was happening. After a while, I realized they were never going to help me. It was just so demeaning to call the counselor on campus or the police and get the same runaround every time. At best, they made me feel completely unimportant, and at worst they made me feel like it was my fault. Every time I spoke with her or the police, I felt like I was right back in the horror of that night. I couldn't keep letting them hold me back, so I decided to stop basing my healing on what *they* were doing... or *not* doing. I had to start moving forward. The only good that came out of me harassing the campus counselor's office is that her secretary referred me to a volunteer support group, where I met a woman named Claire who's helped me a lot."

Chapter 15

SHANE

"THERE ARE SO many things I want to say right now, but I don't want to overwhelm you." I take her hands again. They're so soft and petite, and I can't begin to explain the feeling of seeing them wrapped in my own larger, rougher hands. How could anyone hurt her like that? The thought cuts me in half. "But I have to say this. Whatever unwise decisions you might've made, they don't excuse or justify his criminal actions against you. He is the only one to blame in this."

"I know that," Sydney whispers. "In my mind, I know that's true. The rest of me is getting there, too. Finally."

Keeping my calm in this moment is a monumental feat. It takes every shred of willpower I have to sit here and carry on a conversation with her, when what I really want to do is demand the name of the asshole that hurt her, then get in my car and drive to Phoenix and rip him apart.

Instead, I focus on Sydney. Cautiously, I bring my hand to her shoulder. I wait several seconds, gauging her reaction. She blinks up at me, and I slide my arm across to her other shoulder, my eyes asking the question my voice doesn't speak.

Is this okay?

She nods, and I pull her closer, until her head rests on

my shoulder. It's a little awkward, trying to comfort her when our bodies are still a foot apart, but it feels right nonetheless. And it feels somehow important that she's comfortable enough to let me.

"If I strong-armed you into staying with Caleb and me," I say, thinking about the way I refused to let her get a hotel room after the wedding, "I'm sorry. I can see now how being in an apartment with two guys you didn't really know might've made you uncomfortable, and if I over-stepped, please forgive me."

She leans up and smiles, her eyes lit with warmth and sweetness. "You did make me uncomfortable, but not in a bad way."

I narrow my eyes, silently questioning that statement.

"I was stuck, Shane. Whether I was at home in Grey-son, or in Phoenix at school, I was stuck. I was the victim. And victims are quiet, withdrawn, and solitary. I got really good at being alone. It was so much easier than putting myself out there and risking the ridicule and judgement I knew was waiting for me. I didn't want to keep being the victim. I wanted to smile again, to live again, but I didn't know how. If you hadn't insisted that I stay with you, I'd have just kept right on being alone. Now, instead of that solitary existence I've endured for the last year, I have a whole new set of friends. I feel like I'm coming back to life."

"Sydney." My voice is nothing but breath because her words have knocked the wind right out of me. But she doesn't stop there.

"You've made me feel safe, Shane," she says. "Not just physically, but in here, too." She places her palm over her chest, indicating her heart. "For the first time in so long, I feel safe."

My emotions are all over the place. I'm pissed as hell, incredibly sad, so damn proud of her, and every protective instinct I have is roaring to the surface. Sydney isn't mine. We're friends. Maybe we've even become good friends over the past couple of weeks, but she isn't mine.

And yet, it feels like she is.

"You don't have to worry about rushing to find an apartment," I say. "Caleb and I can make the rent for a while, so don't take the first job that comes along if it isn't right for you. You have a place with us, for as long as you need it or want it."

"Thank you." Her voice is soft and sweet, and it adds to the already perplexing mix of feelings coursing through me.

My mind races for a new subject, anything that will take us away from the emotional minefield we're in. I'm not good at this… this crazy situation where what I want is so completely at odds with what's good and right. Wanting Sydney is selfish, and yet, I can't stop. But now, more than ever, I know she needs someone with so much more to offer than a twenty-something tattooist with a screwed up family history.

Mentally, I tick through the things we talked about on the drive to Albuquerque, when conversation flowed so comfortably between us, searching for a fresh topic. She talked about growing up in Greyson, her parents, her brother, and I realize how close we'll come to her hometown as we drive back to Flagstaff.

"I just realized we'll drive right past Greyson on the way home," I say. "It's just a few miles off the interstate. Would you want to stop and visit your family?"

She takes a deep breath and lowers her eyelids, quiet for a moment as she decides how to respond. I keep my eyes glued to her face, watching her while she's unaware. It's something I've caught myself doing a lot since she moved into the apartment. Despite my best efforts, everything about her mesmerizes me. The gentle slope of her jaw when, like now, I'm looking at her profile. The way her soft blonde hair brushes against the smooth skin of her neck. The way her long lashes rest against the swells of her cheeks when she closes her eyes.

Good lord, I'm in such deep trouble.

"No," she replies after a long minute of silence. "I don't think that would be a good idea."

She looks at me, her expression almost sad. Suddenly, it occurs to me that maybe it's me she doesn't want her family to meet. I'm not stupid, and I know at first glance I don't look like what parents dream about for their little girls, but I'm surprised how much the thought of Sydney wanting to keep me away from her family hurts.

I don't show it, though. "I guess I'm probably not the sort of guy they'd expect you to be hanging out with, am I?" I keep my voice light, letting her know that I get it without allowing the pain to be evident.

"No, no!" she says, scrambling around on the mattress until she sits facing me, reaching out to take my hands again. "It's not that at all! They know you're a tattoo artist, so the ink and piercings wouldn't be a surprise. And they know Asher, so the idea isn't a completely foreign concept to them."

My sense of relief is overwhelming, and I'm forced to acknowledge how desperately I didn't want to be found lacking in her eyes.

"It's just that I know if we stop in to see my parents, they'd try to convince me to come back home. They'd probably even try to get me to just stay there while you went back to Flagstaff. They'd plead their case – and Mom would cry – and I just can't do that."

"Okay." I squeeze her hand and take a look at the clock on the nightstand between the beds. It's past two o'clock in the morning. "We'll just sleep as late as we want to in the morning and head out whenever we get up and moving."

"Sounds like a plan," she says, smiling as I get up and move to my own bed, clicking off the lamp and plunging the room into darkness. "And Shane?"

"Yeah?"

"Thank you," she whispers. "For everything."

My heart lodges painfully in my throat.

Chapter 16

SYDNEY

I HAVE A vague memory of Shane calling the front desk and arranging for a later check-out time. Our late-night marathon conversation lasted until the wee morning hours, so I'm more than grateful for a few extra hours of sleep.

After leaving the hotel and grabbing a late lunch that's closer to an early dinner, we don't roll out of Albuquerque until almost four in the afternoon. With the almost five hour drive back to Flagstaff, it's nearly nine in the evening when we arrive back at the townhouse.

Felicity must still be out of town because Caleb's car is in the parking lot.

Shane grabs both our bags from the trunk while I pick up the small cooler from the backseat, and together we walk through the door.

I can tell immediately that Caleb is in the living room paying Xbox. The TV volume is way up, and I can hear the sound of gunfire and shouting.

I set the cooler on the table, and Shane drops my bag inside my bedroom. Caleb pauses the game and looks over at us.

"How was the family situation?" he asks.

"Sucked." Shane's one-word answer pretty much sums it up. "But it was necessary."

"You two have a fun time?" Caleb narrows his eyes at us.

"I just told you it sucked, douchebag," Shane says, clearly annoyed. "What about that sounds fun?"

Caleb shrugs. "Just thought maybe the trip together was at least enjoyable."

I can tell he's digging for information, trying to decide if there's something going on between Shane and me. Something *is* going on, but I'm certain it's not what he's imagining.

"I was grateful for Syd's company." Shane glances at me, his expression soft. "Made the unpleasant stuff a little easier."

Caleb nods, apparently satisfied with that answer. He holds up the Xbox controller and asks, "Halo? You can join us Sydney."

"Not a chance," I laugh. "Mario is more my speed. You two have fun shooting at people. I'm just going to relax in my room with some Netflix on the laptop."

"You can stream it on the TV in my room if you want," Shane offers. "Bigger screen that way."

"Okay, thanks."

After changing into my standard sleepwear – leggings and another one of my oversized tee shirts – I settle myself against the pillows in Shane's bed and start searching for a movie. It always takes me a while to find something, but finally I decide on an animated kids movie. Somehow, after the gravity of the past couple of days and all that Shane and I have experienced and discussed, something juvenile seems appropriate.

I can smell Shane's scent on the sheets and pillow slips, whatever soap he uses a combination of evergreen and mint. It's almost as soothing as smelling it on his skin when he sits next to me every morning after his shower.

That's the last thought I have before my heavy eyelids descend.

THE SCENT OF coffee combined with evergreen and mint wakes me the next morning. Shane must be up and brewing the first pot, so why do I smell him in the room with me?

My eyes open slowly, blinking to clear the fog from a truly decent night's sleep. It's then I realize I'm in Shane's bedroom. The events of the night before come back to me as I sit up and swing my legs to the floor.

Returning from Albuquerque. Shane and Caleb deciding to play Halo. Shane offering to let me watch Netflix on the TV in his room.

I must've fallen asleep. Sweet of Shane to not disturb me. Turning back toward the bed, I see the other side of the bed undisturbed. Covers not turned down. Pillow not indented from someone's head.

I wonder where he slept?

Quietly, I make my way across the hall to the bathroom, thankful that I started leaving my bag of toiletries in there so I don't have to wander through the kitchen with bed head and morning breath. I make quick work of brushing my teeth and combing my hair, pulling the blonde locks over my right shoulder and fashioning them into a loose braid. Satisfied that I look somewhat alive, I head to the kitchen for the first cup of coffee.

"Hey there," Shane says as soon as I round the corner. "Sleep well?"

I smile. "I did. Your bed is pretty comfy. Where'd you sleep?"

"Caleb and I played pretty late," he answers. "I didn't

want to wake you up, so I just turned off the TV, then crashed in your room."

I grin and pour myself a cup of coffee, stepping to the refrigerator for a splash of milk.

"I hope Halo was a good distraction from the heaviness of the trip to Albuquerque," I say, taking my seat next to him at the counter.

"It was." He takes a long drink from his mug, then turns to me. "But the trip wasn't all bad. Never in a million years would I have wanted to hear what you told me in that hotel room, and if I could I'd go back in time and make sure that it never happened to you. But you trusted me, and opened up to me, and that was a good thing. It meant a lot to me."

"Talking about it with you," I begin, stopping to take a sip and gather my thoughts. "It was the first time I've told the story without feeling shame. Without feeling suffocated. Sharing it with you lightened my load. So thank you for that."

I look up from my mug and our gazes collide. He doesn't blink. Doesn't say anything. It's like we're held there by the sheer intensity of the things we shared with one another this weekend. I'm afraid to move... to even breathe.

Just then, Shane's phone dings with an incoming text, and he looks away from me to pick it up from the counter.

"It's Asher," he says, turning the screen so I can read.

Grace and I got in late last night. We have souvenirs for everybody. Wanna do a get together at your place after the shop closes tonight?

"Sounds like fun," I say.

Shane nods. "The shop's usually closed by nine, but my last appointment should be over by about seven. I'll take care of grabbing the pizza and snacks."

"Or we could cook." The words are out of my mouth before I can even process the idea.

"You don't have to do that," Shane responds.

"We'll do it together," I respond. "I'll hit the grocery later today, then you can help when you get home. By the time everyone gets here, it'll all be ready."

Shane sends a text back to Asher and tells him we have the food under control, so all he and Grace will have to do is invite everyone.

"Hey," he says, looking up from the phone. "Does Grace know you're still in town?"

I hadn't even thought of that. "No, I guess not."

"I'll let Ash know."

I can't help but wonder what her reaction will be, but at least she'll have a bit of warning before showing up here tonight.

An hour later, Shane is headed off to work, and I'm going through the kitchen surveying the possibilities for tonight. Hopefully tomorrow Kathryn will call and I'll have a new job, so I'll enjoy being able to piddle around the house today.

Chapter 17

SHANE

SYDNEY'S IN THE kitchen when I get home shortly before eight o'clock. She's got music cranking, and some sort of folky rock pours from the speaker on the table. The counter is lined with several empty bowls, along with several grocery bags.

She sings along with the haunting melody of the song. Her voice is soulful and lilting and it hits me square in the chest.

She doesn't hear me come in, so for a moment I just watch her. And listen as she continues to sing about a woman searching for truth and meaning. I can't help but think the lyrics are somewhat biographical for her.

She retrieves a skillet from the cabinet, bouncing and shaking her hips as she moves to put it on the stovetop. She's on the way to the refrigerator when she sees me.

"Shane!" She jumps back a bit, startled by my arrival. Her smile is huge. "I didn't hear you come in!"

I can't help but smile back at her. She's cute as hell all flustered like this. I also want to ask her to keep on singing, but I manage to stop myself from blurting it out. "I didn't mean to startle you. I thought I'd be home a little earlier."

"You're just in time," she says, pointing to the stove. "I'm about to start the beef. You can help."

I glance around the kitchen at all the stuff, and ask, "What are you making?"

"Nacho bar," she says. "Who doesn't love a nacho bar?"

"I can't think of anyone," I reply, still grinning like an idiot. "What do you need me to do?"

She points toward the bar. "Go through those bags and find the packages of taco seasoning."

As I'm searching, I go ahead and unpack the groceries. Shredded lettuce and cheese, salsa, sour cream, jalapeños, and several bags of tortilla chips later, I have the seasoning packets in hand and join her at the stove.

Ground beef sizzles away in the skillet, and she gives it one last stir and declares it ready. Together, we rip open the packets and dump the contents in, filling the whole room with the scent of Mexican spices.

"What now?" I ask as she pours a cup of water into the beef mixture, setting the temperature to simmer.

"Let's get the toppings ready."

As we empty cheese, lettuce, and salsa into the bowls on the counter, Sydney begins to once again sign along with the music, this time about a man who lost everything and doesn't even recognize it. Despite the message of the song, the music sort of rolls along in a way that's both upbeat and somber. During the instrumental break, her hips begin to sway, and she accidentally bumps into me.

"Oh, sorry." Her cheeks blush slightly, and she keeps her eyes focused on the jar of jalapeños she's now emptying into a small bowl.

"No problem," I say, bumping into her intentionally with my hip. It's a pretty good excuse to touch her if I'm being honest.

Sydney laughs and bumps me back. It shouldn't pull at me the way it does, her laughter and the slight physical contact. Shouldn't make my chest expand and my head swim. Something so simple shouldn't do that to me.

But it does.

Pulling the largest bowl toward me, I open a bag of chips and pour them in. I tell myself not to bump her again, not to torture myself that way, but damn if I can stop myself. Only this time, I bump her hard enough that she scoots sideways and I have to put my arm around her to steady her.

Yeah, I did that on purpose. I'm a total dickhead.

Her laughter bubbles even louder, and I find myself laughing as well.

Beneath my hand, her slim waist and silky shirt tease me with their warmth and softness, and it's all I can do to not pull her fully against me and wrap my other arm around her.

Sydney stops laughing.

"Shane, I want to say thank you." Her words are almost whispered, but I heard them.

"For what?" I ask. I should be the one thanking her, over and over, for enduring the really awkward and dismal scene with my mom and Greg.

She steps away slightly, then turns to face me, her eyes lifting until they meet mine. "For not treating me any different after what I told you the other night in Albuquerque."

I nod. "You told me once that you'd never kick someone when they were at their lowest. Treating you differently because of what you went through would be the same thing, and I'll never do that."

She smiles, and I feel it in the soles of my feet.

God, this girl gets to me in the most profound ways.

"But I do look at you differently." I can't stop the

honesty from falling out of my mouth so I give up trying. She looks at me with a questioning expression, so I explain. "You're the strongest girl I've ever known. You're the picture of strength and resilience. I can't help but see you as *more* because of all that perseverance."

Her smile is tiny, like she's embarrassed by words and is trying to appear modest. Her eyes fill with moisture, and for a second I'm afraid she might cry. I have no idea what to do here… whether to let her tear up or apologize and try to stop whatever is about to happen.

But then she starts talking.

"I'm not going back to Phoenix to school," she blurts, and before I can even process that bit of information, she continues. "I tried to go back this past year to prove I would not run away, but I've finally realized that leaving isn't running away. It's starting over. And it's taken more strength to do that than to stay put. I have no idea what I'm going to do with myself yet, but I know it won't be in Phoenix. And it won't be in Greyson. I'm staying here, in Flagstaff. I'm going to get a job and a place to live, and I'm going to prove to myself and everyone else that I can stand on my own two feet again, and no one, including the boy who raped me, is going to take that away from me."

I can't decide whether to high-five her or hug her, but Caleb's abrupt arrival puts the skids on either one.

"Gabe and Rachelle pulled in right behind me," he says from the hallway.

He rounds the corner into the living room, heading for the kitchen, and Sydney turns to the stove to remove the now-ready taco meat.

"Ash and Grace are on their way, too," he says, popping tortilla chip in his mouth. "Bing went to pick up Kristy and Ezra."

I'm beginning to really resent Caleb and his shitty timing.

"Nachos, huh?" He grabs another chip. "Great idea, Sydney."

Syd is composed as she brings the pan of beef to the counter, and without a word about what just happened, we finish setting up the nacho bar. I'm dying to ask her about her outburst, and my mind races with the possibilities that exist if she stays in Flagstaff, even though I shouldn't entertain them.

But Gabe and Rachelle come in, followed closely by Asher and Grace, and soon the townhouse is overflowing with the most important people in my life.

Sydney is not only part of that group; she's now at the top of the list.

AFTER THE SOUVENIRS have been distributed and the iPhone pics have been looked at, Asher manages to get away from the crowd and corners me with what I know he's been wondering all day.

"How'd Sydney wind up staying here?" he asks, his voice low so no one overhears.

"I found her in the parking lot during your wedding reception," I begin. "I stepped out to get some fresh air, and she was sitting in her car, so I went over to talk to her. She was about to book a motel room for the night. I figured it was some cheap place, so I offered her your old room."

Asher nods. "Nice of you."

"She tried to say no," I continue. "Told me she was thinking of hanging around indefinitely, finding a job, and spending the summer here. So I told her she should definitely stay with us, since we had the room and wouldn't charge her while she looked for a job."

"Well, Grace and I appreciate you helping her out." Asher takes a long swig of his beer. "Everything going ok? You guys aren't used to having a girl here."

I shrug. "Caleb's gone a lot. When he's not at work he's usually with Felicity. And Sydney and I have gotten to know each other. We get along."

Asher nods, and I know he's considering my words, trying to determine what exactly I mean. The trouble is I don't really know myself.

"She's a nice girl," he says. "She and Grace have been friends a long time."

"Yeah, Caleb's pointed that out a number of times. Warned me not to mess around with her and screw up the whole friendship dynamic we all have. You going to do the same?"

I'm baiting him, and I know it. I know Asher well enough to know he'd never come at me that way.

"No," he says calmly. "I figure you're both adults and can decide for yourselves what you're going to do or not do."

"We're friends." I take a drink of my own beer, looking across the room at Sydney talking with Grace and Kristy. "That's it."

Ash nods again. "You're looking at her like you might want it to be more than that."

I shake my head. "You know me. All about the fun without the strings." The words taste bitter as they leave my mouth.

"I get that. Been there myself, as you know. But that doesn't mean it always has to stay that way." Ash turns to face me. "Caleb says the two of you went to Albuquerque."

Of course, Caleb ratted me out. "Family crisis. I'll fill

you in on it later. Sydney was here when I got the news. I sort of confided in her. She went with me for moral support."

"That's a lot of friendship for only knowing each other for a couple of weeks," he observes.

"I know that." Might as well admit it. This is Asher after all.

"I'm assuming she knows your history since you took her to Albuquerque?" he asks.

"Most of it."

"It's huge that you told her any of it," he says. "You've only told Bing and me."

"I know that, too."

"Sounds like you might have some real feelings for her." Asher's words are spoken softly, but they boom in my ears like canons.

I don't answer right away, because I know he's right. But my feelings aren't the most important here. Hers are, and I can't spell it all out to him without revealing what she confided in me last night. No way am I betraying her trust that way.

"She's not the quick fun type of girl," I answer, as if this explains everything.

Asher raises his eyebrows and just shrugs, if to say *So what?*

"She deserves commitment and faithfulness and all the stuff that goes along with long-term." *And more,* I add silently.

"Some reason you can't give those things to her?" Asher asks.

In the living room, Caleb, who is still sans Felicity, is pulling out the Xbox controllers and shouting at Asher and me to join him. It's the typical way these gatherings always go, but instinctively I look toward the kitchen to make sure

Sydney isn't alone. She's huddled with Grace, talking quietly at the table.

Asher follows my glance, his eyes landing on his new wife. "I'm not suggesting that you should settle down with Sydney," he says, keeping his gaze glued to Grace. "Whether it's Sydney or someone else down the road, your past doesn't exclude you from being able to be a good partner for someone. In fact, if anything, the things you went through as a kid kind of give you a rare perspective on the importance of honesty and family. I think that makes you uniquely equipped to deliver on all those things you said Sydney deserves."

"Gabe, Ash, Shane!" Caleb yells. "Get over here and let's play."

Bing and Kristy gather Ezra up and say their goodbyes, and Rachelle begins making her way toward the kitchen were Grace and Sydney are.

"Just don't sell yourself short, man." Asher slaps me jovially on the back as we walk toward the living room. "You gave me some good advice once. You said I could be miserable without Grace or suck it up and deal with the obstacles, and be happy *with* her." He cuts his eyes toward his wife, then holds up his left hand where the platinum wedding band rests on his ring finger. "It was good advice."

"Totally not the same thing," I argue, plopping onto the sofa with him.

Whispering now, because the other guys are within earshot, he goes on. "Maybe not. But I was determined to punish myself by choosing unhappiness. You told me how stupid that was. Now I'm telling you. Forcing yourself to be miserable to make up for some wrong you think you've committed against the universe? That's just stupid. The only person you're hurting is yourself. And her."

Chapter 18

SYDNEY

IT'S WELL PAST midnight when the night finally winds down. The Call of Duty marathon is coming to an end, and beside me Grace lets out a yawn.

"Not getting a lot of sleep these days?" Rachelle teases, jabbing Grace gently in the side with her elbow.

"Long day of travel yesterday is catching up with me," Grace says, then looks at both of us with a wink. "Among other things."

"I can't believe you and Asher haven't already headed back to the love nest," Rachelle adds. "When Gabe and I came back from Vegas, we were in the apartment by eight o'clock every night for a week!"

The two of them giggle, sharing a little new wives humor. I find myself a bit jealous. Not necessarily because I want to be married, although I do hope for that someday. It's because I'm scared I'll never be able to think about sex this way... as something sweet and wonderful, worthy of early nights and inside jokes. As proud as I am of how I've been able to pull my life back together, I'm afraid that something so personal and elemental may never be normal for me again.

I'm afraid I'll see *his* face. I'm afraid I'll re-live those thirty seconds I remember from my assault every time a guy touches me.

The guys announce that this next mission is their last, so Rachelle excuses herself to the restroom. Once she's gone, Grace scoots her chair closer to me. I knew she'd start the questioning once we were finally alone.

"OK, I want details," she says. "Asher says you've been staying here since the wedding."

"Yes." Of course I can't hide it, but I can try to evade the more personal conversation I'm sure she wants to have. "Shane and Caleb have been really gracious to let me use Asher's old room while I look for a job."

"Why didn't you tell me you were thinking of staying in Flagstaff this summer?"

"I wasn't really certain I was going to do it," I explain. "I'd thought about it, but I didn't decide for sure until that night at the wedding reception."

"Have you had any luck yet?" she asks.

"A few interviews and a lot of applications. I'm supposed to hear back from Beautiful Things tomorrow."

"The place near Ugly Mug?" Her face lights up. "That's a terrific boutique."

"I know," I say. "I'm really hopeful. Kathryn and I hit it off well, and Gabe let me put him down as a reference."

"I heard you went to Albuquerque with Shane." I gasp and raise my eyebrows, my surprise evident enough that Grace rushes to explain. "Caleb told Asher you guys went so Shane could visit his family."

"Caleb has a big mouth apparently," I mutter.

"Sometimes, yes," she agrees. "But these guys are like brothers. They keep tabs on one another."

She's quiet for a moment, and I know she's waiting for an explanation. I'm not sure how much she knows about Shane's family. I know Shane and Asher are close, and that

Shane feels closer to Asher than to the other guys, but I'm unsure exactly how much he might've shared with his friend.

"A bit of a family crisis," I say, repeating what I know Shane said to Caleb about our trip. "I happened to be here when Shane got the news, otherwise I'm sure he wouldn't have told me about it. But since I knew, and he wanted some company for the drive, I agreed. It was most certainly not a recreational road trip."

"Family crisis?" Her voice tells me it's a question, but I know I can't answer.

"You know I can't tell what it was about," I say. "It's his story to share, if he chooses to."

"Keeping his confidences already?" This time her tone is the slightest bit taunting. It's her way of fishing for information.

"Like I said, I was here when he got some unsettling news. I'd keep it to myself no matter whose news it was."

"Listen, Sydney," Grace says, lowering her voice. "Shane is a really good guy."

She told me this before the wedding festivities, and of course I know it for myself now. I also sense there's more to what she's trying to say.

"I hear a *but* at the end of that sentence."

"I adore Shane," she replies. "But he's a single guy and making the most of it, according to Asher. I just don't want you to get hurt."

It's sweet of her to worry about me getting my heart broken. It's also wonderful that she worries only about that, and not about whether I'm going to be able to function in the real boy-slash-girl world. Several times I've considered telling her about the rape, but something always held me back. At this moment, I'm glad I kept quiet, because in

Grace's eyes, I'm exactly like I always was.

"Grace, I know that," I say, reaching the short distance between us to pat her hand. I'm also struck by the desire to defend Shane, to make sure Grace knows he's been nothing but kind and honorable toward me. "Shane's exactly like you said. He's a good, *good* guy. We're friends, I guess. But don't worry. I'm not hearing wedding bells or anything."

✧　　✧　　✧

IT'S BEEN A good night, I think to myself.

One of the best I can remember having in a long time. I enjoyed the food, the conversation, even the noise. I haven't been comfortable in a crowd since spring break of my first year at Malpais College, but tonight, with all of Shane's friends here, celebrating Grace and Asher's marriage and the return from their honeymoon in Hawaii, I enjoyed myself.

True, I'd been around them all at the wedding, but that had been a formal occasion. I did my duty as maid of honor, held the bouquet, and sat next to Grace at the reception. Other than that, there hadn't been a lot of time to interact with anyone, although they were all exceedingly nice to me. They're all so close that it felt like a family gathering. In a way, I guess they are a family, and now it feels as though they've welcomed me into it.

I'm honest enough to admit to myself that my favorite part of the evening was cooking dinner with Shane before everyone arrived. Convincing him that we should cook something, instead of just ordering pizza, had been purely selfish. I'd wanted time with him.

I smile, remembering him bumping hips with me as we assembled the nacho bar. With I sigh, I tuck the memory away in my heart, determined to savor the bit of domesticity he and I had shared.

These feelings for Shane, while confusing and a bit scary, are also incredibly sweet. Regardless of what comes of them – and I'm quite sure that nothing will – these are the first stirrings my heart has felt in a long time, and I'm glad to know I'm still capable of it.

I'm snuggled in my bed, about to turn the light off, when I hear a knock at the door.

"It's me," comes Shane's voice from the other side. "Can I come in? I wanted to talk to you."

Quickly, I sit up. "Of course."

He opens the door and looks in, noticing me already under the covers. "Hey, I know it's late, so if you'd rather just sleep, it's ok."

"No, it's fine. It'll take me a while to settle down anyway." Plus, I'm pretty sure I'd rather talk with him than sleep.

"You sure?" he asks.

I pat the side of the bed next to me. "Get in here."

He slips in and silently closes the door. Before I can blink, he's seated next to me on the bed.

"The other night in Albuquerque," he begins, "I told you about my childhood. I want to tell you the truth about what came after that."

That sounds somewhat ominous. I tilt my head toward him, looking him in the eye. "Shane, if you want to, that's fine, but you don't owe me some kind of full disclosure or anything."

"I want you to know everything," he says, his expression serious and his eyes never leaving mine.

"Okay."

Chapter 19

SHANE

"I TOLD YOU about my mom, how she'd sort of pop in and out of my life once I went to live with Greg," I begin.

"Yes," Sydney says, shifting around on the mattress so that she's facing me, her right shoulder leaning against the headboard. The light blue sheet slips off her and pools on the bed between us, revealing the pink leggings she's wearing.

"At first, I was always glad to see her," I begin. "Happy when she was with us. But the older I got, the more I realized that every time she appeared, it just meant she was going to disappear again."

"Almost made you dread when she'd come around," she whispers.

Once again, she just *gets it*. No judgment, no condemnation. Just understanding.

"After a while, it seemed like I lived in a constant tug of war between the pain of missing her and the guilt of wishing she'd just stay away."

"Shane." Her voice quivers, as if she's on the verge of tears. "You were just a kid."

"I was old enough to make stupid choices, though." I reach for her hand, enfolding it in both of mine. Strange how in the course of a couple of weeks touching her has become some kind of anchor for me. I'd be terrified if I stopped to examine it closely, so I don't. Instead, I just hold her hand and absorb the intense comfort it gives me. "I was about fifteen when I took a page from her book, trying to deal with it all."

"Drugs?" Her emerald eyes peer at me, nothing but compassion swimming in their depths. This girl… she slays me with her sweetness.

"Pills." I nod, acknowledging the truth. "Prescription drugs. They were easy to get. Easy to conceal."

Her fingers squeeze mine, gentle and reassuring. She doesn't ask any questions. She just waits. It's one of the things I've come to love most about her, the way she let's me share with her at my own pace.

"The first time Greg caught me, I got the stern *talking to*. He really made me feel like shit. He set me up with a counselor, because I think he knew it was more about Mom than about any kind of rebellion. It worked for a while."

Thinking about that time in my life isn't pleasant, and I don't do it very often. When I finally got my life together, I put the past in the past and tried not to look back. But for the sake of being honest with Sydney, I'll go there.

"I'd gotten in with a really bad crowd of people, and it wasn't long before I got sucked back in. Didn't help that Mom had breezed in for a few days, then hightailed it out again. Greg knew what to look for that time, so he was on to me a lot quicker. My ass was back with the counselor immediately, and he threatened to send me to juvie the next time."

Closing my eyes, I take a deep breath and let it out slowly, mentally preparing myself to finish the story.

"My good streak lasted a little longer that time, but it's

so difficult to get away from people like that. They just kept coming around, and it was just too easy to give in. Not that any of it was their fault. I made those choices, so I have no one to blame but myself. A few months before my seventeenth birthday I moved out of Greg's and bounced around between my friends' places. I figured he was just going to catch me again, so I beat him to the punch."

She squeezes my hand again and speaks softly. "Obviously, you found your way out of that life."

"I was failing high school," I went on. "No way was I going to graduate. But then my cousin Parker got a hold of me."

"Parker?" She tilts her head to meet my gaze.

"Parker is Greg's son. He's ten years older than me. Greg and his wife divorced when Parker was really small, and Greg and Parker were never really close. I'd just come to live with Greg when Parker started coming around a bit, trying to get to know his dad. He was apprenticing at a tattoo place in Albuquerque. He took an interest in me because I loved to draw and was pretty good at it. We sort of hit it off."

"Is Parker the reason you became a tattoo artist?"

I nod. "When I started in with the pills for the third time, he came looking for me. Drug me out of the house I was staying in and punched the daylights out of me. He threw me in his car and drove me to some isolated spot outside of town." I can't help but smile as I recall the way Parker saved me. "He'd taken some of my sketchpads out of my room at Greg's house and gone to his boss at the tattoo shop. By this time, he'd been tattooing for about five years and had a good relationship with his boss. Parker put his neck on the line to convince the guy to offer me an apprenticeship on the condition that I finished high school.

He'd already looked into some alternative school options so I could catch up and get my diploma without having to go back to my old school."

She scoots closer and puts her hand on my shoulder. "Wow. Parker sounds like an amazing guy."

"Yeah, he is." Her hand moves softly against my shoulder, and through the fabric of my tee shirt the warmth of her touch spreads across my skin. "He's in Dallas now, married and a couple of kids. He threatened to cut my nuts off if I screwed up the deal he'd made for me. He was the one person in my life I didn't want to disappoint, so I got myself back with the drug counselor and worked my ass off. Thankfully, I'd never gotten mixed up with coke or heroin. Kicking the pill addiction was bad enough. That was over five years ago. I've been clean ever since."

"How did you wind up in Flagstaff?" she asks. It astounds me that her expression is the same as if we were talking about our friends' recent wedding or her job search.

"I needed a new start, away from the people who'd been a part of my destructive behavior. After I finished my apprenticeship, I started looking for a new place immediately. Getting out of Albuquerque was my only criteria, the further the better. Bing asked me to come in and talk with him and offered me a job the next day. Bing knows the whole story about me. My mom, the drugs, all of it. He's never treated me different because of it. After Asher came on board, he and I got pretty close. I've told him everything as well. But no one else knows."

"And now me," she whispers. "Why?"

I don't really have an answer for her. I can't explain why it's so easy to confide in her, why I've been compelled to share all the worst parts of my past with her. All I know is how it feels to be transparent with her. My heart feels lighter, and the darkness of my mom's health declining doesn't seem so oppressive. "I shared it all with Bing because he deserved the truth if he was going to give me a job, and I trusted him to keep it to himself. I told Asher because he was fast becoming my best friend, and I wanted him to really know me. With you... it's like telling you frees something inside me. It gives me a sense of peace inside that I haven't known in... forever."

She takes a deep breath, her hand sliding from my shoulder, down my arm until she reaches my hand. "It's the same for me, telling you the truth about what happened to me. I'm so, so grateful for my parents and for the way they've loved and supported me. I told them because I had to, because they're my parents and I need them. But telling you was different. I told you because I wanted to confide in you. Telling you was a giant unburdening, and in the process I think I destroyed some of the power it had over me."

I don't even know what to say, how to respond. This girl, she just *gets* to me in ways I can't even describe.

"Can I tell you something else?" she asks. "Something I've never told anyone before."

"Of course," I say, my insides quaking at what else she might have to say. If something or someone else hurt her, I will absolutely come unglued.

"All the partying I did, before the rape," she begins. "All the guys I was with. It was all about the attention, about looking for some kind of affirmation. I thought that was the way to get it, to feel like I was valuable. But it didn't work. It did just the opposite."

I nod, realizing that since Sydney breezed into my life I've been coming to terms with that exact truth in my own life. The affirmation that comes with meaningless hook-ups is empty and false.

"What's worse is that I didn't even enjoy it," she goes on, leaning closer. No one else is in the room with us, but the proximity seems necessary when sharing secrets like this. "Not any of it. Not emotionally. Not even physically. I didn't feel *anything.*" Her lids drop, and sadness creeps into her voice. "Is there something wrong with me?"

I shake my head, because there is *nothing* wrong with her, but with her eyes closed she doesn't see me. She's so close I can almost feel her breath on my face. Everything in me begs to put my arms around her and pull her to me. Resisting is physically painful, but I manage… barely.

She opens her eyes, and in their depths I see a mix of curiosity, wonder, and apprehension. Whatever it is she's warring with, I want her to be certain of my support, so I pull her hand into mine and envelope it once again.

"Does it make any sense…" She stops, mid-sentence, and lets out a heavy sigh. "That I feel more sitting here with you right now than I ever felt with any of those guys?"

This time I nod and agree, because I can do absolutely nothing else. I know all the reasons why I shouldn't respond to that statement – my screwed-up family, past drug addiction, the fact that until she walked into my life I filled my time with insignificant encounters with girls who were just as messed up as me – but I simply cannot stop myself from uttering my next words.

"Can I kiss you?"

Chapter 20

SYNDEY

*C*AN I KISS *you?* Everything in me sparks at the words. My skin tingles and my heart thunders. I'm thrilled and terrified all at once, and I never, ever want it to end.

Shane's hand comes to rest against my cheek, his touch so soft it nearly breaks me. He leans closer, his icy blue eyes locked on mine, watching for any hint of hesitation. Anxiety races through my system like lightning, but not because I don't want this. It's because I *do.*

"Yes," I say on an exhale, the word more breath than sound.

I expect him to close the distance between us then, but he doesn't. Instead, he keeps his eyes on mine, studying, searching, as if he wants to see to the very bottom of my heart. The air between us thickens, and flashes of excitement explode all over me. The waiting is such exquisite torture. I'd end it myself if I could, and lift my lips to his, but his gaze has me practically paralyzed with anticipation.

The promise of his lips on mine is enough to make any apprehension I might've worried about vanish. He moves toward me slowly, so slowly that I wonder if he'll ever arrive. Finally, *finally,* he does, and my soul practically sings with joy.

He's gentle... so very gentle. He tilts my head slightly and angles his own so his mouth fits over mine with exquisite tenderness. His lips move tentatively at first, his movements mere millimeters as he tests my response to his touch. Despite the fact that something in me threatens to unravel if he doesn't move faster, up his aggressiveness, I'm more than content to let him pace this moment exactly the way he is, drawing out every movement, every breath, every slide of skin.

He's not demanding, although part of me wishes he was. Instead, he coaxes me, using such sweetness, such delicacy, that my lips part of their own volition, inviting him inside with zero doubt.

Something I thought I had lost ignites inside me... the inexplicable desire to connect with another person... the feeling of two puzzle pieces finally falling together... the satisfaction of finding such delight in another human being.

I'm not sure how long the kiss goes on. Shane makes no move to stop, and neither do I. His hand strokes tenderly across my cheek and down my neck, and my hands rest flat against his chest. We stay like that, pressed close together, and gradually his movements slow, until his mouth is still, and the soft flesh of his lips rests unmoving against my own.

A hush hangs in the room, like the silence that follows a loud crash of thunder. My pulse hammers beneath my skin, still jumping with the voltage Shane's kiss set off inside me.

My eyes flutter open to find Shane's icy blues gazing at me with intense focus. I swallow hard, trying in vain to get my breathing back under control. The silence is warm and golden, and I want to stay in it forever, while at the same time wanting to say all the words in the world about what that kiss meant to me.

Shane's expression softens and a smile tugs at the corners of his mouth, and I'm certain he knows just how monumental the last few moments have been for me. His hand covers my own, where it's still pressed against him. Beneath my palm his heart beats as wildly as mine.

"Did you feel that?" he asks, his voice a husky whisper. He pushes my hand more firmly into his chest. "Do you feel this?"

I nod, searching desperately for my vocal cords. "Yes."

"Me too," he answers.

He slides one arm around me and pulls me against his side. My head lowers to rest on his shoulder, and his hand comes up to tunnel through my hair. I feel his lips as he presses a kiss to the top of my head.

No words are spoken as he reaches over to turn the bedside lamp off. The nightlight plugged in next to the door illuminates the room just enough that I can see the outline of his legs as they stretch out on the mattress. We cuddle together, leaned back on the pillows, quiet and content in the afterglow of the kiss that changed everything for me.

At some point, I drift off into a peaceful sleep, still wrapped in his embrace.

And when I wake the next morning, I'm alone in my bed.

BY EIGHT O'CLOCK, I've showered and dressed, hoping that Kathryn will call today to let me know what she's decided about the job. Shane isn't up yet, which is surprising since he's an early riser like me. I know he's still here because his Audi is still in the parking lot, and a small part of me wonders if he's avoiding me.

I start the coffee and begin going over possible conversation starters in my head. When we almost kissed before, my attempt to make our first conversation afterward less awkward only made it worse, but luckily Shane's easy charm – and my spaghetti – smoothed things over. I've just about convinced myself to *not* exhibit diarrhea of the mouth symptoms when I hear Shane's bedroom door open.

I hear him step into the bathroom and turn on the water. By the time the coffee pot is full, Shane is making his way into the kitchen. I'm just about to offer to pour him coffee when he speaks first.

"Morning," he says, reaching over me to grab a mug from the cabinet while at the same time kissing the top of my head.

The kiss catches me off guard. Does it mean something? Is it an acknowledgement of the kiss we shared last night?

And why exactly am I obsessing about it? I give myself a mental lecture, demanding that I not develop any sort of clingy feelings toward Shane. He's a nice guy, and I enjoy his company, but I'm not foolish enough to think that I could be anything long-term to him. I have too much baggage. However, I will allow myself to be happy, thrilled even, at the knowledge that I *can* have physical contact with a man and enjoy it. It's enough to know that *that* part of me isn't completely destroyed.

"Good morning," I say with a smile. "You're up later than usual."

"I left your room about three this morning," he responds, dropping to seat on one of the barstools. I don't ask him why he didn't just stay in my room. With Caleb upstairs, he didn't want to take the chance that anything might be misinterpreted. "Took me a while to get back to sleep after that."

He speaks about last night as if it's the most normal thing in the world. What's more is that's precisely how it felt to kiss him and snuggle into his embrace. *Normal.*

I pour my coffee and take a seat next to him. "What time is your first appointment today?"

"Eleven." He takes a long sip of coffee. "What's on your agenda?"

"Kathryn from Beautiful Things is supposed to call me sometime today and let me know what she's decided about the job."

Shane nods. "She'd be crazy not to hire you."

I smile. His confidence in me is uplifting. "Why's that?"

"You're nice and easy to talk to." He turns to face me. "And you're beautiful. Of course women are going to want to buy clothes from you."

"I'm not sure about all that," I respond. "But thank you for the encouragement."

"Will you text me and let me know when you hear from her?"

I nod. "Sure."

He drains the last bit of coffee from his mug. "I'm going to get ready and head on to the shop. My station was kind of a mess when I left before our trip to Albuquerque, so I need to put it back in order."

"I'm going to follow up on some of the other applications I've put in, so I'm heading out before long, too."

He stands and starts across the living room toward the hallway. Looking back, he adds, "Thanks for the coffee."

Then he winks. And my heart spins around in my chest like a top.

I head back into my bedroom and shut the door, dialing Claire's number as I drop onto the mattress.

"Hello Sydney." Her voice is bright, and I'm glad it appears I didn't wake her up. Her job as an elementary school teacher means she's off during the summer, but her volunteer hours with the rape crisis center in Phoenix keep her busy.

"Claire," I say, keeping my voice low since Shane is still in the apartment. "I kissed a guy."

I feel silly for just blurting it out with no preparation whatsoever, but I couldn't think of any better way to break the ice of that conversation, so I decided on simple bluntness.

"Okay," she draws the word out, as if she's trying to figure out what to say next. "And how do you feel about that?"

"Amazing," I reply with honesty. "And confused."

"Let's start by talking about who you kissed," she suggests.

"His name is Shane. He was the best man at the wedding. I've been staying at the townhouse he shares with another of the tattoo artists. They've been really nice to let me crash in their spare bedroom."

"You like him?"

"I do," I admit. "I like him more than I probably should. He's really very sweet and generous, and we've become close. We've confided in each other. I've told him everything."

"Sydney, that's a big step," Claire says. "How did it make you feel to share that with him?"

"That's the thing. I thought it would be hard to talk about it with him, but it wasn't. I didn't feel any of the shame I used to feel when I talked about it. I felt lighter, freer, like somehow telling Shane about it meant it didn't have the same power over me anymore."

"So, how did the kiss happen?"

"Well, he's confided a lot in me, too. Things I can't share with you, of course, because they're his stories. The kiss just sort of happened during one of our talks."

"And now? How do you feel about it now?"

I take a deep breath. "I'm so relieved because I didn't freak out. I enjoyed it. It felt good. Natural. For so long I thought I'd never be able to enjoy physical contact with a guy again, but after kissing Shane, I know I can enjoy at least that much."

"That's really wonderful, Sydney."

"But part of me is confused by how easy it was. It seems like I should've been nervous or afraid. Like it hasn't been long enough for being physical with someone to be so easy."

"Sydney you can't feel guilty because you're able to enjoy physical contact with a man again. There's no universal timetable for that sort of thing. It's different for every person who goes through something like you did. Some sexual assault victims have a long aversion to physical contact. Others don't experience that at all. Most are like you and develop a cautiousness that keeps physical relationships at a safe distance until the time is right to try again. If you're able to be physical, in even the smallest way, with a man again, that's something to celebrate."

"I don't know if there's a future with us," I whisper. "In fact I'm pretty sure there's not."

"Perhaps that makes him a safe way to test the waters," Claire says. "For a lot of women, opening up physically can be easier than opening up emotionally."

I'm sure she's right, but I've already opened myself

emotionally to Shane. And in no way am I using him to "test the waters". But I'm realistic enough to know that a future between us, even in the short term, is probably not in the cards.

"But since it seems that the two of you became close before the kiss," Claire goes on, "it's more likely that your physical contact is a result of that closeness. And if something more develops between the two of you, the fact that he knows and is a part of your healing process will more than likely give him insight and patience."

"Well, I'm not counting on anything other than con-tinuing friendship," I say. "And I've told myself that I won't regret the kiss no matter what happens, because it's a big victory for me."

"It is a big victory, Sydney. It's huge, and I'm so proud of you." Claire's voice softens. "But be careful going forward. The next steps may not be as effortless. Baby steps."

"I know," I whisper. "I've told myself the same thing already."

Chapter 21

SHANE

I'M WALKING MY first client of the day to the front counter when my phone buzzes in my pocket. The thirty-something guy named Ted is sporting a new hourglass on his left bicep, with plans to add more until he's got a full sleeve. Repeat customers are like gold, so I force myself not to pull out my phone until I've got him successfully handed off to Rachelle for payment and aftercare instructions. Even though I'm dying to see if it's Sydney with news from the boutique.

"Rach," I say, tapping my fist on the counter. "Ted here is all set. He needs all the usual aftercare stuff, plus another appointment in a couple of months."

"Got it," Rachelle winks. "I'll get it all taken care of."

I turn and shake Ted's hand. "Thanks for coming in. Call if you've got any questions, and be sure to let me know when you decide for sure how you want to proceed on the sleeve. I'll work up some artwork for you to look at ahead of time."

"Will do," Ted says, nodding as he returns my handshake.

Making my way down the hall to my room, I grab my phone and open the text.

Syd: *I got the job!*

I'm ridiculously excited for her. One, because I know how much she wanted this job. And two, because it means she's really sticking around.

Me: *That's great! When do you start?*
Syd: *I'm headed down there now. I'll work with her today and then take a shift on my own tomorrow.*
Me: *You'll be great. I'm proud of you.*

She responds with a smiley face emoji.

I'm about to look for some emoji to return to her, one that would likely get my man-card revoked, but just then the phone on my desk buzzes and Rachelle lets me know my next appointment has just arrived.

I think through the rest of my afternoon and realize I've got a bit of a break later on. Perfect time to head to Ugly Mug for some coffee. And maybe even stop in and smile at a pretty clerk in an upscale boutique.

I PUSH OPEN the door of Beautiful Things and immediately feel out of place. This is a designer boutique, and I'm wearing ripped jeans, black combat boots, and a vintage Billy Idol tee shirt. I fit right in at Resolution. Here, not so much.

Sydney and her boss are at the counter, and it looks like Syd is learning about the computer system. At the moment there are no customers in the small store.

Sydney looks up when the bell above the door rings, announcing my entrance, and her wide smile practically punches me in the gut. Kathryn looks up as well, and doesn't bat an eye at my appearance.

"Something tells me you aren't here to buy clothes," Kathryn jokes, moving from behind the counter to shake my hand. "You must be a friend of Sydney's."

"Shane Dawson," I say, my right hand shaking hers while my left holds the latte I bought for Syndey. "I brought Sydney a congratulatory coffee, but now I'm wondering if it's such a good idea with all these clothes in here."

Kathryn laughs. "Nonsense. If there weren't coffee in this place I wouldn't survive most days."

I like Kathryn immediately. She's probably sixty, I'm guessing, slim and fit, with short, sporty hair and bright clothes. She's got that *"cool aunt"* vibe, the one that tells you she'll let you get away with more than your mom ever would.

"I'm going to check the prices on the sale rack," Kathryn says, looking over her shoulder at Sydney. "Enjoy your afternoon pick-me-up."

I walk toward the counter, and Sydney's green eyes lock on mine, her expression one I can't even describe. She looks content and happy and something else I can't put my finger on.

Setting the latte on the counter and leaning one hip against it, I smile at her. "Congratulations."

"Thank you." She pulls the cup to her lips and takes a small sip, and the bottom drops out of my stomach. I've never been jealous of a coffee cup before. "For the coffee and the congrats."

I grin, and I know I must look like a smitten fifteen year-old, but damn if I can stop it. Just looking at her makes me happy. And when she smiles back, forget about it. I'm gone.

Just then, the bell above the door dings and two customers walk in. Looks like a mother and daughter, and Kathryn steps in and smoothly engages the mom. Syd looks at me and takes a deep breath as if to say *here goes nothing.* I give her a quick encouraging hug then head out.

I'm almost to the door when I hear her start speaking with the daughter. The girl looks to be about sixteen, and I imagine being waited on by a beautiful twenty year-old makes her day. Sydney talks to the girl like they're girlfriends sharing all their secrets. I look back, and my breath catches in my throat. She has no idea how alluring she is like this, lit up from the inside, joy glowing across her face. She could hold every red-blooded male in the vicinity in the palm of her hand with no effort at all. She's such a natural at this, so at ease in this role of helping someone else feel beautiful. She's kind and lovely and pure, despite what she may think of herself because of her past.

And I am utterly unworthy... yet so damn lucky to know her and by some miracle have her affection and trust.

Chapter 22

SYDNEY

THREE DAYS LATER, things between Shane and me are exactly the same. That's not necessarily bad. It's just weird. I don't know what it means.

We have coffee together every morning. We talk. We joke. We smile. He's been by the store once more this week to bring me coffee. We even played Mario together last night.

He hasn't kissed me again, but that's not the really strange thing. He hasn't even mentioned that it happened. And because he hasn't, I'm not sure I should. We haven't spoken about it at all. Not that I'm imagining some great declaration of love, but it seems like maybe we should acknowledge that it happened, even if we don't assign some sort of meaning to it.

I'd be lying if I said it didn't hurt. He hasn't necessarily pulled back from me. If anything, he's more attentive. It just seems as if he's making a gigantic, intentional effort to make sure things are precisely the way they were pre-kiss.

On Friday morning, I have a long talk with myself while I'm in the shower. I remind myself how significant that kiss was... that it was more than the evidence of attraction between two people. It was the first bit of proof that maybe I'm not as broken as I had feared. For that reason alone, I can't regret what happened, no matter what.

I don't go into work until after lunch, so my plan is to grab coffee and a quick bite of breakfast, then head out and look at a few apartments. I found a couple that look promising, so I called yesterday and set up appointments to view them. I slide into my favorite boot-cut jeans and a bright green bohemian style shirt from Beautiful Things, and fashion my hair into a loose French braid with wisps hanging down around my face. With a pair of dangly gold earrings and a swipe of mascara, I'm sufficiently dressed for apartment hunting and work at the boutique later.

When I come through the kitchen, Shane is there, two cups of coffee sitting on the bar. His eyes widen when he sees me, like something about me looks different. There's something primal in his gaze, something almost tangible that I've never felt before and can't identify. Unnerved a bit by his stare, I simply smile and slip into my room to slide my feet into my sandals.

I join him at the bar moments later, dropping into my seat without looking at him and taking the first sip of the coffee that he fixed perfectly to my liking. Strange how well he seems to know me. Well, at least *parts* of me.

"That shirt is the exact color of your eyes."

Well, at least now I know the reason behind his staring.

Still too nervous to face him, I respond without looking up. "It's from the boutique. Kathryn suggested it for me."

"I like it," he says, his voice low and quiet with an edgy hoarseness that is anything but unappealing.

Something about his attention and his tone shifts the moment from our normal morning coffee to something with more depth and meaning. For several seconds I wait, thinking maybe he'll go on, say something else, elaborate on whatever it was that caused him to notice my shirt and my eyes and talk to me with all manner of sensuality in his voice.

But he doesn't speak again. He's silent next to me, and I decide I'll have to be the one to switch things back to our typical morning conversations.

"So what's on tap for you today?" I ask, keeping my tone light and so very, very ordinary.

"Headed to the shop around eleven," he answers, slipping easily back into our familiar routine. "Appointments start around noon. What time do you go in today?"

I'm both relieved and disappointed that the intensity of moments ago evaporated so effortlessly. I wish I didn't still feel the heat of his gaze in the pit of my stomach.

"After lunch," I answer, still focusing on my coffee. "I'm checking out a couple of apartments this morning."

"Really?"

The surprise in his voice catches me off guard. He's well aware that finding a job and an apartment of my own has been my plan all along.

"Yes. It's time. I have some income now, or at least I will once I get my first paycheck next week, and thanks to you and Caleb letting me stay here rent free for the past few weeks, I've got enough money to get a place of my own."

"Do you want me to go look with you?" he asks. "I know the city pretty well, I could maybe give you advice about the neighborhoods and traffic and things like that."

As much as I adore the idea of him accompanying me, I know I need to do this on my own. I can't keep depending on him, much less *enjoying* him. I need to get on board with the reality that Shane is my friend and nothing more.

"That's really nice of you, Shane," I begin, shoring myself up to look up and face him like a normal person. "But it's not necessary, and I need to do this on my own."

He takes a deep breath and nods in understanding. I know he thinks my need to do it on my own is about asserting my self-sufficiency, and he's at least partly right. There's no reason to correct him, though.

"Well, tell me where they are, and I'll tell you what I know," he suggests. "That way I can at least feel like I helped a little."

"The first is a place called High Pine Village." I get up from my seat and go in search of a granola bar. "It's pretty close to NAU's campus. It's convenient to work as well. The other place is called Graystone Manor. It's a bit off the beaten path in a quiet neighborhood."

"I know both places," he says, as I return to the bar with my breakfast. "High Pine is going to have a lot of college kids who've moved off campus, so there's the potential for quite a few loud and obnoxious parties. Graystone will be quieter, but it's also secluded."

"So is this place," I respond, referring to the townhouse he shares with Caleb.

"Yeah, but you're not living here alone." He reaches over and grasps my pinky finger. "I don't want you to be uncomfortable."

I try to ignore the zing of electricity that shoots up my arm from his finger touching mine, but it's a lost cause. I may as well just accept that Shane affects me, and do what I can to minimize the damage.

"Shane, listen." I pull my pinky free and turn toward him. "It's sweet that you're concerned, but I know I'm going to have to deal with lots of things like obnoxious college kids and secluded places. I may be a bit nervous at first, but I'm not afraid. Besides, I know from experience that the enemy is most often *not* a stranger in the hallway or a dark parking lot."

Shane closes his eyes and takes a deep breath. "Of course you know that. Give me a second while I pull my foot out of my mouth."

"It's okay." This time I touch him, laying my hand gently on his arm. "It means a lot to me that you care."

"I do," he breathes, eyes still closed, his hand closing over mine.

And just like that the intensity amps back up and I'm once again drawn into the vortex of my ever-growing affection for him. It's such a strange contradiction, being so grateful for these feelings and what they mean about me as a woman, yet at the same time, wishing they would go away so I could avoid the hurt I know is coming.

Caleb's loud descent down the stairs saves the day – or ruins the moment, depending on your perspective – and I'm freed from having to respond to Shane's whispery *I do*.

Without another word, I rinse my coffee cup and grab my purse, getting out of the townhouse before I do something stupid like kiss Shane right in front of Caleb.

Chapter 23

SYDNEY

M Y PARENTS ARE coming to Flagstaff.

For several seconds I sit on my bed, not moving, staring at the cell phone I just hung up.

They're ambushing me, and I know it. Why else would they wait until they've already left Greyson to call and tell me they're *dropping by* to see me?

Mentally, I think through my options. It's Sunday, so the tattoo shop is closed. Caleb already left to meet Felicity for lunch since she's back in town. Shane and I are here alone, which is certainly fine with me, but I'm sure my parents will jump to the conclusion that I'm nervous and afraid being alone with a man.

I need a buffer.

Grace! The answer comes to me swiftly. Grace isn't working today, and neither is Asher. I say a prayer that they don't already have plans as I bring up Grace's contact info and click to dial.

"I need a favor," I blurt out, as soon as Grace's voice comes over the line.

"You sound worried." Perceptive, as always.

"My parents are on their way here," I say. "They'll be here in an hour."

"And?"

For a moment part of me wishes that Grace knew the truth, because it would be so much easier to explain.

"I think they're going to try to convince me to come back to Greyson, and I just don't want to argue with them about it. And I don't want Shane to have to deal with that awkwardness. If you're here I think they'll be less likely to push hard."

"You think they'll be weirded out that you're living with two strange, inked up guys?" I can hear the humor in her voice.

"Well, Caleb's out with Felicity, and they know Asher, so the tattoo thing shouldn't be a big deal. I just don't want them to get the wrong idea about Shane and me."

"I get it," she says, and I breathe a sigh of relief. "I don't mind running interference. Asher and I can pick up some lunch and be over in a bit. It'll just look like a group of friends having lunch together."

"Thank you. I owe you big."

"Nah," Grace replies. "No debts between best friends."

I hang up the phone and make my way to my room to find something suitable to wear. I don't think my yoga pants and oversized tee shirt will send the right message to my parents.

Fifteen minutes later, I'm in front of the mirror inspecting myself when Shane appears.

"Sydney, relax," he says. "It's going to be fine."

He's standing in the door of my bedroom, leaning against the frame while I try to decide which button-up to wear over the baby blue tank top I have on.

"Black or gray?" I ask, ignoring his request for me to relax.

"Well," he begins, a wicked grin on his face. "I think if you wear the black one they're going to think you've become a devil worshipper, so you better go for the gray one. They'll feel so much better about your living situation if you're wearing gray."

"Shut up." I turn and throw the black shirt at him, laughing when it hits him in the face.

"Seriously, Syd, your parents will see that you're happy and excited." He tosses the shirt back to me.

"You underestimate their powers of seeing me as an invalid who needs constant care."

"Then between Grace, Asher, and me, we'll show them how well taken care of you are here in Flagstaff."

A loud knocking sound comes from the front door along with Grace's raised voice. "We're here, and we brought food!"

Shane goes to let them in while I look at the two shirts I've been debating over. For shits and giggles, I put on the black one. If nothing else, it'll be an inside joke between Shane and me.

Sliding my feet into black flip-flops, I head out to the kitchen in time to see Grace and Asher setting large bags from Ugly Mug onto the counter.

"We got sandwiches from the coffee shop," she explains. "And we ran into Gabe and Rachelle while we were there. They'll be here any minute."

"More reinforcements," Shane says sidling up next to me. Nudging me with his elbow, he lowers his voice and says, "Nice shirt. Decide to live dangerously?"

"What can I say? You bring it out in me."

Shane laughs, and the sound of it settles around me like a comforting blanket. He throws an arm around my shoulders as we sit and begin unpacking the lunch Grace and Asher have brought.

✧   ✧   ✧

GRACE AND ASHER thought to bring enough dessert for everyone, including my parents and Devin. Which is why I'm currently brewing a pot of coffee, while Grace and Rachelle take care of the lunch dishes and Asher engages my parents in conversation about Hawaii.

At the moment, Shane is showing Devin his collection of video games and Devin is monumentally impressed. I'm avoiding interacting with my parents by paying close attention to each drop of coffee that drips into the carafe, while at the same time straining my ears to eavesdrop on my brother and Shane.

"Did that hurt when they pierced the top of your nose?" Devin asks, referring to Shane's bridge piercing.

Looking over my shoulder, I watch as Shane leans close, as if sharing a secret with Devin. "Between you and me, yeah. It hurt pretty bad. I even screamed, but don't tell anyone. I don't want to get my man-card revoked."

Devin laughs and his eyes light up. "I'll keep your secret."

The rest of their conversation is drowned out when Grace starts the dishwasher, but I see Shane reach for two Xbox controllers. I'm pretty sure Devin has a new best friend.

I grab the sugar bowl from the cabinet and the milk from the refrigerator and set them beside the coffee pot, thinking that maybe I've dodged a bullet and I won't have to deal with an interrogation or a prolonged discussion with my parents about my living arrangements.

But Dale and Stacy Baldwin don't give up so easily, and just as I'm setting the mugs on the counter, Mom steps up beside me.

"I didn't realize you were having company when I called to let you know we were coming by to visit," she says.

Of course you didn't, Mom, because my friends bailed me out of having to deal with you all alone when I called and begged them. Naturally, I don't say that out loud, though part of me wants to.

"Well, you didn't exactly ask," I answer, doing my best to keep the snark out of my voice. "The shop isn't open on Sundays so get-togethers like this aren't unusual."

"Hmmm," she mutters in way of a response.

I busy myself by fixing a cup of coffee, then grab a cookie. May as well fortify myself with chocolate.

"Grace and Asher appear very happy." Mom turns around to lean on the counter, looking to where Grace has joined Asher in talking to my dad.

"They are." This is an easy and safe topic, so I'll try to prolong it. "Grace is working at a really nice salon, and Asher stays busy at the tattoo shop. They're looking for a larger apartment."

"And that blond young man owns the coffee shop, is that right?" she asks, pointing toward Gabe.

"Gabe, yes. His wife Rachelle is the receptionist and bookkeeper at the shop."

There's silence for a moment, and I rack my brain for a smooth extraction from this little talk, but I'm not fast enough.

"Shane seems very nice." And *there* it is. The real reason she wandered over.

I take a deep breath and remind myself that she loves me and that all she wants is to protect me... and that I need to be gentle in the way I go about helping her realize that she's done her job and now it's time for me to take care

AMY DURHAM

of myself.

"He is nice, Mom. He and Caleb have been very gracious to let me stay in Asher's old room while I look for a
job and an apartment."

"And have they asked you for money?" She already
knows the answer to this. I don't know why she's asking.

"No. Like I told you, I offered and they wouldn't accept. I think Caleb's exact words were *Grace would have our
balls in a vice if we tried to take money from her best friend.* I
stopped trying to pay them after that."

"My goodness!" The shock is evident in her voice.
Having grown up with two sisters, I don't think Mom ever
got accustomed to the way guys so easily throw around
references to genitalia.

I can't help but laugh. "Mom, these are grown men.
Tattoo artists. A little rough around the edges. Their
language can get a little salty. It's not a character flaw."

"And you're not uncomfortable with that?"

"No," I reply. "And I never have been. Being sexually
assaulted doesn't mean you're forever traumatized by
raunchy terms for testicles or penises."

Mom's eyes go wide, and her mouth opens in shock.
Perhaps I went a little too far.

"Sorry, Mom." I sit my coffee on the counter and turn
toward her. "I'm not trying to be crude. I just need you to
start realizing that I'm moving forward."

"Of course you are, darling. I just wish you'd consider
coming home for the summer. I'm sure you could find a
job in Greyson, and then we'd all be together, and –"

"I have a job," I interject, stopping the rest of her
statement. "A job I love. And I know you'd rather me be at
home where you could watch me all the time, but I need to
spread my wings. I need to stand on my own two feet

again."

My dad has broken loose from Asher and Grace and is now making his way to the kitchen toward Mom and me. Grace catches my eye and mouths an apology to me. I know she and Asher tried to keep him occupied for as long as possible.

"Quite a crew you have here," Dad says, stepping up beside my mom. "Very colorful folks."

"I was just telling Sydney how much we wish she'd come home for the summer." Mom repeats her earlier words.

"And I was just telling Mom how it's time for me to stand on my own two feet again."

"Don't you think it's a bit soon to be considering something so drastic?" Dad asks.

"I didn't realize a job and an apartment in Flagstaff were such drastic things." I cross my arms across my chest. "I sort of thought it was a new adventure."

"Yes, but after what you've been through –"

"I was raped." I interrupt my Dad with blunt words that stun him. "Not disabled. I'm still a whole person, and maybe it's escaped your notice, but I'm actually doing okay."

"But it's only been a little over a year," Mom puts in.

"So?" I square my shoulders. "Claire and everyone else who's counseled me tells me there's no set time frame, no set process for moving on after a sexual assault. It's all about when you feel ready to take your life back. I'm ready."

"You've been keeping in touch with Claire?" Mom asks.

"Of course. I call her whenever I need to talk." I pick up my coffee cup and take a sip. "Or even when I just want to tell her something exciting."

Like when I kissed Shane. The thought dances through my brain, and I force myself not to smile.

Dad tilts his head and looks at me, his expression almost as if he's seeing me for the first time after a long absence. "You're really happy aren't you?"

I take a deep breath before answering, because the deep down truth is that I *am* happy. And the knowledge of that pierces my heart in the most wonderful way.

"Yes," I whisper and give him a half smile, tears pooling in my eyes.

"It's been so long since I've seen happiness in you." His voice breaks, and he stops for a moment before continuing. "I guess I forgot what it looked like."

The look in Mom's eyes tells me she's seeing it for the first time, too, so I figure now is the moment to tell them I'm staying in Flagstaff even once summer ends.

"I'm not going back to school in Phoenix."

Both my parents look relieved, which isn't a shock since they didn't want me to go back for my sophomore year. While they're still riding that wave of relief, I give them the rest.

"I'm staying here. In Flagstaff."

"In Flagstaff?" mom gasps. "Why?"

"What about school?" Dad fires his question before I have a chance to answer Mom.

"I'm staying in Flagstaff because I love my new job. I love being here with Grace and Asher, and I love the new friends I've made." Shane's at the top of that list, but I keep that tidbit to myself. "As for school, I'm taking a break, trying to figure out what I want to do with my life. NAU is here in Flagstaff, so when I decide what I want to study, I can apply there."

"Are you sure?" Dad asks.

"Yes." My voice is breathy, but my conviction is strong. "For the first time in a long time, I'm sure. This is what I want."

Mom looks on the verge of tears from a mixture of relief and sadness. Dad notices and puts his arm around her.

"This is what we've wanted for her, Stacy. To be able to live her life unafraid and happy."

"I know," Mom says, dabbing at the corners of her eyes. "I guess I'm the one who isn't ready." She raises her eyes to meet mine. "But I'll be fine. If this is what you want, then I want it for you."

"I know you're only a phone call or a short drive away," I say.

I step closer and hug her, her embrace feeling more like love and affection, and less like pity, than it has in a long time. Over her shoulder I see Shane standing near the bar. His smile says *I told you they'd come around,* but his eyes seem sad and distant.

I want to find out what that expression is all about, but I can't extricate myself from my parents fast enough, and Devin reclaims Shane's attention. Apparently he's dug through the stack of video games and found another he wants to try, and Shane is more than happy to accommodate him.

The rest of the afternoon passes in a comfortable peace. Mom and Dad have stopped looking at Shane suspiciously, obviously charmed by the kind and generous way he interacts with Devin. Dad talks at length with Gabe about the business end of running a coffee shop. Mom settles into a conversation with me, Grace, and Rachelle about the boutique where I work and all the lovely clothing items there.

Finally, my parents decide it's time to load up and head back to Greyson. Devin, of course, complains because he wants to continue raiding Shane's gaming collection. Shane invites him back any time to play Xbox, and Devin seems satisfied with that. Gabe, Rachelle, Asher, and Grace all make their exits just before Mom and Dad, giving us time to say goodbye.

Shane and I walk them outside, but Shane stays on the front steps while I walk to the car with my family.

"Come here, you." I hug Devin first, squeezing him harder than necessary just because it makes him laugh. "I'm glad you came to see me."

"Shane is so cool. He has lots of games, and his tattoos are awesome!"

"Shane *is* cool," I say. "I'm glad you had fun today."

He continues to talk about Shane and the video games as he climbs in the back of my parents' SUV.

I turn to Mom and Dad and we share a group hug.

"I'm so proud of you," Dad whispers in my ear, before pressing a kiss against my cheek.

"Me too," Mom says. "I'll miss you, but I'm so glad to see you doing so well."

After a promise to call more often and keep them informed about my apartment search, they pull out of the parking lot with Devin waving wildly from the backseat, more than likely at Shane rather than me.

Watching them drive away, I let my mind linger on how Shane interacted with Devin. How he welcomed him with open arms and treated him like he was just like any other kid… like autism didn't exist and all kids ask overly personal questions about your facial piercings and tattoos. My heart warms, overflowing with feelings of all kinds, and every last one of them involve Shane.

This burgeoning love I feel for him is a struggle to keep in perspective. As much as I believe everything I told my parents about being a whole person and feeling ready to take my life back, I'm also realistic enough to know that what Claire told me is absolutely correct. The next steps in a romantic, especially *physically* romantic relationship, might not be as easy as kissing Shane had felt. And the last thing I want is to start something with him and have him regret it if my sexual pace slows to a crawl.

Yet I can't help what swirls inside me when I turn back to look at him. I can't help but feel gratitude for the way his presence makes me feel undeniably female, in a way I haven't felt in a long time, and I know without a doubt that if he gave me any indication that he was willing to take a chance on me, I'd jump at the opportunity.

Chapter 24

SHANE

STANDING ON THE front steps, I watch Sydney say goodbye to her family, a growing knot of dread forming in the pit of my stomach. I tell myself to go inside and not watch the exchange of love that happens between them, but I can't tear my eyes away. I knew she had a family with two parents and a sibling, but seeing them together... it's like I finally *know it.*

The knowledge of it grew on me all day long, creeping up like moss on a tree trunk, and while I've never felt the need to apologize for who and what I am, I'm helpless to combat the feelings of inadequacy now that the differences between Sydney and me are staring me in the face.

Her family unit is complete. Two parents who love each other and both their kids. She's had the kind of family that offers security and belonging her whole life.

And mine's been shit since the day I was born.

What a fool I've been to think for even a moment that I could offer her anything. I have no idea how to be a part of a real family. No idea how to manage a healthy relationship. No idea how to be good enough for a woman like Sydney. She needs someone who grew up the way she did. Someone who can give her the kind of love and commitment she deserves.

I've known it since the night I kissed her. That's why I haven't kissed her again, even though every cell in my body craves the feeling of her lips on mine. So, I've kept my distance physically, but damn if I can keep her at a distance emotionally. She's under my skin, that much I admit.

But I don't need to be under hers. She needs to be free and clear of me so she can build a life worthy of someone so beautiful.

Though it burns like a hot knife in my gut, I know there's nothing left to do but call a halt to whatever's brewing between us, before it snowballs into something I can't control.

I slam my eyes shut and make up my mind to do it.

When I open my eyes and see her walking toward me, that sweet smile on her face, I want to collapse and die.

She breezes into the townhouse, and I follow, thankful that Caleb isn't home. This conversation is going to flay me open and I sure as hell don't need his commentary.

When Syd reaches the living room she turns to face me, her expression bright and full of all the joy I know she possesses.

"I don't think I can even express how much I appreciate the way you were with Devin." I see the moisture gather in her deep green eyes.

I swallow hard. "It was easy. He's a great kid."

"And my parents," she goes on, heading over to the kitchen and dropping on to a barstool. "You managed to win them over as well. They're confident I'm fine here in Flagstaff."

"Sydney," I begin, hating myself before the words are even out of my mouth. "We're friends."

"Of course we are," she replies.

I remain rooted to my spot on the other side of the

room from her but force myself to look her in the eyes. "I mean we're *just* friends. That's all we are."

As I watch, she takes a deep breath and closes her eyes, gathering her thoughts before she responds. My heart races, one half trying to kill me for hurting her, the other half insisting I'm doing the right thing.

When she finally opens her eyes, the joy is gone.

"Okay." Her voice is flat, yet firm.

"I'm no good for you." It's cliche, I know, but I can't think of a better way to word it.

"You sell yourself short an awful lot," she says.

I shake my head. "You deserve someone better than a former addict who learned the art of drug abuse from his own mother."

"Shane, you are not your mother," she insists. "And you are not defined by your past choices, no matter how bad they were."

"After everything you've been through –"

"Stop it right there." She hasn't raised her voice, but the anger is evident. "I wasn't mad before, but now you've pissed me off."

"Sydney –"

She interrupts again, this time standing up and squaring her shoulders. "I'm not fragile, Shane. I'm not breakable. People have treated me that way for the past year, and I won't have it from you. You won't break me. I promise you. I'm stronger than that. You can be an adult and acknowledge what's happening between us or you can ignore it and run away. Either way, I'll be fine. But don't you dare use what happened to me as an excuse because *you're* afraid."

And with that, she walks calmly to her bedroom. She doesn't slam the door. She closes it quietly.

Then she clicks the lock into place with a firm finality that echoes around in the empty spot where my heart used to be.

Chapter 25

SYDNEY

FOR THE PAST week, I've gone on about my business. I go to work each day. I've looked at a few more apartments, all of which had both positives and negatives. While I don't need anything extravagant, not having a roommate means the rent is the deciding factor, which makes the search more difficult because things like security and peace of mind come with a price tag.

I've done my best to be civil to Shane. It's hard, because what I'd like to do is just avoid him, but I'm determined to be more adult than that. I'm not mad at him for rejecting me. Well, not much anyway. I mean, after all, I'd been telling myself over and over to not to start spinning fantasies about happy endings and all that.

For whatever reason, we still have coffee together every morning. Neither one of us has made a move to change our morning routine, even though it's awkward and strained. Maybe it's because it's the one time we can count on Caleb not being around since he's not an early riser. Maybe it's because despite his big "just friends" declaration the other day, the two of us genuinely like each other and enjoy one another's company.

Although, as I sit next to him at the bar this Monday morning, I'm not sure how much either of us is enjoying this.

"Work okay?" he asks.

"Yes," I reply.

Same conversation we've had every morning for the past seven days.

"Day full of appointments?" I ask.

"Several," he answers. "Kind of spread out, though. Might stop by Ugly Mug for lunch during one of my breaks."

Well, this is new. He hasn't even hinted that he might come near me at work in the past week, much less returned to his habit of bringing me an afternoon coffee when his schedule allowed. Not that I'm going to ask him if he's bringing me coffee. Nope. Not happening. I might be fumbling my way back into dating mode, but I'm not desperate enough to beg.

Shane starts to say something, but he's cut off by a knock at the door. He looks at me questioningly, but I just shrug. He hops up to answer the door before whoever it is knocks again. No need to risk waking Caleb up early. He's never very happy when that happens.

I'm pouring a second cup of coffee when Grace comes in, immediately plopping down next to me in the seat Shane had been occupying. I pour a cup for Grace, and Shane drops into a chair at the small dining table.

"So, I have news," Grace says, her eyes glinting.

"You're not pregnant are you?" I'm sure she's not, but it's too good an opportunity to pass up.

"Of course not," she says, laughing. "But we did find an apartment."

"Great news. Where?"

"The Spring Meadow area. It's really convenient to Resolution and my salon. It's got two bedrooms, so we can have guests."

She's clearly excited about their new place, and I'm glad for her. It gives me hope that my apartment search will be successful in the near future.

"And guess what else?" she asks. When I look at her with raised eyebrows, she goes on. "Aunt Becca says they'll be more than happy to rent the garage apartment to you."

"Oh my gosh. That's perfect!" And it is. I've seen Grace's little studio-type apartment above her aunt and uncle's garage. It's small, but it's just what one person needs. "How much?"

She quotes me a price that's well below what I'd been hoping for, and I lean over and throw my arms around my friend. She hugs me back, and I'm reminded all over again how good it is to be in a place where I have true friends.

"That's really nice of your aunt and uncle," Shane says. I look over to the table and notice that his expression is blank, like he's disappointed somehow.

"It is." Grace swivels around on the barstool to face him. "I mentioned to her once that Sydney was looking for a place to rent, and as soon as I told them Asher and I had found a bigger place, she asked if I thought Syd would be interested."

"I guess it's a pretty nice neighborhood." Shane cuts his gaze from Grace to me, his eyes softening just a bit, and I can't help but be a little bit touched that he's still trying to look out for me.

"Oh yeah," Grace assures him. "Lots of families, some with kids still at home, some like Aunt Becca whose kids are grown. It's really quiet and peaceful."

I'm seriously relieved to know I'll be living in an actual neighborhood, not just a rental property area. Not that I've got anything against college students, but it's nice to imagine a quiet place to unwind at the end of a day.

"They're always really selective who they rent to," Grace explains. "That's why they never advertise it, but they know Sydney because of me, so it's a perfect scenario for them and for her. The furniture all stays. Asher and I are using some of our wedding gift money and buying a new bed and sofa. It's not a lot of furniture, of course, since it's a tiny apartment, but you won't have to buy anything except maybe a coffee pot and a couple sets of sheets."

Shane nods but says nothing. He seems almost sullen about it, but he has nothing negative to say about Grace's old apartment. For half a second I wonder if he wishes I'd stay here, but quickly dismiss that thought. It'll be so much easier to get back to the business of being friends once there's some distance between us.

"Asher and I are moving this weekend, so you can move in next Monday."

A week from today I'll have my own apartment. Paid for by money I'm earning myself. In a place I want to be, a place that makes me happy. It's what I'd hoped for when I took the risk to stay here after the wedding, and things are panning out much better than I could've ever hoped.

Shane congratulates me, gets up to put his coffee mug in the dishwasher, then exits the kitchen and returns to his bedroom. Grace stays a while longer, while I get ready for work.

Shane doesn't return.

Chapter 26

SHANE

ON FRIDAY MORNING, I pull into the back lot at Resolution an hour earlier than I anticipated.

Throwing the car into park, I look over my shoulder and take stock of the purchases I made on my early morning spree through the home goods store.

A coffee pot, a couple of mugs with quirky sayings on them, two sets of super soft sheets, and a memory foam pillow. Later this weekend, I'm grocery shopping, and Grace has agreed to let me in the apartment so I can stock Sydney's kitchen.

My gut is all twisted up over Syd moving out of my townhouse. I want her to feel independent, but at the same time I want to protect her. I know we need to put some distance between us, but part of me wants nothing more than to pull her closer.

It's maddening.

I finally decided that the best thing for both of us was for me to help her set up house… to let myself to be a part of her new living situation so at least I wouldn't have to imagine where she lives while I'm sitting alone playing Xbox and drinking Heineken.

You wouldn't have to be alone, the voice inside my head says. *You never were before Sydney, so once she's gone you can just resume your old life.*

The thought leaves me cold and empty, and I shut it down immediately.

Is this what it means to really care about someone? To want to do for her even if it hurts me or takes her further away from me? I'm not sure what it looks like for one person to sacrifice for another. My mom certainly didn't sacrifice for me, and although Greg was good to me, that just wasn't the same.

For a second I wonder if this is what it means to love someone.

The next second, I'm pissed as hell that I'm twenty-three years old and still have no idea.

Pushing thoughts of love and sacrifice aside, I remind myself that regardless, I'll continue to help make Sydney's transition easier. That means I owe her more than a coffee pot and a pillow.

I owe her an apology for the way I acted the day of her parents' visit, so I gear myself up for the pride-swallowing that will commence after work.

I'm about to climb out of the car when Asher pulls in next to me. He's out of his car in a heartbeat, so I hit the button to lower my window. Naturally, he immediately sees what I've got in the backseat, and his eyebrows raise in silent question.

"Housewarming presents," I say.

Ash nods. "Grace says Sydney's looking forward to moving in."

"Yeah. She's pretty stoked to finally have her own place." I tilt my head toward the items in the back. "Figured I'd help her get set up."

"Grace also mentioned you told her you want to stock the kitchen for Sydney."

I shrug my shoulders. "Just want to make sure she has what she needs."

"You've got feelings for her."

It's not a question, so I know there's no use denying it. Instead, I just close my eyes and lean back against the headrest.

Asher moves around the front of the car, then slides into my passenger seat. I roll up the driver's side window, because whatever conversation is about to happen doesn't need to be overheard if and when Caleb rolls into the parking lot.

"Why is this such an issue, man?" Asher asks. "It's obvious she has feelings for you, too."

"I talked to Greg this morning." I divert away from Asher's question. "Mom's getting worse. It probably won't be long now."

Ash takes a deep breath. "I'm sorry about that man. It's got to be tough on you."

I nod. "I'm never really sure how I'm supposed to feel. I mean, it sucks and I hate it, but sometimes I think I'm not sad enough about it."

"You've always had a complicated relationship with her, and that's not your fault. Makes sense you'd have mixed up feelings about the fact that she's dying. Don't beat yourself up so much over it. She made her own bad choices. She doesn't expect you to atone for them."

"I've been sending Greg money the past few weeks. I know Bing would give me leave from the shop to stay in Albuquerque, the same way he did for you when your brother died, but I just can't go back there. I feel like my money's a pitiful substitute, but it's the only way I can think of to help."

"No one expects you to stay in Albuquerque and help

take care of her. Greg included. He knows better than anyone why you can't be there, and I'm sure he doesn't blame you."

"That's what he told me," I admit.

Asher is silent long enough that I think maybe I've succeeded in making him forget his original question. But then he sighs and turns toward me in the seat. I can feel the intensity ramping up before he even opens his mouth.

"So this business with your mom," he says. "It's what's got you all jacked up and unable to admit what you feel for Sydney."

"Asher," I begin, but he cuts me off.

"Because if it is, that's bullshit, Shane. Total bullshit."

"It's not bullshit." I don't shout, but there's force behind my voice that makes his eyes widen. "It's my reality. It's tainted and ugly, and she's everything that's beautiful and good."

"You're not the same guy that left Albuquerque years ago. I never even knew that guy. I've only know you the way you are now. Honest and hardworking with a wicked sense of humor. You've got to stop punishing yourself for the mistakes you made back then."

"It's not just the drugs or my crazy mom, Ash." I scrub my hands over my face and hit my palms against the steering wheel in frustration. "It's how I've lived since. Life's been a constant party with a steady stream of girls, and I've never taken anything seriously."

"You take your job seriously," he says. "And your friends. And as for the partying and the girls, let me give it to you straight. I did the same. You know that. I doubt any of us were prepared for the sort of celebrity that came with being a tattoo artist at a place like Resolution. I felt like a freaking rock star with a bunch of groupies. I lived in it for a while myself."

"Yeah, and you straightened your ass up when Grace came into the picture," I say, as if that settles that.

"I did," Asher agrees. "And you can too. What do you think I've been trying to get through that thick skull of yours? Just because you acted like a horny shit for a while doesn't mean you can't change. It doesn't mean you don't get to have something really good. And Sydney is really good."

There's a part of me that knows Asher is right. I trust her in a way I've never trusted anyone, and for whatever mysterious reason, she seems to trust me too. But even if I could get beyond my own baggage, there's still the matter that Sydney needs to stand on her own two feet again, and I'm afraid I'd only get in the way of that.

"It's more than my own crap, Ash. For reasons I can't explain to you, she needs this. She needs to be independent. She needs a fresh start. I'm not going to mess that up for her."

"Ok, I'll grant you that you probably know a lot more about Sydney at this point in her life than I do, so I'll just say a couple more things and then I'll drop it. You willing to listen?"

"You mean I have a choice?" I ask, rolling my eyes.

Asher laughs. "You've always got a choice, man."

"Then go ahead," I say. "Fire away."

"All right. Number one. Sydney has obviously confided in you about something important. That says something about how she feels toward you. You refuse to break her confidence, and you're currently stocking her apartment for her. All that says something about how you feel for her. Number two. Yes, you have a past. I'd wager she does too. Neither one has to screw up your present or your future.

Number three, you say she needs a fresh start and a new independence, but that doesn't mean that your affections would screw that up. I'm suggesting that you be honest with her about how you feel, not ask her to move in with you permanently. And last, since it's completely apparent to everyone, except maybe you, that she is crazy about you, maybe you ought to let her make up her own mind where and how you fit into her life. Don't make decisions for her, especially ones that involve her heart."

"Okay," I reply, not looking at him. Everything he said is true, and I know it, but that doesn't mean I can act on it.

"Okay what?" Asher asks. "Okay you'll think about what I said?"

"Okay, I hear you," I answer. "I hear you."

Asher nods. "Fair enough. Just so you know, you're my best friend, and I want you to be happy, whatever that means for you."

I'm about to thank him for the heartfelt words, but that just seems out of character for me. Instead, I raise one eyebrow and grin. "Enough mushy stuff, princess. Let's go do some tattoos."

Asher laughs and punches me half-heartedly in the shoulder. "You're right. Let's go douchebag."

Chapter 27

SYDNEY

THE CHINESE TAKE-OUT I ordered arrives just as Shane pulls in to his parking spot. I make quick work of paying and tipping the delivery guy, thankful that I ordered extra just in case one or both of the guys came home. No sign of Caleb yet, which means he's probably with Felicity. I'm sure I have way more than Shane and I will finish on our own, but who doesn't love Lo Mein leftovers?

Shane's on the phone, so I don't wait for him. Instead, I head to the kitchen and drop the take-out boxes on the bar. Grabbing a can of soda from the refrigerator, I hop up onto a barstool, open my chopsticks and dig in.

A moment later I hear the front door open.

"Plenty of Chinese if you want some," I call out.

"Thanks," he says back. "Be there in a sec."

A moment later he appears, grabbing a carton of sweet and sour chicken and taking a seat on the furthest barstool from me.

I cringe inside. We've maintained a level of civility since his "just friends" declaration, but the awkward tension that hangs in the air whenever we're alone together is so uncomfortable. I've come to the conclusion that it's a good thing I'm moving out. I genuinely like Shane, even if we're never anything more than friends. I value his friendship, and I like the rest of his crew, too. Asher, Grace, Bing, Kristy, and Caleb have all become like a second family to me. Somehow, they've let me in and accepted me as one of their own, and I want to keep it that way. I don't want the weird vibes currently buzzing between Shane and me to affect my growing friendships with everyone else. Once I'm in my own place, out from under Shane's roof, hopefully the tension will abate and things between us will return to normal.

We eat in companionable silence for several minutes, and I'm thankful not to have to engage in small talk. If nothing else, we can at least have coffee or a meal together and not stumble over useless conversation.

"I owe you an apology," he says, out of the blue.

My eyes widen, surprised, and I ask, "Why?"

"For being a dick to you the other day," he answers. "When your parents and Devin came to visit."

I agree. He'd acted like a dick, but I keep that thought to myself. "You were being honest." Which was true enough.

He shrugs one shoulder and takes another bite of chicken. I wait, not exactly sure how to proceed.

He points his chopsticks at me and goes on. "Honesty doesn't justify being a jerk. So, for that, I'm sorry."

I nod. "Accepted."

What else can I do? I'm so hopelessly infatuated with this man that there's no way I wouldn't forgive him.

Shane starts to respond, but keys in the front door halt whatever he was about to say. His eyes narrow. "He met Felicity for dinner an hour ago. Why's he back already?"

Definitely odd. Caleb rarely comes in this early when he and Felicity are together.

"Caleb?" Shane calls.

He doesn't answer, but a second later he steps out of the hallway and into the small living room. He looks like crap, shoulders slumped and eyes almost blank.

Shane turns his barstool to face him. "You okay, man?"

Caleb shakes his head. "It's over."

Those two words carry a ton of weight. Clearly, he'd been serious about Felicity, so whatever happened to end their relationship must've been big.

"Hell," Shane mutters, jumping up to grab a beer from the refrigerator. He places the drink and a pair of chopsticks at one of the barstools across from where he and I are sitting, then nods toward it, inviting Caleb to sit down.

To my surprise, he actually sits. Caleb has been kind and welcoming to me, but not quite an open book. He's exceedingly private, which I get, but the entire time I've been here, I've not been able to get a read on his personality.

Caleb picks up the carton of dumplings and pops one into his mouth. I don't know whether or not to expect him to talk, and Shane doesn't press him. For several moments the three of us simply eat.

"Old boyfriend." Caleb makes the declaration as he picks up the beer and takes a long swig.

"That sucks," Shane says.

"Absolutely." I'm not sure how much I should enter into this conversation, but I figure agreeing that the situation sucks can't hurt.

"They hooked up when she and her sister when to Tucson to visit their brother. Apparently, the flame had never really gone out for either of them."

He uses a sarcastic tone of voice and makes air quotes when he says *the flame,* so I assume those were Felicity's words.

"You catch her in a lie, or did she admit it?" Shane asks.

"She'd been distant since they got back, so I had a feeling something happened. I just never imagined she cheated, though. When I asked her what was up, she came clean."

"So, on a scale of one to Brenna, how bad is this?" Shane's question comes with a wicked glint in his eye.

"I should've never told you about that, asshole," Caleb replies.

I'm sure I look confused because I have no idea who or what Brenna is. My eyes move back and forth between the two of them, waiting to see if one of them is going to fill me in.

"Good grief, Shane, you've got a big mouth." Caleb swivels on his barstool to face me. "Brenna was a girl I knew in Kentucky. She was the younger sister of one of my high school friends. I had a sort of crush on her, but she was too young for me. Her dad was a major shithead, too, so it's not like I stood a chance. One night after one too many beers, I mistakenly told idiot boy here, and Asher, all about how I'd been so heartbroken to leave her behind when I moved to Arizona. They've never let me live it down."

Wow. I have no idea how to unpack all that Caleb just revealed. I wonder just how deep his feelings had been for Brenna, or if perhaps they were simply the sweet, yet typical, longings of the teenage heart.

Regardless, I'm not close enough to Caleb to ask, and I most certainly don't want to add to his frustration.

"So on a scale of one to Brenna…?" Shane, naturally, isn't going to let it drop.

"Four, okay?" It's not a shout, but he definitely raised his voice. Shane seems satisfied. "I wasn't in love with

Felicity yet or anything, but I liked her a lot. And I was digging the idea of settling down into a steady relationship. So, yeah. A four."

Caleb is annoyed, and Shane is enjoying it. I'm sure to them this is all normal fun and games, but it's rather uncomfortable for me. I decide to diffuse the situation.

"I'm sorry, Caleb. It stinks even if it wasn't super serious."

"Thanks, Sydney." He shoots me a small smile. "You order the Chinese?"

"I did."

"Thanks for that, too."

Chapter 29

SHANE

SATURDAY MORNING. SYD'S last full day living here. I tell myself I'm fine, but the truth is, the closer she gets to moving out, the closer I get to losing my shit.

Asher and Grace have gone back to Greyson for the day to pick up some things from their parents' houses. I've got their key in my pocket and the go-ahead to take Sydney over and show her the stuff I bought her, as well as the stocked kitchen.

I make my way to the kitchen, fully dressed and ready to go as soon as she appears. I hear her moving around in her bedroom, so I know she's awake. I take a seat at the bar, pull out my cell phone, and shoot her a text.

Me: You up yet? I've got a surprise for you this morning.

She doesn't answer via text, but she does stick her head out the door.

"Surprise?" she asks. "What is it?"

"It's not here," I reply. "You'll have to get dressed and come with me to find out."

"Give me ten minutes!" The smile on her face is worth every penny I spent on her new apartment and then some.

Sure enough, ten minutes later she's ready to go, in a pair of jeans that fit her like a glove, a pink tee shirt, and a pony tail. I secretly love that she doesn't go to a lot of trouble to doll herself up for me. Not that she's not smoking when she's rocking a full make-up job and sexy hair-do, but it's not necessary at all for her beauty to shine. And though I know I don't deserve it, I love that she trusts me enough to throw her hair up and come with me on a moment's notice without make-up or fancy clothes.

Once we're on the road, she shifts in her seat to look at me.

"No hints?" she asks.

"Nope." I glance at her for half a second, then put my eyes back on the road.

When I turn into the subdivision where Grace's aunt and uncle live, Sydney eyes me with suspicion. "My apartment is this way."

"I know."

I pull into the driveway and put the car in park, just as she says, "I don't even have a key yet."

I smile and wink, then reach into my pocket and pull out the key Asher gave me last night. Hopping out of the car, I jog around and manage to get to her door before she opens it herself.

"What's going on?" she asks, stepping out onto the driveway and propping her fists on her hips.

I don't answer. I just take her hand in mind and begin leading her around the side of the garage to the steps that lead up to the apartment, all the while doing my best to ignore the way her hand feels small and perfect in my own.

"You know Asher's not here, right?"

"Yes, I'm aware. He's the one who gave me the key. I doubt he'd have given it to me if he and Grace were going to be up here this morning."

Unlocking the door, I push it wide so Sydney can step in ahead of me. The place looks the same as it did when I left last night. Bed on the far wall, partially blocked by a folding wardrobe. Bathroom and laundry through a door in the back right corner near the foot of the bed. Brown leather couch that's seen its better days, along with a large coffee table, immediately to the left of the front door, and a tiny kitchen to the right.

Asher and Grace have moved most of their stuff already, except for a couple of duffel bags of clothes on the floor near the bed and a few boxes sitting beside the couch. Sydney looks around, and I know she's seeing the beginning of her new start. This tiny garage apartment is so much more to her than a place to live.

"It'll take me a while to make it homey, but that's all right," she whispers. "I'll be able to buy a few new things each month after I've paid the rent."

"Might not take as long as you think." I take her hand again and pull her toward the kitchen.

On the counter next to the sink is the coffee pot I bought for her. It's red, because I thought the color matched her bright spirit. I keep that to myself because I know it sounds stupid. Beside the coffee pot are the two mugs I picked out. One says *I'm mentally rolling my eyes at you,* and the other reads *Coffee Snob.*

Sydney picks each one up and giggles as she reads them. Above the coffee pot, she opens the cabinet and sees the filters and three kinds of coffee, as well as several boxes of cereal. Moving the only other cabinet in the kitchen, she opens it to reveal several varieties of pasta and sauce, canned soup, crackers, and four boxes of brownie mix. Next she opens the refrigerator and sees the milk, juice, cheese, and eggs.

So far she's said nothing, and I'm beginning to wonder if maybe I overstepped. Grace had seemed to think this was a great idea, but perhaps we both miscalculated.

But then Sydney turns around. Her eyes are misted over with unshed tears, but her lips form a smile. "You stocked the kitchen for me?"

I nod. "And a few other things as well."

I walk toward the wardrobe, where I stashed the sheet sets and pillow.

She looks closely at each set, one pink and white striped, the other solid sunshine yellow, then turns back toward me.

"I'm overwhelmed." She closes her eyes for a moment and takes a deep breath. "Thank you so much."

My hands itch to reach for her, to pull her to me and wrap my arms around her, so I shove them in my pockets and shrug my shoulders. "I want this for you, Sydney. I want this new beginning to be everything you want and need it to be. I just thought maybe I could do a little something to make things smoother for you."

She looks toward the kitchen where the coffee pot sits on the counter. "Share the first pot with me?"

I can't help the smile that spreads across my face. "Yeah, sure."

Ten minutes later, on opposite ends of the couch, Sydney and I sip coffee from the mugs I picked out for her.

"I'm going to miss this," she says, gesturing toward me with my cup of coffee. "You and the Resolution crew, you've become such good friends in such a short amount of time"

"Yeah, me too." I smile. *Friends.* I'm both relieved and sad that she includes me in that category. "You're part of our family now. That's not changing just because you've got your own place. I'd wager my townhouse will still be the meeting place for everyone, so I'm sure you'll be back from time to time. And I'll still bring you coffee to the shop if I have time in the afternoons."

She laughs, and it almost sounds like a girly giggle. I love that. "And I'll come by every now and then and cook something for you and Caleb, so you don't go back to existing on pizza and beer."

"That would be most appreciated." I take a long drink, then set the mug on the coffee table. "You'll be missed too, Syd."

Chapter 30

SHANE

SYDNEY IS IN her room packing. She's moving first thing in the morning. She doesn't have a lot to move. Just her clothes and some of the things she bought. Towels, dishes, and that sort of thing. I told her I'd help her get everything over there and unpacked tomorrow, but honestly, I'm dreading it. It means she won't be with me all the time anymore, and I dislike that idea the closer it gets to being reality.

I can't begin to imagine my days without her here. In such a short span time she's woven her way into my life to the point that I can't imagine this apartment without her presence. The thought leaves me empty and sad.

I occupy myself with *Call of Duty* to avoid thinking about the inevitable. I hear her in her room, singing softly, that rich, sexy voice of hers winding around me like strings of honey.

Yeah, I'm going to miss that, too.

Half a dozen times I almost put the controller down and go in there and tell her how I really feel about her. Half a dozen times I stop myself, forcing myself to remember all the reasons I've convinced myself that I'm no good for her.

My arguments get weaker every time.

At midnight, I've exhausted every logical reason to stay

away, and I can't stop myself. Before I talk myself out of it, I kill the Xbox and leap up from the couch, making a beeline for Sydney's room.

She's folding the load of clean laundry she just washed, placing each item in a duffle bag laying open on the bed. I force myself not to look at the lacy bits of fabric in the bottom of the laundry basket, but it's an effort. Shampoo and all manner of female bath products are also scattered on the mattress.

I just stand there for a moment, the peace that's come with this decision settling into my bones. I may still believe Sydney's better off without me, but Asher's right. She can decide that for herself. I'll never be the one who takes her choices away.

She doesn't see me, or if she does she doesn't show it. I know she's not ignoring me. The tension between us abated after I apologized for being a dick. But we're both aware that this is her last night under my roof, and it's strange for both of us. I think, at this moment, she's like me and just doesn't know what to say.

Except I do know what to say.

"We need to talk about how you moving out affects our relationship." I blurt it out, the words racing out of me so fast I wonder if she even understood them.

"We're friends, Shane," she says without looking up. "We'll still be friends once I'm in my own place. Just like you said this morning when we shared coffee at my new place."

"No, I mean our relationship." I know I'm not making any sense to her, but I can't stop myself. "As in you and me."

She stops folding and turns her face toward me. I can see her breathing speed up, and she takes a deep breath to slow it before she speaks.

"I wasn't aware we were in a relationship." Her voice is shaky, yet the words are strong. She's not going to make this easy on me, and I'm so proud of her for that. "In fact, the last time we even tip-toed toward a conversation about such a thing, you very quickly nixed the idea."

"Well, I was wrong." Admitting it is so much easier than I imagined it would be. "And we *are* in a relationship."

I step into the room and close the distance between us. Taking her face in my hands, I lean in and lay my lips against hers. The shirt she was holding falls, landing on my bare feet, and her hands press flat against my chest.

Whatever crazy connection we've been dancing around practically explodes between us and for the life of me I can't figure out why in the world I ever resisted it. I angle my head, deepening the kiss, sliding my arms around her while her hands curl and grip handfuls of my shirt. The meld of our mouths is hot and wet, but the depth of the intimacy runs much deeper. It's me, letting go of my past, all the baggage I've accumulated, and it's her, taking control of her life, taking the first tentative steps back into her womanhood.

I pull back, just enough that I can look her in the eyes, but I don't let go. I keep her right where she is, wrapped up in my arms.

"I have no idea how to do this. No idea how to be a good boyfriend. But I want to try. I want to be with you, and I want to do right by you. You'll have to be patient, because I'm probably going to screw up regularly, but if you'll give me a chance, I promise, I'll…"

"Shane," she interrupts, smiling up at me. "You're selling yourself short again."

I shrug my shoulders and press a kiss to her forehead. "Just trying to be honest."

"I have no doubt that you'll be a great boyfriend. You're kind and funny and attentive, and you've made me feel more special than anyone ever has." She takes a deep breath and closes her eyes. "But me? I don't know if I can be your girlfriend."

My knees nearly buckle, and she sees the panic on my face.

"I mean, clearly, I want to," she clarifies. "But I don't know if wanting to is enough. I know I told you not to use what happened to me last year as an excuse to ignore what's between us, but the truth is I don't know if I can..."

She stops, not finishing her thought.

"Don't know if you can what, Sydney?"

"I don't know when, or even *if* I can... respond to you." Her lids lower, and her chin drops, and I can tell how much it hurts her to say those words. "In *that* way."

In this moment, I know that my response to what she just said is of the utmost importance. I have the power to break her, or to help her start building that confidence again. I'm humbled that she trusts me that much.

Bringing my hands to her face once again, I place my palms gently against her cheeks and trace soft lines beneath her eyes with my thumbs. I lock my eyes on her bright green gaze and speak.

"Sydney, you just did respond to me. There is *nothing* wrong with you. *Nothing.*" I emphasize the word and tilt my head closer to hers. "And I completely understand that some things between us will have to move slowly. Trust me when I say that's not even an issue you should be worried about. I've done the fast and loose thing, and it's not something I care to repeat. *Ever.* I would rather wait years for you than hop into bed with the next willing female that comes along. I'm done with meaningless hook-ups. I want something real. I want *you.*"

"But what if I can't ever?" she asks, her voice breaking.

"Stop it, Syd," I whisper. "Stop expecting the worst. I don't believe for a single second that you're going to be handicapped in *any* way because of what happened to you. I'm not worried at all that you won't be able to be with me intimately someday. In the meantime, there's *so much more* to us than the physical. We have fun together, or at least we did before I acted like a jerk. We trust each other. There's so much more we can learn about each other. I want all those things. I want to go on dates and see movies. I want to have picnics and Netflix binges. I want to get together with all our friends and be able to hold your hand and let them know that you're mine. I want *all* that."

I kiss her again, a brief whisper of my lips against hers. "Please tell me you want those things too."

Her eyes are still closed, but the corners of her mouth turn up. "I do. I want all those things."

Relief buzzes through my system like electricity, and I bend my head to kiss her again.

"I want those things," she says against my lips. "But I want to be a normal woman… in *every* way."

"Sydney," I whisper, leaning my forehead against hers. "Do you like kissing me."

She rolls her eyes. "Of course."

"Do you think about me? About kissing me? Being with me?"

She nods, a pink blush rising on the skin of her neck.

"Then don't you see? You're already responding in *that* way. Everything else will come later, when the time is right. You have nothing to worry about."

One side of her mouth tilts in a half grin. "What if that's not enough for you?"

"It is enough," I answer, tightening my arms around her. "*You* are more than enough."

Chapter 31

SYDNEY

WHEN I OPEN my eyes the next morning I'm greeted with the first, soft wisps of sunlight peeking through the blinds in my window. It's early, and no one is stirring in the townhouse yet, but rather than getting out bed and starting my day like I normally would – by beating Shane to the coffee pot – I take a few moments to remember all that transpired last night and soak in all the warm, sweet feelings bubbling inside me.

Shane is mine, and I am his.

I still can't believe how fast it all happened. One moment I'm packing my things, happy that we seemed to be back on friendly terms, and the next he's declaring all the reasons we should be together. Doubts still swirl around in my head – about me and my ability to *be* someone's girlfriend – but I shove them all down and refuse to listen to them. The pain of what happened to me raises its hand, demanding to be acknowledged, but I ignore it, refusing to give it attention. There will be plenty of time to overthink things down the road. For the moment, I just want to enjoy the fact that the guy I've been crushing on for weeks actually returns my feelings.

When he put his lips on mine, and defined exactly what he meant when he said *relationship,* well, I very nearly turned to jello right then and there. Kissing Shane is like nothing I've ever experienced, and for that I'm grateful. For all the experience I racked up during that first year of college, I never knew what it felt like to be kissed by someone who respected me and cared for me until Shane.

I'm glad there are some firsts I can still give him.

When I hear Shane in the kitchen starting the coffee, I know the time has come to start my day. Everything is packed and ready to be loaded in the car, so all that's left is for me to get up and going.

I grab the clothes that I laid out for today and step out into the kitchen.

Shane looks up from the dripping coffee pot and a huge smile spreads across his face. He walks toward me, and before I know what's happening, I'm wrapped in his embrace, my arms and the clothes I'm holding trapped between us, and he's lowering his face to mine.

I shake my head and clamp my lips shut, turning my face away from his. He looks at me with narrowed eyes and curious expression. I wiggle one hand out from between our torsos and cover my mouth.

"Morning breath," I whisper.

He chuckles. "Well hurry up and brush your teeth, because I'm kissing you in the next five minutes."

He lets me go with a peck to my forehead.

"It'll be longer than five because I'm taking a shower, too."

He groans. "Don't say stuff like that."

"Seriously Shane. It's not like this is new. I've been showering here for weeks."

"And I've been painfully aware of it every single time."

"You're a teenage boy," I say, laughing as I turn down the hall toward the bathroom.

"One who's crazy about you," he calls after me.

I'm still grinning like an idiot when I step out of the shower several minutes later, towel drying my hair and pulling it up into a messy bun. I pull on my shorts and tank top, then brush my teeth so I'm not dealing with morning breath the next time my boyfriend tries to kiss me.

Boyfriend. It seems so surreal. I've had boyfriends before, but with Shane the word means so much more.

When I return to the kitchen, I notice that Shane has already poured my coffee and toasted a blueberry bagel for each of us. I toss my sleep clothes through the open bedroom door so that they land on the bed, then turn and head for the bar where Shane has breakfast set.

He stops me before I get there, sliding his arms around me and kissing me with all the soft, gentle sweetness I've come to expect from him. He may look like a hard ass with his tattoos and piercings, but there's a sweet side to him that melts me every time I experience it.

We're both so lost in each other that we apparently fail to hear footsteps coming down the stairs. Our first clue that Caleb is up way earlier than usual is when he steps into the living room.

"Holy shit!" he exclaims.

Shane and I spring apart, like we've been caught by our parents or something. But as soon as we do, Shane reaches for my hand and laces our fingers together, as if to say to Caleb, *yes we are together.*

Shane takes a deep breath and starts talking. "Remember that night we all stumbled out the back door of Resolution and found Gabe and Rachelle kissing in the parking lot?"

Caleb nods, but says nothing.

"And nobody freaked out or blew up. We all just said,

'hey, it's cool that two of our good friends are dating', and then we all went out for hot wings."

Caleb nods again.

"Well, I expect the same from you in this moment. Sydney and I are together, and we're going to stay that way. We haven't told anyone yet, and I'm going to let her decide how we let that information out, so for the time being I'm going to ask that you keep this to yourself and be supportive."

Caleb looks back and forth between the two of us, then goes to grab a coffee mug. "I figured since it's your last day here, I'd come down and have breakfast with you guys. Obviously, you weren't expecting me."

I laugh. "It's not like you've ever graced us with your presence this early in the day."

Shane adds his thoughts on the matter. "He was home early last night since he and Felicity are splitsville. Easier to get up early when you get to bed at a decent hour."

"Like you ever called it a night early before Sydney moved in," Caleb says, dropping onto a barstool with his mug full of black coffee.

Shane looks like he could commit murder over Caleb's crack about his previous dating habits.

"Caleb, I know," I say, sitting down to my own coffee and bagel. "Shane and I clearly both have histories that don't involve each other. What matters now is what's ahead of us."

Shane sits down beside me and puts an arm around my shoulder, leaning over and pressing a kiss against my cheek. He looks over at Caleb. "You said last night you were digging the idea of settling down into a relationship. Well, so am I. I hate that things went sour with you and Felicity, but the truth is Syd and I have had a connection since day one. It took a while for me to come around to it, but I finally got there, and I'm not going anywhere."

"No doubt there's something different about you, man," Caleb replies. "You're good for him, Sydney. I'll keep quiet about it until you guys go public. And if it's important, you have my stamp of approval."

"It matters," Shane says. "Thanks Caleb."

"You'll be missed around here, Syd." Caleb takes a drink of coffee and continues. "You've spoiled us with the nacho bar and spaghetti."

"I'll be around, so no worries. You don't have to go back to beer and pizza all the time."

"You could just stay," Shane says with a grin. I can't tell if he's serious or joking, or maybe a bit of both. "Just keep your room here and cook for us in lieu of rent."

"I think it's a bit early to be talking about moving in together," I joke, nudging him with my shoulder. "Besides, I need the fresh start."

He smiles, that warm, knowing smile that I've come to adore, and says, "I know you do." He follows that up with a soft kiss on my lips.

Caleb makes gagging noises. "At least I'm not going to have to watch you two be all over each other all the time."

Shane laughs. "Don't bet on it, dude."

Chapter 32

SYDNEY'S BEEN IN her apartment for a couple of days. I've been fighting the urge to stop by fifty times each day. I don't want her to feel like I think she can't do things on her own. I know she can. I just miss her. Fortunately, we stay in contact all day through text messages, and I took her coffee at the boutique this afternoon when I had a break between clients.

She and Grace are having dinner tonight since Asher and I both have appointments until late this evening. We agreed that we'd each tell our best friends and let the information about the two of us filter out from there. So, while Sydney and Grace are having girl time at their favorite sushi place, I'm going to tell Asher, between clients, over the pizza that's sitting on the break room table.

"Sydney adjusting to her new place?" Asher asks, grabbing a slice of pepperoni and dropping it on a paper plate.

I pop open a can of soda. "Yeah. She's thrilled."

"You don't sound thrilled," he smirks.

I shrug my shoulders. "I miss her."

"I knew you would."

I open my mouth to tell him about Syd and me, but stop when Rachelle breezes into the room.

"You guys have fifteen minutes until your next appointments, so hurry up with your dinner." She opens the fridge and takes out a bottle of water, but stops and pretends to chastise us. "And no gossiping while I'm not in the room."

I love Rachelle, but no way do I want her hearing about this before Asher. Caleb knowing is one thing, since he's my roommate and a super decent guy despite the fact that he tried to warn me off Syd when she first moved in. But I want to tell Asher myself.

"Since when do we gossip?" Asher asks with a snide voice.

"Oh please," she responds, sitting down in a chair next to him. "You guys are just as bad as girls. Don't even try to hide it."

I'm beginning to wonder how long she's planning to stay back here and shoot my plan to talk privately with Asher all to hell. Just then the bell on the front door dings.

Rachelle sighs. "Duty calls. You two eat fast."

Once she's back in the lobby, I lean back in my chair and push the door shut. At least now we'll have a split second of warning if someone else decides to interrupt.

"Before Sydney moved out," I begin, then find myself not knowing how to put it into words. Asher takes a second slice of pizza and waits for me to continue. "Before she moved out, I told her how I felt. And we made things official."

He drops his pizza back on the plate. "Wait? Like, the two of you are an item now?"

I nod. "She's telling Grace tonight."

"Shane, that's great." He reaches over and slaps me on the shoulder. "I knew there was something between you two."

"It's brand new, but it's important." I look at my best friend and give him the honest truth. "The most important thing ever for me."

Because I know. I know that even though we've only known each other a few weeks, and we only decided to be together a couple of days ago, Sydney is like no other woman has ever been or ever will be to me.

"I'm scared shitless," I admit. "Scared I'll screw it up somehow."

Ash nods. "I get that. I do. When something matters this much you want to protect it, make sure it's unharmed."

"How do I do that?" I ask.

"You don't." He finishes his drink, then goes on. "There's no way to keep a relationship in a bubble, no matter how hard you try. Grace and I tried that, and it blew up in our faces. You just have to trust each other and in the feelings you know are real. The rest will fall into place. If it doesn't, you figure it out together. And we're all here for you. Both of you."

"Is Grace going to bust my chops and tell me not to hurt her friend?" I'm only half joking.

"She'll be ecstatic," Asher says, smiling. "But not surprised. We knew it was only a matter of time."

"Well, let's just hope Sydney doesn't come to her senses and realize what terrible boyfriend material I am."

Asher laughs. "I have faith in you, man."

The fact that he means it gives me confidence.

Chapter 33

SYDNEY

BING PROPOSED TO Kristy last weekend, which is the reason I'm at Shane's getting things ready for a barbecue.

I've been in my own place for a couple of weeks, and I've settled in nicely. I love the independence I feel, going to work each day, making a living, paying my own bills. It's satisfying in a way I never imagined.

Shane and I have created a nice pattern as well. We have dinner together several times a week, even if it's just me bringing take out to the shop on nights he has appointments until late in the evening. When he has a break in the afternoon, he stops in at Beautiful Things with coffee and some kind of cookie from Ugly Mug. And throughout the day, we text and talk as much as possible.

It's Sunday afternoon, and the entire gang is coming over today to celebrate Bing and Kristy's engagement. Last night, when Shane finished at the shop, he and I hit the grocery and picked up everything for burgers, hot dogs, and a traditional summer cook out. Since Kristy's son, Ezra, will be there, we wanted to something kid-friendly.

Shane is currently out back, getting the charcoal going for the grill. Caleb's upstairs taking his time getting ready, which means he's probably avoiding everybody for as long as possible. Everyone else should be arriving shortly.

I'm at the stove stirring macaroni and cheese when I hear the first knock at the door.

"Come on in!" I call, and the door immediately opens.

A moment later Gabe and Rachelle arrive in the kitchen and place a large box of cookies from Ugly Mug on the counter.

"Dessert!" Rachelle exclaims, then envelopes me in a huge hug. "You and Shane? I'm so glad it finally happened! I was beginning to wonder if you two were ever going to get your heads out of your asses!"

I love her exuberant response. I've learned that Rachelle is kind of the "mother hen" of this bunch, and her greatest desire is to see everyone happy.

"Thank you," I say, hugging her back. "I guess you are all stuck with me now."

"And we're thrilled about it," she says, releasing me.

"You two are a good match, Sydney," Gabe says. "I'm glad to see you both happy."

Rachelle retrieves a platter from the cabinet and begins arranging cookies while Gabe heads out back to join Shane at the grill.

"I can't believe Caleb and Felicity broke up the same night you and Shane finally got together," Rachelle says. "I almost had all my boys successfully and happily paired up. Now it's back to square one with Caleb."

"I felt really bad for him that night." I move to the counter alongside Rachelle and begin transferring the macaroni from the pot into a serving bowl. "He was really bummed. Not heartbroken, but just sad."

"He doesn't talk about it much at the shop," she says. "But I can tell it's on his mind."

"In all the time I stayed here, I never really got to know

him much," I reply, grabbing mustard, ketchup, and pickles from the refrigerator. "He keeps his cards pretty close to his chest it seems."

"He's a tough one to crack," Rachelle agrees. "He's been at the shop longer than Asher and Shane, and still sometimes it seems like he intentionally keeps himself on the outside. Someday, he's going to fall in love, and that woman will open him up for real."

"I'd just like to see the smile back in his eyes."

The bar is now set with macaroni and cheese, all the fixings for burgers and hot dogs, various potato chips, and cookies for dessert. Rachelle and I are setting the paper plates and plastic cups out when we hear the front door open and the rest of the guests arrive.

Asher and Grace set their assortment of soft drinks on the table, and the guests of honor, Bing, Kristy, and Ezra, are instructed that they don't get to help in the least.

There are more hugs for me, along with words of congratulations about my relationship with Shane. In all my life, I've never seen a group of people more excited for other people's happiness. Part of me still can't believe I've somehow been included in this circle of friends, but I'm eternally grateful that I have.

Caleb emerges just as Shane and Asher come in from the back with the burgers and hot dogs.

Bing grabs him before anyone else has a chance to. I can't hear what they say to each other, but it's clear that Bing takes his role as honorary big brother to these guys seriously. Whatever words he's saying, Caleb is smiling and nodding, and their conversation ends with a man hug and back slaps.

Later in the evening, after everyone is stuffed and Shane has Ezra occupied with the Xbox, and the rest of us sit around the table sipping soda, the conversation turns to

Caleb's new single status.

"I'm sorry about Felicity," Kristy says.

Caleb just nods in way of acknowledgement.

"She wasn't the girl for him," Bing says. His tone leaves no room for argument.

"I have to admit, I wondered what the connection was," Rachelle agrees. "But I would've never said anything because you seemed happy."

"I was happy. Just not in that soul deep way all of you seem to be," Caleb responds, gesturing around the table at the happy married or engaged couples.

"It'll happen for you," Asher says.

Caleb just shrugs his shoulders. "I don't know if it ever will."

"He knows what he's looking for. He just has to go after it." Bing's words hang in the air and no one questions the meaning behind them. Clearly, he knows something about Caleb that the rest of us don't.

"New subject," Caleb announces. "Let's talk about the morning I came in here and found Shane and Sydney with their tongues down each other's throats."

"No making my girl uncomfortable, Caleb," Shane shouts from the living room where he and Ezra are engrossed in some kind of game where they skateboard across the screen.

Everyone at the table laughs, and lets Caleb's description of catching me and Shane kissing drop.

"Seriously, Sydney," Bing begins, "it's good to see the two of you together and happy."

"Thank you," I answer. "For everything, including being so welcoming to me. I feel like I've fallen into a brand new family."

"You have!" Rachelle says, her voice bubbly and full of joy. "It's a crazy family, but now you're one of us."

Chapter 34

SHANE

IT'S JULY 8. Four days ago we celebrated Independence Day with all our crew, heading downtown for the annual parade, then watching the fireworks together, sitting on picnic blankets and eating popcorn. The weather was perfect, sunny and bright during the day, cool and crisp in the evening. Sydney and I shared a blanket, among all our friends, and she laid her head on my shoulder as I slipped my arm around her waist. The brilliant lights exploding in the sky couldn't touch the brightness of the sparks in my heart.

Life with Sydney is beautiful.

Today is her birthday. She didn't tell me. Grace did. At first, I'd been a little irritated, but keeping it to herself is such a "Sydney" thing to do. She's not comfortable in the center of attention. Whether she's always been like that, or whether it's a result of what happened to her in college I'm not sure. But regardless, Sydney deserves to be celebrated, so that's what I'm about to do.

Rachelle gave me the name of a great bakery, so on my afternoon break I drove over and ordered cupcakes. When my last appointment finished at just after eight, I picked up pizza and headed to her place.

She thinks I'm just stopping by to hang out after work,

but the cupcakes and birthday gift in my backseat say otherwise. I slide the handles of the gift bag over my arm, then balance the cupcakes on top of the pizza box before heading up the stairs to her garage apartment.

She opens the door when I'm halfway up the steps. She must've been watching for me to arrive.

I love that.

Her eyes drop to the cupcakes, the chocolate frosting decorated with bright pink sprinkles and small, red candy disks in the shape of a heart. She brings her gaze up to mine, and a slow smile begins to spread across her face.

"Happy birthday," I say, finally reaching the top step. I lean down and place a kiss on her lips. "Grace told me."

She steps back to let me enter the apartment, and I quickly place the pizza and cupcakes on the kitchen counter, along with the bag that holds her gift.

"You didn't have to make a big deal," she whispers, stepping up beside me.

I wrap her in my arms and look down into her gorgeous green eyes. "Your birthday is a big deal, Sydney. To me anyway. You should've told me."

"I didn't want to seem like I was asking for a birthday present or something." Her gaze drops, as if she's embarrassed. "I know that probably sounds stupid."

"Not stupid at all." I kiss the top of her head. "But now you know that I didn't bring cupcakes and a present because you asked. I did it because I want to."

"Well then," she begins, pulling away from me to grab two plates from the cabinet, "let's not let your efforts go to waste."

We sit together on the couch, pizza, cupcakes, and soda on the coffee table in front of us, and thirty minutes later half the pizza and four cupcakes are gone. I'd attempted to sing "Happy Birthday", but I'm no singer, so Sydney joined me halfway through. Her voice, with it's warm, smooth sound, made my pitiful attempt to serenade her infinitely better.

I can't help but think how that's almost an analogy for my life. Just like Sydney's voice combined with mine made me sound better, having Sydney by my side makes my life better in every way. If my life is a melody, a tune made up of single, individual pitches, Sydney is the harmony... the notes that accompany mine and make them richer and fuller.

"Present time," I announce, hopping up from the couch to get her gift from the kitchen. When Grace told me last week that Sydney's birthday was coming up, I'd given her gift a fair amount of thought. We haven't been together long, but I've known from the beginning that she's special in a way that no one ever has been.

Placing the bright yellow gift bag in front of her, I drop back onto the couch and scoot closer. She peers inside the bag, moves the white tissue paper around a bit, then looks back up at me with a grin.

"Open it," I say, nudging her with my elbow.

She reaches inside and pulls out the rectangular box, recognizing it immediately as a jewelry box. "Shane, what did you do?"

"I didn't go overboard, if that's what you're asking." I take the bag and toss it on the coffee table. "Go on. Take a look."

She lifts the lid, gradually revealing what's inside. I watch as her eyes travel over the brown leather bracelet, landing on the silver bar in the middle. Choosing a word for the inscription on the bar had been difficult. Sydney is so many things... beautiful, smart, kind, and courageous.

In the end, I'd decided on the word that I believe encompasses all of her beauty and courage.

Strength.

Because she is so strong, and I want her to always, always remember that.

Her eyes remain glued to the bracelet, to the word on the silver bar, and as she stares, a single tear rolls down her cheek.

"Shane…" she begins, but doesn't say more.

"You're strength is the most beautiful thing about you," I tell her. "And if you ever doubt that, I want to be the one to remind you."

She lifts it from the box and hands it to me, stretching her arm out so I can put it on. Circling her dainty wrist with the leather band, I work the clasp until the bracelet rests gracefully against her skin.

"Thank you," she whispers, threading her fingers together with mine.

"Happy birthday," I reply, leaning close.

"You spoil me." She brushes the tip of her nose against mine.

"You've remade me." I tilt my head and slide my lips onto hers.

The kiss is soft at first, reverent and unhurried. Sydney moves her free hand to my neck, pulling me closer until I'm forced to unlace my fingers from her other hand and slip my arm around her back. Before I know it, both of her arms encircle my neck and she's somehow gotten to her knees so that our chests are plastered together.

All this and our lips haven't unlocked once.

The warmth of her mouth envelopes my entire body, and I feel the heat to the soles of my feet. She's taking charge of the kiss, and her eagerness ignites something primal and deep inside me, and I struggle to keep it under control.

I'm always so careful in moments like this, balancing my very real and palpable desire for her with the yearning I have to make her feel safe and cared for, and not in any way pressured or rushed.

I want nothing I do to ever trigger a memory of the bastard that hurt her.

Which is why, despite the crazy feelings barreling through me, I slow the pace of the kiss and loosen my hold on her body.

Slowly, her eyes open and she focuses that brilliant green gaze on me.

"Is something wrong?" she asks.

I shake my head and smile. "Everything's right. Just letting up off the accelerator for a bit."

Her eyes narrow. "Why?"

I lift my hand to her face, brushing a strand of her golden blonde hair behind her ear. "There's no rush."

She takes a deep breath and takes my hand, squeezing it in both of hers. "Shane, you're sweet and so considerate. But you don't have to be so careful all the time."

"And you don't have to be in a hurry."

"Listen." She presses a quick kiss to my lips. "First off, I don't want you to ever be worried that you're going to remind me of *him*. I could never mistake you for the piece of trash who hurt me. Second, if I need to slow things down, I'll say so. I trust you enough to know you're not going to be pissed if I have to put the brakes on."

I pick up her hand and glance at the bracelet on her wrist. *Strong.* I couldn't have picked a more perfect word for her. "Okay."

"Now that that's settled," she says, resuming her seat on

the couch and snuggling into my side, "have you talked to Greg lately?"

I take a deep breath. Definitely not my favorite subject, but I'm so thankful I have Sydney to share it with. "Yesterday. It's still just a steady decline. He doesn't think it'll be much longer. She sleeps most of the time."

"How's he handling it all?"

"He says he's doing okay. The hospice folks take care of most of her care, so he can still go to work most days. His boss has been flexible, which is great. He always tries to stop me from sending money, but I know it has to be helping, especially when he has to take unpaid days off."

"You're a good man, Shane," she whispers, sliding her arm across my chest and hugging me close.

"I don't know about that," I say. "I'm here and not there. I'm glad about it, and yet I feel guilty at the same time."

"You're doing what you can. Your mom never sacrificed anything for you, but here you are, sacrificing for your uncle so he can care for her. The fact that you can't be there is for your own well-being, and no one, including Greg, faults you for that."

"And this is just one reason why you're so good for me." I wrap both arms around her and haul her into my lap. "You keep me out of the dark places in my head."

She giggles and leans in to kiss me. And for the next hour or so I reacquaint myself with the sheer joy of making out with my girlfriend without the pressure or expectation that anything more will happen.

Chapter 35

SHANE

RESOLUTION IS SLAMMED tonight. In addition to a full slate of appointments for all four of us, we've had quite a few people stop in to make appointments and talk about design. Asher's managed to take a couple of walk-ins that weren't too complicated. I've got a twenty minute breather coming up, and Sydney's bringing dinner. I can't wait.

On my way to the back room I notice that Bing, Asher, and Caleb are all still busy with their clients. Hopefully that means Syd and I will have a few minutes alone. I'm always happy for private moments with my girl, but tonight I also want to tell her what I found out yesterday. I don't know how she'll react, but I'm hoping she sees it as an opportunity to…

I stop cold when I push into the break room.

Dex.

"Scrotum face!" Dex shouts.

Usually I laugh, because it's such a guy thing to call your buddy an indecent name, but this time I inwardly groan at his nickname for me.

"What are you doing here on a Friday night?" I ask.

"On my way to Holbrook," he answers. "Stopped in to check the appointment calendar for next week, and to say hi to all you shitheads."

"Listen, Dex," I begin. "Sydney's coming in any minute with some dinner. Try not to completely offend her, okay?"

"What?" He feigns shock. "Me, offend someone?"

Just then, the door pushes open and Sydney walks in, a tote bag over one shoulder and a small bag from Ugly Mug in her hand.

"Oh, hey!" Syndey says, her voice cheerful as she looks from me to Dex. "Since we haven't met yet, you must be Dex."

"Yeah, Syd," I begin. "This is Dex. Dex. This is Sydney."

"Nice to meet you, Sydney." Dex extends his hand. "You were right Shane. She *is* hot."

"Damn it, Dex," I mutter.

Sydney just laughs and sits the tote and the Ugly Mug bag on the table. "It's nice to finally meet you, too." She shakes his hand. "Shane and Caleb have told me a lot about you."

"Knowing Shane, it involves tales of me bringing even the manliest of men to tears when they come in to have their dicks pierced."

"Good grief, Dex." Can the ground just open up and swallow me now?

Once again, Sydney laughs. "I've heard a few stories." Then she looks at me. "Relax, Shane. I'm not scandalized or anything."

Dex laughs. "She's awesome, Shane." He swipes his keys and ball cap from the table and goes on. "As much as I'd like to stay and tell you more about the world of genital piercing, I've got to get on the road." He grabs a soda from the refrigerator and slaps me on the back. "I'll see you ass cracks next week." He glances at Sydney. "And maybe you as well."

Dex makes his exit and I breathe a sigh of relief. I still have twenty minutes to spend with Sydney before my next client is due to arrive.

Opening the refrigerator, I pull out two bottles of water while Sydney unpacks what looks like some kind of sandwich, potato chips, and cookies from Ugly Mug.

Pulling up seats next to one another, Sydney unwraps the sandwiches and opens the bag of chips between us.

"BLTs?" I ask.

She nods. "With avocado. A little bit of healthy stuff to balance out the bacon."

"Sounds awesome." I'm seriously spoiled by this girl.

It's so pleasant, so sweet, to eat dinner together on a regular work night, and I'm enjoying her company and our conversation so much that I almost decide to forget about what I'd planned to talk to her about. But then a brief lull presents itself, and I decide to go ahead.

"This is probably going to sound weird," I begin, "but I was flipping the channels yesterday, and I caught a bit of a documentary."

I stop there, taking a deep breath. Sydney tilts her head and says nothing, waiting for me to go on.

"It was about campus sexual assault."

She doesn't gasp or flinch or have any kind of strong reaction. She just closes her eyes for a moment, then sits her sandwich down on the paper plate.

"Doesn't sound very uplifting." She takes a drink of water.

"Well, no," I agree. "I was just… I don't know… I've never been to college, so I had no idea how common it is."

Sydney exhales slowly. "Unfortunately, it's more common than anyone realizes. Claire, the counselor I worked with in Phoenix counseled with lots of girls who'd been victimized at school or on a college campus."

"I can't get over how so many times no one helped the victims. Not the police. Not the college. So many of the people on the documentary had stories like yours, where everyone protected the rapists, and no one stood up for them."

"That's why I left Phoenix. Hard to move forward when everyone is holding you back."

"Couple of the girls filed a Title Nine complaint against the colleges because the schools created a hostile environment by not addressing what had happened."

Sydney picks up her sandwich and starts eating again. She says nothing, so I continue.

"You ever heard of Title Nine?"

She shakes her head.

"I thought maybe you hadn't, since it seemed like it wasn't common knowledge to the girls on the documentary, at least until someone else told them. I thought maybe you might want to look in to that."

I don't say more. I just let that sit between us, giving her the time to let it sink in. She finishes her sandwich, then reaches into the Ugly Mug bag for a cookie.

"I don't think I can consider anything else at this point," she says, reaching across to put her hand on top of mine. "I left Malpais College on purpose, because it was draining the life out of me. I'm finally in a good place, on a brand new path. And I'm happy." She squeezes my hand and smiles at me. "That's where I want to focus all my energy. I don't want to look back. I just want to look forward, with you."

It's difficult to find fault with that logic, so I simply thread my fingers through hers and lean close enough to place a soft kiss on her lips.

"Okay," I whisper.

"Okay," she whispers back.

"Thanks for bringing me dinner."

"Any time." She kisses me again, then holds up the cookie so I can take a bite. "I love that you care enough to think about things like that."

"I do care," I say, biting the cookie. "About you and everything that affects you."

Chapter 36

SYDNEY

D EVIN'S BIRTHDAY IS almost exactly a month after mine. As soon as my birthday is over, he starts dreaming and planning for his own celebration. This year, all he wanted was to play video games with Shane again.

And so, Shane arranged for a day off from the shop, and he and I made the drive to Greyson for Devin's birthday.

They are currently engaged in a bowling tournament via Xbox Kinect. It's hysterical to watch, and it warms me to the bottom of my feet. My brother is in heaven.

Meanwhile, Mom, Dad, and I sit in the kitchen, following up the birthday cake with coffee. I've filled them in on my job, my new apartment, Grace and Asher's new place. They've been really supportive, excited even, about the way my life is rebounding. I haven't told them about Shane and me. It's not that I don't want to, it's just that I wonder how they'll react. Will they see this relationship the way I do, as not only a victory for me as a sexual assault survivor, but also as something that just plain makes me happy as a woman? Or will they be skeptical of Shane because he's a man, more specifically a man who probably isn't exactly the type they thought I'd wind up with?

"Shane is very kind to do this for Devin," Mom says,

nodding her head in the direction of the living room where we can hear shouts and high-fiving going on.

"Don't think for a minute this was a sacrifice for him," I reply, laughter in my voice. "Shane loves any excuse for a video game marathon. He and the guys play video games the way girls go shopping. It's their thing."

"You and Shane seem… close," she says, dropping her eyes to the coffee in her mug.

Dad is suddenly interested in some article in the newspaper that's been lying dormant on the table until this moment.

I should've known I couldn't hide it. Feeling the way I do about Shane, a person would have to be completely oblivious not to realize something's between us.

I take a deep breath and answer. "We are. I hope you'll both be happy for us."

Mom looks up from her coffee, at me, then across at Dad. It's clear they've already discussed the possibility of Shane and me. I can't imagine what it must be like for them to consider their daughter opening up to a man after experiencing a sexual assault.

"I know I've exercised some pretty poor judgement in the guy department in the past." I talk quick, just in case she was about to launch into all the reasons she's concerned and thinks this is a bad idea. "But not this time."

From the living room Devin's shout of victory rings out, and Shane's voice follows. "Devin, you are the bomb, and I'm not worthy."

I look directly at my mom and say with conviction, "Shane is special."

She nods. "I can tell that he is."

I breathe a huge sigh of relief.

"I won't ask for personal details," she continues, "but I

do hope you are keeping in contact with Claire. A new relationship and all the… well, all that goes with it could be tricky for you."

"I talk to Claire regularly." I smile across at her, touched by her concern. "Shane knows everything. He's incredibly caring and patient."

"You've shared all of it with him?" Dad asks, finally speaking up.

"Yes. I told him the whole truth before things moved beyond friendship. I don't know how to explain it, but the trust was just there between us from the beginning."

Tears form in Mom's eyes, and she reaches for my hand. "I was so worried that boys would treat you badly because of what you experienced. It makes me so happy to know that's not true."

I turn my wrist over so she can see the word *strength* on my leather bracelet. "This was my birthday present from him. He told me that to him my strength was the most beautiful part of me."

Dad clears his throat. "I guess it's safe to say that we approve."

The grin that breaks across my face must be enormous.

"Not that you needed our permission," he adds, "but your mom and I are very glad we can be happy about your new relationship."

"Thank you." My words are soft, and I manage to keep my voice from breaking.

Just then Shane and Devin appear in the doorway.

"The champ here says he needs another piece of birthday cake," Shane says. "I told him only if you all okayed it."

Mom looks at me, blinking the moisture in her eyes away, then turns to Shane and Devin. "Oh why not? It's your birthday, so what's a little more sugar?"

Devin jumps up in the air and pumps his fist. Shane looks down at Devin with something very much like love in his gaze. And my heart expands and spills over with an emotion very, very similar.

✧   ✧   ✧

HALFWAY THROUGH THE drive back to Flagstaff I'm still floating. My parents know about Shane and me, and they approve. Devin responds to Shane in a way I've not seen him respond to anyone other than family. Shane genuinely adores Devin. And something inside me grew exponentially watching Shane look at my brother with such affection in his eyes.

Yet even in my happiness, I'm aware of place inside me that's still hidden away. A room with a door that's kept locked, where I keep the hurt and the pain. As always, I can't decide if I want that place to disappear and leave me alone, or if I want to open the door and let out everything that's inside so it will stop creeping up on me during the happy moments. Now is not the time to wrestle with those options, so I do what I always do… push the thoughts away and turn my attention back to what's happening in the *now*.

"You know the documentary I told you about the other day?" Shane's question comes out of the blue and for a moment I simply stare out the window, unwilling to visit that subject after having just shut down the thread of darkness.

But this is Shane, who cares for me and wants the best for me. So for his sake, I'll engage in this conversation. At least long enough to reiterate what I'd said the last time he brought it up.

"Yes, I remember." I keep my gaze on the landscape

passing by my window.

"I think maybe I didn't explain what a Title Nine complaint is," he continues. "I know you said you weren't interested in thinking about it, but I thought I'd at least clarify what it is, since I did a crap job of it before."

I turn in my seat, enough that I can look at him as he drives. Taking in his profile, my breath catches. The uniqueness on the outside is just the tip of the iceberg compared to what's inside him, and I remind myself that if this is what it means to be cared for by him, I'm a lucky woman.

"It's not a police report," he says. "It's not like you're filing charges against someone. It's a complaint to the U.S. Department of Education. It probably doesn't end with anyone being arrested, but it holds the college accountable, to some degree, and it does sort of force them to acknowledge what's happening and at least try to improve things."

For a long moment I don't say anything, and neither does he. I can tell he thinks this is an idea with merit but doesn't want to push me. It's not like I wouldn't want to shine a light on how Malpais protected the wrong person and did nothing to help me, I just don't know if it's a road I can walk without opening the door inside me that only moments ago I slammed shut.

"I'm sure for the victims who filed a complaint, it was validating to have the Department of Education not only believe them, but also attempt to do something about it." In the interior of the car, my hushed tone is easily heard. "But when I think about the day you and I just had, and how happy I am, I think there's just no way I can turn back the clock and live in that place where I'm literally begging someone to take me seriously."

Shane nods, and turns briefly toward me and smiles before putting his eyes back on the road. "I just want you to know that if there's ever another step you decide to take, I'll be beside you. And if not, I'll still be beside you."

"Thank you," I whisper, leaning across the console to kiss his cheek.

He doesn't mention it again during the drive home, but it's swirling in my mind like a whirlpool. The possibility that someone might see the wrong in what happened to me and how the college treated me is alluring. But the thought of revisiting the darkest part of my life is enough to make me abandon even the tiniest bit of consideration.

Chapter 37

SYDNEY

"**YOU'RE SHITTING ME!**" Shane's voice is a mix between excited and shocked.

He and I, along with Asher, Grace, Dex, and Dex's apparent fiancee, Sarah sit at a table in the back of Ugly Mug, having lunch together.

"Not a bit," Dex replies. "We're headed to Vegas right now to tie the knot."

Across from me, Grace smiles and congratulates them, and Asher laughs, happy for his friend, yet not at all surprised at the unconventional way he's going about getting married.

Sarah is the complete opposite of Dex. Where he is tatted and pierced like the rest of the Resolution crew, Sarah is all manner of prim and proper. Chin length brown hair with blunt bangs, purple-framed trendy glasses, black dress slacks and a button up white blouse. She's almost nerdy, but in a really cute way. And by the way she's blushing, she's clearly crazy about Dex.

Since the guys are busy congratulating their buddy, I lean close and whisper my own words of congrats.

"I'm really happy for you two," I say. "This is an amazing group of people, and I hope we'll get to see you more often."

On the other side of Sarah, Grace echoes my sentiment. "Absolutely. You should come to town when Dex is working and hang out with the girls."

Sarah's chin dips, and she smiles. "I'd like that. Since he comes only once or twice a month, I can probably arrange my work schedule to be able to come with him."

"What do you do for a living?" Grace asks.

"I'm a librarian at a public library," she answers.

Of course she is. She looks every bit the part.

"I'm a cosmetologist," Grace replies. "And Sydney works at the boutique right down the street.

"Speaking of." I reach for my to-go latte and stand up from my seat. "My lunch break is almost over, so I better head back."

Shane grabs my hand and stops me. "Hang on. I'll walk with you."

He takes our lunch trash and drops it in the garbage, then comes back, laces our fingers together, and walks out with me.

"Hey, I had a cancellation, so I'm off a bit early tonight. You wanna come over for dinner?"

I look up at him and smile. "Of course. Want me to pick up something on the way?"

He shakes his head. "I'm going to cook."

"You? Really?"

"I'm not totally helpless, you know." He pretends to be wounded that I doubted him. "I learned a lot watching you, and I figure it's time I did the cooking."

"Well, I'll happily be your guinea pig." I tip toe to kiss his check and start to open the door to Beautiful Things.

"Listen, Syd," he begins. "Caleb's off for a few days, visiting his folks in San Diego, but I don't want you to think I invited you over just because we'll have the place to ourselves."

I can't help but chuckle. "Shane, we're alone every time you come to my apartment. You're sweet to reassure me, but I know I don't have to worry about you pressuring me."

He squeezes my hand. "Okay then. See you at eight?"

"I'll be there."

✧   ✧   ✧

I ARRIVE TO the fantastic smell of oven roasted chicken, and the adorable sight of Shane in an apron putting together a green salad. What I'm certain are baked potatoes rest on the bar, wrapped in foil and still steaming as if they've just been pulled from the oven. The chicken, perfectly browned, sits on a serving platter beside them.

"Wow," I say. "You've really been practicing."

Shane looks up and smiles as I walk into the kitchen. He leans over and kisses me, then returns to tossing the salad greens with the dressing.

"Caleb agreed to let me test it on him the other night. I didn't kill him, so I think you're probably safe."

"I'm impressed." I open the cabinet and pull out two plates. Walking toward the table, I notice that he's got a candle and a vase of flowers in the center. "And now I'm doubly impressed."

"I'm good like that," he says, turning to wink at me over his shoulder. "And seriously, the chicken is pretty easy because there's nothing to mix. Same with the potatoes. The salad isn't too complicated because you just throw stuff together. I just followed instructions."

"Which is more than a lot of people dare to try." I return to the kitchen for utensils and glasses, but Shane stops me before I can pull the tall glasses from the cabinet.

"I've got glasses already," he says, nodding toward a pitcher and two long-stemmed glasses sitting next to the refrigerator. I can't help but smile. "It's just lemonade."

"Perfect." I take the glasses, lemonade, and utensils and finish setting the table.

Shane brings dinner to the table and slices the chicken like an expert. "I watched some dude on the food channel," he admits.

"Better than I could do. I've never even tried. Dad always did it with the Thanksgiving turkey."

"That's why I figured I ought to learn," he says. "It's a man thing."

I chuckle as I fill our salad bowls, forcing myself not to imagine Shane carving the turkey at Thanksgiving while the kids and I watch from our seats at the family table.

His dinner is outstanding and made even better because of the easy, flirty conversation that flows between us. Everything with him just comes so naturally. Sometimes it scares me a little, like maybe I don't deserve to be this happy so soon, but then I remember what Claire told me. Everyone recovers and moves on a different pace, and I shouldn't feel guilty because I'm able to feel this way again.

I eye the pocket watch and angel tattoo on Shane's right arm. I've always wondered what it meant, but never asked. I guess it seemed to personal, which is stupid since we've each shared the worst parts of our pasts with each other. I figure there's no danger in asking him now.

"Can you tell me about the pocket watch tattoo?"

"Parker did it for me, while I was apprenticing at the shop in Albuquerque." He slides his arm closer to me. "I'd gotten myself clean and finished high school. I guess the watch reminds me that life is short so time shouldn't be wasted or thrown away. I'd done a lot of that and didn't want to do it anymore."

I reach out and trace the watch with my fingers. "What about the angel?"

"The people who helped me," he replies. "Greg, Parker, the guy who took a chance and let me apprentice with him, they all pulled me out of the situation I'd gotten myself into. Cared enough about me to not let me destroy myself. I'm grateful for all of them."

"I'm grateful for them, too," I whisper, resting my palm over the angel above the pocket watch. "So much."

He rests his forehead against mine, his eyes closed, and raises his hand to rest against my cheek. He says nothing, and I follow suit, basking in the sweetness of this moment.

"I'm lost in you," he finally whispers, eyes still closed. He nuzzles his cheek into mine until his lips land near my ear. "Lost in you and finally home."

Chapter 38

SHANE

THERE ARE MOMENTS when I cannot believe that Sydney is mine. That this sweet, strong, amazing woman chooses me above all others. I don't know that I've ever done anything to deserve someone like her, but I'm not going to argue with the universe for giving me a chance to try.

We're cuddled together on the couch after dinner, a movie playing on the TV. Syd's head rests on my shoulder, my hand running through the soft blonde strands of her hair. She's so much stronger than she realizes, and I want to help her prove it to herself.

Gently, I untangle myself from her and stand. "Be right back."

She smiles up at me with that stunning goodness that I'll do anything to protect and champion.

From my bedroom, I retrieve the papers I printed out earlier. Heading back to the living room, I sit down next to her and take a deep breath.

"I took a look at the website that was mentioned on that documentary," I begin. Immediately, Sydney's eyes close and I can see her begin to shut down. "Please don't think I'm trying to make you do anything. I just thought you might like to read some of the stories that were shared on the site."

She glances at the papers in my hand. "You mean stories like mine?"

I nod, thinking she's coming around.

"Why would I want to read about a girl being raped, when I've experienced it for myself, firsthand?"

I can tell I miscalculated. "These aren't play by play accounts of what happened to them. They're more about what these girls did afterward. How they didn't let the college off the hook."

"Is that what you think I did?" she asks, standing up from the couch to pace back and forth across the room. "That I let the college off the hook?"

"Of course not." I pop up from my seat and stand in her way. "I think you did everything you could at the time."

She stops, crossing her arms across her chest and staring at me. "At the time? What is that supposed to mean?"

"It means exactly what I said. That you did everything you could at the time to tell the truth and pursue justice." I try to put my arms around her but she steps backward, out of my reach. "And it means that now that you're here, in a better place, with your strength built back up and a huge support system around you, maybe you can take the next step. It means that maybe doing something else to hold the college accountable would be further proof of how strong you are and how far you've come."

"I don't really feel the need to prove anything to Malpais anymore. I tried for a year to prove to them that I was telling the truth, that I deserved to be protected, and it got me nothing." She pauses, making direct eye contact with me. "Nothing, except feelings of worthlessness and defeat. Why would I ever put myself through that again?"

"If you'll just take a look," I plead. "Read how these women were empowered when they took this step. There's even a step-by-step guide to filing a Title Nine complaint."

"A step-by-step guide?" Her voice is raised now, and I can feel the incredulousness rolling off her. "Do you seriously think I can just go through and check off a bunch of boxes and be magically all right again? Is that really what you believe about sexual assault recovery?"

"No, that's not what I meant..." I break off mid-thought, knowing the conversation needs to slow down before it gets out of hand.

Sydney sighs heavily and closes her eyes. "What is it that you see in me that makes you think I need more in order to recover?"

"Syd, this isn't about you lacking anything." I step closer and she doesn't back away. "I just think you're strong enough to shine the light on Malpais's cover up and hand their asses to them via the U.S. Department of Education."

"I know I'm strong enough to do it," she agrees. "I'm also strong enough not to. I'm strong enough to leave them in the dust and start over, take control of my life and my own recovery. That's the whole reason I left. To take my life back."

"Syd," I whisper, lifting her chin to bring her eyes to mine. "I can't stand the thought that no one has been held accountable for what happened to you. The thought of that bastard's hands on you, taking from you without your consent, it slices me open."

My voice breaks on the last word, and I don't try to hide the watering in my eyes.

The muscles in her jaw clench and her breath hitches. When she speaks, her voice is soft but full of conviction. "You think it doesn't do the same to me? Except I don't have to imagine it. Those few seconds, after I woke up, are burned in my memory forever. What's more, I have no idea what happened to me before I came to, and that haunts me."

Her eyes narrow as she waits for me to respond. I believe every word I've said about her being strong, about holding the college accountable for abandoning her at her most vulnerable, but there's something else beneath the surface... a truth I owe her.

"I wasn't there for you then." I don't even try to stop the quiver in my voice or the leaking from my eyes. "I know I hadn't even met you at the time, but that doesn't mean I'm not devastated that I couldn't protect you from what happened. And now that you're here and we're together, I feel driven by the *need* to do something."

Silent tears stream down her face, and she nods as if she accepts what I've said. But then she flays me to the bone with her next words.

"I can't talk about this with you anymore right now. It seems like every time we're alone this is what you want to talk about, so maybe we just shouldn't talk for a few days."

"Sydney, no —"

She cuts me off before I can finish the thought.

"Take a couple of days to cool off, then have a new conversation."

I reach for her, but she backs away, all the way to the table where she left her purse and car keys. "Please, Shane. A couple of days." Her voice is shaky, and I can tell I've pushed her too far.

So, even though it kills me inside, I nod.

Then watch with a shattered heart as she walks out the door.

✧ ✧ ✧

IT WAS MIDNIGHT the last time I looked, and I have no idea what time it is now. I'm still on the couch, staring at the walls, and I haven't even attempted to sleep. I'm filled with regret over what happened with Sydney. My heart is screaming at me to go to her, apologize and grovel and whatever else it takes to make things right again, but my brain tells me to honor her request. To give her a few days before we deal with all the things that were said and done tonight.

But make no mistake. I *will* grovel. I took a tragedy that happened to and made it all about me and my need to feel heroic, as if my big idea of her filing a Title Nine complaint would be the magic wand that suddenly punished Malpais for not protecting her.

I can't even begin to describe how much of an asshole I feel like right now.

Maybe I should text her. Not expecting a response or a conversation or anything. Just to let her know how sorry I am. I'm reaching for my phone, trying to convince myself that a text will be okay and not violate her request for a couple of days, when my phone buzzes with an incoming call.

Greg.

I swallow hard before answering.

"Hello."

"It's me," he says. "Your mom's gone."

Chapter 39

SYDNEY

AFTER A FITFUL and restless night of little to no sleep, I give up at just after six o'clock and shuffle to the kitchen to make coffee. The thought of caffeine lifts my spirits for half a second until I see the red coffee maker and think of Shane.

I regret the way things got out of hand last night. I realize he wasn't trying to upset me, and I wish I hadn't been so short tempered. He looked so broken when I told him I needed a few days of radio silence.

The coffee begins to drip, and I consider calling him. I know he's up making coffee, the same as me, but I decide to wait until later in the day. Maybe I'll go by the shop and speak to him in person. I don't want to jump headfirst into a Title Nine complaint, but I also don't want the distance that opened up between us last night to have time to grow.

When my cell phone rings, I grab it quickly thinking perhaps it's Shane. An unfamiliar number appears on the screen, and I almost let it go to voicemail. At the last minute I decide to answer.

"Hello."

"Is this Sydney Baldwin?" The girl's voice on the other end of the call is quiet and timid, and I don't recognize it.

"Who's this?" I ask, not willing to divulge my identity

just yet.

"My name is Allie," she answers. "I'm a student at Malpais."

"Do I know you?"

"Not really. I think maybe we had a class together, but we never talked. I heard about you from a girl who lived on your floor last year."

For a moment I'm almost offended that she *heard about me,* because it means people are still talking, but something in her tone of voice gives me pause. She sounds sad.

My muscles begin to quiver. I remain silent.

"Someone told me you might know Chad Brooks." Allie's voice trembles as she says the name.

Beneath my skin my blood turns to ice. The room begins to spin around me. Immediately, I slide to the kitchen floor, lean back against the refrigerator door, and force myself to take long, slow breaths.

Allie must sense my distress because she doesn't press me to reply.

Of all the possible reasons that a female student from Malpais would go to the trouble to find my name and number, call to ask about Chad Brooks, and sound haunted as she says his name, only one reason has a ring of truth to it.

"Yes," I whisper. "I know him."

I don't confirm that I know him because he raped me. Neither does Allie. The reality of it settles on us, connecting us with an invisible bond that spans the distance between us.

Allie speaks first. "It was a party. The week after spring break."

I slam my eyes shut, forcing tears to spill down my cheeks. "Same," I reply, my heart splintering at the familiarity of her story.

"I think he put something in my drink," she says.

"A pattern of behavior." I don't know why the thought had never occurred to me before. I suppose I'd been caught up in what I was going through, and the thought of the same thing happening to someone else just never entered my mind.

"I reported it," Allie goes on. "I've gotten nowhere with Malpais or the police."

Yet another pattern of behavior. How many other Chad Brooks victims might be out there? All kinds of feelings clash inside me at the thought. Sadness that more people have been hurt by this animal. Outrage at how we've all been mistreated by the people who should've helped us. A sense of belonging to a sisterhood none of us ever asked to be a part of.

My entire body starts to shake. "Are there others?"

"I know of one," she says. "I've heard of two others."

Five. And possibly more.

My gaze falls on the bracelet around my wrist. Even after our argument last night, I couldn't bring myself to take it off. The word *strength* stares up at me, and I hear Shane's voice, reminding me that I am strong and capable and worthy.

"Allie," I say, pushing myself off the floor and over to the sofa. "How are you doing?"

On the other end of the call, she begins to cry, and I just wait, giving her the time she needs. When she starts to talk, her story sounds much like my own. Not only the aftermath of the attack and trying to deal with the authorities, but the emotional journey as well. Those moments when it doesn't even seem real, when you try, for just a little while, to pretend it didn't happen. The times you wake up in a sweat, heart racing, because in your dream you were right there, in the situation all over again. The blind belief that someone with the power to help eventually will because it's the right thing to do, and the slow awareness that it isn't going to happen.

Before we hang up, I give Allie the number to the volunteer crisis center where I met Claire and encourage her to reach out. I save her number in my contacts as soon as we hang up, and immediately dial Claire.

Claire answers on the second ring. "Hey Sydney."

I love how bright she sounds every time she answers a call. I hate that I'm about to deliver awful news.

"Claire, I got a call this morning," I begin. "From a girl at Malpais who was raped by the same boy who raped me."

Her quick intake of breath tells me that I've taken her by surprise. Before I allow my emotions to get out of control, I launch into the story, telling her everything Allie told me, without using her name of course. Claire asks me how I'm feeling, and for several moments we talk about the implications of knowing I'm not the only one. She's such a calming force for me, objective, yet so compassionate, and talking with her seems to bring these revelations to a level where I can deal with them in a healthy way.

However there's one final, nagging sliver of truth I need to tell her. "I feel guilty, Claire."

"Sydney, you can't hold yourself accountable for the actions of a sexual predator."

"I know." I close my eyes and lean back against the couch cushions. "But if I'd said something, if I'd done more, maybe he wouldn't have been free to do this to another girl."

"Listen to me." Claire's voice is stern now. Not at all unkind, but enough for me to know she means business. "You did everything right. You reported it to the police.

You went to the hospital and had the exam. You and your parents kept in contact with the college and the authorities. And at every turn you were met with a brick wall you couldn't get past. That's not your fault."

"But maybe if I'd talked about it more, if I'd let other girls know –"

Claire cuts me off. "No, Sydney. You are not the one who dropped the ball here. You are not the one who shirked your responsibility. That's on *them*. Not you."

A heavy sigh escapes my body. "You're right. I know you're right. I guess I just feel really protective of her now, especially since she sought me out."

"I'd be surprised if you didn't feel that way," Claire says. "It's the kind of person you are. You care, and you nurture."

Care and nurture. Those two words strike a chord somewhere deep inside me, as if they hold some kind of value that needs to be explored. A knock at my door diverts my attention, so I tuck them away to examine later.

"Syd, it's me, Grace," comes the voice from outside my door.

"Claire, I've got to go. My friend Grace is here. I'll call you again soon, though."

I toss my phone on the couch and head for the door, certain I look like death warmed over after tossing and turning all night. I wish I had a few minutes alone, to start the process of absorbing everything that's happened this morning, but Grace never stops by this early, so I figure it must be important.

I open the door, intending to apologize for my ragged appearance, but Grace speaks first.

"Shane's mother died last night. He's already gone to Albuquerque."

Chapter 40

SYDNEY

"**W**HAT?" THE WORD comes out as a strangled cry as I try to process the fact that Shane's mom is gone, and he didn't call me.

Then again, I did request a two-day communication hiatus.

I'm so angry at myself for how I reacted last night. Telling him to leave me alone for a couple of days solves nothing. And now we're each dealing with an enormous crisis and can't lean on one another.

Grace steps in and closes the door behind her. "He called about four this morning when he was headed out of town. Asher convinced him to stop by before he left. I made him some breakfast and coffee for the road."

I sink onto the couch and drop my head into my hands. "Thank you," I whisper. "For taking care of him."

Grace sits down beside me. "He said you two argued."

I nod but don't look up. My heart is lodged in my throat.

"Are you guys going to be all right?"

I shrug my shoulders. "I don't know. Last night, I was sure we would be, but now I don't know." I let my voice trail off, then lean back against the cushions before continuing. "I told him we needed to take a couple of days to cool down before we talked again, which means I'm not there for him when he needs me the most. Not sure he'll be able to forgive that so easily."

"He told us you guys were taking a day or two to cool down," Grace says. "I told him to call you anyway, but he said he wanted to honor what you asked and didn't want you to feel pressured to talk to him because of his personal crisis."

I laugh, but it's not out of humor. It's because that's typical Shane, to put aside his own issues so I don't feel pressured. "He's infuriatingly considerate sometimes."

Grace chuckles. "You should go," she says. "To Albuquerque."

"Do you think he even wants me there after the way we argued?"

"I'm sure of it," she answers. "But he won't ask you to come if it means going against what you told him you needed."

She's right. He won't ask me, but he's alone. I have to go.

"It's almost a five hour drive," I say, pushing to my feet as I think of all the things I need to do in order to leave town. "I've got to call Kathryn and ask off for tomorrow, and pack a few thing, and…"

Grace cuts me off. "If I can get you to the airport in an hour, there's a flight you can get on."

I stop in my tracks and turn to stare at her.

She shrugs her shoulders. "I checked before I came over here. It has a stop in Phoenix, but it's still shorter than the five hours it'll take to drive there. The one-way ticket isn't outrageous, and you can ride back with Shane that way."

"You are seriously the best friend in the entire world."

"You call Kathryn and pack a bag. I'll use my credit

card to book the ticket for you, and you can pay me back later."

I dial Kathryn's number, and Grace clicks away on her iPhone, reserving my ticket on the flight to Albuquerque. Kathryn picks up while I'm in the bathroom throwing my toothbrush, make up, and shampoo into a bag, and I explain to her that my boyfriend's mom passed away during the night. She's completely understanding, as I knew she would be, and I thank my lucky stars for a boss who is willing to give me time off. I promise to update her once I'm in Albuquerque and let her know when I think I'll be back in Flagstaff.

"Ticket is taken care of," Grace says just as I step out of the bathroom and start digging through drawers, throwing clothes on the bed.

"I have no idea what to pack."

"Don't worry about anything dressy. Shane said they aren't planning any sort of formal service."

I nod, but throw a navy blue sundress in anyway, just in case. I fill the rest of the duffel bag with jeans, solid color tank tops, and various color lightweight cardigans. I dress myself in pretty much the same fashion, then jump back into the bathroom for a quick hairbrush and ponytail job. I forgo the makeup, since it's already packed, thinking I'll just use my compact and dust some powder on my face on the way to the airport.

"I'm texting you Greg's address, in case you don't already have it." Grace is throwing a granola bar into my purse and grabbing a bottle of water from my fridge. "You can call an Uber to get you there once you land."

"All right." I grab my purse, throw my duffel bag over my shoulder, and Grace and I head out the door and down to her car. "While you drive, I need to tell you something."

Grace narrows her eyes and nods as I throw my bag in her back seat. Once we're in the car, I begin.

"I was raped my freshman year at Malpais."

BY THE TIME we arrive at the airport, I've given Grace pretty much all the details of what happened to me and the fall out afterward. She's understandably shell-shocked.

She puts the car into park and turns to me. "If I'd had any idea, I'd have been there for you from the beginning."

"I know that. That's not why I didn't tell you. Everyone in my life treated me differently. People at Malpais. My parents. I just needed to have a few people who acted just like they always had around me."

"It was your story to tell," she replies. "In your own way and your own time. I can promise you things will be just the same between you and me, except that I'm more proud of you than I ever imagined I could be."

She leans across the console to hug me, and I whisper a word of thanks in her ear.

"Now, go to Albuquerque and find your man."

"Absolutely," I say with a smile, grabbing my bag from the back and heading inside.

THE THREE AND a half hours to Albuquerque seem to take a lifetime when I know that Shane is at the other end of this journey. I take the opportunity to think about everything that happened this morning, from learning about Allie and the other girls Chad Brooks hurt, to the knowledge that Shane left for Albuquerque without calling me because he's honorable enough to respect the wishes I expressed last night.

That he was willing to do this alone… come to Albuquerque and say the final goodbye to a mother he had such a complicated relationship with, completely alone, proves what I've always known. He will always put my needs first and always have my best interest at heart.

Which forces me to acknowledge that talking to me about Title Nine and what it means to file a complaint came from that same place in his heart. The part that wants the best for me.

Deep down, I know he wasn't trying to pressure me to file if I truly didn't want to. He just wanted me to consider it.

And now I am.

For myself, I might never have pursued it. But knowing he's hurt other girls, that the college knows of at least two of us, and still allows him on campus where he's free to target more young women… I don't think I can sit idly when I know there's at least one more step I can take.

Before we're asked to turn off all cell phones as the plane prepares to land, I search online and read about a few Title Nine complaints that the U.S. Department Education accepted. It may not solve the problem completely, but it at least shines light on a problem that has been allowed to thrive in the darkness for far too long.

I shoot a quick text to Claire and asked if she's heard of Title Nine. She says she knows a little, but hasn't had any experience. When I ask if she thinks it might be a good idea, especially if Allie and possibly the others would file it jointly with me, she replies that anything I feel helps me keep moving forward is a positive step.

As the plane taxis along, approaching our terminal, I know I've decided to pursue it. I'll talk with Allie after I'm back in Flagstaff, and hopefully together we can take more of our lives back while at the same time holding Malpais accountable for turning a blind eye to the sexual predator on their campus.

Chapter 41

SHANE

B Y THE TIME I get to Greg's house, the hospice people
have come and gone and have walked him through
what happens next. They'd helped him do some of the
paperwork at the crematorium ahead of time, and this
morning, assisted with starting the process of getting a
death certificate.

He's on the phone when I come in and motions me to
take a seat at the table with him.

"That was the funeral home," he says, laying his phone
face down on the table. "Her body's arrived there, if you
want to see her one last time."

I shake my head. "I said my goodbyes to her when I
was here in the spring. I just want to help you with these
final steps. I think I owe her that much."

"Well, I'm not sure how much you owe her, but I'm
glad you're here."

"Do you have plans for her ashes?" I ask.

"Not yet," Greg answers. "Hadn't really thought that
far ahead. Now that you're here, maybe we can decide
together."

I nod and close my eyes, weary from lack of sleep and
the long drive here.

"You had anything to eat today?" he asks.

"I had some coffee and a peanut butter sandwich some-time after four this morning, as I was driving out of Flagstaff."

"I think I'm going to make pancakes. Why don't you kick back in the recliner for a few while I put some food together."

"Deal," I say. "And after we eat, you get some rest."

✧   ✧   ✧

ONCE THE PANCAKES were consumed, Greg headed for the shower and a little rest afterward. I told him I'd take care of the dishes, and I've just finished washing the plates and forks when I hear a car door outside.

Dropping the dishtowel onto the counter, I head to the front door to see what's going on.

A car and driver I don't recognize sit in Greg's drive-way. The back door is open, and it appears someone is taking something out of the back seat. The driver waves in greeting, but I keep my eyes on the back door, wondering who it is.

When the person stands up, duffle bag in hand, and shuts the car door, my breath backs up in my lungs.

Sydney.

Just the sight of her makes my heart explode. The rest of the world falls away, and my vision narrows in on only her. She's here. In front of me. I didn't realize just how badly I wanted her with me until this moment. Even after all that we said last night, she came anyway. For me.

She hasn't moved from her spot on the black top, but the car has backed away and left while we've been staring at one another.

"Sydney." I step off the front porch, but don't move further.

She shrugs one shoulder. "I took an Uber from the airport."

The sound of her voice, the lightness in her tone, somehow assures me that she's happy to see me and whatever unpleasantness passed between us last night is forgiven.

My feet move of their own volition, and in seconds she's in my arms, her duffel bag tossed to the ground beside us. I bury my face in her neck, reveling in the feel of her skin against mine. Her arms surround me, pulling me to her, cradling me in their warmth.

"How are you here?" I ask, turning to press a kiss to her ear, then resting my forehead against hers so I can look into her intoxicating green eyes.

"Grace," she says. "She found me a flight."

"I didn't want them to tell you." I press a kiss to her lips. "I didn't want you to feel like you had to be here." I kiss her again. "But I'm so glad you are."

"I'm so sorry about last night Shane. So sorry I overreacted."

Shaking my head, I silence her with a kiss. "I'm the one who's sorry. I overstepped, and I shouldn't have. It won't happen again."

"I'm glad you told me about Title Nine complaints." Her words surprise me, but I don't say anything. I just wait for her to continue. "We'll talk about it all when we're back in Flagstaff. Right now, we're just going to focus on you and what you need in order to get through these next few days."

✧ ✧ ✧

PARKER ARRIVED THAT night. I wasn't expecting him. He and Shaneen never really knew one another, but I'm glad to see him anyway. I know he came for Greg and me, and I appreciate it more than I can express.

We managed to throw together some sandwiches for dinner, and now we're all in the living room, mugs of coffee in our hands to counteract the effects of this long ass day. Sydney and I are on the sofa, while Greg and Parker occupy the two recliners.

"Given any thought to her ashes?" Greg asks.

I shake my head. "I don't know of any place that was really special to her, so it's hard to imagine picking a place to scatter them. I'm guessing neither one of us wants to keep them with us in an urn."

The look on Greg's face mirrors my own. "They'll have the ashes ready day after tomorrow."

"Shaneen have a favorite food? Or favorite restaurant?" Parker asks suddenly.

I look across to Greg, while I search my memory for anything that might stick out. "She loved Chinese take-out."

Greg sits up straight. "Right. Every time she'd stay with us here she wanted to order from that place with the dragon on the logo. What was it?"

"The Wicked Dragon," I say, snapping my fingers at the memory.

"The place still open?" Parker asks?

"Pretty sure," Greg answers. "I drove by there the other day and there were cars in the lot."

"So tomorrow we have Chinese take-out in Shaneen's honor, and maybe we can each recall something positive we remember about her." Parker looks from me to Greg, and seeing no resistance, continues. "I know she lived a hard life and good memories are few, but there has to be something you can think of."

"That's actually a really good idea," Syd says from beside me. "I completely understand not wanting to have a formal service, given the circumstances of her life and death, but maybe eating her favorite meal will be your own personal memorial."

Parker speaks again. "And maybe while we think about some of the good things about her, we'll come up with a way to handle her ashes that makes sense."

"Greg and I were both up most of the night, and it's been a stressful day, so why don't we all sleep in and get together early afternoon tomorrow?" I pick up Sydney's hand and look at her. "I reserved a room at the same place we stayed last time. Is that okay?"

"Of course."

The difficulties of the day can't dim the anticipation I feel knowing I have alone time with Sydney in my immediate future. And it has nothing to do with hormones – well, very little anyway – and everything to do with just needing to be with her and hold her, and let her goodness and affection wash over me.

"Ready to head that way?" I ask.

She takes my hand, and we say our goodbyes, grabbing her duffel bag on our way out.

I PUSH THE door to our room open and hold it wide so Sydney can walk in. I step in after her and lock the door behind me. Then I notice there's only one bed.

"I made the reservation over the phone in the car between here and Flagstaff. You weren't with me, so I didn't think to ask for two beds. Do you want me to call and ask them to switch us?"

"Shane, it's fine." She tosses her purse on the dresser

and turns to face me. "Don't worry."

"No expectations," I say, just to be clear. "You know that right?"

"I know you'll never pressure me." She steps closer. "As much as I wish I could snap my fingers and… well… I think you're more patient about it than I am."

"Everything about you is worth waiting for. The things I already have," I say, wrapping my arms around her and pressing a kiss to her forehead. "And the things we're looking forward to. But if I said I wasn't super happy about falling asleep with you in my arms, I'd be lying. I think it's exactly what I need after this day."

And thirty minutes later, that's exactly what I do.

Chapter 42

SYDNEY

WHEN SHANE AND I arrive at Greg's the following day, the table is set for four, with pristine white plates, red cloth napkins, and tall, clear tumblers. A short vase with red roses sits in the center of the table. Greg has gone to some effort to honor his sister and make this transition easier for everyone. I find it extremely admirable.

"I sent Parker out this morning to get the flowers," he says as Shane and I enter the kitchen. "Figured why not."

Shane smiles and hugs his uncle. "She'd have liked them."

"I ordered the food when you called and said you were on your way. It should get here any minute."

"Let me take care of the drinks." I pick up two glasses from the table and take them to the ice dispenser on the refrigerator door. "What are we drinking?"

"Well, I made…" Greg says, then stops and looks at Shane. "It sounds stupid, but Shaneen loved Kool-Aid, the tropical kind. So I made some of that."

"Perfect." Shane pats Greg on the shoulder. "Good memories. That's what today is about."

The doorbell rings, and from the living room Parker announces that he'll get it.

A moment later, he enters the kitchen with four bags

from The Wicked Dragon and sets them on the counter.

Greg must notice Shane and I staring at the amount of food. "I ordered her favorites, and some of the things I knew you and Parker liked. I hope I got something Sydney will eat."

"I'm not picky," I reply. "And I love Chinese, so I'm sure it'll be fine."

We fill our plates and take our seats, and Parker begins the trip down memory lane.

"I don't have a lot of memories of Shaneen, since mom and I moved away when I was pretty young, but I do remember she always had gum. Lots of it. And she'd always give me a piece."

Greg laughed. "Covered up the cigarette breath."

"Probably so," Parker says. "But still, even today I can't taste spearmint gum without thinking of her. And it's always a happy thought."

Greg shares some of his childhood memories of Shaneen, things they did when they were kids, places they went with their family. I can tell Shane is thinking, mulling over memories of his mom, trying to find the right one to talk about.

"When I think about Mom, one of the times I always go back to was the first summer after I came to live here." He leans back in his chair and throws his arm across the back of mine, his hand settling on my shoulder. "It was one of her good stretches. She was here with us for several weeks. She really paid attention to me, you know? It wasn't always like that. A lot of times when she was here she slept a lot, watched TV, and didn't really interact with me. But that time she did. We'd play out back in the yard, and we planted that little flower garden. Remember that, Greg?"

Greg smiles and nods his head. "I remember. Looked

real pretty out there."

Shane closes his eyes. "She loved those flowers. I had no idea what kind they were, and she probably didn't either, but they were colorful and beautiful and we'd spend all afternoon out there. When she looked at the flowers, she didn't look so defeated. She almost looked hopeful."

"Shane, that's it!" I exclaim, the excitement in my voice causing everyone to look at me. Reigning in my enthusiasm, I continue. "What if you plant that flower garden again? You could go find a nursery, pick out the flowers you want to use, and we could plant it this afternoon."

Shane sees where I'm going with this and picks up the rest. "And tomorrow, when we have her ashes we can put them in the flower garden."

"Sydney, that's a great idea," Greg says.

"I'll find us a nursery close by," Parker says, grabbing his phone from the counter.

And without even clearing the dishes, we head out to Bickett's nursery, Greg and Parker in Greg's truck, and Shane and I following behind in his car.

✧   ✧   ✧

SHANE PICKED OUT several plants that reminded him of the things he planted with his mother when he was a child. Though he wasn't sure if they were exactly the same, the fact that they looked similar was enough.

Now the four of us are elbow deep in potting soil, as the flower garden in Greg's backyard begins to take shape. Parker hauls the heavy bags of soil, Greg spreads fertilizer, and Shane and I dig holes for the flowers and shrubs and fill the soil around them. When everything is planted, Parker empties the mulch into the wheel barrow and rolls it close, so that all four of us can fill it around plants.

The dark fuchsia flowers called Jupiter's beard bloom atop tall stems. The Apache plume, a gentle white bloom that gives way to feathery pink whips, is a shrub that will continue to fill and grow. And Shane's final selection, the butterfly bush, is a shrub with brilliant purple cones of flowers. The combination of colors and textures is really lovely.

Once everything is planted, and mulch spread around the plants, we all step back and look. Greg grabs the water hose and begins a gentle watering of the plants now in the ground. It's hard not to feel hopeful looking at the beauty, as Shane said his mother had once done. I lace my dirty-covered fingers through Shane's and hope that it's doing the same for him now.

Chapter 43

SHANE

THE ACTUAL SPRINKLING of the ashes the next day turns out to be really chill compared to the emotion I experienced yesterday when we planted the flower garden. There was a moment, when I first picked up the small, standard urn from the funeral home that I thought *this is all that's left of my mom.*

After all she'd been through, all she'd put us through, she's now reduced to a small container of ashes.

But then I took a good, hard look at my life, my job, my friends in Flagstaff. And Sydney. Especially Sydney. And I know that the ashes in the urn aren't the sum total of my mom's life. Despite her best efforts to completely destroy herself, in the very end, she's more than the string of bad choices she made.

She didn't thrive, but I am, and for whatever part she had in making me into who I am today, I'm grateful.

The four of us step outside into Greg's backyard. I hold the urn in my left arm, and my right hand holds on to Sydney. We stand around the small flower garden, none of us speaking. Perhaps it might've been wise to have made some kind of plan for what we were going to do in this moment.

Eventually, Parker breaks the silence. He takes the urn

from me and carefully removes the lid, handing it to Greg. "Thanks for the endless gum supply," he says, shaking some of the ashes into the mulch. He reaches into his pocket and pulls out a stick of spearmint gum. Breaking it in two, he puts one half in his mouth and tosses the other into the flower bed. "It may seem small, but it made a little boy smile, and I'll never forget it."

Greg goes next, and more of Mom's ashes make their way in and around the things we planted yesterday. "Here's to Saturday morning cartoons and eating all the marshmallows out of the cereal. And here's to you finally being free of what you could never break away from in this life. Godspeed, sister."

He hands the urn back to me, and suddenly, I realize I have no idea what I'm going to say. I stand there, still as a statue, trying to come up with something appropriate, when Sydney takes the urn from my hands.

"May I?" she asks.

I nod.

She sprinkles a few ashes around each flower. "Thank you for your son. For the beauty and sweetness and hope he brings to my life. He'll never be alone. I promise."

God, this girl. She undoes me.

She hands the urn back to me, and I step forward, sprinkling the remaining ashes. "It wasn't always easy Mom. For you or for me. I was angry at you a lot, probably still am a little bit. But I loved you. And I always knew you loved me, even though it was hard for you to show it. Thank you for letting Greg raise me when you couldn't anymore. Thank you for spending the time that you could with me. And thank you for giving me love in the best way you knew how. I'll carry that love with me always. It won't go to waste."

The urn now empty, I look at Parker and nod. He takes the mulch left over from yesterday's landscaping and begins putting it around the plants, effectively securing the ashes into the flower bed. Mom will be a part of these flowers. I like the thought of leaving her in a place of beauty and hope.

✧　✧　✧

It was nine in the evening before Sydney and I finally left Albuquerque. After scattering Mom's ashes, we pulled out the Chinese leftovers and had a nice dinner together, with lots of reminiscing and lots of laughter. Parker and I talked shop, each of us filling in the other about our work in the shops we call home. I invited him and his family to Flagstaff for a visit, told them they had a place to stay whenever they wanted to come. Of all the things that have come of mom's death, reconnecting with Parker is perhaps the best. I hope we can maintain contact once he's back in Texas and I'm back in Arizona.

The drive home didn't seem so endless with Sydney in the passenger seat. She stayed awake as long as she could, but about the time we rolled into Winslow, I could tell she was struggling to stay awake. I told her to go ahead and rest, and she managed to sleep the last hour of the trip. Stealing glances at her as she snoozed filled me with an incredible contentment.

Now I'm turning into her subdivision, and she's opening her eyes, sitting up, and realizing where we are. We're quiet as we get out of the car, shutting the doors quietly so as not to wake up Grace's aunt and uncle in the house. I carry her duffel bag up the stairs and use the flashlight on my phone to make it easier for her to unlock the door.

Syd unzips the bag and pulls out her sleep clothes, then

looks over to me. "Wait here just for a minute."

She slips in the bathroom to change. It takes her all of about two minutes. But in those two minutes I all but fall asleep on her couch.

"Shane," she whispers, pulling me out of my near-REM state.

"Sorry," I say, dragging myself off the couch. "I'll head on home, let you get to bed."

"You're not driving any further tonight." She pushes me the opposite direction of the door. "You're exhausted, so just stay here. We can sleep as long as we want. No Caleb to disturb us."

"You sure?"

"We've been in the same hotel room the past two nights," she reasons. "What's the difference?"

"I'll run down and grab my backpack out of the car."

"Why?"

"Um, my shorts?" I'd been sleeping in a pair of gym shorts in Albuquerque, hoping that made her feel a little more comfortable.

"You think your gym shorts really hide anything?" she asks with a giggle. "Gym shorts, boxer briefs, same difference. Just drop your pants and get in bed before you collapse from lack of sleep."

With that, she turns and walks around the partition to the bed, climbing in the side closest to the wall. The thought of sleep, especially sleep next to Sydney, is far too attractive for me to argue.

"Yes ma'am."

Chapter 44

SYDNEY

THE LIGHT STREAMING in the window tells me it's well into the morning. Thankfully I'm not working until tomorrow, and Shane isn't going into the shop until late this afternoon. After rolling in at nearly two in the morning, we both needed the chance to sleep in.

I'm on my left side, and behind me Shane's body shifts, his arm sliding around my waist and hugging me to him. He was dead on his feet when he pulled into my driveway, and I hadn't had the heart to make him drive across Flagstaff to his townhouse.

So he'd crashed here.

Thus, the morning snuggling.

I'm not complaining.

"Three mornings of waking up next to you has spoiled me." His voice, deep and raspy from sleep, rumbles softly in my ear as his breath tickles the skin of my neck. "I never should've let you move out."

Laughing, I elbow him in the ribs, just hard enough to make him laugh as well.

He flips over onto his back, then pulls me so that my cheek is resting against his chest. For a long moment he says nothing, just runs his hand through my hair. I close my eyes and soak in the feeling of being cherished by this man I adore.

His other hand comes to rest gently against my face, his thumb tracing soft lines beneath my eye. He tilts my face up toward him, then shifts so he's looking at me. "I'm not going anywhere. You know that, right?"

"Shane." My voice is nothing but breath.

"Seriously. You're the only one for me, Sydney. Always." He pauses and smiles. "I'm in love with you."

Everything inside of me lights up, glowing like the shimmer of a million candles. Finding love was something I'd dreamed of growing up, but after what happened at Malpais, it was something I thought was lost to me forever. It had been so easy to think I wasn't worthy or capable of receiving or returning something so wondrous. Yet here it is, offered to me by the only man to ever, ever touch my heart.

"I love you, too, Shane," I whisper, reaching up to cover his hand with my own.

He leans down to kiss me, and I think to myself... *to hell with morning breath.*

"This is forever," he whispers against my lips. "I know we're only a few months into this relationship, but I know."

I blink up at him, drawing heavy breaths as his words sink in.

"Don't worry." He plants a soft peck on my forehead. "You don't have to respond. I know it's a lot. I've always been a handful, more than most people can handle." He winks and kisses my forehead again. "But I want to be completely honest with you. Someday I'm going to ask you the question. Emphasis on *the.* I hope you'll be ready to say yes when I do."

Joy blooms inside me in a way I never thought possible, and I can't help the smile that spreads across my face.

Falling in love is so much sweeter than I ever could've imagined, and that it happened following what was the most traumatic year of my life makes it so, so precious.

I want Shane to know that not only has he given me love and confidence, but he's also empowered me to push even further for the justice I know I deserve. The justice Allie deserves. The justice that every girl who's ever suffered at the hands of a rapist and the college that protects him deserves.

"I love you, Shane." I press a kiss to his lips, and sit up in the bed. "Will you make a pot of coffee while I get dressed? I want to talk to you about Title Nine."

Chapter 45

SHANE

THE COFFEE IS brewing, so I pull on my jeans and run down to the car to grab my backpack. Syd's still in the bathroom when I get back, so I use the kitchen sink to brush my teeth. She'd probably kill me if she knew, but she can't be the only one with fresh breath this morning.

She said she wanted to talk about Title Nine. I can't help but wonder what that's about, since she'd seemed so against the idea every time I brought it up.

But this time it's different. She's bringing it up. Whatever she has to say, whatever she wants to do, I'm going to listen and be supportive. No more caveman hero shit.

When she comes out of the bathroom, she's still in the leggings she slept in, but she swapped the oversized tee shirt with a sleeveless, flowery top that billows around her when she walks. Her hair is braided and hangs down her back, and she's wearing flip-flops.

"Want some breakfast?" She glances at the clock and sees that it's almost noon. "Well, more like lunch, but I have some bagels, cream cheese, and blueberries."

"Sure," I say, catching the bag of bagels she tosses me and popping a couple in the toaster.

A few moments later, we're seated on the sofa, two plates of bagels on the coffee table in front of us, mugs of coffee in our hands.

"The morning after you and I argued, I got a phone call," she begins. "It was really early, just after six o'clock, but I hadn't slept so I was awake. The number was unfamiliar, and I almost didn't answer it, but something changed my mind. It was a girl named Allie. She's a student at Malpais."

I don't say anything. I just sip my coffee and wait for her to continue. I can tell it's something important by her tone of voice and the expression on her face. She takes a bite of her bagel and a few more drinks of coffee before continuing.

"She said she'd heard about me. At first I was upset, because that must mean people are still talking about me and speculating and gossiping. But something in her voice sounded so sad that I couldn't be pissed off. Then she asked me if I knew Chad Brooks."

My stomach clenches and anger boils inside me. I can tell by the way she says the name – like it's poison coming out of her mouth – that this is the name of the asshole who raped her.

"I knew it then, you know?" She swallows hard and tears gather in her eyes. "I just whispered into the phone that yes, I knew him."

I sit my cup on the coffee table, then reach for hers and do the same. I take both her hands in mine so that she knows I'm here, knows I won't let her go.

"She didn't even have to say it out loud," she goes on. "She just said it was at a party, and she thinks he put something in her drink."

"Sydney." I say her name with reverence, because that's exactly how I feel about her. I bring her hands to my lips and kiss each one.

"She knows of one other girl for certain who was raped by him, and she's heard of two others."

"Shit." I bite the word out like the curse it is, because I'm infuriated that this son of a bitch is still walking around, free to assault women whenever the hell he wants.

"I asked her how she was doing." She grabs a napkin from the table and dabs at the wetness beneath her eyes. "It seemed like the right thing to do. I'm a year ahead of her in terms of recovery, so I wanted to help her if I could. Everything about her experience is the same as mine, including the lack of response from Malpais. I gave her the number of the crisis center where I met Claire. I hope she'll call them."

"I'm sure reaching out to you helped her." I tilt my head until I catch her gaze. "Knowing she's not alone, that's got to be a positive thing for her."

"I want to file the Title Nine Complaint," she announces, shocking the heck out of me. "I thought about it on the flight to Albuquerque, even texted Claire about it. I'm going to talk to Allie and see if she'd be willing to file it with me. Maybe even ask the others."

"Sydney, if I pushed you in anyway…"

She stops me with a gentle hand against my lips.

"You do push me, Shane. You push me to be strong, to be an individual, to be me. You push me to fight for what I deserve. And that's what I'm going to do. I know it may not do any good. The Department of Education may not take the case, and even if they do, Malpais and their public relations cronies will spin their story to make themselves smell like roses, but at least my story will be out there. Someone else will read it and know it. Chad Brooks is out there hurting women, over and over again. I can't know that there's another step I could take, and just choose not to take it."

For a moment, I'm speechless. I just stare at her, chin dropped in surprise, her hands still gripped tightly in mine.

"Shane?" She gives my hands a shake to snap me out of it. "What are you thinking?"

"I'm so proud of you." I can't even be ashamed of the tear escaping from my eye. "And so in awe of the person you are."

She smiles and it illuminates her entire being. "So you think it's a good idea?"

"Whatever you want to do, however you want to proceed, I'm behind you one hundred percent." I take her face in my hands. "But yeah. I think it's a great idea."

"The next thing is…" she takes a deep breath. "I want to tell everyone else. All our friends. I told Grace that morning while she drove me to the airport. But I want to tell everyone else. It's possible there may be some negative publicity for me once the complaint is filed, especially if the Department of Education takes it. I want them all to hear the truth from me beforehand."

"If that's what you want, I'm with you all the way. We can invite everyone over to my place, tell them all at once if you want."

She nods, her body shivering slightly at the thought of telling everyone else. I know it's a daunting idea, and I'm so proud of her for getting to the point that she can talk about it.

"It won't make a difference to any of them."

"I know. I just want to be sure I continue being just plain Sydney, not Sydney the rape victim."

"There's nothing plain about you," I say, kissing her cheek. "But trust me when I say, they will not treat you like a victim. They will see you as this amazing, fierce creature, and they'll be proud of you. Just like I am."

Chapter 46

SYDNEY

IT'S BEEN A month since Shane's mom died, and a lot has happened in those four weeks. I spoke to Allie about the Title Nine complaint. She took a day to think about it, then called me with a very affirmative *yes*. She spoke with two other Malpais students who'd been assaulted by Chad Brooks over the last three years, a senior named Misty and a sophomore named Olivia, both of whom are still enrolled in the institution that has swept everything under the rug, and both of whom agreed to join us in filing a complaint with the U.S. Department of Education.

The fifth girl Allie had heard about is nowhere to be found. She dropped out of Malpais shortly after the assault, and no one knows where she is. I pray she's somewhere where she's loved and cared for, somewhere she feels safe.

The four of us have corresponded via email, each of us writing our own story which included details of all the ways Malpais had violated our rights under Title Nine, such as dragging out investigations, disciplinary hearings being put off or forgotten about entirely, keeping victims in the dark about the progress of investigations, and failing to intercede when victims faced backlash and harassment from other students on campus.

I read it in its entirety once it was finished. My own

story and the others'. It was chilling. It was heartbreaking. It was raw and honest. And it was *ours*.

Before the complaint gets officially filed, Shane and I are telling our group of friends here in Flagstaff. They're all coming over to Shane's once the shop closes tonight. I'm nervous, but also relieved. Relieved that in a few short hours I won't have to hide it any longer, and relieved that I'm in a place, both physically and emotionally, where I know it's safe to share.

Shane declared early on that under no circumstances was I cooking for this get together, so he's currently picking up a variety of pizza, soft drinks, and beer. I'm here in the townhouse, digging paper plates and plastic cups out of the cabinet and setting them out on the bar.

I've just finished checking the ice situation in the freezer when I hear the doorbell. As I head down the hallway, I hear Grace's voice.

"It's me," she calls. "I brought dessert."

Opening the door, I take one of the shopping bags from her, and we make our way to the kitchen.

"Good grief, Grace," I say, pulling out hot fudge, cherries, marshmallow cream, and crushed peanuts. "Did you rob the Baskin Robbins?"

"It's a sundae bar!" She holds up a gallon of vanilla bean ice cream in one hand and a gallon of cookies and cream in the other. "How fun is this?"

"I'm sure it will be a hit. I'm not sure what exactly we're celebrating tonight, but at least there will be pizza and ice cream to enjoy."

"We're celebrating the fact that you are an amazing woman, with more determination and courage than anyone I know. We're celebrating that you are one of us now, that we're your family, and that the Resolution crew has your back always. No matter what."

"Yeah," I say with a smile, "being a part of the Resolution crew is definitely something worth celebrating."

"Sydney, Asher knows." Grace's voice drops to a whisper. "I wasn't planning on telling him until I asked you if it was all right, and things were so rushed the morning I drove you to the airport that you and I didn't even discuss it. But when I got home later that morning, I was just so upset and heartbroken, and he knew something was wrong. I broke down and cried, and I just couldn't not tell him."

"Syd, it's okay," I assure her. "I never expected you to keep it from your husband."

"He promised he wouldn't say anything, or even let you know that he knew, until you were ready to tell everyone yourself."

"He's a good one, Grace," I say. "You lucked out in the guy department."

She moves to stand next to me and slings an arm around my shoulder. "So did you."

My heart warms at the thought of Shane. "I did."

Keys rattle in the front door, and half a second later, we hear, "Pizza!" Shane comes down the hall with six pizzas stacked on top of each other. "Asher rode over with me. He's bringing the drinks in."

He stops and kisses me on his way to the bar, balancing the pizzas with one hand and touching my face with the other. "Hey," he whispers. "You good?"

"I'm good." And I am. I really, really am.

GRACE AND ASHER sit beside Shane and me on the couch. They look indignant on my behalf, but not blindsided.

Caleb is sitting backwards in a chair he drug into the

living room from the dining table. His head is hung low, one hand kneading the back of his neck in frustration.

Rachelle sits on Gabe's lap in one of the recliners, silently wiping tears from her eyes, while the muscles in Gabe's jaw clench over and over.

Bing, who came sans Kristy since it's a school night for Ezra, sits in the other recliner, hands flexing in and out of fists.

I've just told them the whole story, the rape, the lack of response from Malpais and the police, connecting with Allie, Misty, and Olivia. I've also told them about the Title Nine complaint we plan to file in the next few days, and how some assault survivors have experienced negative blowback and unflattering publicity if the Department of Education actually takes their case. I've assured them that I'm prepared for it if it happens, but I love all of them enough to give them a heads up about the potential for crap to hit the fan.

And now, I'm waiting for a response.

Caleb speaks first. "Tell the haters to bring it. Who gives a shit what they say on the news? We know you, and we're going to stand behind you."

"Absolutely," Gabe agrees. "And let me just say, I think it's an incredibly brave thing you're doing."

"Yes," Rachelle says between sniffles. "Very brave. And, Sydney, I'm just so angry that this happened to you."

"That was my reaction too," Grace replies. "So proud, but so pissed off."

"Mine as well," Asher agrees. "No one should experience what you did, Syd."

Bing's been silent, but finally scoots to the edge of the recliner. "Whatever we can do to help, just name it. If the organization that's helping you all file the Title Nine complaint has publicity materials, we'll hang them in the shop. We'll make a donation as well. And most of all, we're going be beside you all the way, whatever happens."

"I can't express what you all mean to me." I reach for Shane's hand, squeezing it tight in mine. "I've never had friends like this. Knowing you, becoming a part of your family, it's helped give me the strength to take this step."

I dab at my eyes and breathe deep, trying to keep the crying at bay.

Shane leans over and kisses me softly on the cheek.

"Sorry to be such a downer," I say. "I know it's not exactly the kind of story you want to hear at a party."

"But this is a celebration," Grace reminds me, then turns to everyone else. "We're celebrating how awesome Sydney is and how glad we are that she's a part of our little circle. And we're having ice cream sundaes, so everybody just put a smile on your face and get ready for hot fudge and marshmallow cream!"

And just like that, the mood turns from somber to celebratory, as Grace breaks out the ice cream and all the sundae toppings, and topics of conversation move from the serious to the lighthearted.

I look around at each one and think how much they all mean to me.

These people, they're my tribe.

I've never been happier.

LATER THAT NIGHT, Shane and I are alone in my apartment. He insisted on following me home, since it was so late. His protectiveness is sweet, plus I think we both just wanted some alone time.

We're on the couch, and some late night talk show that

we aren't paying attention to plays on the TV.

"I was really proud of you tonight," he says.

"It's not an easy story to tell, but I don't feel ashamed when I tell it anymore," I reply.

"This crew of people saved my life as much as Greg and Parker did." Shane slides his hand behind my neck and gently toys with my hair as he talks. "If I hadn't found a strong, healthy place to land, I might've wound up sliding back into the same crap I'd been into in Albuquerque."

"I've been thinking about you and me." I tilt my head into the palm of his hand, enjoying the feel of his fingers brushing against my scalp. "About all we've been through. The really great thing is that we get to decide what defines us. The places and situations we come from, the things that happen to us, they all play a part, but we get to decide which things really define who we are and which things we leave in the past. And what's more, we get to decide whether those things make us better or worse, whether we learn from them or let them drag us down. *We* get to decide."

Shane smiles. "You're pretty smart, you know that?"

"So are you." I grin back at him. "You're the one that taught me all that."

"Me?" He narrows his eyes.

"When I told you about being raped, you didn't back away. You didn't treat me like I was going to break if you looked at me wrong. You didn't treat me like a victim. You showed me that I'm not defined by what happened to me. Just like you're not defined by your mom's choices or your past mistakes."

"Your love defines me," he whispers, leaning in to lay his lips against mine. "Gives me purpose."

"I'm so glad we decided on each other." I press my lips

more firmly against his. "I love you, Shane."

"And I love you, Sydney. Now and always."

Epilogue

SHANE

IT'S THREE O'CLOCK on a Saturday afternoon, and Resolution is hopping. Back to back appointments, consultations, and walk-ins are keeping all of us busy. I'm grateful for the full schedule, since it keeps my mind from wondering all day long about the status of Sydney's Title Nine complaint.

There's been no word from the Department of Education about whether or not they'll take the case, and we know that even if they do the process can take years. However, Sydney and the others all received calls from lawyers from the Office for Civil Rights, asking questions about their complaint. I'm hopeful that's a good sign.

But regardless, Sydney's doing great. She's still working at Beautiful Things and considering going back to college to study education. I think she'll be an amazing teacher, if that's what she decides she wants to do. No one in my life has cared for or encouraged me more than Sydney, and I know she'll be the same way for her students.

I've been looking at rings. The day is coming, sooner rather than later, when I'll ask her to marry me. I smile, imagining what it will be like to see my ring on her finger and pick out a wedding date with her.

I'm walking a client out to the front counter so that

Rachelle can take care of his payment and aftercare instructions, when Sydney and Grace come through the door with to-go coffees and snacks from Ugly Mug.

"We heard from Rachelle that you guys were slammed, so we thought we'd bring some fuel."

"You're an angel," I say, kissing her on the cheek. "I can so use a shot of caffeine right now."

Rachelle takes care of my client, then helps Grace and Sydney set the coffee and cookies out on the counter behind her desk. My next client hasn't arrived yet, and Bing has just finished with a consult, so he and I take advantage of the coffee and snickerdoodles. Asher comes out next, and Rachelle gets his client taken care of quickly.

"Save something for Caleb," Sydney reminds us.

For as much grief as he gave me in the beginning, Caleb's been super supportive of our relationship and of Sydney's search for justice. And my girl has a soft spot for him. She won't be happy until he's settled with a girl who appreciates him.

We manage to leave a coffee and two cookies un-touched for Caleb, who emerges several minutes later. Bing's client has just arrived, and the two of them are still in the lobby, looking at the design Bing has come up with. The bell over the door dings, and I figure it's my next appointment, Ted, who's coming in for the next piece in what will eventually be a full sleeve.

But when I turn around, I know that the petite young lady with brown curly hair is absolutely not Ted. A quick look at Asher and I know it's not his next client either. Caleb's back is to the door as he picks up his coffee, completely uninterested in who just came through the door, so I figure he must not have another appointment for a bit. There's no recognition in Rachelle's face either. Must be a walk-in.

The girl looks around, scanning the room as if she's looking for someone specific. A look of uncertainty crosses her face, like she has no idea what to say or how to approach us.

But then Caleb turns around, and the electricity in the room sparks with a tangible flare. The two of them are across the room from one another, yet completely connected by something invisible and incredibly strong.

Caleb nearly drops his coffee, and the girl's hand flies up to her mouth, as if she's surprised or overcome with some kind of emotion. I've never witnessed anything like this before.

Beside me, Sydney slips her hand in mine.

Caleb takes a step toward the girl, then stops, like he's afraid to get any closer.

And then Caleb says her name and everything makes sense.

"Brenna".

THE END

AUTHOR'S NOTE

Often times people say "write about what you know". I've done that before, but not this time. There's nothing about Shane and Sydney that I have known personally in my own life. The things they experienced, the journeys they took, were both very, very different than my own upbringing and life experiences. But for so many…too many… people in our world, they are familiar journeys.

When the idea of this story came to me, I initially put it aside because I thought, *"There's no way I can do justice to the people who've lived through that."* But the story just would not let me go, and I came to the conclusion that any story that shines light on the issue of campus sexual assault and the way it's so often swept under the rug is a good thing. I told myself that I would do my absolute best. I would read and research, and I would go to the hard places to make this story as authentic as I could. I'm sure there are ways in which I have not accurately portrayed a woman's recovery after a sexual assault, but my prayer is that the overarching message of the book – that you are NOT defined by what was done to you, that you CAN take your life back, that you are NOT damaged and unable to move forward – shines through.

My writing is not dark. Sometimes I wish it was, because I like a good, dark story as much as anyone. But it just isn't my "voice". At times during the writing of this book I thought that lack of "darkness" in my writing meant I wasn't telling the story right. I hope that my "voice", the aspect of my writing that I've always loved the most comes through in this story. HOPE. Perhaps it's my personality. Perhaps it's my heart, but I can't help but write stories that carry a thread of hope. And my greatest desire is that Shane and Sydney's story, one that came from places of great darkness for these characters, will be imbued with a sense of hope that I believe is available to EVERYONE, regardless of their circumstances.

EROC (End Rape on Campus) is an organization that envisions a world without sexual violence, particularly on college campuses. Their website, www.endrapeoncampus. org, is one of the places I found a wealth of information to aid me in writing this book. If you or someone you know is interested in learning more about Title IX, or connecting with other survivors, visit their website.

And if you've experienced sexual assault, please don't suffer alone and in silence. Find the support you need, whether it's a friend, minister, counselor, or support group. And please know that you are beautiful. You are valuable. And you are enough.

If you enjoyed this book, please consider leaving a review at your place of purchase and/or any other online review site you frequent. Customer reviews are one of the best ways to show an author you enjoyed his or her work and can be invaluable for other readers as they browse for reading material. This author reads all reviews and greatly appreciates each one.

CALEB'S
Chance
Resolution Series, Book Four

AMY DURHAM

DEDICATION

To Amy E
for many years of being Amy^2
I love you big!

2017

Flagstaff, Arizona

Caleb, age 25

Brenna, age 21

Prologue

CALEB

R ESOLUTION INK, THE tattoo shop where I've worked for the past six years, is running at full capacity tonight. Every artist – me, Shane, Asher, and Bing, the owner – has a full slate of appointments, not to mention future pieces to work on between clients.

I've got one a few more appointments tonight, but right now I'm in the lobby grabbing a cookie and quick cup of coffee, courtesy of Asher's wife and Shane's girlfriend. Between the two of them, plus our receptionist, Rachelle, and Bing's fiancee, Kristy, the ladies of Resolution take good care of us.

It doesn't escape me that I'm the only one without a lady.

I thought maybe I'd been on the right track with Felicity, but it fizzled out like a popped balloon after she went back to Tucson for a visit and hooked up with her old boyfriend. My pride was more damaged than my heart, a fact that made it clear I hadn't been as invested in her as I thought.

In fact, at this point, I've pretty much given up hope that I'll ever feel that all-encompassing, breath-stealing, heart-pounding affection for a girl. I felt it once and nearly died when I lost it, so the notion of never going there again doesn't upset me all that much.

The bell on the front door rings, but I've got a bit of time before my next appointment, so I don't turn around, figuring this client belongs to one of the other guys. Several seconds pass and no one speaks. Whoever opened the door must be in the lobby right now, but so far none of the guys have greeted the person. Maybe it's a walk-in. If so, I might be able to squeeze in a small piece before my next client, provided it's nothing super complicated.

I chew up the last bite of my cookie and turn around, coffee still in my hand.

My heart stops. My knees nearly buckle. I almost lose my grip on the paper cup in my hand.

How is she here, right in front of me after all this time? Six years. It's been Six years. And nothing about the way she affects me has changed.

I take a step closer, but stop myself, afraid that if I move too quickly she'll disappear. I swallow past the huge lump in my throat and take a breath, willing my voice not to break as I open my mouth to speak.

"Brenna."

2005

Clayton, Kentucky

Caleb, age 13

Brenna, age 9

Chapter 1

BRENNA

MY BROTHER AND his new friend are jerks.

I'm sitting at the kitchen table all alone because ever since Hunter brought Caleb around the first time, all they do is play video games and ignore me. Caleb is thirteen, a year older than Hunter, so Hunter thinks he's some kind of big shot now.

Mom's been sleeping a lot these days, so I try to keep myself busy doing things that don't disturb her. Usually Hunter and I play outside, or watch movies in the basement if it's raining or cold, but since Hunter and Caleb became friends, I just keep to myself.

I try not to feel jealous over how much fun they're having, but it's hard, when I can hear the laughter from my spot at the kitchen table. To distract myself from how lonely I am, I pull out my coloring pencils and pass the time drawing flowers in all sorts of bright colors.

I'm putting the finishing touches on a pink rose when my dad's car pulls up. Quickly, I try to gather my things into neat stacks that can be easily moved, but I'm not fast enough. I can tell he's angry by the way he glares as he walks in the back door.

"Brenna, how many times have I told you not to clutter the table with your junk?" He doesn't really want an answer. "Clear those silly drawings off so we can heat up the last of the leftovers."

Footsteps pound on the basement steps as the boys make their way upstairs. Usually Hunter tries to be the first one my dad sees when he gets home. I think he does it so Dad won't snap at me so bad.

"Hey Dad," Hunter says, distracting him from his irritation that I was drawing at the table again. "I'll take care of getting things heated up."

Hunter begins pulling dishes from the refrigerator as Dad heads down the hallway to change clothes. A few days ago Mom felt good enough to cook, and she made a huge pot roast and mashed potatoes. The leftovers have lasted most of this week.

"Sorry Caleb," Hunter says in a soft voice. He must've told Caleb about Mom being so sad all the time, and Dad being really mean when she's like that.

"It's okay," Caleb replies. "I'll head on home."

I'm busy stacking my papers and putting my coloring pencils in the box, so I don't see Caleb walk up to the table.

"These are really nice," he says, pointing to the two drawings still visible in the stack. "I like to draw, too."

I shrug my shoulders. "I'm not very good at it."

"I think you are." He smiles when I look up at him, and I decide maybe he's not a jerk after all. "And they're not silly drawings."

Right then and there, Caleb Hanson becomes my hero.

2009

Clayton, Kentucky

Caleb, age 17

Brenna, age 13

Chapter 2

CALEB

THE MALONE'S BACKYARD is full of people. Apparently Hunter's dad invited their whole neighborhood for this cookout. Mrs. Malone is having one of her good spells, and for the past week she's been in the kitchen every time I've come over after school. She's currently laughing with a couple of other ladies over on the patio.

It's good to see her like this. Hunter and I have been best friends for four years, and I know from everything he's told me that it's only a matter of time before her depression flares up again. When that happens, she'll spend weeks in the bed while Hunter and his sister, Brenna, basically fend for themselves.

Their dad is a top notch asshole when his wife is down for the count. He's all kinds of nasty to Hunter and Brenna, and if not for the fact that both kids learned to cook at an early age, they'd probably go hungry. I know Mr. Malone's a cop, which isn't exactly an easy job, but in a small town like Clayton, Kentucky it can't be that stressful.

At least he makes an effort when Mrs. Malone is feeling good. Like today.

Hunter is at the grill flipping hot dogs, so I grab a can of soda and head over to join him. On my way across the yard, I catch sight of Brenna putting a tray of cupcakes onto a picnic table. They're chocolate with some kind of white frosting that looks like a swirl of snow on top. I'm sure she made them herself. She's gotten pretty good at baking over the last year, and Hunter and I are always happy to be her taste testers.

Brenna is thirteen now, but sometimes it's hard to remember that she's not in high school like Hunter and me. She had to grow up quick. I think she's felt the strain of her mom's depression even more than Hunter and has taken on the role of caretaker. She always make sure there are snacks after school and hounds Hunter about getting his homework done.

"Those look great, Brenna," I say, coming to a stop next to the table.

"Chocolate with cream cheese frosting," she replies.

"My favorite."

"I know." She looks up at me with lowered lids, one corner of her mouth turned up in a slight grin.

For a second I wonder if she made them because she knows I like them, and I'm surprised how much I like the idea that she might've done something special just for me. She turns and heads back toward the house, and I watch her go. I've known Brenna for four years now, and always thought of her like a kid sister, the little girl who ran after her brother and me and refused to leave us alone.

But that's kind of difficult these days, since she doesn't seem so little anymore. She seems more like a lady. I'm seventeen, and she's more mature even than the girls my age. I remind myself again that she's thirteen years old and Hunter's baby sister, then continue walking to the grill.

Chapter 3

BRENNA

THE COOKOUT IS in full swing, and Mom is enjoying herself.

I've learned to appreciate these moments and keep them stored in my memory to think back on later, when she spends days in her bedroom suffering.

For a while, when I was younger, I'd get really mad when she'd go into one of her spells. Now I understand that she can't help it. I asked dad once if she needed counseling or medication. He yelled at me and told me that Mom just needed to get a hold of herself. I never asked again. I think he's embarrassed by Mom's depression. I know now that Mom can't get help because Dad won't allow it, so I try to do what I can to help during her sad times, and make her good times as positive as they can be.

I make my way back outside with a fresh pitcher of lemonade and notice Caleb helping Hunter out at the grill. For the past four years he's been a regular fixture at our house. I'm grateful that Hunter has such a good friend. Mom's illness is harder on him that it is me. He wants to be able to help her, and I know he feels useless. I try to show him that he helps *me* and because of that he's also helping Mom, but I know it's not the same. Caleb is a good friend to Hunter, which gives him some companionship during the really dark moments.

For a long time Caleb has felt like another brother to me. He looks out for me just like Hunter, and he helps around the house when Hunter and I have to handle everything from the laundry, to cooking, to cleaning the bathrooms.

But lately I've started to see Caleb in a different way. When I see him I don't automatically think *there's Hunter's friend.* Now, when I see Caleb, I just see *him.* And the things I feel for him are more about the relationship I have with him myself than the friendship he shares with my brother.

Obviously, Caleb is a cute guy, and I'm not blind. I've noticed. But it's more than just the fact that he's good looking. It's the fact that I know him, and I like the person he is on the inside.

It's confusing, and I sort of feel guilty. Like maybe I'm betraying my brother by having these secret feelings for his best friend. Not that it matters when there's four years difference between Caleb and me. I'm certain he still sees me as Hunter's little sister and nothing more, so it really doesn't matter how I feel.

But still, I made chocolate cupcakes with cream cheese icing because I know he loves them.

THE SUN HAS set, and the barbecue is long over, when I head out to the backyard by myself. Mom went to bed early, claiming she was tired from all the activity of the day. It's a reasonable enough idea, but I can see her slipping back into the sadness. Rather than being upset by it, I choose to be thankful that she had so many good days in a row.

Dad and Hunter went down to the community center to shoot basketball with some of the other guys from the neighborhood. Part of me hates the way Dad puts on such a show when Mom is feeling well, pretending like he's father of the year or something. But another part of me is thankful for the peaceful days, and the moments when he actually acts like a father, at least to Hunter.

The bench swing that hangs from a low tree limb near the back of the yard sways gently as I pull my feet up and wrap my arms around my knees. In my mind, I begin making a list of all the good things that happened today so I can think about them tomorrow when things have returned to our *normal.*

I hear the footsteps behind me before I see him, but I already know it's Caleb. He's the only one that sneaks through the backyard to get here.

"Hi Caleb," I say, just as he comes around to the front of the swing.

"Hi Bren." I secretly love it when he shortens my name. He's the only one who does it. He looks at the empty side of the swing. "Can I sit?"

"Sure." I scoot a bit to make more room for him. "Hunter and Dad are down playing basketball at the center."

Caleb nods. He's used to the routine by now. "How's your mom?"

The sun dips lower, disappearing behind the trees across the road from my house, tinting the sky with pale orange. The humidity of the September heat lifts just a bit, and the slightest breeze moves across my skin. I recognize the sensations for what they are... the beauty before the darkness.

"In bed." I release a heavy sigh and point toward her

bedroom window just beyond the patio. "Tired from the day, she said."

"I'll be around after school next week." He knows without me saying it out loud. "To help you and Hunter."

I nod and say nothing, because I have no words to really express how much Caleb's presence in our lives means.

"What's that pink flower thing right outside her window?" he asks. "I've always thought it was pretty."

"Rhododendron," I answer. "It's her favorite flower. She planted it outside the bedroom window as soon as we moved into this house. I like to think maybe she looks out here sometimes and it makes her smile a little, but who knows."

"I'm sure it does. I guess sometimes those small things are big deals to her."

I change the subject, needing to get away from the reality of my family. "Have you made plans for after you graduate in the spring?"

"I'm thinking about taking a year off." He shrugs his shoulders. "Hunter and I have talked about rooming together, but he's got another year of high school after me. Plus, I have no idea what I want to study, so I figure maybe I'll get a job and hang around here until Hunter graduates."

My stomach does a little flip-flop at the knowledge that Caleb won't be gone this time next year. I don't even try to pretend I'm only happy about it because I'm glad Hunter will still have his friend around. I'm happy because Caleb will still be close to *me*.

"Hunter doesn't know what he wants to study either. He just wants to get out of here."

"What about you?" Caleb asks. "You'll be in high school next year. You must be looking forward to that."

I turn my head and stare at him. "I don't think there's any such thing as looking forward to high school, but at least I won't be stuck in class with all the idiots anymore. I can take advanced courses."

"You're ahead of the kids your age in a lot of ways." Caleb shifts a little closer. "Smarter. Nicer. More mature."

"Thanks." I drop my eyes and bit the inside of my cheek to keep from smiling. "I guess."

"I meant it as a compliment," he whispers.

I gather his words and brand the memory into my heart, knowing I'll relive it over and over again in the lonely moments. I try to think of a response that's not stupid, but come up empty.

The sound of my Dad's car pulling in the driveway interrupts my thoughts, and Caleb pushes to his feet.

"I should go," he says. "Let you guys enjoy your dad while he's in a good mood. Tell Hunter I stopped by, and I'll see him Monday at school."

He turns and heads through the trees before I even get a chance to say goodbye, his words of praise still ringing in my ears.

2010

Clayton, Kentucky

Caleb, age 18

Brenna, age 14

Chapter 4

CALEB

"WHY'D YOU MAKE me leave so early," Hunter complains from the passenger seat of my car.

The fourth of July pool party at Mark Sizemore's house sounded like a great idea, until I realized his parents were out of town and the party was really just an excuse to drink a crap ton of beer.

Not that I've never had a beer. I enjoy one now and then, but I've never found getting stupid drunk to be a super fun pass time.

Hunter, on the other hand, seems to think getting drunk is the best thing in the world. Until the next morning, when he swears he'll never do it again.

But he always does.

Which is why, at midnight, I'm driving him home, despite his protests.

"We're leaving because if you drink anymore you're going to puke it all up, and then your dad will know exactly what you've been doing."

The mention of his dad always shuts down any argument. I try not to play the dad-card any more than I have to, because I know that Hunter's relationship with his father is pretty messed up. But sometimes that's all that gets through.

"You're right. I know it." His speech is slurred, but at least he's agreeing with me now. "Dad will just yell at me, and I hate that."

I'm sure that if Mr. Malone had any idea about Hunter's drinking he'd do more than just yell at him. However, the man never has any idea what's going on with his children. I guess in Hunter's current situation, that's kind of a blessing.

"Hunter, man, you've got to quit doing this." I keep my voice low and non-accusatory, because it won't do any good to antagonize him. "Before he finds out, or worse yet, you hurt yourself."

Hunter just nods, and from the corner of my eye I can see his shoulders slump.

I pick up my cell phone and dial Brenna's number. She always keeps it near her – and on silent – because this isn't the first time I've had to bring Hunter home in this condition.

Her voice is soft when she answers. "Caleb."

"What's the situation at your house?" I ask. "I'm headed there now with Hunter."

She sighs, and even on the other end of the cell phone call, I can feel the heavy sadness of it. We've had this same conversation before, and it sucks every time.

"Dad's on patrol for another hour," she answers. "So we'll be able to get him in the house and in bed."

Luckily, Hunter's a sleepy drunk and is likely to sleep until early afternoon once he gets in bed. Lord knows what would happen if he got up and started stumbling around the house after his dad got home.

"Ok. I'll see you in a few."

After ending the call, I drop my cell into the cup holder and look over at Hunter.

He's shaking his head. "Brenna's going to be mad at me."

"Probably so." I put on my left turn signal and pull up to the intersection that turns into Hunter's neighborhood. "But she'll still help you get into bed and keep you out of trouble."

"I'm a shitty brother."

Hunter is my best friend, and I'd do anything for him, but he's right. Sometimes he's a real shitty brother to Brenna. She's taken on enough responsibility thanks to their mom's illness and their dad's nastiness. She shouldn't have to be responsible for Hunter's ass, too.

"Yeah, sometimes you are," I agree. "But she loves you. Maybe you ought to try showing her you love her too by staying sober a little more often."

He nods his head, and I say a quick prayer that he means it – and that he remembers it in the morning.

Chapter 5

BRENNA

M OM SLEEPS LIKE the dead when her depression flares, so there's no danger of her waking up to find Caleb and me walking a staggering Hunter down the hallway toward his bedroom. Thankfully, he's quiet as we open the door and usher him inside.

What happens next is, unfortunately, a routine Caleb and I have down pat. I head to the kitchen and fill a glass with water and retrieve a hefty dose of ibuprofen from the medicine cabinet. When I get back to Hunter's room, Caleb's got him in the bed and covered up, jeans tossed to the floor just like Hunter would've done it if he'd been sober.

I put the water and pills on his nightstand, and sit down on the mattress beside him. He's almost out, but manages to mutter a weak *I'm sorry.*

"I know you are," I whisper. "Just sleep it off, okay."

I stand, leaving him sleeping in his bed, and follow Caleb out of the house and into the driveway. We stop beside the driver's side of his car, and just look at one another.

"This is the third time this summer," I say.

"I know." Caleb's voice is stricken. "I'd never have taken him there if I'd realized Mark's parents were out of town."

I shake my head. "It's not your fault Caleb. None of it is. He makes these choices."

Caleb shoves his hands in his pockets. I can see the frustration rolling off him. He loves Hunter, and he hates this just as much as I do. And just like me, Caleb is powerless to stop Hunter's destructive behavior if he's determined to continue.

Deep down, I know Hunter is using alcohol as a way to escape the reality that we live with. Part of me can't even blame him. Living with a mom who suffers from clinical depression and a dad who won't help her and treats us all like garbage is enough to drive anyone crazy.

But that doesn't change the fact that I need him. Even if he can't help Mom and can't please Dad, *I* need him. Until he started drinking he was always here for me. We tackled this life together.

"I'll talk to him," Caleb says. "Again. Maybe this time I'll get through."

It occurs to me that where I have always felt like it was Hunter and me against the world, it now feels more like Caleb and me taking on the situation. Because here he and I are, standing in the driveway, discussing how to help my brother, while he sleeps of his drunken stupor down the hallway from the bedroom my mom has been holed up for most of my life.

Hunter's troubles with alcohol have forced me into an even closer alliance with Caleb, given us a common goal, and created a bond between us that goes beyond the fact that I'm his best friend's little sister. It's more than just friendship, but it's not quite *something else* either.

I stopped denying that I wanted *something else* with him a while ago. Being honest with myself about my feelings for

Caleb does nothing to change the fact that, as Hunter's sister, I'm off limits to him, but it also doesn't change the way that I feel.

Over the past five years I've seen him step up and be more a part of our family than either one of my parents. He's done it just because he cares about us. Not many teenage boys would do such a thing, and the small seed of affection that planted deep in my heart the day Caleb told me that my drawings weren't stupid has grown exponentially ever since.

"Thank you for bringing him home." I look up into the eyes that have become as familiar to me as my own. "Tonight, at least, I know he's safe."

Caleb nods, hands still in his pockets, dark brown hair falling across his forehead. "I should go before your dad gets back. Call me tomorrow and let me know how he is."

Without waiting for an answer, he turns and gets in his car. Moments like this one, when we deal with Hunter's increasingly poor judgement, are difficult and tense for both of us. Add to that my conflicted feelings for Caleb, and I'm as relieved to see him go as I am desperate to have him near.

2011

Clayton, Kentucky

Caleb, age 19

Brenna, age 15

Chapter 6

CALEB

HUNTER GRADUATED HIGH school last month. We've both been accepted to a small college about an hour away from Clayton. We're supposed to move in to the dorm mid-August. While I'm not exactly stoked about starting classes, especially after taking a year off after I finished high school, I am looking forward to getting Hunter out of this town and away from his father.

But then I think about how available alcohol will be once we're at school, and I wonder if putting Hunter on a college campus is a good thing at all.

His drinking slowed down a bit once he started his senior year, but he never quit altogether. More than once Brenna found some kind of liquor stashed in his bedroom. She'd quietly get rid of it, never telling him she'd found it, and he never said a word to her about his missing alcohol.

Hunter's drinking is the elephant in the room that they never talk about. The worry of it wears on Brenna, and all year long I've watched her spirit sink lower and lower.

It kills me to see the spark in her dim. Brenna is special. Special in a general sense, because she's very smart and extremely nice. But she's also special *to me*. I haven't put words to my feelings toward her, partly because I don't really understand them and partly because I realize how dangerous it would be to actually admit what I have in my heart for her.

She's my best friends sister, and she's four years younger than me. And her dad is the biggest asshole on the planet.

Yet none of that stops my heart from turning over in my chest the moment she walks into the room.

Hunter and I met up with a group of guys at the Community Rec Center a couple of hours ago for a few games of basketball. Not that playing ball is my thing, but it seemed safer than a lot of stuff Hunter's wanted to do these days, so I agreed. I'm sitting in a chair on one side of the gym, chugging a Gatorade, when I see Brenna walk in.

She's never come here, that I know if, so the fact that she walked her from her house immediately raises a red flag for me.

As well as sending my pulse into overdrive.

I dart my eyes from one side of the basketball court to the other, looking for Hunter. He's not here.

I push to my feet and practically sprint across the gym. I can see her looking around for her brother and not finding him. Panic begins to set in across her face.

"Brenna!" I shout, just before I reach her.

"He called me," she says, her voice breathless. "He sounded drunk. Like, really drunk. He was talking all kinds of nonsense."

"He's been here the whole time," I reply. "Playing ball and laughing with the guys."

"Where is he now?" She continues looking around the gym.

I grab her hand. "Let's go out back."

The feeling of her hand in mine is electric and almost covers the fear coursing through me as I imagine what we may find in the back of the rec center. No one pays any attention to us as we make our way around the side of the gym to the back of the building. We pass by the locker room door, and finally push out into the back parking lot.

Hunter is there, along with some guy I've never seen. The dude's trunk is open and inside is enough beer to make everyone in the gym drunk.

"Shit." It dawns on me then, that the couple of times Hunter said he was hitting the restroom, he was coming out here to drink. "I thought he'd gone to the bathroom a little while ago, but he must've out here drinking."

Brenna's hand tightens around my fingers, and, in this moment I want to forget about her idiot brother and wrap my arms around her. Hunter may be my best friend, but he's hurt his sister way too many times for me to overlook his behavior.

"I can't believe I didn't realize what he was doing." I shake my head, forcing myself to stand still and not pull Brenna into my embrace.

"You couldn't have known," she whispers. "The rec center has always been a pretty safe place."

"He needs help, Bren." I turn to face her, keeping her hand locked in mine. "More than we can give him."

She nods, and I can see the wheels turning in her head as she imagines trying to convince Hunter to go to rehab or join some kind of support group. Even if we wait a month and bring it up to him after he turns eighteen, there's still no conceivable way we'd be able to hide it from their father. And what an ugly mess that will be.

But Hunter and his safety have to be the most important thing right now, even if it means dealing with Mr. Malone's temper.

He sees us then, and shoves the beer in his hand behind

his back, as if that will somehow erase what we already know.

The unknown beer supplier jumps into the driver's seat and speeds away, obviously not wanting to be a part of whatever is about to go down.

Hunter walks toward us with a big, stupid grin on his face. "Is your dad on duty, Bren?" I ask under my breath.

She nods, just as Hunter reaches us.

"What're you doing here, Brenna?" he drawls, his words slurring together.

"Just came to say hi," she answers, keeping her voice light.

Hunter and I both drove here, and I know his car keys are in the pocket of his shorts. Somehow, we've got to get them from him, or at least get him into my car.

"Let's not make her walk back home in the dark," I say. "Hop in my car and we'll drive her home."

If I can get him to agree, we can get him into bed, and I'll walk back here and bring his car home.

"Nah," he argues. "Let's go get pizza. She can come with us."

Not that I want to hang out at Pizza Palace with a drunk Hunter, but if it gets him into my car, I'll agree to it.

"Sounds good. I'll drive." I let go of Brenna's hand to dig my keys from my pocket.

"I'll meet you there." Hunter palms his own set of keys.

"Hunter, just ride with us." Brenna's voice is pleading. "There's no sense taking two vehicles."

"You two looked pretty cozy there, holding hands," Hunter says, attempting to wink but only accomplishing a clumsy blink. "Thought maybe you wanted some privacy."

"Don't be stupid, Hunter." I clap my hand on his shoulder. "Hop in and we'll go get pizza."

"I said I'd drive myself." He shrugs my hand from his shoulder. "You two are always ordering me around like I'm a baby."

"Hunter, I'm worried about you," Brenna says. "Let us drive you over to Pizza Palace and get some food in you. You can't be this drunk when Dad gets home after his shift."

"Maybe I don't give a shit about Dad, anymore." His voice rises. Clearly the mention of his father has agitated him. "It's not like he gives a shit about me."

"But I do Hunter." Brenna's voice wobbles, and I can tell she's on the verge of tears. She's carried the burden of Hunter's drinking for over a year, and the weight of it is crushing her. "I care about what happens to you."

"What do you know about anything?" Hunter snaps back at her. "You're fifteen. You're still just a stupid child."

He turns toward his car, and Brenna grabs his arm, desperate to stop him. He slings her away, and her butt lands on the blacktop.

"Brenna!" I yell, stepping over to help her up.

"I'm fine. Just stop him!"

But Hunter has a head start on me, and before I can reach him, he's in the driver's seat with the doors locked. I pound on his window, shouting at him to get out of the car, but he doesn't listen. He's so far gone with beer and a general bitterness for the reality of his life that he refuses to hear me.

He cranks the car, and I turn and sprint toward my own. Brenna is already there, climbing into the passenger side. We take off after Hunter, buckling our seat belts as we turn out onto the street.

Hunter turns left at the end of the street onto the main road that bisects the town. We follow, watching as he weaves from one side of the road to the other, somehow making it through the sleepy downtown area. He keeps driving, heading north of Clayton, and for several miles he seems to hold it together. I have no idea where he's going, and honestly, Hunter probably has no idea either, but I'm praying he stops at some point so we can get him out from behind the wheel.

Beside me, Brenna wrings her hands. More than anything I want to reach across the console of my car and comfort her, but I know that if I truly want to help her, the best thing I can do is keep my eye on Hunter's car and both hands on the steering wheel so we can stay with him.

We're headed down the hill that leads to the county fairgrounds when Hunter suddenly speeds up, barreling full blast toward the intersection at the bottom. If he doesn't let up on the gas pedal there's no way he's going to manage to stop at the stop sign at the bottom of the hill.

He doesn't stop.

He plows toward the stop sign without slowing down.

The cross traffic has no stop sign, and Hunter flies into the middle of the intersection without regard to the huge farm truck approaching from the left.

The crash as the truck t-bones Hunter directly in the driver's side of his car is deafening. I slam my brakes, pulling to the side of the road as quickly as I can. I grab my phone, dialing 911 and bounding out of the car as Brenna does the same. For a moment we stand there on the shoulder of the highway, frozen in place as we watch the driver of the farm truck climb down from the cab.

I give the information to the dispatcher and beg them to send help as fast as possible. Beside me, Brenna vibrates with emotion as she watches the other driver approach Hunter's now crumpled car.

He moves as close to the driver's door as he can and peers inside. Even from this distance, his voice is crystal clear as he cries out, "Oh my god!"

Brenna takes off running toward Hunter's car, and I'm behind her at once.

"Brenna, no!" I shout, afraid of what she might see once she gets there. If it's as bad as it looks, I don't want her to see her brother in that condition.

She's on a mission and despite my longer legs, I can't catch up to her quick enough. Luckily, the other driver intercepts her and holds her back.

"Don't look," he says, holding her by the shoulders. "You don't need to see."

"He's my brother!" she cries.

I wrap my arms around her from behind, pulling her back against me. My cell phone falls to the ground at my feet as I hold onto her. She stops struggling and slumps in my arms, her shoulders shaking with the force of her sobs.

In the distance I hear the sirens of the approaching emergency vehicles as I pull Brenna against me once more, leaning down so I can put my face right next to hers.

"I'm here," I say over and over again, because what more can I really say?

My mind goes blank, refusing to process the reality in front of me. Somewhere inside I know a terrible sadness is waiting to swallow me, but in this moment, Brenna's breathing is all I'm aware of.

I stare at Hunter's mangled car, knowing I won't see him climbing out. Knowing without really *knowing* that what we've feared the most has finally come to pass.

Chapter 7

BRENNA

THEY PRONOUNCED HUNTER dead shortly after he arrived at the hospital.

Caleb drove us both there. Dad arrived only moments later and blew us right past us, not even acknowledging us as he stormed back into the exam rooms.

The police officer that arrived at the scene is sitting with Caleb and me. We'd agreed on the frantic drive to the hospital that we had to tell the truth about Hunter's accident. They'd find out anyway, so it was better that it come from us.

Caleb just finished giving his statement, and now it's my turn.

"You can wait until tomorrow if you need to," the officer says, his voice soft and compassionate. "I know this has been a terrible night for you."

For a moment I consider waiting. It almost seems like I should, like maybe I'm too devastated at this moment to speak coherently. But the truth is, I'm so numb that I'm not sure I'm feeling anything right now. Maybe tomorrow I'll feel all the overwhelming sadness that I know is coming, so I think to myself that tonight is the perfect time to tell my story.

"I can talk," I reply. "I'm okay."

"Bren, are you sure?" Caleb asks, taking one of my hands and wrapping it in both of his.

I nod. "I'm sure. I need to do this now."

I take a deep breath and begin. I start with how Hunter began drinking a year ago and how Caleb and I have tried to help him, the way that Caleb brought him home so many times, how I'd plead with him to stop. I tell him about tonight, about Hunter leaving to meet Caleb at the rec center to play ball with a group of guys, and how he'd drunk-dialed me, which prompted me to walk the few blocks to the rec center to check on him. I describe how Caleb and I found Hunter in the back parking lot with some guy we didn't know, drinking beer from the guy's trunk. Finally, I end with Hunter getting in his car to drive, despite our protests, Caleb and me following close behind him.

"We just kept hoping he'd stop somewhere and we could get his keys away from him." I pause for a moment and take a deep breath. "But he didn't. He just sped up as he went down the hill toward the fairgrounds. He didn't even slow down as he came to the stop sign."

"Did you see the impact?" the officer asks in a gentle voice.

I nod. "It all happened really fast, but when I realized he wasn't going to stop at the intersection I looked to the left and saw the truck coming toward him."

"And you have no idea how much he'd had to drink?"

"No," I answer, shaking my head. I go through it all with him again, reiterating how Caleb and I tried to stop him from driving.

As the officer finally wraps things up, I see my dad standing on the other side of the room. The look on his face tells me he heard enough to know the truth about what happened.

I glance around the waiting room as the officer gathers his things and leave, thankful that we're the only ones here. I'm not looking forward to the conversation that's about to happen. I want to tell Caleb to leave, to just get up and walk out before the explosion starts, but I know he won't go. He's always been here for Hunter and me, and I know he'll stick around for me regardless.

The outside door has barely shut when my dad begins.

"Your brother is dead and you sit there lying to the police?" His voice is quiet, but the contempt can't be missed.

"I'm not lying," I say. I knew he'd accuse me of lying. Why he thinks I'd make something like this up is beyond me, but I suppose it's easier to think his daughter would fabricate this story than it is to admit he's so oblivious that he had no idea what was happening in his own son's life. "Hunter's been drinking heavily for a year. We tried to help him, but nothing we did ever worked."

"You expect me to believe that my son practically became an alcoholic under my own roof and I didn't know about it?"

I laugh, but not out of any kind of humor. I laugh at the incredible irony of what my dad just said. "You have no idea about anything, Dad. Mom suffers every day, and you pay no attention. I get good grades, and you never notice. Hunter spiraled out of control, and you were clueless. That's nothing new. You've been clueless about us our whole lives."

"Why didn't you tell me what was happening!" he yells, startling the clerk behind the counter.

"Because you wouldn't have helped." I keep my voice calm as the honesty pours out of me. "You never help

Mom, so why would I think you would help Hunter? You'd have just gotten angry and yelled at him, and that wouldn't have helped. You would've just made things worse."

I can see his chest rising and falling with increasing speed. I've never talked to him this way, and he has no idea how to respond. I like to think that his momentary silence is because he knows I'm right, but I know he'll never admit it.

Then he turns on Caleb.

"This is all your fault." He points his finger at Caleb, shaking with rage. "Everything Hunter got himself into is because of you."

Even if that were true, Dad would have no way of knowing. Caleb says nothing in his own defense. He knows it's pointless. But I won't let it slide.

"No." My voice is loud and firm. I push to my feet and stand. "None of this is Caleb's fault. Caleb's been Hunter's friend through the good and the bad. He's driven him home more times that I can count, because my brother was too drunk to drive himself. He tried over and over again to get through to Hunter, to try to get him to stop drinking. Caleb has been there, with Hunter and with me, more than you ever have, so don't you dare blame this on him."

I make the short walk across the waiting room to stand toe to toe with my father before delivering my final truth.

"Hunter made his own choices, chased his own demons. He was driven by sadness and helplessness, because one of his parents couldn't be a real parent for him and the other parent just chose not to. I'll let you figure out which is which."

For once, my dad is speechless. I take advantage of the moment and turn to Caleb. "Will you drive me home?"

"Of course," he says immediately.

We exit the tiny hospital and ride in silence to my house. Neither one of us knows what to say, so we just say nothing. The weight of everything that's happened tonight sits in the car like a heavy fog.

It's after three in the morning when he pulls into the driveway and puts the car in park. I don't move to get out of the car, instead turning to face him. The streetlight across from my house illuminates the interior of the car just enough that I can see the devastated look in his eyes.

"You want me to walk you in?" he asks.

I shake my head. "I don't want to take a chance on you still being here when Dad gets home."

"I'm not worried about him, Bren. He can say whatever he wants to me. I just want to make sure you're okay."

"I'm not okay," I reply. "And neither are you. Both of us need a little time to process everything."

"All right," he answers with a sigh. "Will you call me and check in later?"

"I will." For a second I look at him. *Really* look at him. His chocolate brown eyes are swimming in sadness, and yet, I still see the infinite kindness that I've come to love about him.

He reaches across the console to hug me, and I respond, burying my face in the crook of his neck, snaking my arms around his shoulders. The feel of his embrace is so warm, so sweet, and so *right,* and I know if I stay here much longer I'll dissolve into the ugly cry that I know is coming.

I definitely want to be alone with that happens.

"Thank you." I turn my head so that my face is close to his ear. "For everything you've done for us. Not just tonight, but always."

His arms tighten around me. "It doesn't stop now, you know. Hunter may be gone," he stops, his voice breaking. He takes a moment to get himself under control, then continues. "I'm still here for you."

I force myself to pull back from him, knowing it would be far too easy to stay wrapped up in him until my father parks his cruiser in the driveway. Caleb loosens his hold enough that I can look at him. Our faces are only inches apart, the same tears that are threatening in my eyes are also pooling in his. We've shared many things over the past six years, but this grief… witnessing Hunter's death… it's created something in us that will never break.

This boy, who saved Hunter and me when we didn't even realize we needed saving, is still here, holding on to me on the worst night of my life. I have no idea where I'd be or what how I would survive without him.

So I do the only thing I know to do to express just how important he is to me.

I press my lips against his.

It's horrible timing. Caleb is too old for me. I know this. And yet, something in me craves genuine contact with another human, and my affections for Caleb already run so deep.

So I chose not to even think about it. Don't stop to measure my actions or weigh the consequences. I just do it, because this moment feels too significant to hold back.

I don't move. I just hold myself there, my mouth gently aligned with his, our breaths mingling together. Slowly, he brings his hands to my cheeks, his touch soft and tender. I could stay in this moment for the rest of my life, forgetting the reality that awaits inside my house, the torture of the next few days as we say goodbye to my brother.

But I can't. I know I have to face what's coming, and more than that, I know Caleb needs to be gone from here before my dad gets home and opens fire on him again with his verbal assault.

Pulling back, I look up at him, blinking as a tear rolls down my cheek. "I'll call you."

He nods, lifts one corner of his mouth in a half smile that doesn't reach his eyes, and lets me go.

And I walk into my house, bracing myself to wake up my mother who already lives in a world of oppressive sadness, and tell her that her son is dead.

Chapter 8

BRENNA

I T'S BEEN TEN days since we buried Hunter.

Mom was devastated when I told her what had happened. Dad came home and found her curled up on the couch, whimpering inconsolably. I begged him to call the doctor, and he finally did. She had enough medication to make it through the funeral without falling apart. It mostly just made her stare off into space with a blank expression in her eyes, but at least she stayed upright.

If there's a silver lining to all this, it's that once the doctor got involved, he managed to convince my dad that Mom isn't crazy. She's just suffering from major clinical depression. The doctor explained that chemical and hormonal imbalances were probably the culprits, and that sometimes there's no visible reason for a person's depression. Maybe now Dad will get out of the way and let her get the help she needs.

Caleb came to the funeral. His parents were with him, so thankfully Dad couldn't make a scene like he did at the hospital. But it was impossible for me to speak to him. I couldn't take a chance on setting my dad off, plus I didn't want to leave Mom's side.

That night I'd gotten a text from Caleb. I assured him we were managing as well as possible. He asked when my dad was going back to work. I told him he was returning to evening patrol the next week. He told me he'd see me then.

So here I am, sitting on the patio, close enough to the house so that if Mom needs me I'll hear her. She's sleeping, as she usually does, but at least now I have hope that she'll soon be receiving the medical help she's needed for so long.

Caleb appears from the tree line at the back of the yard. This first time seeing him come through the trees since Hunter's death is bittersweet.

"Hi, Bren," he says, holding his arms out.

I stand up from my seat and let him hug me, wrapping my arms around his middle in return. For the first time in over a week, I feel my body relax, as Caleb shares this burden with me.

"I brought snacks." I gesture to the cookies and soda on the small table between the two patio chairs.

With a grin, he sits down and pops open a can.

We talk for a long time, mostly about nothing significant. It's nice to just chat. But eventually I do tell him about the doctor and how Mom may finally get some help.

"How are things with your dad?" he asks.

I shrug my shoulders. "Basically the same. He hasn't gotten angry at me again. He's just pretty much left me alone, which is fine."

"So you support your mom while your dad ignores you, and nobody really supports you." His voice holds a trace of anger, and knowing it's there on my behalf warms my heart.

"Mom's cousin flew in from Seattle," I reply. "She and mom were really close growing up apparently. She was here for the funeral and a couple of days after. She realized pretty quickly what I was dealing with. She was really kind to me. Before she left, she gave me her phone number so we could keep in touch."

"That's something, at least."

"And I know you're always here," I whisper. "Even when we couldn't see each other."

He reaches for my hand, where it rests on the arm of the chair, and threads his fingers through mine. That small contact sends tingles up my arm, and I feel goosebumps break out over my skin.

Caleb has been a part of my life for six years, but this soft touch means so much more than anything I've experienced before. That he came here, even though Hunter is gone and my dad is an asshole… that he takes my hand and holds it in his… it's both comfort and affection.

For a long moment we sit in silence, our hands laced together, his thumb tracing gentle circles against my palm. I feel the tension of the past several days melt away, replaced by a calming warmth that I only experience in his presence.

As the sun disappears below the trees, casting shadows in the backyard, Caleb stands.

"I should go." He pulls me to me feet to stand in front of him. "Can I come back tomorrow?"

I nod. "Dad works the same time."

"Okay."

He leans down and places a kiss on the top of my head, then silently makes his way across the yard before disappearing into the trees.

I stay on the patio after he's gone, my heart both broken and full all at the same time.

Chapter 9

CALEB

I'VE BEEN TO Brenna's almost every night for the past two weeks. Even on the nights her Dad doesn't have patrol, he usually goes somewhere. We're not exactly sure where he goes, but it's nothing new. He avoided dealing with his family before Hunter died. Why should anything be different now?

Brenna and I rarely talk about anything heavy. Sometimes we reminisce about Hunter, but I try to focus on good memories, the things that make us laugh, the times we shared that make us smile.

I tell myself that I'm spending time with her because of Hunter, because he'd want me to look after her. I know that's true, but with every step that takes me closer to Brenna's back yard, I know that's not all of it.

I have feelings for this girl. Real, genuine feelings. Feelings that started long before Hunter died. My mind is completely aware that she's four years younger than me, but that doesn't seem to make any difference to my heart.

I don't know what the answer is, if there's any logical way forward for the two of us. I realize the situation between is probably a lost cause. I just know that I can't abandon her.

When I step out of the trees, I see Brenna in the swing

at the back of the yard. My chest expands at the sight of her curly, dark brown hair tumbling over her shoulders. She looks sadder than she did last night.

"Hi there." I ease down next to her on the swing. "You okay?"

"Mom had a bad day," she says. "She finally took the medicine the doctor prescribed for her, and now she's sleeping. I sort of feel guilty for being glad she's asleep."

I slip my arm around her shoulders and pull her closer, until her head rests on my shoulder. Every night I've been here, I've only touched her in comforting ways. Even though my heart would like nothing more than to be with her – really be a with her, the way a guy and a girl are together when they feel something so strong – most of the time I just hold her hand. Tonight, I get the sense that she needs more.

"Don't feel guilty, Bren," I whisper. "You're allowed to grieve, too. You're strong for you mom every day, but you don't have to hold it together with me."

I feel her take a shaky breath, and her shoulders begin to tremble. She's been a rock for everyone else, and it's about time she let herself cry. I don't say stupid things and try to convince her it's all going to be okay. I just hold her while her tears fall.

"I'm so thankful you're here," she whispers. "I think I'd be lost if you weren't."

"Not going anywhere, I promise." I press a kiss to the top of her head. "Rhododendron looks great. I can tell you've been taking care of it."

She looks up at me then, and in her amber colored eyes I see a kind of trust and affection that I've never known. Something deep and true that means more than either one of us can put words to.

She raises her hand and places it against my cheek, and her touch completely undoes me. I lean closer, watching her expression for any sign of hesitancy, but all I see is belonging.

When my lips meet hers, everything around me shifts, tumbling and moving and clicking into place, fitting together like pieces of a puzzle. Nothing in my life has ever made more sense than this moment. Whatever the reasons that we shouldn't be doing this – and I know there are many – I can't stop the way I feel.

Brenna moves even closer and slides her arm around my neck. She's not tentative as she opens her mouth under mine, moving with me as I deepen the kiss.

"I never knew it was possible to feel so much for one person." I say the words against her skin.

"Me either," she says, pulling back enough to look into my eyes.

A smile breaks out on her face, the first one I've seen in weeks. I lean my forehead against hers, smiling back at her. For several seconds we stay like that, eyes locked, arms around one another.

I know she's too young for me. Four years is a huge difference at this point in our lives. I know she's grieving her brother, and that what she believes is affection for me may well be only some kind of misplaced attempt to hang on to Hunter. I know all this, and I know that at some point I'm going to have to take a step back and figure out a way to put the brakes on, to put these feelings on a shelf until she's older and the time is right.

I've just about worked up the courage to say all this to her when she tiptoes and presses her lips to mine once more, and I decide I can wait one more minute.

And then the back door of her house slams.

Cold dread spreads over me.

Her father.

Quickly, we stand up from the swing.

He stalks toward us, malice pouring off him, and instinctively I push Brenna behind me. Whatever he's about to unleash, it's going to come at me, not at her.

"Mr. Malone," I say, willing my voice to stay even. "I care very deeply for your daughter."

He doesn't respond, instead he continues his march toward where we're standing. I watch him curl his right hand into a fist, and as he gets closer to us, he begins to pull it back.

I brace myself.

At the last moment, Brenna moves from behind me and jumps between her father and me.

"No!" she screams, and shoves her dad in the chest.

She's small, and he's stout, so her action doesn't do much to move him, but it's enough to stop him from driving his fist into my face.

"Brenna." I yell her name at the same time I shove her behind me again.

"Get the hell away from her." His voice seethes with anger. "You corrupted my son, and now he's dead. I won't let you do the same to my daughter."

"Dad, stop it!" Brenna cries, stepping out from behind me and taking my hand. "None of this Caleb's fault. You just want to blame someone because you feel guilty for never being around. Caleb was Hunter's best friend. Stop trying to make him responsible for Hunter's death."

He looks at her, narrows his eyes, then cuts his gaze toward me. He takes a step closer. Brenna flinches, but I hold my ground. When he's practically toe to toe with me, he drops his voice and speaks.

"If I catch you with my daughter again, I will end you. I have the resources to throw your ass in jail and make sure you rot. You'll never see it coming." He pauses, pointing to the badge on his uniform. "One day, the police will show up with a warrant to search your car. And inside, they'll find cocaine, maybe even a stolen weapon that was used in another crime. They will haul you off to jail, and I'll make damn sure there's someone to testify that they saw you buy those drugs."

Brenna's sharp intake of breath echoes the disbelief that I feel. I can't wrap my mind around the threats, can't even begin to imagine a way around them.

I feel Brenna's hand tremble in mine, and I know that for the time being, all I can do is diffuse the tension in this moment.

"I'm leaving," I say, letting go of her hand and taking a step backward.

"Caleb no!"

"Brenna, it's for the best right now." I stress the words *right now,* hoping she understands my meaning.

She wraps her arms around herself, and tears begin to pool in her eyes. I look at her once more and nod, trying without words to send some kind of message of comfort.

Then I turn and walk out of her yard, with no idea how the two of us can possibly fix this.

Chapter 10

BRENNA

I'M MEETING CALEB tonight. Not in my backyard. Even though my dad's on patrol, we can't take a chance on being seen together. Not after what happened two nights ago when he came home early and saw Caleb and me kissing.

My stomach clenches at the memory. I've always known my dad wasn't nice, but I never knew he could be so ugly.

I make my way through the yard, past the tree line in the back, and wait in the small cluster of trees that separates our yard from the one directly behind us. I think it technically belongs to the Petersons, who live in the house whose back yard joins ours, but they don't have young kids at home anymore, so no one ever comes here.

Caleb and I arranged it via text this morning. I deleted the conversation immediately afterward because I don't trust my dad not to go through my phone.

Our current situation seems hopeless, but I tell myself to have faith that somehow everything will be all right, eventually. My heart almost believes it.

Caleb appears only seconds after I get there, and without a word we go into each other's arms. In that instant, I feel the stress and heartache I've been living with evaporate.

Two days without him have seemed like an eternity.

If it were possible to solve every problem simply by being in Caleb's arms the world would be a much better place. However, as wonderful as it feels to be wrapped up in this boy who has my heart, I know we have to deal with the reality in front of us.

"Things will cool down," I say, ignoring the doubts trying to creep in. "Once you're at college, Dad will go back to his regular routine. Everything will be fine."

Caleb takes my hands, and we sit down on the grass underneath one of the trees. He doesn't let go of my hands once we're seated, and the hollow look in his eyes sends a chill across my skin.

"My dad's being transferred to Phoenix," he says, his voice flat and void of emotion.

Caleb's dad has worked for a manufacturing company in Louisville for the past six years. In fact, it was the job that brought them to Clayton in the first place. Since they didn't want to live in a big city while Caleb was still in school, they chose a small town within a reasonable commute, and during busy weeks, Mr. Hanson would stay in the city with one of his co-workers.

Now it seems the job is taking them somewhere else, and I'm not sure what this means for Caleb.

"How long have you known?" I ask.

"Since about a week before Hunter died." His voice lowers on the last word, the pain of losing Hunter still fresh on both our hearts.

"Why didn't you say anything?" I squeeze his hands.

"At first, it didn't seem important," he replies. "I wasn't going to Phoenix with them. I was going to college with Hunter. And after Hunter died, well, it still just didn't seem very important."

My mind whirls, wondering why he's bringing it up now. I'm almost afraid to ask, but I know I have to.

"And now?" My voice is barely more than breath.

"Mom and Dad think I should go with them." He closes his eyes and drops his head. "They've left it up to me, of course, but after I told them what happened with your dad, they think getting out of town would be best."

"You told them?" I ask. "Everything?"

He nods his head. "I didn't know what else to do. I had to talk to someone, and I've always been close with my parents. They weren't weirded out about the you and me part of it, although I'm sure under normal circumstances they'd have had some very specific advice. They were just concerned about your dad's threats."

An invisible fist reaches into my chest and squeezes my heart, pain coursing through my system at the thought of Caleb being on the other side of the country.

"Are you going?" The words are like shards of glass in my throat.

Caleb swallows hard. "I don't want to. I don't want to leave you here alone, and I sure as hell don't want to be so far away from you. But if I stay here, even if I go on to college like Hunter and I had planned, I don't think I can stay away from you. I don't think there's any way I could do what your dad insisted."

"What about college?" I choke the words out as my heart splinters into a thousand pieces, the jagged edges slicing and scraping as they bounce around inside my chest.

"I'm not even sure I'm going. I have no idea what I want to study. The only things I really like are drawing and painting. And I was never super stoked about college, anyway. I just wanted to go with Hunter."

I do my best to stop the torrent of sadness and look at

this situation not as a fifteen year-old girl who's about to lose the boy she loves, but as a nineteen year-old boy who could be hurt in a very real, irreversible way. My dad is a monster, and Caleb is in his crosshairs. No way do I want Caleb suffering at the hands of my father.

The thought of my dad ruining Caleb's life hurts worse than the thought of Caleb leaving.

I have to let him go.

The tears start then, and they're not pretty. Huge, ugly sobs rack my body, and Caleb quickly scoops me up into his lap, his arms holding tight to me. He presses his cheek to the top of my head and I can feel the wetness from his tears as they dampen my hair. Of all the things my father has done to hurt me over the years, ripping Caleb and me apart is by far the worst.

"I won't go," he says suddenly. "I can't leave you. I'll figure something out."

But I know it's futile. In a small town like this, a cop's word is gospel, and a reputation damaged stays that way forever, even once the truth comes out. I can't let that happen to Caleb.

"No," I whisper, sitting up and gathering every shred of courage I possess. I continue speaking while the tears keep falling. "You have to go. My dad will make good on his threats. He'll hurt you. Get you arrested and thrown in jail. Ruin your reputation. I couldn't live with myself if you were hurt because of me."

He leans down, pressing his forehead against mine, dark brown eyes filled with sorrow. I can tell by his expression that he knows I'm right, that he probably knew it even before he came here tonight.

"I can't leave, Caleb." I inhale slowly, my body shaking with the effort to calm down. "Even if I wasn't only fifteen,

I couldn't leave my mom right now."

"I know," he says, nodding in agreement. "And I wouldn't want you to, especially now that she's got a chance at getting better. She needs you."

My tears have subsided, but the incredible ache in my chest remains, as I know it will for a long time to come. Every time I blink, a new tear rolls down my cheek. "I don't know how I'm going to do this without you."

"You can and you will." Caleb takes my face between both his hands. "Because you're the strongest person I've ever known. You will thrive in spite of your dad. You will help your mom because you're kind and loving. And one day, it will be *your* time, and you'll get to decide for yourself what you want to do."

"Same goes, you know?" I smile, because even though my heart is breaking, I believe in Caleb in ways I can't even begin to explain. "You'll find your place. Figure out the right path for yourself. And you'll be fantastic."

"This won't be forever." His voice is full of conviction, but deep inside the small tendril of doubt spreads, and I know it may very well be.

I nod and agree with him, even though I'm very aware that Caleb is leaving to start the next chapter in his life. He'll go to college or start a job. He'll be in a new place, and he'll meet new people… new girls. And I'll still be here. Still fifteen years-old. Still in high school. Still stuck in the same dysfunctional family.

Caleb will be living his life, and despite the fact that his absence will cut me in half, I wouldn't have it any other way. He shouldn't be stuck here in a town with nothing much to offer him except a too-young-for-him girl and her out-for-revenge father.

He should go find his destiny.

We get to our feet, knowing our time here is quickly coming to an end. I can't be out of earshot from the house for very long while Mom is inside. She wants us to have dinner together when she wakes up from her nap, and surprisingly enough, that's actually happened a couple of times lately.

Caleb is silent, and so am I. We just sort of stare at each other for a long moment, both of us aware of the agonizing reality that we are about to say goodbye, for a long, long time. If not forever. How exactly are we supposed to do that?

Instead of saying anything, he leans down and kisses me, crushing my body to his with the strength of his embrace. Knowing this is the last time, I throw every bit of myself into that kiss… all of my energy and all of my heart. I memorize every sensation so that I can recall them in the lonely moments I know lie ahead of me.

Then, without a word, Caleb turns and leaves, walking out of the grove of trees and through the other yards, never once looking back.

And I very quietly go to pieces.

2017

Flagstaff, Arizona

Caleb, age 25

Brenna, age 21

Chapter 11

CALEB

"BRENNA." ONE WORD is all I manage. Just her name. And suddenly my heart feels like it's outside my chest, out in the open for everyone to see.

"Hi Caleb." Her voice is soft, tentative, like she's unsure what my reaction will be.

I'm not sure what my reaction will be. Standing here like a speechless fool is a definite possibility, as is grabbing her and crushing her in my arms. I've also given thought to turning around and walking out the back of the building, just to avoid humiliating myself further.

But she's *here*. Brenna, *my* Brenna, is here. Whatever the circumstances that brought her here, I can't behave like an idiot.

So I smile, because, really, what else can I do? This isn't some random pretty girl. This is Brenna.

"What are you doing here?" I ask. I realize after the fact that those words sound a bit accusatory, but I hope the stupid grin on my face conveys that I'm anything but irritated.

Her eyes dart around the lobby, and I remember that we're not alone. The entire Resolution crew is here – well, minus Rachelle's husband Gabe and Bing's fiancee Kristy – and they're all looking at us with their mouths hanging open.

I should introduce her. And I will. But first I need to know what brought her here.

She looks back at me, her amber colored eyes locking on mine the same way they used to. I feel her gaze in the soles of my feet and the center of my chest.

She takes a shaky breath and says, "My mom's dead."

All the air leaves my lungs in a giant whoosh. Brenna's mom has been her entire world all her life. I see all kinds of sadness in those gorgeous eyes, and quite a bit of uncertainty, almost as if she's wondering if coming here was a mistake.

It absolutely was *not*.

Without another thought, I sit my coffee cup on Rachelle's desk, and close the distance between us. When I'm near enough, I open my arms and she all but launches herself at me.

"I'm so sorry, Bren," I whisper, holding her tight, letting her absorb whatever comfort and strength she can from me. I have no idea how long it's been since someone was strong *for* her, so I'll happily take the job.

She buries her face in my neck and says nothing, and for a long moment we stand there like that, breathing each other in, reacquainting ourselves with what it feels like to be together this way after so long.

When she steps back from me my first instinct is to keep my arm around her, to pull her to me and keep her by my side, but I stop myself. For all I know she's got a boyfriend or husband outside parking the car. A little part of my heart dies at the thought, but I have to acknowledge the possibility.

I look around the lobby at my friends… my family, really. My parents are in San Diego now, but the people in this room are every bit my family as well. My eyes land on Shane and Sydney, then move across the room to Asher. They knew who Brenna was soon as I said her name. But everyone else has no idea. Introductions are in order.

"This is Brenna Malone," I begin, eyes scanning the room. "Her brother Hunter was my best friend when I was growing up in Kentucky."

The room erupts in a chorus of *nice-to-meet-yous.* I give Brenna a quick rundown of everyone's name, and she smiles politely and greets each person. Thankfully, Shane and Asher don't let on that they know that Brenna is more than just my friend's sister.

Looking up at the clock above the counter, I notice that it's mid-afternoon and I never took a lunch break. "Have you eaten?" I ask, turning back to Brenna.

She shakes her head. "No. I came straight here from the airport."

"Rach," I call over my shoulder. "When's my next appointment?"

"Thirty minutes," she answers, looking at the computer screen. She must've already looked it up in anticipation that I was going to ask. "It's Zeb Martinez."

I give Brenna a wink. "Give me just a second."

She nods, and I step over to the counter and ask Rachelle to dial Zeb's cell number. He's a regular client. I've been working on his full sleeve, and this afternoon was supposed to be the final piece of it. We've got a good relationship, so I figure he'll be okay about rescheduling. She hands me the phone once she dials.

"Zeb," I say when he answers. "Caleb Hanson. I've had an unexpected emergency come up, and I need to reschedule. I know it's last minute, so I'll give you a sweet discount when you come back in."

As I suspected, he's totally cool with it, and even tells me the discount won't be necessary. I'll it give to him anyway, because that's just good business.

"I've got a few more this evening. Can you reschedule them for me?" I ask Rachelle.

She nods, her eyes telling me that eventually I'm going to have to give her the rest of the story about Brenna.

Quickly I step over to Shane and lower my voice so no one but him and Sydney can hear me. "How long before you head home?"

"Couple of hours."

"Do me a favor? Check my room and straighten it up if it looks like crap? I'll owe you one."

His eyes widen, and he nods.

"And make sure there are sheets on Sydney's old bed for me. I don't know what her plans are, but I'm going to offer her my room."

"Understood," he says. "No problem."

I lower my voice even more. "There's a lot I've never told you about Brenna, but once she and I are out of here, you and Asher can fill everyone else in on what you know. Maybe it'll keep Rach off my back for a while."

He nods again, and Sydney puts her hand on my shoulder. "I'll go with him and make sure everything looks nice at the townhouse."

"Thanks," I say. "Both of you."

I turn back to Brenna. She seems at bit more at ease now, and I hope that's because she realizes that I'm glad she's here.

"Let me just get my room closed up and we can grab something to eat and catch up."

"I've got your room, Caleb," Asher says from across the room. He tosses my jacket to me, and I realize he must've gone back to my room to retrieve it when I wasn't paying attention. "You go ahead. Take your time."

God, these guys. They are the best friends anyone could ever ask for.

"Thanks, man."

He gives me a smile that says he knows just how important this is to me.

I step up next to Brenna and gesture to the door. She turns back to the lobby and says, "It was nice to meet all of you, even though I'm sure I won't remember all your names tomorrow."

"No worries there," Rachelle says. "I'm sure we'll see more of you, and you can figure us all out then."

Brenna smiles and looks up at me. I hold the door open for her, and the two of us step out onto the sidewalk.

Together.

Chapter 12

BRENNA

"THERE'S A SMALL Italian place one street over," Caleb says, once we're outside. The November air is crisp, cooler than the Kentucky weather I left behind. "We can walk over there, or we can take my truck and drive somewhere else."

I look up at him, trying to keep my breathing even and my face pleasantly neutral. When he left Clayton six years ago, he was a nineteen year-old guy, legally an adult and almost a man. He'd been breathtaking then. He's even more so now. His shoulders are broader, and his chest is firmer. And don't even get me started on the beard. Wow.

After six years, to be standing next to him is so surreal. The amount of happiness currently bubbling through me is ridiculous.

"Italian's fine with me."

We step up to the cross-walk and wait for the light to change, and Caleb notices as I adjust the straps of my small backpack. "Here, let me take that."

"You don't have to," I say, but the argument dies as I feel him slip his hands between the straps and my shoulders.

"It's no problem." He hikes the navy blue backpack onto one shoulder. "Did you take a cab from the airport or rent a car?"

"I called an Uber." The light turns just as I answer, and we make our way quickly across the street.

"What about luggage?" he asks. "Is this all you have?"

"My suitcase didn't make it here. The airline said they'd deliver it to me, so I gave them the address of your shop." I stop walking, and shrug my shoulders. "I hope that was okay. I've never flown before, and it was the only address I had. Since I don't have a hotel room yet, I didn't know what else to tell them."

"It's totally fine." He places a hand on the small of my back as we begin walking again. My insides threaten to turn to jello. "I'll shoot Rachelle a text and let her know to be on the lookout."

We pass two more buildings before we get to the restaurant. The sign reads *Lucca,* and the smell as Caleb holds the door for me is incredible.

The inside of the restaurant is quaint and charming. A few of the tables are occupied, but it's not crowded. The hostess greets Caleb by name and leads us to a quiet table near the back.

"Wine?" the hostess asks.

Caleb looks at me. I shake my head. I know next to nothing about wine, so I decide to just stick to something familiar.

"Just water for me," I answer. "Thank you."

"Same," Caleb says.

She lets us know that our server will be right with us, then leaves us.

"Everything's good here," he says, not even bothering to open his menu. "They have all the regular pasta stuff, plus individual sized pizzas."

I nod, and quickly scan the menu, settling on a pizza

with grilled chicken and mushrooms. After seven hours of only airline peanuts, anything sounds delicious.

"There are a thousand things I want to ask you." He puts his elbows on the table and leans closer. "But let's start with the basics. Are you traveling alone?"

"Yes." I shrug my shoulders. "Just me."

He nods. "And you said you don't have a hotel yet, correct?"

"That's right. I was hoping you could give me a few suggestions of decent places."

He shakes his head. "You can stay at my place."

"Caleb, that's not necessary," I argue, even though my heart leaps at the prospect. "I don't want to impose."

"It's not an imposition. Shane and I share a townhouse, and right now our third bedroom is empty."

"Caleb." I start to put up a fight again, but the waitress appears and interrupts. She delivers our water glasses, and we quickly place our orders. As soon as she turns away, Caleb speaks.

"No more arguments about staying in a hotel." He picks up his glass and takes a long drink. "If you've got some reason why you don't want to stay with me, say it now, and I'll drop it. Otherwise, I'm not letting you spend money to stay in a hotel when I have room for you."

I can't help but smile. This is *so* like him… helping me, making sure I have what I need, that I'm not alone. He's so much like I remember, and yet, there's a rough edge that wasn't there before. I wonder if I'll have the chance to find out what put it there.

"I'll stay with you." I lift my own glass and take a drink to keep the giddy expression off my face. Despite the nerves that are jumping around inside me, I'm secretly thrilled at the prospect of staying at his place and having that much more time with him.

"Glad that's settled." He reaches across the table and takes my hand in his. My belly flip-flops, much the same as it did when he hugged me in the lobby of the shop earlier. After so much time, every touch from him is like lightning through my system. "When did you lose your mom?"

I swallow hard. Even though it's still difficult to talk about, throughout the entire journey of Mom's illness, Caleb is the one I longed to talk to, to confide in. And now I'm here, and he wants to listen. I feel a peace settle in my soul, one that's been missing since Caleb left six years ago.

"A month ago," I whisper. His hand squeezes mine. "Respiratory failure, which is how it usually goes with ALS." Amyotrophic Lateral Sclerosis, more commonly known as Lou Gehrig's disease, is a neurological disease that attacks the nerves that control muscle movement, eventually even the muscles that control swallowing and breathing. It had been a cruel twist of fate that just as Mom was seeing real improvement in terms of her clinical depression, she was diagnosed with ALS. "She just sort of went to sleep one day and didn't wake up."

"I'm so sorry," he says, squeezing my hand once more. "My parents kept in touch with the older lady who lived next door, Mrs. Patterson. She told us when your mom was diagnosed. I wanted to come back then, but I was afraid I might just make things worse for you. Part of me has always felt guilty for staying away."

"No, don't feel that way. If you'd tried to come back, I would've sent you away. My dad, he never really got over Hunter's death, and if you can believe it, he was even worse the more time that passed. I would've never let you put yourself in a position for him to hurt you."

"Mrs. Patterson died shortly after we found out about

your mom. My parents didn't keep in touch with anyone else from Clayton, and they moved to San Diego that same year, so I never heard anything more." He drops his head. "I should've found a way to contact you."

"Stop it, Caleb." The firmness in my voice causes him to raise his head and look me in the eye. "We said our goodbyes that day behind my house. We both knew what your leaving meant. I never expected you to wait around for me to be old enough or to pine away for me until I could get away from my dad. I wanted you to start over, to live your life."

"But you went through that all alone. With Hunter gone, it was just you. I can't imagine what it was like, caring for your mom like that." He laces his fingers through mine, pressing our palms together. "I wish I could've been there for you."

Of course, I had wished that too, but I won't ever say that to him. I know very well that staying away was the best thing for him. Knowing that he wanted to be there for me, that he grieved for me and all I'd been through, warms something in me that has been cold for a long, long time.

Everything I'd ever felt for him is right there on the tip of my tongue. Every ounce of longing I'd buried six years ago blossoms in my heart, and I can't find the words to express to him what his thoughtfulness means to me.

Our waitress arrives with our dinner, saving me from stumbling through a response that I'm certain would've been a spectacular epic fail. She places my pizza on the table, sits Caleb's lasagna in front of him, and after refilling our water glasses, leaves us alone again.

For several minutes we eat in silence. The food is delicious, the perfect combination of flavor and comfort, and I take the opportunity to appreciate the beauty of being in

Caleb's presence again.

"How are you?" he asks, putting his fork down and looking across at me. "Since losing your mom?"

"I'm okay." I finish off my piece of pizza and take a drink. "I mean, considering everything, I'm doing okay. I miss her every day, but her life was hard. ALS made it harder. She's at peace finally, and that gives me peace, too."

"Does your dad know you're here?"

I shake my head. "I knew eventually Mom would be gone, and I needed to have a plan. I've been putting money away for a couple of years so I'd have enough to start over somewhere, and a few months before Mom died I got a new cell phone that Dad knows nothing about."

"Do you think he'd try to cause you trouble?"

"I doubt it, but who knows. He's a retired, small town cop without a lot of friends. It's not like he could do anything to stop me. I just didn't want to deal with whatever bullshit he'd have to say about me leaving, so I left him a note, and walked out before he got out of bed."

"Wow." Caleb leans back in his chair. "I'm sure the past six years with him haven't been easy. Eventually you'll have to tell me about it. But let's not waste anymore time tonight talking about him."

I smile, and grab my last piece of my pizza. "Agreed."

Caleb goes back to his lasagna as well, and for a while we talk about the people I met back at the tattoo shop. I learn that Asher and Grace just got married a few months ago, and that Rachelle eloped with her husband Gabe over New Years. Bing is engaged to a lawyer named Kristy, who has a little boy named Ezra, and that Shane and Sydney fell in love after Grace and Asher's wedding.

I enjoy hearing about his friends, and it's obvious that these people are incredibly important to him. He found his place, just like I knew he would, and I know that letting him go six years ago was the right thing to do.

He orders tiramisu with two spoons, and insists on paying when the check arrives, even though I assure him that I'm okay financially.

"I never got to buy you dinner in Clayton," he says, his chocolate eyes soft as they land on mine. "Let me do it now."

And how can I argue with that?

Chapter 13

CALEB

BRENNA AND I linger over our dessert. My appointments have all been rescheduled, so I'm in no hurry, and though the crowd at Lucca is picking up as the dinner hour gets nearer, there are still several empty tables. I realize that she's coming home with me, but we've created a cozy bubble here in the restaurant, and I'm reluctant to leave the comfort and laughter that's buzzing between us right now.

I really want to know more about the past six years of Brenna's life. How did she manage after her mom was diagnosed with ALS? Was her dad any help at all, or did he abandon her yet again to deal with all her mom's needs? But I put off those questions for another time.

"You said you'd made plans," I say, steering us to what I hope is a safe topic. "You mind sharing?"

"You remember me mentioning Mom's cousin?" She relaxes back into her chair and absently toys with the strands of curly brown hair that hang over her shoulder. "The one from Seattle, who flew in when Hunter died?"

"I remember." As long as I live I'll never forget those nights spent in her backyard. We'd both been devastated by Hunter's death, and our young, broken hearts had clung to each other to drown out the pain. It hadn't been smart. I knew it then, and I know it now. But looking at her now, I

367

can't help but believe those feelings had been real, although incredibly ill-timed.

"We kept in touch pretty regularly after that. She came to visit several times. When Mom was diagnosed, she came more often. I think she realized how useless Dad was." She shakes her head at the memory of her father's lack of interest in anything having to do with his family. I know it's pointless, but I'd still like to slam my fist directly into his face. "She and her husband own a hotel, one of those trendy, boutique style places. She told me when I was ready to move, there would be a job for me there, along with a place to live there in the hotel."

"So you're going to Seattle?" I ask, dread landing heavy in my heart. She just got here. She can't be leaving already.

Brenna nods, and I feel a kind of misery I've only known once before in my life: when I left her six years ago.

"I told her I'd be there by next week," she says. "I wanted to catch up with you first. I didn't mean for you to have to cancel your appointments."

"Don't worry about that. I'll get them rescheduled." My phone buzzes with an incoming text, so I pick up to look. "Rachelle says your luggage arrived. Why don't we walk over and pick it up, then I'll drive you over to my place so you can get settled in."

As we leave the restaurant and head back toward Resolution I decide that if she's only going to be her for a few days, I'm going to make the most of them. We're going to talk about Hunter and about her life after I left Clayton. She's going to get to know all my friends and see the family we've all become. And if nothing else, before she leaves for Seattle, she'll know that what I felt for her when we were teenagers was real, and that she can always count on me.

SHANE AND SYDNEY are just coming out of the townhouse when Brenna and I pull into the parking lot, which means hopefully my room is straightened up enough that I won't look like a slob when I take Brenna up there.

"Where are you two headed?" I ask, when we meet them coming down the steps.

"Grocery shopping," Sydney says. "I'm out of coffee, which is kind of an emergency for me."

"I'm tagging along." Shane gives me a nod. "Then I'll hang at Syd's place for a while."

So they're giving me more time alone with Brenna. Sweet.

Shane continues. "Rachelle said to tell you that you're first appointment's at eleven tomorrow, in case you hadn't looked at the schedule yet."

"Should I get a rental car?" Brenna asks.

"Not necessary." I turn my head toward her, still so astounded that she's here. "I can grab a ride in with Shane and leave you my truck."

Shane and Sydney say their goodbyes, then hop in their respective cars and take off. I unlock the door and hold it while Brenna steps inside. I drop her bag and backpack by the steps and lead her down the hall.

"This is Shane's room," I say, pointing toward his bedroom door. "And across the hall is the bathroom."

When we reach the back of the house, the layout is pretty self explanatory. One big, open space, kitchen to the left and living room to the right.

Brenna points to the door off the kitchen. "Is that the spare room I'm sleeping in?"

"That's the spare room," I tell her. "But I'm sleeping

there. I'm giving you my room."

"Caleb, no," she argues. "You don't need to give up your room."

I shake my head. "No arguments. Upstairs is just the bedroom and another bathroom, so you'll have plenty of privacy. I'd have let Sydney use the upstairs when she stayed with us earlier this year, but Shane had her moved into the spare room before I even knew she was here. Plus, I think he liked having her downstairs close to him."

Brenna nods, a small smile on her face, and says, "Okay."

I gesture to the living room, inviting her to have a seat. She sits on one end of the couch, and I move to occupy the opposite end. She seems unsure what to say or what to do, so I decide to ask what I've been wondering since the day I left Clayton six years ago.

"While we've got the place to ourselves," I begin, "would you tell me what happened after I left? What was life like for you?"

Chapter 14

BRENNA

"IT WAS ABOUT like you'd imagine." No sense sugar coating it with Caleb. He knows exactly what my dad is like. "Dad pretty much stayed in his own world, and I took care of Mom. It seemed he had even less use for me after the big blow up with you."

"I'm so sorry about how that all went down," Caleb says. "I've always felt really guilty about the fact that I got out of town and away from your dad's bullshit, and you had to stay there live with it."

I shake my head. "You had to go, Caleb. We both knew it. And we both knew I couldn't leave. Not only was I just fifteen, I couldn't leave Mom."

Caleb starts to argue again, but I cut him off.

"Stop." My voice is firm, leaving no room for negotiation. "Let's not relive that last conversation we had. Please." Because truly, my heart could not take that.

Caleb nods. "Your mom, did she get some help for her depression?"

"She did. Once the doctor got involved and Dad agreed to let him treat her, she started on some antidepressants and other vitamin supplements that helped. She still had her down times, but they were a bit less frequent and not as severe. And she seemed to enjoy the times in between more than she did before. It was good. We had a few good years together, she and I. I'm grateful for that."

His chocolate brown eyes soften, and he smiles. "I'm so glad. The two of you deserved that."

Part of me still can't believe I'm sitting here with him. In many ways those last few days with him in Clayton seem like yesterday, the memories imprinted in my brain and my heart forever. In other ways, it seems like a lifetime that I've been without him, feeling like a piece of my heart was missing. After just a few short hours with him, I don't know how I'll ever be able to leave for Seattle next week.

I force myself not think about leaving, and just enjoy these moments with him. "Mom wanted me to go away to college. She never talked with me about Dad and the way he treated us, but I know she was aware. How could she not be? She really encouraged me to look at colleges all over the country. She promised me she'd be okay. I was starting to believe her. She was doing so much better, and she had a good counselor and a support group she was a part of. I started to get really excited about going away, starting over somewhere new. I'd even been accepted to several places. Then, just before I graduated, she was diagnosed with ALS. I knew I couldn't leave her. She tried to convince me to go, but I knew Dad wouldn't take care of her. That eventually he'd just put her in a nursing home so he didn't have to deal with her at all. I couldn't do that to her." I look across the couch and notice the way his dark hair falls across his forehead, wishing I could run my hands through it. "So I stayed."

"Yeah. You couldn't leave. I totally get that."

"I did some online classes through the community college. Mostly just some general education stuff, but when I go back to school eventually hopefully it'll give me leg up."

"How did you handle your mom's illness?" he asks. "With no help from your dad."

I take a deep breath, and figure there's no reason to hold back with Caleb. "It sucked. Majorly. Most of the time I felt like I was the only one who was grieving the decline in her health or the fact that her illness was terminal. Dad gave me money each week to take care of all Mom's expenses, but that was the extent of his involvement. He didn't even ask how she was doing."

"Shit," Caleb spits out. "Not that I'm surprised. I just hoped for better for you. No wonder you left with only a note for him."

"What about you?" I ask, wanting to get away from talking about my dad. "What have the last six years been like for you?"

Caleb sighs. "At first it was pretty boring and lonely. Phoenix was this huge city, but I was all alone, or at least it felt that way. I started working for a contracting company, painting houses. Eventually word got out that I could really paint, and someone hired me to do a mural on the wall of their nursery. That job lead to another, and pretty soon I was doing a lot of baby nurseries."

I can't help the giggle that escapes me. "I can't picture you painting a princess mural."

"I did," he says with a wink. "Several, actually. And they were damn good."

"How'd you wind up here?"

"Tattooing was always in the back of my mind. Eventually I worked up enough nerve to put together a portfolio and hit the pavement looking for an apprenticeship. Bing and I clicked right away, so when he offered, I accepted."

"Bing's the owner, right?"

He nods and shifts on the couch, stretching his arm along the back of it. My elbow is propped on the back as well, and if I lowered my arm I could put my hand on his. The temptation is strong. *Really* strong.

"The dude with the buzz cut hair you met this afternoon. Super guy. Getting married in February."

"When did you move to Flagstaff?" I ask, still fighting the intense urge to hold his hand.

"Couple years after I left Clayton," he replies. "By that time I was twenty-one and it was high time I moved out of my parents' house and started my own life." His foot slides across the floor and nudges mine playfully. "It took me a while to get motivated and get my shit together after leaving you behind."

"Caleb." My voice takes on a reprimanding tone. "No regrets. We did what we had to do."

"I should've figured out a way to keep in touch with you," he says with a sad smile. "At least a little bit."

"It would've killed us both," I counter. "As much as I wanted to stay in contact with you, I'm not sure my heart could've handled it. The clean break was brutal, but it was best."

He sighs, heavy and deep. "I know you're right. But it still cuts me in half, knowing what you went through all alone."

I shrug my shoulders, not because the hurt and disappointment I lived with don't matter, but because I chose my own path, knowing full well what awaited me. I chose it knowing that Caleb would be safe from my father and I would be there for my mom when she needed me most. I also chose it knowing that it wouldn't be forever, and that eventually the time would be right for me to strike out on my own. I never imagined it would come because of my mother's death, but it had, and despite the pain that her absence caused, I couldn't help but feel some comfort that she was free of the pain – both physical and emotional – that she'd had to endure.

"I'm here now," I whispered, those three words full of hope for all kinds of things I couldn't even express.

"Yeah." His voice is soft, the warmth of it surrounding me. "You are. I do have one question, though. Why didn't you let me know you were coming?"

Chapter 15

CALEB

A SLIGHT BLUSH works its way from her neck to her cheeks, and I can tell that whatever the answer to my question is, it makes her uncomfortable. But then the corner of her mouth kicks up a bit, and she speaks.

"It's silly, really," she says, dropping her eyes to the floor. Her next words are so soft I almost don't catch them, but when I do, they nearly stop my heart. "I was afraid maybe you'd be married."

All day I've been wondering if her feelings are the same – or even close to the same – as they were six years ago. For me, what I felt for her never went away. It just got buried underneath a crap ton of stuff I did to try and forget, and under the knowledge that letting her go meant that she might never come back to me. But if she'd been afraid I'd gotten married...

I force myself to maintain a light, neutral expression. "Obviously not married."

She smiles, and some of the tension that began when she made that admission eases up. "I was afraid if I got in touch and told you I wanted to see you, that you might not want to see me for some reason. Maybe because you were married, or maybe you just didn't want to revisit the past. I couldn't tell much about you from the short bio on

Resolution's website, and you are annoyingly absent from all social media, so I had no way of finding out. I told myself I'd just show up and surprise you, and if it seemed like seeing me wasn't something you really wanted, I'd just say hi, give you a brief catch-up conversation, then go on to Seattle straight away."

"So you didn't call because you were afraid I'd tell you not to come?" How could she have thought for a second that I wouldn't want to see her?

"It sounds ridiculous now. I know it does. But I guess I sort of have a fear of rejection. Some kind of 'daddy issues' probably. At least I'm aware of it, though, and I choose how I handle it."

I scoot a little closer so that I can reach her arm where it rests on the back of the couch. "You know I'm happy to see you, right? Like, insanely happy."

The blush reappears on her cheeks, and her lips break out in a brilliant smile. "It's mutual."

For several seconds we just stare at each other, lost in the wonder and astonishment of being together again after six long years. I'm not sure what the future holds, or what her presence here means, but it's infinitely better than the years spent apart, with no contact whatsoever. Especially knowing that she's free to go where she wants and do what she wants.

The spell is broken when Brenna yawns. A look at my cell tells me that even though it's not late by my standards, for someone who spent a good chunk of the day traveling and who is more than likely feeling the fact that the time zone she left this morning is three hours ahead of this one, it probably feels like the dead of night.

"You're exhausted." I stand up and reach for her hand. "I shouldn't have kept you up talking."

She shakes her head. "No. Don't be sorry about that. I'm thrilled to be able to talk to you finally."

"Well, you're not leaving first thing in the morning, I assume, so we'll have more time to catch up once you've slept."

She takes my hand and I help her to her feet, the feel of her palm against mine creating a warmth that spreads all the way to the soles of my feet.

"Glad to know you're hanging around for a bit." I lead her gently back down the hall to where I left her bags by the steps. "Let me get you settled upstairs and you can crash."

In my room, I'm ecstatic to see that Shane and Sydney picked up the random tee shirts and jeans that had been scattered on the floor, and a quick peek into the bathroom tells me that my deodorant, toothbrush, and various other items have been put in the medicine cabinet rather than being piled on the vanity.

I owe the two of them big time.

I place Brenna's bags on the bed, and she sits down beside them. "It's really nice of you to give up your room for me."

"Just want you to be comfortable while you're here." The words *while you're here* taste bitter coming out of my mouth, and for the first time I admit to myself that I don't want her to go. Crazy, she's only been in Flagstaff part of the day, and already I don't want to think about her leaving.

I reign in those thoughts and tell myself to get a handle on my emotions. The last thing I want to do is scare her off when she just got here.

"I'm just going to grab a few things so that if I'm up before you in the morning I don't have to come in and disturb you."

Pulling open the middle drawer of my dresser, I grab a clean pair of jeans and a tee shirt. From the top drawer, I take a pair of socks and boxer briefs. In the bathroom I grab my toothbrush, and figure that I can use whatever toothpaste and soap Shane has in the downstairs bathroom. As an afterthought, I slide open the closet door, kick the dirty laundry out of the way, and grab the black Chucks from the floor.

"I'm all set." I turn back to face her, clothes and shoes in one arm. With my free hand I reach in my pocket for my cell and toss it to her. "Put your number in, then text yourself from my phone so you'll have my number. If you need anything during the night, or anytime while you're in town, all you have to do is call or text."

When she finishes, she stands and brings the phone back to me. I slip it back into my pocket, say goodnight, and walk toward the door.

"Caleb." Her soft voice stops me and I turn back to her.

Without a word, she walks to me and slips her arms around my torso, her face laying flush against my chest. The arm not holding my clothes envelops her. It's so natural I don't even have to think about it. Bending my head, I put my cheek on the top of her head, the softness of her hair a balm to the callouses that have built up on my heart during the past six years.

"I've missed you." Her voice is quiet, uncertain almost, like she doesn't know how I'm going to respond.

Everything in me wants to jump and shout in victory at the knowledge that after all this time she still misses me.

I tamp down on my enthusiasm and answer her as honestly as I possibly can. "I've missed you too, Bren." I place a kiss on the top of her head. "So much."

Chapter 16

BRENNA

I HEAR CALEB moving around downstairs, and I wonder how he normally spends his evenings. Does he go on a lot of dates? Does he casually hook-up on a regular basis?

I hate the thoughts of both, so I make myself stop pondering such dumb ideas. It's not like he's been living in a cave since he left Clayton. Of course there have been girls in his life. I managed a few dates myself over the years, but nothing that even came close to matching what I feel for Caleb.

For a split second I consider going back downstairs to be with him, because seriously, I can't get enough of being in the same room with him, but my eyelids are growing heavier with every blink, and I know my body is about to collapse in need of sleep.

I unzip my bag and dig around, looking for something to sleep in. I've just put my hand on a pair of polka-dotted pajama bottoms when an idea occurs to me. A wicked idea. But a great idea.

Walking to the dresser, I slide it open silently. I look for a long moment, then reach in and pull out a tee shirt, disturbing the rest of the clothes as little as possible. Satisfied that he'll never know, I stand up and take a look at the shirt I've just commandeered.

It's red, but it's so worn that it's almost heathery looking. The fabric is soft, and across the chest it says "Resolution" in a fancy scroll that I assume mimics some kind of lettering commonly used in tattooing. Slowly, I bring the shirt to my face and inhale. The shirt smells fresh, like laundry detergent. I'd noticed a similar, but faint scent, a moment ago when I hugged him.

I make quick work of brushing my teeth and washing my face. I throw my pajama pants and tank top on the bed just in case I need to do a quick change. Then I undress and slide Caleb's tee shirt over my head.

I close my eyes and imagine the way it felt to be in his arms tonight. I call to mind the memory of his lips on mine. It's stupid, I know. It's been six years and who knows what's different inside him when it comes to his feelings toward me, but I can't help myself. It's possible this is as close as I'm ever going to be to him again, and I want to take full advantage.

I pull back the covers and lay down in his bed, resting my head on a pillow that also smells like him. The feel and the scent of him surrounds me, and before I know it I'm drifting off to sleep, more at peace than I ever remember feeling.

✧   ✧   ✧

I'M AWAKE REALLY early, thanks to my body still functioning mostly on the Eastern time zone, rather than the Pacific. I take the opportunity to shower and put myself together so I look a bit more like myself, and less like someone who spent half a day on airplanes and rushing through airports. I stash Caleb's shirt in the bottom of my bag and refuse to think too much about how juvenile I'm being.

Dressed in a pair of skinny jeans and an oversized sweater, I make my way downstairs. I'd have bet money that I was the first one up, but the scent of coffee tells me I'm not. When I turn toward the kitchen, I see Caleb's roommate, Shane, pouring a cup.

"Morning," he says when he notices me. "Coffee?"

I smile. "Please."

He takes another mug from the cabinet and pours it full. "Milk or sugar?"

I shake my head. "Black is fine."

He takes a seat at the bar and nods to the seat across from him, inviting me to join.

"I didn't figure any of you for morning people," I say, sliding onto the barstool.

Shane shrugs his shoulders. "Most days I wish I wasn't, but it can't be helped." He inclines his head toward the door I know leads to the room where Caleb's sleeping. "Him, not so much. If we wake him up he'll probably give us the look of death."

I laugh, silently of course. "Well, to be fair, I'm sure me showing up here yesterday has screwed up his schedule."

Shane leans across the bar and lowers his voice. "Trust me, that's not a problem for him."

I narrow my eyes, questioning his words.

"I don't know a lot about you, but I do know that you were important to him," Shane says. "I imagine you still are."

"It's been a long time," I reply. "There's a lot of water under the bridge."

Shane winks. "But there *is* a bridge, right?"

I just smile and sip my coffee. From inside the bedroom, I hear movement. Shane's eyes light up.

"Just a word of warning," he says, a bit louder than

before. "He's not nice in the mornings, especially this early. He just sort of grunts and grumbles."

"Seriously, Shane?" comes Caleb's voice from the bedroom door. "Throwing me under the bus already?"

I turn his way and very nearly swallow my tongue. In the doorway is a shirtless Caleb, one arm braced on the door facing above his head, wearing nothing but a pair of low-slung jeans. The tattoos that I saw peeking out from under the rolled up sleeves of his shirt yesterday go all the way to his shoulders, the colorful artwork winding its way across his skin like some kind of fine fabric. His torso is free of ink, but the lean muscles there are no less a work of art.

I realize I'm staring, so I quickly turn back to my coffee.

"Just keeping it real, man," Shane says.

"Morning, Bren." Caleb steps out of the room and turns toward the hallway. He looks back and pins Shane with his gaze as he nods toward the coffee pot. "There better be a cup of that left when I get out of the shower."

"See what I mean? He's a grouch!" Shane's voice calls out as Caleb ignores him, making his way to the bathroom. With Caleb out of the room, Shane returns his attention to me. "So what are you getting into while you're here?"

"No idea, honestly. I've never really been anywhere."

Shane heads to the cabinet for a bowl and a box of cereal. With a raise of his eyebrows he asks if I want to join him, but I shake my head. Coffee is enough for me this early. He makes quick work of pouring his cereal and milk, then returns to the bar and digs into his breakfast.

For several moments we're quiet. "Flagstaff is a cool city," Shane says, nearing the bottom of his cereal bowl. "Some unique restaurants and neat shops. Sydney works at a great boutique called Beautiful Things. It's just up the street from Ugly Mug, the coffee shop that Rachelle's husband, Gabe, owns."

"Sydney's your girlfriend, right?" I ask. "I met you all so quickly yesterday."

Shane nods. "The blonde standing next to me in the lobby. And Rachelle is our receptionist. The one who was behind the counter."

Slowly, but surely I was beginning to sort them all out. Hopefully by the time I saw them all again I'd have their names memorized.

Shane continues. "And if you're into more touristy stuff, there's the Lowell Observatory. If you go in the evenings they have telescope viewings. It's pretty cool. There are some pretty sweet mountain views, and a Native American monument as well. And of course, the Grand Canyon is just a little under two hours away."

"That's something I've always wanted to see," I admit.

"We'll head up there Sunday." Caleb's voice comes from behind me. I turn to see him, still shirtless, walking through the living room toward the bedroom off the kitchen. His hair is still damp, and his feet are bare, and I'm about to turn into a puddle of hormones right here. "Make a day of it."

"Sounds great!" Shane says, forcing a really cheesy grin. "I'll text everybody and let them know."

Caleb gives Shane what must be the *look of death* Shane mentioned earlier.

Shane cracks up laughing. "Kidding, dude. Totally kidding. I'm sure you two have plenty of catching up left to do. I'd never butt in on that."

Caleb grumbles under his breath – once again, Shane was right – and heads into the bedroom to finish getting dressed. I'm getting the idea that Shane enjoys giving Caleb a hard time. I find it all very endearing, and I'm so glad he wound up with such a warm, tight-knit group of friends. It's what I wanted for him that day in the grove of trees behind my house when I said goodbye to him.

And secretly, I adore the idea that Caleb wants to spend the day alone with me.

When he emerges from the bedroom, he's in a long sleeve black tee shirt with the name of some diner I've never heard of screen-printed across the front. It's not tight, but it clings to him in a way that accentuates the fact that this Caleb is not nineteen years-old anymore. *This* Caleb is very much a man. On his feet are the Chuck's he dug out from under the pile of dirty laundry last night.

He walks to the coffee pot and pours his cup, then comes to sit on the barstool next to me. The stools are close enough that his thigh brushes mine, and I feel my heart begin to beat faster. Proximity to Caleb seems to still have that effect on me.

"What time you heading in, Shane?" he asks.

"Around ten. You need a ride?"

"Thought I'd ride with you so I can leave Brenna my keys."

"Actually," I interrupt, before Shane can respond. "Would it be okay if I tagged along? I don't want to be in the way or anything, but it looked like maybe there were some things within walking distance. And if I needed to, I could drive your truck somewhere from there."

"You wouldn't be in the way," Caleb says. "There's a break room in the back where you could hang out, but I don't know how exciting it would be for you."

"Well, since I've never been in a tattoo shop before, it'll at least be a new experience." I shift so that I'm turned toward him. "There haven't been a lot of those for me, you know."

Caleb nods, his lips set in a firm line. He takes a deep breath before speaking again. "So we'll make sure you have plenty while you're here."

I smile at him, my heart doing it's best to beat out of my chest. For the first time in my life, I'm on my own, free to do and see what ever I want. And the fact that I'm here, and get to share it with Caleb, is so incredibly special.

"Be prepared for the onslaught, Brenna," Shane interjects, then turns to Caleb. "I mean, you know Rachelle's got a million questions, and if Brenna's at the shop while you're working on a client, she's going to pounce."

Beside me, Caleb chuckles. "Rachelle's a little bit of a mother hen to all of us."

"I'm sure I can handle it," I assure them. "It's not like I'm that interesting."

"Don't be on it." Shane finishes his cereal and loads his bowl and spoon in the dishwasher. "You have a history with Caleb, and that makes you a prime target."

Caleb cuts his glance back to me. "You don't have to talk about anything you don't want to."

"If you mean about Hunter and the rest of my family, it's okay. I can be honest without showing all the ugly parts."

"I'm not going to ask questions," Shane says, leaning on the bar and facing us both. "Naturally, I hope you'll tell me at some point, Caleb, because I do give more than two shits about you." Next, he looks at me. "For now, I'll just say this. Caleb's glad you're here, Brenna. That means the rest of us are, too."

Chapter 17

BRENNA

I SPENT THE better part of an hour in the break room at Resolution before Rachelle realized I was back there. Now I'm up front with her, a chair from the waiting area dragged behind the counter, sipping a latte and nibbling on a scone that she had Asher pick up on his way in.

"So you knew Caleb when he was a kid?" she asks.

"Yes. He and my brother Hunter were best friends." I know this is opening up the subject of Hunter, but talking about it isn't so difficult anymore.

"Where's your brother now?"

"Hunter died not long after he graduated high school." Rachelle's eyes go wide in shock at the honesty of my words.

"Oh, Brenna, I'm so sorry. I shouldn't have asked. I'm so nosy sometimes. Ask the guys. They'll tell you."

I can't help but give her a small smile. "It's fine. Don't worry. I don't mind talking about it."

Her gaze softens, and she reaches to pat my hand. "Still. It can't be easy."

"He drove drunk." I stop and let that sink in for a moment, breathing deep before I continue. "Hunter and I, we didn't have the ideal family or childhood. Life wasn't rosy for us. That's not an excuse for his behavior, but it gives a little context. He started the summer before his senior year, I'm sure to ease the pain or to make himself forget. Caleb and I tried for months to help, but we were just kids really. Caleb was nineteen, and had graduated the year before Hunter. I was just fifteen. The night it happened, we begged him not to drive. We even tried to take his keys from him. But he got behind the wheel anyway. We followed him. We saw it happen."

"How terrible for you both." Tears shimmer in her eyes, but the phone rings before she can say more.

She answers the call and schedules an appointment for Bing, then replaces the receiver. "I'm so sorry. I can see why you and Caleb are bonded so tightly now. It was obvious yesterday that there's more than just old friendship between you. Now I get it."

Hunter's death is part of it, but not all.

"It was over six years ago. I've had time to deal with it."

"I doubt you ever get over something like that."

I shake my head. "No, I don't think you do. It just becomes a part of the landscape of your life, and you go on living in a new normal."

"Okay," she says, sitting up straighter and putting a big smile on her face. "New subject. What can we talk about that's happy?"

I eye the large photo books on the counter above us. I'm certain those are portfolios, and one of them belongs to Caleb. "Can I see Caleb's work?"

"Oh my gosh, yes!" Rachelle exclaims, standing up to look through the albums until she finds his. "He's ridiculously talented."

I open the portfolio and immediately lose my breath. His work is exquisite. I'm not an artist, but even I can tell that his skill with shading gives a realistic, three-dimensional quality to the artwork he creates. There are daggers and chains, skulls and pin-up girls, and even an eagle with its wings spread across a guy's back. But what I'm drawn to most are the pictures in the back. Granted, they're clearly feminine based on the sizes of the ankles, wrists and shoulder blades they're placed on, but it's the way the images seem to just float on the skin that has me mesmerized.

I'm running my fingers lovingly across a gorgeous tattoo of a purple Iris when Rachelle finishes up with Shane's client, taking his payment and handing him a sheet of instructions for taking care of the ink work.

"Those are watercolor," she says. "It's a different technique than typical tattooing. Caleb's really good at it."

"Everything looks so soft."

"That's because there's no outlining," she points out. "The color just sort of fades in."

"Rachelle will get you all taken care of," Caleb says, walking into the reception area with his client. "Thanks again for coming in."

The fortyish man shakes Caleb's hand and tells him more than once how pleased he is with the artwork. Since there are other tattoos visible on his skin, I imagine this won't be his last visit with Caleb.

"Rachelle wearing you out yet?" he asks me, winking at Rachelle when she feigns shock.

"Not at all," I reply. I nod my head toward the open portfolio. "I've just been admiring your work."

One corner of his mouth lifts, his eyelids drop. I can tell he's pleased that I like his work. "I've got a break right now if you want to take a look at a tattoo station."

I smile. I wanted new experiences. Wish granted.

✧   ✧   ✧

CALEB ORDERS SANDWICHES from a nearby deli and we eat a late lunch eat together in the break room. It's quick, eaten quickly between clients, but I can't remember the last time I enjoyed lunch so much. So far, this day has been better than anything I could've imagined. Rachelle embraced me like we'd known each other all our lives. Bing and Asher both greeted me and told me they were happy I'd be hanging out with them today. Of course, Shane had been the same jolly guy I encountered over coffee this morning.

I seriously can't get over these people and how they interact with each other, how they care about and support each other. It's really beautiful, and, again, I find myself so incredibly thankful that Caleb landed here.

We've just finished our sandwiches, and Caleb is throwing our trash away, when Grace, Asher's wife, and Sydney, Shane's girlfriend, open the door to the break room.

"We're here," Grace says. "Just as you requested."

I know she's not talking to me, so I look at Caleb.

"Thanks ladies." He looks at me and wiggles his eyebrows.

"What's going on?" I push up from my chair and turn to face him.

"It's a surprise," he replies, moving to stand right in front of me. "For you."

"Caleb, what did you do?"

"Have fun." He winks, then walks right out of the room.

Grace and Sydney both take seats at the table, so I do as well, completely confused about what is happening.

Grace speaks first. "It was super quick when we met

yesterday, but I'm Grace, and I'm really happy to meet you."

"And I'm Sydney. We're really glad you're here."

"We've been instructed to pamper you," Grace explains.

"Pamper me?" I'm lost. "I don't understand."

"Let me explain," Sydney says. "I work at a clothing boutique, and Grace is a cosmetologist. It's like girl nirvana. Caleb told us to make sure you got the star treatment."

"His exact words," Grace pipes up, "were 'definitely a massage and whatever else you do at the salon that she wants, and send the bill to me'."

"And to me," Sydney adds, "his exact words were 'get her suited up for a trip to the Grand Canyon this weekend, and whatever fancy outfit she likes, with all the stuff that goes with it, and send the bill to me'."

I'm stunned. "You're kidding me."

"Nope," they say in unison.

"This is too much," I argue. "He can't do this."

I stand up, intending to march right up to him and insist he stop this craziness. The girls won't let me.

"Listen, Brenna," Sydney begins. "I know this probably seems overwhelming, but what you don't understand is that this is the most spark we've seen out of Caleb in, well, forever."

"Caleb is a really private person," Grace adds. "In fact, other than Asher, Shane, and Sydney, none of the rest of us even knew you existed until yesterday. We didn't know anything about his life in Kentucky. Now you're here, and there's life in his eyes that none of us have ever seen."

"I don't know the whole story with you two, and I don't expect you to tell me." Sydney steps closer. "But I do know that Caleb is a special guy, one we all adore and want to see happy. This will make him happy, Brenna. Let him do this for you."

It's the knowledge that this will make Caleb happy that has me walking out the back of Resolution with two girls I barely know, about to experience my very first girls' day.

Another new experience.

Thanks to Caleb.

Chapter 18

CALEB

PIZZA AND BEER have been consumed, but Asher, Shane, and I are still sitting at the bar, rather than in the living room in front of the Xbox. The girls are still out treating Brenna to the day of pampering I arranged. Naturally, our conversation has turned to her, and if I'm honest with myself, I'm glad. I need to talk about her.

"I told you this morning I wasn't asking any questions," Shane says, tipping his beer bottle in my direction, "but I'm hoping since it's just us, you'll decide to give us the details."

"Her showing up here yesterday has to have thrown you for a loop," Asher adds.

"Nearly caused a heart attack," I say, downing the last of my beer. I set the bottle down and look across the table at my friends. What they know about Brenna is only the tip of the iceberg, and for the first time since I left Clayton, I realize I'm ready to tell the whole story. Brenna's appearance here yesterday spurred something inside me, a need to acknowledge what we felt, what happened. "But in a good way."

"Yeah, I could tell you were all kinds of happy." Shane flips the pizza box closed and leans his elbows onto the table. "That hug between you two in the lobby of the shop was intense."

"Brenna's brother, Hunter, was a year behind me in school, but when I moved to Clayton we became best friends pretty quickly." I take a deep breath, mentally preparing to revisit those memories. "Brenna's four years younger than me, so we never would've met had it not been for Hunter. Their family situation wasn't great. Their mom suffered from severe depression, and their dad was a local cop, a complete asshole who paid no attention to his family and refused to get his wife the help she needed. Hunter and Brenna basically fended for themselves all the time."

Shane bites out a curse, and Asher just shakes his head.

"I was just thirteen when I got to know them," I continue, "so I didn't really know what to do to help. I just kept hanging around, making sure they had some company while their dad ignored them and their mom slept most of her life away."

"So Hunter was your best friend," Shane says. "Where does this crazy connection with Brenna come in?"

"I don't even know when my feelings for her changed from simple friendship to something more." I take a moment, remembering. "Sometimes I think maybe I've loved her from the beginning, although at first it was a different kind of love. She was this little nine year-old girl who was smart and sweet, and her dad treated her like garbage. I just wanted to take away some of that sting, you know?"

"I think that's natural," Asher says. "To want to help when you see a child mistreated."

"Somewhere along the way I started to look at her differently," I go on. "Not just as Hunter's little sister, but as a girl. I told myself I was an idiot for even entertaining the idea. I mean, she was only thirteen or fourteen years old at the time, and I was almost grown. But she'd had to grow up fast living in that family, and she never seemed that much younger than me."

"Make sense," Shane says. "Once I got over my rebellion into drugs, I didn't feel like a kid anymore. It was like I'd seen some of the bad the world had to offer and decided I'd be better equipped to deal with it if I just went ahead and grew the hell up."

"Hunter started drinking really heavily his last year in high school." I drop my head, letting it sag from my shoulders, and lift my hand to knead the muscles at the base of my neck. Revisiting Hunter's death is always hard. "I'd graduated the year before, but I hung around Clayton so he and I could go off to college together."

"Clearly that didn't happen." Asher's tone tells me he sees where this story is headed.

"Brenna and I, we tried to intervene. We rescued him more times that I want to remember. He was always so sorry the next day, and he'd promise never to do it again."

Shane sighs and shakes his head, more than a little aware of how stories of addiction can play out.

"The summer after he graduated things weren't any better. I kept thinking if I could just keep him together until we went to college, that maybe getting away from his dad would solve the problem. I realize now that it wouldn't have, but I was just nineteen and had no idea what I was dealing with."

"There's no saving someone who doesn't want to be saved," Shane says. He knows that better than anyone.

"The night he died, Brenna and I tried everything to stop him from driving, but it was no use. He wouldn't listen to reason, and we couldn't get his keys away from him. We jumped in my car and followed him." I almost wish I had another drink of my beer left as I prepare to finish the story. "He ran a stop sign and got hit in the driver's side by a big farm truck. Brenna and I watched it happen."

"Man," Asher says, shaking his head. "That's awful."

"Completely," Shane agrees.

"It was right after that when things with Brenna and me changed. It was like we'd been choosing to ignore our feelings for the sake of propriety, but after Hunter died, acting on our feelings seemed like the only logical response. I mean, who knew if we were even going to wake up the next morning, so what did it matter if I kissed her in the car when I drove her home?"

"Proof of life and all that," Shane whispers.

"Something like that." I nod my head, agreeing. "We had a couple of weeks together, if you can call sneaking in backyard visits while her dad was out of the house *together*. I had no idea how we were going to maintain any sort of relationship until she was old enough for people to think it was appropriate, but those details seemed so unimportant at the time. We were both so devastated over Hunter's death that all we could do was cling to each other, even though it was far from the smartest thing in the world."

"What happened after those couple of weeks?" Asher asks.

"Her dad came home early one night." I swallow hard, the memory of that night still a painful wound. "Caught us kissing on the swing in the backyard. It was ugly. He already blamed me for Hunter's drinking, because it was easier to do that than to accept that he'd ignored his son to the point that he'd practically become an alcoholic. Then he told me that if he caught me with his daughter again he'd ruin me, that he'd use whatever resources he had as a cop to land my ass in jail. He was livid, seriously beyond crazy. I was sweating bullets. Brenna was crying and begging him to stop."

"Could he have done that?" Asher asks. "Managed to get you arrested for something you didn't do?"

"Who knows." I shrug my shoulders. "But in a small town like Clayton, nobody really questions what the police say, and people have long memories. I was nineteen and scared shitless. I knew he meant business. He could've made things really difficult for me."

"So that's why you left," Shane says. "To avoid her dad's wrath."

"My dad had been transferred to Phoenix just before Hunter died, so I moved out here with my parents."

"Couldn't have been easy leaving Brenna behind." Asher's eyes are full of sympathy. He knows some of what it's like to leave the girl you love behind when you leave home.

"Hurt like hell," I agree. "But I held out some hope that she'd find me when she was eighteen. But then her mom was diagnosed with ALS and I knew she wouldn't be able to leave."

"Because Daddy Dearest sure wasn't going to take care of Mom." Shane's voice drips with sarcasm.

"And now her mom's gone," Asher says, "and the first thing she did was come find you."

"She's got a job and a place to live waiting for her in Seattle." I watch as both their eyes widen. "With her mom's cousin."

"So she's just passing through?" Shane asks, his voice incredulous.

"What did you expect? That she was just going to show up here after six years of no contact and want to relocate to city she's never even visited so we can pick up where the left off?"

"I think that's probably exactly what she wants," Shane says, his eyebrows raised as he points his finger directly at me. "Whether she says it or not, whether she even realizes it or not, I think that's probably exactly what she wants deep down."

Asher nods in agreement. "I know this situation is all kinds of tricky, but I've got to agree with Shane. Her presence here in Flagstaff speaks volumes."

"Question is, what do you want?" Shane asks.

I don't answer. I can't. The things I want where Brenna is concerned go beyond words. And I'm scared to death to speak them out loud for fear of jinxing everything.

Thankfully, they don't push.

"When's she supposed to leave?" Asher lays a supportive hand on my shoulder.

"Next week," I answer. "Thursday."

"So you've got a few days to figure things out and make a plan," Asher says, ever the logical, reasonable one of us. "You don't have to have all the answers right this minute."

Shane's phone buzzes with an incoming text. He picks it up and reads, then declares, "The girls are pulling in the parking lot. Time for Ash and me to head out."

"You guys are leaving?" I ask.

"They're in Grace's car, so I'm driving Sydney home." Shane answers.

"And I'm going home with my wife," Asher says.

"And you're leaving me here alone with Brenna." I both love them and hate them for it.

"You need the time with her, man." Asher pushes his chair back and stands up. "Whether you've got a few days or a lifetime with her, it's been six years. The two of you deserve some time to yourselves."

✧ ✧ ✧

ASHER AND SHANE meet the girls in the parking lot of the townhouse, and the four of them wave as they drive away. Brenna makes her way to the door, garment bags in hand, and I hold the door open for her to enter. Once she's inside, I take the bags from her as she turns to face me.

"Caleb," she begins, "this was too much."

For a second, I can't speak. Her hair, still a riot of dark brown curls, now has subtle streaks of caramel running through it, and her face, while not covered in make-up, seems to somehow glow from beneath the surface. All I want to do is bury my hands in her hair and put my mouth against those lips and mess her all up.

"Did you have fun?" I ask, dodging her admonishment about the day being too extravagant.

She rolls her eyes and grins. "Of course I did."

"Then it wasn't too much."

"I can't even imagine what the price tag on all this stuff was."

I shake my head and chuckle under my breath. Typical Brenna, worrying about everything and everyone else.

"Brenna, I make good money doing what I do. I'm not rich by any stretch of the imagination, but I have plenty." I shift the garment bags to my other hand and take a step closer to her. "I live pretty simple, and I don't need a lot. My truck is nothing special, and it's paid for. This townhouse is a nice place to live, but it's not lavish. Plus, I share the rent and expenses with Shane, and up until a few months ago, with Asher as well. Money's not an issue for me, so it was nice to have someone worth spending some of it on." She starts to argue with me again, but I cut her off.

"I can't imagine what the last three years have been like for you, caring for you mom during terminal illness, especially considering the situation with your dad. You deserved a day that was all about *you*."

Her eyelids lower, and she breathes deep. "Thank you."

"You're welcome." I reach out and lift her chin so she's looking at me. "It was my pleasure."

"You're so much like I remember," she whispers. "Taking on other people's burdens like your own."

I haven't felt like that version of myself in a long time. Losing Hunter, then Brenna, dug a hole in my heart, one that never really healed properly. It just covered over with scar tissue. It's why I've maintained a certain amount of distance between me and the people I care about. It's why I've never shared much of anything with them about my past in Kentucky. Talking about it would make it real, and I just wanted to forget it every happened.

Fat lot of good that did me, because standing here in front of Brenna, my feelings for her are every bit as real as they were six years ago. And strangely enough, I'm starting to feel like *that* Caleb again. The one who helped his friends through all sorts of dysfunctional family drama, then walked away to keep the peace in her family, even though it broke his heart.

I nod in the direction of the living room. "Watch a movie with me?"

"Sure." Her smile widens, and her eyes light up. "Just let me go hang these things up and put on something more comfortable."

I barely stifle a groan at the thought of her in something *more comfortable*, but somehow manage to keep it inside as I had the garment bags over.

"Comedy, romance, mystery?" I ask.

She stops halfway up the steps. "Surprise me. Just not horror."

Odd, how I can know so little about her and yet love her the way I do. And yes, I figure I might as well admit – at least to myself – that I do love Brenna, and I have for as long as I can remember. I guess knowing someone's favorite color or favorite movie and knowing their heart are two different things. And regardless of all the things I don't know about Brenna, I know her heart. And she knows mine.

I've just settled on a rom-com that I think she'll enjoy when she returns to the living room wearing dark grey pajama bottoms and a baby pink tank top. My mouth practically waters, but I force myself to act normal.

"Did you have dinner yet?" I gesture to the table where the pizza box sits. "There's pizza left."

"Thanks, but Grace and Sydney took me to Ugly Mug after we finished at the boutique."

"It's one of our regular haunts," I say.

"I met Gabe," she replies. "Rachelle's husband. He seems nice."

"He is," I agree. "Runs a top-notch business."

For a moment we stand there, two feet apart but joined by some invisible bond that pulls at every cell in my body. I may have less than a week with her, so I know I can't waste a minute.

"Let's sit," I say, taking her hand and walking toward the sofa.

Before I sit, I pick up the remote and hit play, starting the movie. I plant myself in the corner of the couch, and Brenna takes a step to sit in the opposite corner.

But I still have hold of her hand, so I tug her back to me. She's still standing, eyes lowered to look at me.

"Sit with me." I know the pleading in my voice is giving a lot away, but I can't find it in myself to care.

I see her swallow hard, eyes darting between my face and the spot next to me on the sofa. Her hand tightens on mine, but she doesn't sit down.

"I know what you're thinking," I whisper. "I know you're wondering 'what exactly does this mean'. I don't have all the answers right now. All I know is that I want you in my arms."

Her other hand lifts to land on her chest, just above her heart. "Caleb," she breathes.

"Will you do that?" I ask. "Will you let me hold you? It's been such a long time."

Her nod is slight, almost imperceptible, but I see it. Her descent to the spot next to me is agonizingly slow, but finally she's there, her back snuggled up to my chest, as I wrap one arm around her shoulder, pulling her close, while the other hand threads her fingers through mine.

For the first several minutes of the movie, she holds herself still, almost stiff, as if she's afraid of relaxing against me. I don't force it. Now that she's next to me I'm more than content to let her move at her own pace. Eventually, though, her muscles begin to loosen and her head lays back onto my shoulder.

We don't talk, but I'm not sure we watch any of the movie either. I'm paying attention to every movement, every breath, memorizing the way she feels in my arms.

Eventually, she falls asleep in my arms, and for the first time in six years, I feel a spark of hope that maybe, just maybe, the universe is finally going to align for us.

Chapter 19

BRENNA

'M GOING TO see the Grand Canyon.

I realize that it's on practically everyone's bucket list, but seeing any of the world outside of Clayton, Kentucky was something I was almost scared to dream of, and now here I am, in Caleb Hanson's truck, heading toward the South Rim of a place I've imagined seeing all my life.

He's driving with his left hand while his right hand rests on the back of the seat directly behind me. He's been toying with my hair the whole way, and if I said it didn't have everything inside me stirred up, I'd be lying.

"Your hair looks great," he says, eyes not leaving the road. "I meant to say that the other night when you came home from the salon, but I forgot."

"Thank you." I close eyes, and just like when we were kids, I find myself drowning in his compliment. "And no worries about forgetting. It's just nice that you noticed."

"I always notice you, Bren." He tunnels his fingers deeper into the curls at the nape of my neck. "Sometimes I'm just shit at expressing stuff."

"I've never thought you were bad at it." My voice is just above a whisper. It's all I can manage with his fingertips making circles on my scalp. This new level of attention from him is both confusing and wonderful.

"Believe me. I haven't expressed nearly enough."

I hold my breath and wait for him to go on, but he doesn't. He just keeps playing with my hair, and I keep squirming in my seat, for the next twenty minutes.

He pays the vehicle entrance fee and parks in a lot near the visitor's center. I look around, expecting to see... something... but all I see are cars and trees. I had thought a giant hole in the ground would be visible, but so far I'm seeing nothing.

Caleb hops out of the truck while I'm still staring at the tree line a short distance away. He opens my door and notices the puzzled look on my face.

He grins, taking my hands and helping me out of the truck. "You thought you'd see it as soon as we pulled in, didn't you?"

"Kind of," I admit.

"I thought the same thing the first time I came here." He locks the doors, keeping my hand in his as he takes of walking toward the trees. "I think the surprise of the first view is one of the coolest things."

"Surprise?"

"Just beyond those trees," he says, nodding in their direction, "the earth opens up."

We cross a road that's thankfully free of traffic, not surprising since we're in a national park. I notice the crowds all walking away from Caleb and me. "Where are they all going?"

"One of the lookout points," he answers. "Probably Yaki or Grandview. I thought we'd take the first look without anyone else around."

We step into the trees, and a moment later my stomach drops to the soles of my feet.

"Oh!" I exclaim in a swift intake of air. My hands fly

up to my mouth, as if to express some sliver of the disbelief I'm feeling.

"Yeah," Caleb says, his voice soft as he steps behind me. "I know."

My eyes can't take it all in, but that doesn't stop me from trying. Stretched before me is the most beautiful sight I've ever seen. Colors, vibrant and striking. Shapes so magnificent they could've only been carved by nature. And the vastness…. it nearly takes my breath away.

For long moments we're silent, as my head moves in one direction, then another, and then back again, absorbing every possible detail. The way the blue sky collides with the deep reds and browns of the canyon. The tiny streak of blue that can barely be seen at the bottom as the Colorado River winds its way through.

Caleb's arms slip around my waist and he steps closer still, until my back is flush against his chest. His chin rests gently on the top of my head. The gorgeous white sweater from Beautiful Things that had been the perfect defense against the cool November temperatures now seems an inferno in the face of Caleb's body heat.

"The first time I came here was about six months after we moved," he tells me. "It was almost Christmas, and I'd been in a funk since leaving Clayton, going from work to home but nothing else, unless moping around counts. Mom and Dad wanted to do something to snap me out of it, so they planned a trip up here."

"Did it work?" I ask, my voice still a mere whisper. For some reason, it seems appropriate to talk softly while looking at such a wonder of nature and being held by the man I've loved since he was a boy.

"No." He takes a deep breath and tightens his hold on me. I bring my hands to where his rest on my stomach, and link my fingers with his. "All I could think about was how much I wished you were here with me."

"Caleb." I breathe his name and lean my head back against his shoulder.

"I don't know what the future holds for you or for me," he says. "But I know that it won't be another six years before I see you again."

Despite the beauty in front of me, I close my eyes against the moisture gathering in them. One tear trickles down my cheek, and my breath shudders. Caleb turns me to face him, his arms going immediately around my back, keeping me close.

"I'll come to Seattle." He bends down, pressing his forehead to mine. "I'll fly you to Arizona. I promise."

My heart is racing, and my mind is buzzing with all the possibilities of what he means. Does he mean he wants to maintain our friendship? Is he hinting at a relationship? Not for the first time I bemoan the fact that my twenty-one years on this planet have not prepared me in the least for navigating the tricky waters of boy-girl relationships.

What I do know is that I don't want him to say things in the emotion of the moment and regret them later.

"You don't have to make me promises, Caleb." I flatten my hands on his chest, the flannel of his shirt soft beneath my palms. "It's enough to be here with you now."

He shakes his head. "It's not enough."

I close my eyes again, pondering why I feel the need to give him a way out. Why I want to stop him from saying the things I so desperately want him to say. The love torpedoing its way through my system is telling me to stop it right now, but the logical part of my brain insists that it's too soon, and that anything that develops between us should happen slowly, so that we can be sure it's real.

"Seeing each other again after so long has both our emotions all out of whack," I say, eyes still closed. "We shouldn't say things when we're…"

His lips crash down on mine, the heat of his mouth searing as he moves against me, angling his head so he can get even closer. He traces the seam of my lips with his tongue and I open for him without a single thought to the contrary.

Somewhere in the recesses of my mind, I know that I had been having a perfectly reasonable thought process about why we shouldn't rush, why slow and steady was a better idea, but with the magic of his kiss swarming my senses, my heart has overruled everything else with a resounding *YES!*

Eventually, our kiss slows, and Caleb turns us to the side, his arms still locked tight around me, so that we can both look out over the canyon. My cheek is pressed against his chest, over his heart which beats in time to my own. The beauty of the canyon in front of me, the beauty of the man surrounding me, the beauty of the moment we're sharing, is almost too much to contain.

"I don't want to talk about Thursday," he whispers. "I want to pretend Thursday doesn't exist. And for the next few days, I want to behave like we're together. Which includes holding your hand, putting my arms around you, kissing you, whether we're alone or with the rest of the crew. You good with that?"

What else can I possibly say?

"Yes."

Chapter 20

CALEB

W E HOP THE shuttles and ride the Hermit's Rest Route, stopping at a few of the lookouts to take pictures. Eventually, we wind up at the Hermit's Rest Snack Bar, where we grab some hot chocolate and sit by the giant fireplace. Just like I told her, I hold her hand when we walk, pull her close with an arm around her shoulder, and take her lips in a kiss as we stare out at one of the breathtaking views.

To everyone around us, it appears we're on a date.

And I guess we are. Our *first* date.

On the shuttle's return route, we decide to hop off at Hopi point and watch the sun sink. Even on a semi-cloudy November day, the glow bathes the canyon with such brilliance it almost seems to be on fire.

Brenna, backdropped by the image of the sunset along horizon, is enough to make my heart explode. I'm about half a second from doing something insane, like drop to my knees and beg her to marry me and have my babies, when she breaks the silence that had settled around us.

"Will you do a tattoo for me?"

Of all the things I thought she might say, that was *so* not it. A million images run through my mind, all of them consisting of Brenna's skin under my hands. And yeah... I need to stop.

"Really?" I congratulate myself on finding my voice and not sounding like a thirteen year-old going through puberty.

She nods, but doesn't say more.

"Okay, well," I begin, wracking my brain, looking for the will to talk to her like the professional I am. "Is this something you've been thinking about for a while, or did you just decide? Because if it's something you've just decided, you should probably wait and think about it. Make sure it's really what you want."

"I've been thinking about it for a long time," she says.

"All right then. What did you have in mind?"

"A rhododendron bloom."

And suddenly it all makes sense. "For your mom."

She smiles. "You remember."

"Of course I remember." Pulling her to me, I lift one hand to caress her cheek and press a soft kiss against her lips. "The pink flower outside your mom's window. The one you took care of when she couldn't because you knew it would make her smile."

"I knew as soon as she was diagnosed that when the time came I would do something to honor her. I considered a lot of things, including doing a garden of rhododendron bushes in the park or on the kids playground. But I knew I wouldn't stay in Clayton once she was gone. I wanted something that I could take with me, wherever I went, so the idea of a tattoo was a natural fit. Then when I found out you were a tattoo artist, that settled it."

"How did you find me?" I ask, a little embarrassed that I haven't asked her before. "Not that I was trying to hide from you or anything."

She grins and lowers her eyelids. "Google."

"You googled me?" I can't help the amusement in my voice. "Seriously?"

"Not like every day," she says, laughing. "Just every so often, I'd google *Caleb Hanson Arizona* and see what came up. For a long time there was nothing. I sort of gave up hope. But one night, when I was sitting alone in my room after mom had gone to bed, I decided to try again. We were about six months into her ALS diagnosis, and she'd had a particularly bad week. Not necessarily physically, but emotionally. She'd lost so much already, and she was about to lose even more. She had some really rough spells. And I was just depleted. I needed a distraction from it all, so I thought I'd google you again and see what happened. It looked like Resolution had updated their website, and there you were. Picture and a vague bio. You looked a little different, but I knew it was you. Even with the beard."

Just like I'd hungered for every small piece of information Mrs. Patterson could give us on Brenna, Brenna had taken to the internet to try and find me. It seems we'd both had a hard time letting go of one another.

We move from our spot to wait for the next shuttle bus arrival, and I consider what it will be like to tattoo Brenna. The smart thing would be to ask Asher or one of the other guys to do it, because no doubt I'll be nervous as hell, but she asked me, and that means something. To both of us. Not to mention that there's no way I could sit back and watch anyone else – even my best friends – put their hands on her.

"Where do you want this tattoo?" I ask.

"Somewhere I can see it everyday," she says. "Maybe my wrist."

I don't know whether to thankful or sad that the wrist is a safe place and she won't have to remove any clothing. I settle on thankful, because it will make the task so much easier.

"That's a good spot," I agree. "It'll look really feminine."

"Can you do it like the ones in the back of your portfolio? Rachelle says they're watercolor style."

I nod. "I was thinking exactly that. I'll make it beautiful for you. And your mom."

IT'S DARK WHEN we pull into the back lot of Resolution. No cars around this time on a Sunday night. I'd called Bing on the way home to let him know that I'd be in the shop for a while, so he wouldn't think there'd been a break in if someone told him lights were on in the building.

Shutting the door and locking it behind us, I take Brenna's hand and lead her to my room. I flip the lights on, and turn to her and smile.

"You're sure, right?" I ask. "Because this is permanent."

"I'm sure. It's for Mom."

I nod, then sit down and get to work. It doesn't take me long to get something drawn up for her. I've been thinking about it the whole way back from the Grand Canyon, picturing the blossom, with its delicate petals playing across the soft skin of her wrist. I've imagined the pink color, and the way I'd shade it so that it will look delicate from every angle.

The finished product is a large pink bloom, slightly larger than a half dollar. The petals on the bloom are dark pink in the center, and the color gradually lightens toward the tips. A few muted green leaves form the backdrop of the flower, the edges fading slightly so they'll disappear against her skin.

Tears well in her eyes when I hand her the drawing, and she speaks in a hushed whisper. "It's perfect."

"Ready?"

Her answer is to climb onto the tattoo chair and smile. I position the chair where I need it, then create the transfer that will go onto her skin as a reference while I work.

I take several deep breaths and say a prayer before I begin. I don't like the idea of hurting her, and there's no way for this not to sting a bit. But more than that, I want to do a good job for her. I want this to be my best work.

She doesn't flinch at the first needle hit. I can't help but be proud. Her arm is still, her palm and fingers relaxed, and her breathing stays steady the entire time I work. As long as she's okay, I'm determined not to rush. I take my time, making sure each petal is perfect.

When it's done, I wipe the skin, leaving behind the image of her mom's rhododendron blossom. She sits up and studies it for such a long moment that I begin to wonder if she's disappointed.

"The purple lines will fade in a couple of days," I explain. "That's just the outline that the transfer left behind. That part's not permanent."

When she looks at me her eyes are filled with tears, but her lips are smiling. "It's beautiful," she whispers. "Even more so because you did it."

Then she leans forward and kisses me, a gentle brush of lips so soft it makes my heart ache with the enormity of everything I feel for her. In the back of my mind, Thursday looms like a dark cloud. I shove those thoughts away, and concentrate on right now, Brenna's lips on mine, my ink on her skin, and my heart in her hands.

Thursday is not today. And it's not tomorrow either.

I still have time.

Chapter 21

BRENNA

M Y TIME IN Flagstaff has been incredible. The mountains and the evergreens are breathtakingly beautiful, and the people I've come to know here are even more so. Tomorrow I fly to Seattle, to begin my job and new life there. Bittersweet feelings have been bubbling inside me all day. Gratitude for both the new start Kate, my mom's cousin, is offering me and for the wonderful time spent here with Caleb and his friends... and also sadness that my time here is coming to an end.

Everyone insisted that we have a get together tonight, a kind of send-off party for me. The plan is pizza and drinks, so while Caleb is working, I've spent several hours in his kitchen, baking cupcakes and cookies for dessert. Being back in the kitchen feels good. I've loved baking since I was a child, and I enjoyed working part time at the bakery in Clayton. But when Mom's health took its final turn for the worse, I had to give up my job in order to take care of her. I still have some tricks up my sleeve, though, thanks to the things I learned while I worked there, and I'm happy to put them to good use and share them with my new friends.

Caleb insisted on riding into work with Shane this morning and leaving me his truck for me, and it's good he did. I've got twelve more cupcakes to frost, but I've run out of cream cheese. So, I'm heading to the store to pick up supplies, with a few sample cupcakes and a couple of cookies to give him and the crew a little taste test.

Maneuvering his truck in the streets of Flagstaff takes some getting used to, but I get the hang of it quickly, and in no time I'm pulling into an angled spot across the street from the tattoo shop.

I step into the lobby just as Caleb walks a client up counter. He sees me and immediately smiles, although the happiness doesn't exactly reach his eyes. I get it. The reality of tomorrow weighs heavy on me, too.

I hang close to the door while Caleb and Rachelle finish up with the client, then make my way to the counter.

"Samples," I say, sitting the box with the cupcakes and cookies in front of Caleb. "I've got to pick up a few things to finish the last batch, so I thought I'd let you guys be my taste testers."

"Glad to," Caleb says, wiggling his eyebrows at me.

"Absolutely!" Rachelle agrees.

Lifting the top of the box, Caleb peers down at the cupcakes, and I watch a small grin lift one corner of his mouth. "Chocolate with cream cheese frosting?"

I lift one shoulder. "Maybe."

Of course I made his favorite cupcakes.

"You remember," he whispers, pulling one from the box.

"I remember everything," I whisper back. "But these are a more grown up version. Some are filled with chocolate ganache and the others with raspberry."

"I'm game for either," Rachelle declares, picking up one of the cupcakes.

Caleb grabs the other, and they each take a bite, then collectively moan in pleasure. I give myself a mental pat on the back.

"That is spectacular, Bren," Caleb says, turning his cupcake toward me so I can see that he has the one with chocolate ganache. "I always loved your chocolate cupcakes, but this is a whole other level."

"This raspberry is to die for," Rachelle says, going in for another bite. A moment later she asks, "You did these from scratch?"

I nod. "And the cookies, too. They're pecan shortbread with maple glaze."

Caleb takes a cookie and breaks it in half, handing part of it to Rachelle.

And they moan collectively again.

"Brenna, you are so talented!" Rachelle's voice rises in excitement. "Bing, get out here and try some of this stuff!"

And before I know it, the entire Resolution crew is in the lobby, breaking off bits of cupcake and cookie. I'd forgotten how satisfying it is to feed people something they enjoy.

Caleb slips an arm around me, and I lay my head on his shoulder, as I watch these people who have come to mean so much to me in such a short time enjoy something I made.

My heart is full.

THE PARTY IS in full swing. Caleb and Shane's townhouse is full of all the wonderful people I've come to know during my short time here in Flagstaff. Shane's girlfriend, Sydney, is one of the sweetest, kindest people I've ever met. Caleb shared a bit about her history with me, and my heart ached to know she'd been a victim of a sexual predator on her college campus. I'm in awe of the way she's thriving in spite of the things she's been through. She's an inspiration.

Asher and Grace are the perfect example of young, married, and in love. Thanks to Caleb, I also know that they were basically high school sweethearts who found their way back to each other after some pretty bumpy obstacles.

Bing, and his fiancée Kristy, along with her little boy Ezra, will be another sweet example of a loving family once they tie the knot in February. Bing treats Kristy like a princess, and he and Ezra, though not biologically related, could not love each other more. The three of them are beautiful to watch.

Rachelle, Bing's half-sister and the receptionist-slash-bookkeeper at Resolution, is hands-down one of my favorite people I've ever met. Funny and sarcastic, a little bit bossy and over-involved, she takes her role as mother-hen to this crazy crew seriously, and they love her. Her husband Gabe owns Ugly Mug, the super cool coffee shop near Resolution, and though I haven't spent as much time with him as I have the others, I can easily see what a genuine, caring man he is. He clearly adores Rachelle, and Caleb, Shane, Asher, and Bing consider him their brother.

Caleb has been attentive all night, either by my side or maintaining eye contact at all times. We're both doing a lot of smiling and laughing – because what else can you do when you're in a room full of your favorite people? – however, I know we're both thinking about tomorrow.

When I leave for Seattle.

"So, what's in Seattle?" Bing asks. He's sitting in one of the recliners, Ezra perched on his lap.

Beside me on the sofa, Caleb's body stiffens.

"My mom's cousin." I reach up to push an errant curl out of my face, tucking it behind my ear. "She helped me a lot through my mom's illness. Well, as much as she could from across the country. I've spent the last three years, since graduating from high school, pretty much doing nothing but caring for my mom, so I don't really have any marketable skills. She's offered me a job and a place to live while I figure out what my next step is."

"These cupcakes are marketable skills," Rachelle calls from the kitchen.

A chorus made up of everyone's voices agrees.

I smile and drop my eyes, a bit uncomfortable with all the attention and praise. "I worked part time at a bakery for a while, until my mom's condition got so bad that she needed me full time."

"She's being modest." Caleb's voice is firm, but full of tenderness. He cuts his eyes to me, and in them I see everything I've always wanted. "She's been baking since she was eleven."

"You and Hunter were my guinea pigs." I laugh, hoping to infuse some humor to lighten the mood. "I'm sure you ate plenty of things that tasted like cardboard before I figured out what I was doing."

He smiles, but doesn't say more, and thankfully the conversation picks back up among the others, taking the attention off me.

A few moments later, Shane turns on the Xbox, and he and Caleb engage Ezra in some kind of skateboarding game. Ezra is having the time of his life as he listens closely to the directions the two guys give him. Caleb smiles so sweetly at the little boy, both his eyes and his voice full of gentleness and patience. My heart lodges firmly in my throat, and I can hardly breathe. All sorts of crazy images and thoughts rush through my brain… Caleb with a child of his own, of our own, patiently teaching him something new… Caleb and me at the table with a loud, rowdy group of kids that belong to us, the two of us holding hands and smiling at the chaos we created and loving every minute of it.

I force those thoughts away, desperate to regain some amount of composure, no matter how small. Out of the corner of my eye, I see Gabe step up beside me.

"Rachelle is right, you know." He keeps his voice low so that no one but me hears. He holds a cupcake up between us. "These cupcakes are marketable skills. The cookies, too."

I take a deep breath and pray my voice doesn't tremble when I speak. "Thank you."

"We've been outsourcing our baked goods at Ugly Mug," Gabe continues. "Using a local bakery to supply our muffins, scones, and desserts. It's been a good arrangement, but I'd really like to have someone at the shop. Someone who could create things unique to Ugly Mug."

I turn my head and look at him, unsure what he's getting at or how to respond.

"I want to offer you a job," he says, knocking the breath out of me. "Part-time at first, so you can figure out if it's something you want to keep doing. We could re-visit the terms if you decide you want to stay."

My eyes widen, and I can feel the expression of shock as it makes its way across my face. Gabe keeps going.

"I know you have a job and somewhere to live in Seattle, so I'll understand if you want to pass on this. But if you're interested, please don't think I've manufactured this potential job out of thin air just to help you out. Hiring a pastry person has been on my list of potential upgrades ever since I bought the shop. I've just been holding back until I was certain. Rachelle told me before we got here how great your cupcakes and cookies are, and once I tasted them myself, I knew I'd have to talk to you."

"Gabe, that's so…" I stumble over my words, stopping for a second to gather my thoughts. "That's so generous. I don't know what to say."

"Are you interested?"

Was I interested? Of course. But there was so much to consider. Staying in Flagstaff would mean paying rent on an apartment, which I wasn't opposed to, but I'd been counting on the money I'd saved by living in the apartment at the hotel in Seattle to be able to take some college classes. But, if Gabe were to hire me full-time eventually, I might be able to swing rent and a college class or two without going into debt.

But there's also Caleb to consider. Of course, the idea of staying near him appeals enormously, but how can I be sure he wants that? I mean, sure he's been very kissy and touch-feely the last couple of days, but does that translate to *I want a longterm relationship with you?*

He's already talked about coming to Seattle over Thanksgiving, and has even mentioned flying me back to Flagstaff at some point during Christmas. Maybe he'd rather things be that way, long distance, at least for a while. It would give us a chance to figure out if we want to move forward together.

Being completely honest with myself, I admit that I don't need any time or distance to know what I want. I want what I've always wanted. Caleb, and a life with him.

But what does Caleb want?

"Can I think about it?" I ask. "I mean, if you find someone before I can give you an answer, I'll understand completely. It's just a lot to consider all at once."

Gabe nods. "Sure. There's no rush. And I won't hire someone until you decide. We're still using the local bakery, and I'm happy to keep doing that until you know for sure what you want to do."

"Thank you," I whisper.

"Even if you go to Seattle," Gabe goes on, "then decide you'd rather be here, just call me."

"Okay."

And with that, Gabe walks off, leaving me completely stunned, and joins his wife on the couch.

Could I do it? Could I stay here in Flagstaff with all these amazing people? With Caleb? Should I talk to him about Gabe's offer and hopefully get a read on what he'd think about me staying? My flight isn't until four o'clock in the afternoon tomorrow, so we'll have time to talk.

I make up my mind to do just that first thing in the morning.

Chapter 22

CALEB

ASHER AND GRACE are the last to leave. Brenna says her goodbyes to them, then heads upstairs to get ready for bed. Tomorrow will be a long day for her, and I know she needs the sleep.

Although, I admit that I was hoping she might sit up with me a bit, since it's our last night together for a while. The thought of her not being here makes me feel empty and hollow inside, and I can almost sense myself returning to the shell of a human I was when I first left Clayton.

I step outside with Asher and Grace, just as Shane shuts the driver's side door of Sydney's car. Sydney backs out and drives off, headed in the direction of her apartment. Shane walks toward us, and Grace quietly makes her way to the car, leaving me alone with my two best friends.

"You going to let her go without telling her how you feel?" Shane asks.

"She knows how I feel," I say. "I haven't made it a secret. I've even made plans to go to Seattle later this month for Thanksgiving."

"It's obvious to the rest of us how you feel about her," Asher says. "But if you haven't said the words to her, the kisses and hand-holding aren't going to be enough. She needs the words if she's going to be sure."

I run a hand through my hair and to the back of my neck in frustration. I've got all the words in the world for Brenna, but I don't want to say them too early and scare her off. Or maybe I'm just a chicken shit, and I'm hoping she'll say them all first.

"If you don't want her to leave, you should tell her so." Sometimes I hate it when Asher makes so much sense.

"What've you got to lose, man?" Shane shoves his hands in his pockets and leans casually against the hood of Asher's car. "Obviously, she's got feelings for you. Best case scenario, she agrees to stay in Flagstaff. That's a big win for you both. Worst case, she goes on to Seattle and the two of you do the long distance thing for a while. That might suck a little, but not as bad as the complete separation you went through before."

"Shane's right," Asher agrees. "And if you don't ask her to stay, you'll never know what her answer would've been. You'll constantly wonder if you screwed up by not making your feelings known."

"This is your chance, Caleb." Shane slaps a hand on my shoulder. "The chance you've wanted for six years. Don't be a fool and not take it."

I TAKE THE steps two at a time, dashing up the stairs as if that will make the difference between Brenna staying or going. The door is slightly open, and in my hurry to get to her, I push it open without knocking.

Just as Brenna comes out of the bathroom in nothing but an oversized tee shirt. Red, with the word *Resolution* printed across the front.

"Caleb!" She jumps back, startled, crossing her arms across her chest. The shirt falls to mid-thigh, so nothing's exposed, but it's clear that she's not wearing pants or shorts beneath it.

"Sorry," I say, quickly turning around to give her a moment of privacy. I expect to hear her moving around the room, looking for pants, but she doesn't.

A moment later, her soft voice whispers, "It's okay."

Slowly, so slowly it feels like an hour instead of seconds, I turn back to face her. She's still in the doorway of the bathroom, the light behind her framing her in a muted, yellow glow. Her arms are still crossed across her chest, hiding the word on the tee shirt.

"I should've knocked." I force myself to keep my eyes off her bare legs, but that means I'm looking at the shirt she's wearing. Something intensely primal bubbles inside me. "Is that my shirt?"

She nods. Her shoulders fall, and she drops her eyes to the floor as if she's embarrassed. She shouldn't be. I want to shout in victory. I'm pretty sure the grin that spreads across my face is of the shit-eating variety.

"I'm sorry," she says. "I know it's stupid, and I should've asked, but I just…"

"I don't mind." I interrupt her, finally letting my eyes travel down her body, taking note of the lean length of her smooth legs and the gentle way the fabric of my shirt drapes across the curve of her hip. "I like the way it looks on you."

Her skin blushes, the pink beginning on her neck, then traveling up to her cheeks. Her bottom lip is trapped between her teeth, but one corner of her mouth still manages to lift in a smile. For a long moment we just stand there, smiling at each other like two lovesick fools, which, I suppose we are. Or at least I hope we are.

Then I remember what I came up here to say.

"I want you to stay, Brenna."

Her eyes widen, the amber of her irises alive with fervor. She stays silent, her gaze locked on mine.

"I want you to stay here," I repeat. "With me."

I watch as she takes a deep breath and lets it out, her body trembling slightly.

When she still says nothing, I keep going. "I know you've got plans in Seattle, and I know it's up to you. It's your decision, and I realize I don't get a vote, but…"

She cuts me off. "You get a vote." Her voice is a mere whisper, but I hear her loud and clear.

Still, I ask her to repeat it. "What?"

"You get a vote, Caleb."

I take a step toward her, just enough that I'm fully inside the room, and then shut it behind me. "I realize there's a job and a place to live in Seattle, but you have a place here, too, as long as you need it. You can stay here while you figure out what's next. You can stay here even after you've figured it out. If you want to get a job or go to school, whatever. You've got a place."

"Gabe offered me a job tonight," she says, taking a step toward me.

"Seriously? At Ugly Mug?"

She smiles. "Yes. Doing the baking for the shop. Making things exclusive to Ugly Mug."

"Brenna, that's perfect!"

Her smile expands. "Part-time at first, to give me a chance to see what it's like. He said we could revisit the terms if I decide I want to stay."

My heartbeat races under my skin, my mind alive with possibilities. I try to keep in all in check until the deal is sealed.

"Did you accept?"

"I told him I'd consider it," she says tilting her head as

she looks me over. "I wanted to talk to you first, hear your thoughts. I was planning on bringing it up first thing in the morning. It's a big decision."

"I know it's a big decision for you." I move another step closer, barely resisting the urge to grab her and pull her against me. "I realize you have family in Seattle, and…"

"No," she says, stopping my next words. "I mean, it's a big decision for *you*. Having me here, with you. Figuring out what this is between us. It's a big decision."

"No it isn't." I lean my head, putting myself at eye level with her. "It's not. It's the easiest decision I've ever made. And for the record, I know exactly what this is between us."

She lifts a hand to her mouth, her breath shaky and her eyes filling with tears. The emotion shining from those beautiful, whiskey colored eyes matches the feelings that are about to explode out of me.

"I want to stay," she whispers. "I want to stay here with you. It's what I've wanted since the moment I stepped on the plane last week, since the moment I booked the flight, since the very moment I started saving money and making plans to leave Clayton once my mom was gone. In the deepest part of my heart, the part I was afraid to acknowledge, even to myself, this was what I wanted. For you to want me still."

It's my turn to have tears in my eyes. I reach out a hand, placing it gently against her cheek. After six years of agonizing separation, longing so acute sometimes it threatened to rip me apart, we are here. "I do, Brenna. I want you still. I've never stopped."

"We don't really know each other," she says, her hand lifting to rest on mine. "Not like we used to."

I consider her words for a moment. She's right, in a way, but it's not a deterrent. There's a lot we don't know about each other, but I see it as an exciting journey, discovering one another all over again. "We may not know each other's favorite movies, or whether or not one of us snores," I say, shrugging my shoulders. I take her hand and place it against my chest, directly above where my heart is pounding, beating strong and true. For her. "But you know me here, where it matters most. And I think I know you the same way."

She swallows hard, blinking as a tear escapes to roll down her cheek. "You do."

I bring my other hand to her face, wiping the tear away with my thumb. "All the other stuff, we'll learn. Meanwhile, I'll get the privilege of learning all about you at the same time I'm loving you." I take another step, bringing our bodies almost close enough to touch. "And I do, you know. I love you. I always have."

"Caleb." The word comes out on a whoosh of breath as she throws her arms around my neck and launches herself into my embrace. I catch her, of course, lifting her off the ground as she buries her head against my neck. "I love you, too. So much."

Then she's kissing me, and I'm kissing her back, and we're laughing and smiling and holding on to each other.

And all the pain of the past six years melts away.

Epilogue

CALEB

FEBRUARY IN FLAGSTAFF is cold, but the inside of Ugly Mug is warm and inviting.

Just like he did for Asher and Grace's wedding reception, Gabe closed the coffee shop for the night so that Bing and Kristy could hold their reception here. The crowd is intimate, just the way the two of them wanted it, consisting of their family and close friends. In the back of the dining area a small appetizer bar is set up, along with a selection of wine, beer, and soda. But the focal piece of the entire reception is a three tiered display of cupcakes in the pastry cabinet.

Bing and Kristy hired Brenna to bake cupcakes, in lieu of the traditional wedding cake, and the results are simply stunning. The tiny cakes are arranged to look like the layers of a wedding cake, and from a distance you can't tell the difference. Since I'd been the official taste tester, I know that the cakes are a variety of flavors, ranging from red velvet to chocolate to lemon, all with white buttercream frosting piped on top in delicate patterns, and sprinkled with white, sparkling sugar.

The traditional first dance for the bride and groom already happened, along with the father-daughter dance, and after that all the guests were invited onto the dance floor. Which is why I'm currently enjoying the feel of Brenna's body in my arms as we slowly sway to the soft jazz music pumping through the speakers.

"They look so happy," Brenna whispers, looking across to where Bing and Kristy dance together, with Kristy's son, Ezra, in Bing's arms between them. "Such a beautiful family."

"Yeah," I agree. "It's good to see Bing happy. He loves Kristy something fierce, and he may not be Ezra's biological father, but he couldn't love him any more if he was. Fatherhood suits him."

Bing, with his hair buzzed close to his skull and tattoos up both arms and across his back and chest, might appear at first to be a complete bad ass, created to scare women and children and send them screaming in the opposite direction. In reality, he is everything a man should be... a loving son and brother, a fair and honest boss, a loyal friend, and a now a devoted husband and father.

Kristy, fair and blonde haired, is the consummate professional. An attorney who spends her days helping people navigate their way through the complex and difficult-to-understand legal system, she's not the sort of woman you might expect to see with a man like Bing. But regardless of whatever preconceived notions others might have about what type of people fit together, Bing and Kristy just *do*. Looking at them in this moment, I couldn't imagine two people more suited for one another or more perfect together.

Except of course for me and the woman currently in my arms.

Her head is tucked under my chin, her wild, dark brown curls gently brushing against my neck. Sometimes I can't believe she's only been back in my life for three months, because it feels like she's always been here. In a way I guess she has. Even throughout the six years we spent apart from one another, her memory – her presence – was always alive in my heart. The love I feel for her, the love that developed so easily and naturally over the course of our shared childhood that I had never been able to truly imagine myself with another woman, will never go away. Of this, I am certain.

After a few more songs, Bing and Kristy hand Ezra off to his grandparents and make their way to the door, saying their goodbyes. We all gather at the door to see them off, wishing them safe travels and all the happiness in the world.

Gabe cranks the music back up once the happy couple is gone, and the party continues. I lead Brenna back out the dance floor and wrap her up in my arms once more. I love that there's no hurry, no urgency, just the two of us and all the time in the world.

I'm just about to whisper in her ear, when she gasps, her head lifting. "Oh my gosh, Caleb." She nods toward a table in the back corner of the room. "Look!"

In the quiet, secluded part of the room, with no one but Brenna and me paying attention, we watch as Shane gets down on one knee holding an open ring box in his hands. From her spot in the chair, Sydney's hands fly up and land on her chest, covering her heart. We're not close enough to see her eyes, but I'm sure they're tearing up.

I smile, looking down at Brenna. "I knew he was planning that," I admit. "He swore me to secrecy though. And I'm not supposed to make a big deal or draw attention."

"I'm so happy for them," she sighs. "They're so perfect together."

Shane and Sydney have each been through so much, from Shane's drug addicted mother who died of AIDS earlier this year to a campus sexual assault that could've pulled Sydney under forever, the two of them have overcome and found strength together. Watching them together now, it's hard to believe that I once gave Shane grief for pursuing her.

"They are." I press a kiss to Brenna's temple, as I watch Shane slip the ring onto Sydney's finger. "Perfect."

On the other side of the room Asher and Grace, along with Gabe and Rachelle, sit around a table sipping on glasses of wine and soda and laughing together, unaware that across the room, Shane and Sydney just got engaged. All of my friends are happy and settled down, building lives together. For a long time, as I watched from the sidelines, I wondered if it would ever happen for me. I had tried, and failed, to manufacture that kind of relationship, and now I couldn't be happier that I never succeeded.

Because Brenna – *my Brenna* – is here, and she is mine.

The song changes, the tempo picking up a bit, and as I move with her, I maneuver the two of us away from the other couples on the dance floor to the edge, out of the lights, to a more secluded spot.

I keep one arm around her, my hand splayed across her lower back, while my other hand is clasped with hers. She snuggles against me once more, her head tucked neatly beneath my chin. I lean down, putting my lips against her ear.

"I've watched all my best friends fall in love the past few years," I begin. "And I was so happy each time one of them found their one."

She doesn't say anything, but her arm tightens around me, squeezing me in a gentle hug.

"But I was so jealous," I admit. "Because I wanted the same thing. Of course, I never said anything. They all probably just thought I had typical male commitment phobia. But the truth was, and always has been, that there was no one for me except you, Brenna."

"Caleb," she says, her voice soft and sweet as she lifts her head to look up into my eyes.

"I never thought we'd be here, together." I bend down and press my forehead against hers. "I thought you were lost to me forever."

Tears shimmer in her eyes at my words. It's not like I've withheld my feelings. The words come so easily now, and I tell her every day that I love her.

"Marry me?" My voice is steady, my nose brushing hers, my gaze locked on her liquid amber eyes. "Be my wife."

Her quick intake of breath and widened eyes tell me that I've surprised her. While I'm sure she wasn't expecting me to propose this quickly, in my mind the time has never been more right.

"Caleb," she says, her voice no more than a breathy whisper.

"I know you're thinking this seems quick," I say. "That we've only been together for three months, But Bren, even though this part of our relationship is young, the truth is, we've been together practically all our lives. I've loved you since we were kids, since before I could even put a name to what I felt for you. I knew when I left Clayton six years ago that I'd never love anyone the way I love you. So when you think about it that way, we've been together longer than any of our friends."

I press my mouth to hers, lingering there for a long moment, letting my words sink in.

"All my life, Brenna," I whisper, my lips moving against hers. "It's been you all my life. Marry me."

She pulls back slightly, her eyes glistening with unshed tears. She smiles, and it reaches right into my chest and grabs my heart. "You don't have to convince me, Caleb. I'd have said yes if you'd asked me the first moment I stepped into the lobby at Resolution." She lifts her left hand and places it against my cheek. "Of course I'll marry you. I've been waiting to marry you my whole life."

I reach into my pocket, pulling out the small velvet box that holds the ring. I hold it up between us, pressing our bodies close and keeping the ring box out of sight, so we can keep this moment to ourselves. We'll share the news with everyone in a few days, so our engagement doesn't become part of Bing and Kristy's wedding story. Shane and I had agreed on that when we realized we were each planning to propose.

I flip the box open with my thumb, revealing the princess cut diamond set in a simple platinum band.

Brenna blinks, a tear escaping to roll down her face. "It's so beautiful, Caleb."

"You never had a lot pretty things," I say. "And you never complained. You just went right on taking care of your Mom and Hunter and sometimes even me. But you deserve all the beautiful things in the world, and I'm a lucky man to get to give them to you."

I slide the ring into place on her left ring finger, taking a moment to reflect on all we've been through and what the ring on her finger symbolizes.

"Forever, Brenna."

"Forever, Caleb."

THE END

ABOUT THE AUTHOR

After spending every work day with classrooms full of tweens and teens, then going home to three boys of her own, two of whom fall into the tween/teen category, you'd think that Amy Durham might like to leave the world of teenagers and young adults behind.

Not so! Instead, she spends her spare moments – which sometimes consist of waiting twenty minutes for her kiddos to get out of band practice – with her laptop and a multitude of teenage characters trying to navigate their way through the twisted, difficult road of adolescence.

You might ask… "Why Young/New Adult Fiction"? Well, because it's what she knows. As a teacher and a parent, Amy is around teens on an almost constant basis. And while it's true they can be – ahem – challenging, they are also full of life, vision, and dreams. And that's a really cool place to be.

Young Adult and New Adult Fiction allows young readers the opportunity to find hope for the situations they find themselves in, find determination to keep on going, and courage to pursue their dreams. It also allows adult readers the chance to revisit the exuberance of youth, remember the joy and poignancy of first love, and recall how it felt to dream with abandon.

Amy Durham is a wife and mother, an author, a teacher, an avid reader, and a musician. If she weren't writing books, she'd be a celebrity chef!

Contact Amy online at:
www.amybdurham.com
amybdurham@gmail.com
www.facebook.com/AuthorAmyDurham
Twitter: @Amy_Durham
Instagram: @AuthorAmyDurham

If you enjoyed this book, please consider leaving a review at your place of purchase and/or any other online review site you frequent. Customer reviews are one of the best ways to show an author you enjoyed his or her work and can be invaluable for other readers as they browse for reading material. This author reads all reviews and greatly appreciates each one.